Dear Reader,

This month we have four wonderful new *Scarlet* romances for you which we hope will help chase away those winter blues.

Share *That Cinderella Feeling* with Anne Styles's heroine and find out if 'Cinderella' Casey really does live happily ever after . . . When the lawyer meets the dancer, sparks are bound to fly – and they do in *The Marriage Dance*, as author Jillian James brings us a new slant on the old problem of reluctance to commit. We are delighted, too, to bring you *A Darker Shadow*, the latest long novel by Patricia Wilson, in which Luc Martell is forced to remain in England with computer buff Amy Scott – the bane of his life. And finally, *Slow Dancing* by Elizabeth Smith shows us that life in Hollywood isn't always the stuff of dreams.

As always it has been a pleasure *and* a challenge for me to select these latest *Scarlet* titles for you and I hope that you enjoy reading these books as much as I did.

Keep those letters and questionnaires flooding in, won't you? We are always happy to hear from you. And don't forget, if you want to write to a favourite *Scarlet* author, I'll be glad to pass on your letter.

Till next month,
Best wishes,

Sally Cooper

SALLY COOPER,
Editor-in-Chief – *Scarlet*

ANNE STYLES

THAT CINDERELLA FEELING

SCARLET

Enquiries to:
Robinson Publishing Ltd
7 Kensington Church Court
London W8 4SP

First published in the UK by Scarlet, 1998

A copy of the British Library Cataloguing in
Publication data is available from the British Library

ISBN 1-85487-982-0

Printed and bound in the EC

10 9 8 7 6 5 4 3 2 1

With grateful thanks to Laurence Pearce for his endless patience in sorting out my PC, to Pat and Roy Semark for their insider knowledge of Barbados and to Benita, for listening every time I had a problem!

CHAPTER 1

Of all the clients on Marty's lists, Casey hated advertising agencies the most. The costume didn't help, either, she thought ruefully, wrapping her long coat closer around her to try and hide the tight-fitting green satin basque and black fishnet stockings. Not quite normal visiting wear for the foyer of Havilland Gracey she decided, grinning as she looked around the elegant marble-lined lobby. However, two jobs on the run in the same outfit had made her decide to take a chance and grab a taxi. It certainly saved struggling back into her jeans and walking.

A tall, florid-faced young man straightened up from his position leaning over the desk to chat to the pretty receptionist. 'You the Kissagram?' he enquired, with a leer at Casey's long, sleek legs revealed by the swinging coat. Casey put on her best professional actress's smile, and nodded.

'At your service!'

'Hmm . . . better than the usual scrubbers we get from Marty,' he said, approvingly. 'Quick, come on

1

up to my office and I'll give you the low-down on our birthday boy. We don't want to spoil the surprise, do we?'

'Or let Alex Havilland catch you,' the receptionist reminded him with a grin.

'Our beloved boss doesn't approve of us having a bit of fun in working hours,' the man grimaced. 'I'm Tony, by the way.'

'Casey Taylor, hi!'

'Unusual name. Is it a stage name?'

'No, it's short for Cassandra, I had a literary-type father who liked the name, but it never fits on forms so I shortened it. I *am* an actress though.'

'Out of work?'

'Would I be doing this if I wasn't?'

'Some girls like it.'

Well, this one didn't! But Casey was a realist – she had rent to pay and when Marty had offered her good money to work for him there had been very little option. Jobs were hard to come by for an out-of-work actress with a teaching qualification but no computer or secretarial experience.

Swiftly she discarded her coat and touched up her immaculate, though stagey, make-up in Tony's office while he filled her in on the details of his friend's life. 'I don't strip!' she reminded him tartly, as his requests grew more suggestive.

Tony eyed the generous curves displayed by the tight basque, with regret. 'Not even a little bit?' he wheedled, hopefully.

'Not even a little bit!'

2

'But Marty *said* you would!'

'Marty was pushing his luck as usual!' Casey snapped. 'The answer is quite definitely *no*!'

'Oh, well, worth a try!' he sighed. 'I must say you look pretty good like that, anyway. Come on, how about a kiss for booking you?'

'I don't give freebies either!' Casey picked up the gift for the birthday boy, and tossed her bag of street clothes behind his desk together with her coat. 'Can we get on?' she asked, more sweetly. 'I do have a schedule to keep to, you know.' A really exciting one – she had a few hours in a local pub behind the bar to look forward to, but like everything else it was work and unlike Marty the pub paid in cash, and on the night.

Pasting a confident smile on her face, she followed the grinning Tony into a room seemingly overflowing with a noisy crowd liberally awash with champagne and her heart sank. She would be unlikely to get out of this crowd with her costume untouched, and she cursed her ill-luck – and Marty in particular – the last job had been a nightmare, this could well be worse.

With as much aplomb as she could muster she delivered the gift and a kiss, made her little speech and posed for the required photographs with an obviously well-oiled birthday boy before she called time and managed to slip out, to recover her bag and coat from Tony's office along the corridor. Confused, in the silent grey carpeted corridor with its line of identical black ash doors, she paused, conscious suddenly of the brevity of her outfit and wished she had taken her coat into the party room with her.

With relief, she realized the door behind her had opened and, assuming it was Tony at last, she turned around, smiling. 'Tony! About time, where on earth is your office? I need my bag. Let's get going.'

'And where exactly are you expecting to go, young woman?' It wasn't Tony's teasing tones, instead, it was a voice that could quite certainly freeze boiling water. Startled, Casey looked up into the coldest brown eyes she had ever seen, below heavy dark brows, their owner a tall man, topping her five foot nine by five inches at least. Immaculately dressed in a grey Savile Row three-piece suit that shouted money; he was no ordinary office worker, that she was horribly sure of. Why was it, she thought, that some people had complete confidence in-built, hardly knowing that it was there, yet using it instinctively? This man had it in abundance! With his almost black hair and tanned, classically chiselled features, he was a handsome man in every sense of the word, though the thinned twist of his mouth spoke volumes for his current mood.

'Oops! I'm sorry.' Casey grinned to hide her embarrassment. 'I thought you were someone else.'

'*You* are sorry!' A hand shot out and caught at her arm, its grip hard and unforgiving. 'You walk around this building dressed like the whore you

4

probably are – and tell me you're sorry? The hell you are!'

'I am *not* a whore! I'm an actress! I came here to do a job!' Casey wrenched without any effect at the hand that held her. 'How dare you insinuate anything else?'

'I'll insinuate anything I like! Look at you – almost naked – at two o'clock in the afternoon!'

'So what? I'm doing a job, that's all! Let go of me!'

'What job? Who employed you?' The voice dripped acid. 'I don't recall a casting call in costume for anything.'

'Oh, hell, I don't know! A guy called Tony, Tony something.'

'Go on . . .'

'Tony . . . Sorensen . . . that's it . . . Sorensen.' She struggled desperately to break free, as his grip tightened.

'I might have known it!' With his free hand he picked up the phone. 'Mary-Jo, get me Tony Sorensen in here, *now*!'

Casey began to struggle more fiercely as his attention was diverted for a moment. 'Let go of me, you disgusting pervert!' Frantic now, she beat her free fist at his wide chest only to bruise her knuckles on the hard bone and muscle that it seemed to consist of.

'Sit down and shut up!' He hurled her into a chair and to her horror her breasts fell out of the strapless top. Scarlet with embarrassment she flung her arms across her chest to cover herself, only just managing

5

to make herself decent again when there was a knock on the door and a very apprehensive Tony appeared. Sweating profusely, he hovered in the doorway.

'You wanted me, Alex?' he stammered as he pulled his tie straight.

'Yes, I did!' The voice was ice-cold as its owner faced the hapless Tony. 'Can you explain *that*?'

'How *dare* you?' Having made herself as decent as she possibly could, Casey leapt up from the chair she had been so summarily thrown into. 'You can't talk about me like that, as if I don't exist.'

'I'll do what the hell I like,' he retorted coldly. 'Since this is *my* company, and *my* building!'

'Cool it, Casey,' Tony pleaded. 'This is Alexander Havilland!'

The boss, Casey realized. The one who didn't approve of fun. But, she felt she had right on her side – she had, after all, been asked to do a job, it was hardly her fault that the boss was a spoilsport! 'I will *not* cool it!' she retorted, furiously. 'What on earth have I done wrong? And you . . .!' She turned on the fuming Alexander Havilland. 'You should know better than to throw a lady around like a sack of potatoes! OK, this may not be the best way to earn a living but it's all I have at the moment, and believe me, I'm very grateful for it!'

'Lady? I doubt that very much!' snapped Alex Havilland. 'And as for you, Sorensen . . .'

Tony looked sheepish as Alex's cold eyes met his. 'It was only a little birthday party for Jake,' he

6

protested, mildly. 'Half an hour at the most, Alex.' And the rest – Casey thought, beginning to see the funny side of it. Laughing with sudden amusement, she faced Alexander Havilland, her dazzling chestnut-coloured hair tumbling out of its fastenings into a thick cascade down her back after his rough handling of her.

'Look, you two, sort it out between you,' she said, with far more confidence than she felt inside. 'I have another job to go to.'

'Another session of revealing your assets?' Alex Havilland asked sarcastically.

'No! As it happens I work in a pub from four until closing time, again through necessity! I prefer it to starving, distasteful though it may seem to you!' Casey snapped back.

'So what happened to the dole? Or do you claim that as well?' Alex asked. 'I understood you could do very well out of that these days.'

'Then you are *well* behind the times!' Casey could just imagine how the expensive Mr Havilland would cope with living on the dole. 'Quite frankly I'd really rather starve than get into that situation!'

'Or prostitute yourself?'

'So why should you care?' she demanded. 'Oh, for goodness' sake! Tony, get my coat! I'm out of here – now!'

'Just one moment, young woman.' Alex Havilland caught her arm as she made for the door and jerked her round to the light from the window. 'Is your hair real? Or is it a wig?'

'Of course it's not a wig!' The idea revolted her. 'Here – feel it!' She grabbed a handful of her abundant hair and thrust it at him. 'Does that feel like wig hair?'

With a faint inner glimmer of amusement, Alex Havilland let the coil of hair brush his hand for a moment as he stared intently at her, seeing and assessing for the first time the beauty under the heavy make-up. Casey's brilliant green eyes disconcertingly stared right back at him with undisguised venom spitting from their emerald depths. There was, he thought suddenly, a great deal of truth in the saying *if looks could kill*! 'Tony – is Ross still doing the Keara auditions?' he asked then, still holding the fuming girl as if he thought she might just bolt.

'Er, yes Alex, I think he is,' Tony stammered as he looked from Casey to his boss in complete bewilderment.

'And you are an actress?' Alex demanded of Casey as she again struggled to be free of his iron grip.

'I told you I was, Equity and everything. Now let go of me, you great ape!' Casey shouted back. Tony's face was a picture of fear as Casey and his irate boss faced each other, the loathing mutual and almost vibrating in the ominously quiet room.

'Oh, for heaven's sake!' Alex was totally exasperated. 'Will you *shut up* and *listen* to me for a moment?'

'Why should I?' She was belligerent now and well past caring. Alex Havilland could well be the owner of the agency but to a furious Casey he was simply a bombastic and arrogant man who needed to mind his manners.

'Because I say so!' Firmly he propelled her towards a door in the corner of the room. 'Now get in there and wash that muck off your face! Do you have any other clothes? Or did you intend walking the streets in that get-up?'

'No! Of course not! He's got them in his office.' Casey indicated Tony, standing there still staring at the two antagonists in complete bewilderment.

'Then get them, Sorensen. I want her to see Ross Kenny right now. She has the height and the hair; cleaned up she might just be what he's looking for.'

'Will you stop treating me like an object and tell me what the hell is going on?' Casey demanded, her sea-green eyes flashing dangerously between the two men.

'What is going on, young woman, is that I want to see you in your normal clothes and without make-up, because we are casting for a commercial and you may just be right for it – much as it goes against the grain for me to say so! Now get in there and *wash your face*!' Stunned, Casey stared at him as he opened the door to what proved to be a shower room. 'And don't take all day about it!' he added, just in case she thought he'd softened.

'Pig!' she muttered furiously and thankfully shut the door on him. She had nothing with her but there were expensive-smelling soaps and lotions on a shelf by the basin so she made free with them in wicked delight. A few minutes later a knock on the door brought Tony with her rucksack of clothing. Hastily she threw off the much-maligned basque and thankfully dressed herself in her more familiar and comfortable jeans and a sweatshirt. Brushed out, her long, gleaming, chestnut hair fell halfway to her waist and really was her most noticeable asset and she smiled as she finished washing the make-up from her face. Marty always insisted on a really stagey make-up especially round the eyes and though she loathed it, she complied as they all did – too frightened of losing a job to argue.

Finally clean, and respectably dressed, she stepped back into the office, looking round for the first time and realizing just how spacious and luxurious it was compared with Tony's, or indeed the large office where the party-goers had gathered. Alex was seated behind the huge bird's-eye maple desk, leaning back in his leather chair completely at ease as he looked her up and down like a prize animal or something, she thought amusedly. It was getting more and more difficult to take this seriously.

'Well, well,' he said at last, his fingers steepling together as he appraised her. 'Not bad at all – now all that paint is off. What do you think, Tony?'

'I thought so the minute I saw her, Alex,' Tony admitted. 'She's a knockout!'

'Pretty, anyway,' Alex agreed. He made Casey walk the length of the office, to turn and then swing her hair as he watched her with seemingly half-closed eyes, yet Casey was aware all the time of his unrelenting observation of her. 'Yes, take her down to see Ross,' he told Tony eventually, after Casey thought she would scream with frustration at his arrogant treatment of her.

Tony, however, moved swiftly at his instruction and hurriedly ushered her from the office. 'Jeeze, Casey! I thought we'd had it then. You have no idea how lucky you were that he thought about that audition.'

'Lucky?' Casey stared at him. 'Pushed around and shouted at like some half-wit – you call that lucky? He was damned lucky not to get his face slapped!'

'Well thank goodness you managed to control that little urge! Do you *know* who he is?'

'So, he's Alexander Havilland, ad-man extraordinaire, darling of the tabloids, *big deal*! He still needs a lesson in manners!' She smiled suddenly at Tony's horrified face. Of course she had heard of the *enfant terrible* of the advertising world. At the tender age of twenty-eight Alex Havilland had risen to be MD of a large advertising company, raking in new accounts at an unheard of rate until a furious row with the two owners had led to him walking out, and on setting up his own company several major accounts had followed him. Since that event, some ten years ago she remembered, he and his partner Paul Gracey had never looked back and their business had gone from strength to strength. Ruthless and endlessly ambitious, he had used every opportunity to build and consolidate his company, and

11

with admirers in high places it was even rumoured that he would soon be offered a knighthood – an enormous achievement for a man not yet forty.

'He could kill *your* career stone dead, my girl, and don't you forget it!' Tony pressed the button for the lift, as Casey laughed bitterly.

'What career? I'm a bit-part merchant! Forever the glamour bit on the side!'

'You deserve better – on looks alone. You're an absolute cracker, Cassandra Taylor, and this audition he is sending you down for could help you enormously if you got it.'

'What is it?'

'Kear Cars. The "Keara" is a new model, a departure for them, a fast glam sports car and the campaign is *huge*! Robin Faulkner, the racing driver, is headlining – they're looking for his "muse", the girl he drives all over America looking for and keeps losing!'

'Sounds careless to me!' Casey commented, flippantly.

'It's big bucks and instant stardom!' he protested, appalled that she could be so casual about it all.

'You're kidding!' Casey stared at him. 'That guy called me awful names, he wasn't serious. *Was he*?'

'He's no fool, Casey, he saw what you looked like, and they want someone with long hair – and tall. Robin is six foot one after all.'

Ross Kenny had obviously been told to expect her. He showed no surprise when Tony ushered her into the meeting room he was using for his auditions.

Grinning at her, he removed his wire-rimmed glasses and rubbed at his eyes.

'So,' he said, 'the Bossman thinks you might work for Kear?' He had a light American accent and a pleasant smile.

'So I'm told.' Casey smiled back, liking his open friendly face. He was in his late forties, she guessed, with already thinning dark hair and a comfortingly scruffy appearance.

'Well you're the last, thank goodness,' he sighed. 'I don't suppose you have any photographs? Or a composite?'

'I do happen to have a composite.' Casey never went anywhere without at least a couple in her bag. She dug around in its capacious interior and produced the glossy folder of her physical details alongside photographs of her recent roles.

'Great!' He flipped through it with interest. 'And an agent?'

'Yes, Jessie Marks at TSA.'

'Poor you,' he sympathized. 'Get a new one, that old witch is past it.'

'Don't I know it!' Casey groaned. Jessie was a lazy old crone, but Casey had been passed on to her from a colleague who had quit the business, and agents were hard to come by if you were unknown and without any pedigree.

'Nothing will happen if you don't get out there and make it happen,' he commented drily. 'Now, take a seat over there and we'll put the interview on video.'

Glad that she was wearing jeans and could perch decently on the stool he indicated, she obeyed him. Hitching herself into a comfortable position, she faced the camera. The operator winked at her and she was quickly at ease. Auditions on video were quite common, and Casey had done several.

'OK, Casey,' Ross smiled. 'Let's have the biz.'

Casey returned his smile, turning her face to the camera to give him both profiles. 'Hi,' she said, calmly. 'My name is Casey Taylor – short for Cassandra. I'm twenty-seven years old, single, unattached, an actress but at present I'm out of work. The last thing I did was a tour of a play called *The Trials of a Vicar's Wife* – needless to say, I *didn't* play the vicar's wife! It finished about a month ago. I did a tiny part in Brett Kennedy's latest film last year, and bit parts TV, some sit-coms, a few commercials, lots of pop videos and some modelling.' She struggled to make three years of bits sound busy and interesting, knowing that Ross would easily see through it. But he still seemed interested, smiling encouragingly at her.

'And what about your family background, Casey?'

Casey stared. This was a fairly unusual question, but after all, she excused, he was American. Maybe he took *Chorus Line* seriously, she thought to herself! 'I come from a small town on the Sussex coast,' she said. 'My father was an English teacher at a prep school, my mum worked in a local book shop. They both died within a few months of each other two years ago. I grew up with Dad's love of literature and I have a degree in English, and a teaching certificate, though I've never used it.' Supply teaching was hard to come by when you needed constant time off for auditions and Casey had really only done teacher training to make her father happy. She had hated every minute of it. 'Since then I've shared a flat with a girl-friend in Kentish town.' Flat – she grinned to herself. It was a glorified bed-sit with the bathroom one floor down! She and Liz led far too precarious an existence to risk taking a more expensive place, and the rent *was* incredibly cheap.

'Can you drive a car, Casey?' Ross ran through his set list of questions, tiredly rubbing at his eyes, a frequent habit of his.

'Of course! I passed my test when I was eighteen, and I can also ride a motor bike.'

'Great, well that helps with a car commercial! Though the girl only drives a couple of times, mostly she floats around looking beautiful, hair flowing – that sort of thing.'

'Sounds fairly straightforward,' she commented, wishing she had been allowed to put on some make-up before she left Alex Havilland's office. She was certain Ross was not going to be interested in her pale complexion and the tiny mole at the corner of her mouth that, to Casey, marred her skin.

'It is in a way, but the girl must be right, something of an enigma, and visually perfect in every way.'

'Flattering!' Casey raised an ironic eyebrow. 'I think I look better with make-up though!'

'Sorry, honey,' Ross grinned apologetically. 'Client's request, to see the real thing, no paint! And it's no hardship, believe me!'

It was more than flattering and Casey found herself responding easily to his interest. He was drawing her out expertly and unknown to her it was visible on camera as she relaxed. She listened intently as he outlined the details of the four-week shoot, hardly believing that she could be lucky enough to get the job. It seemed like the impossible dream as she heard him talk about filming all over the West Coast of America; unusual enough in these days of computer generated commercials, but Kear wanted the real thing, it transpired.

'The car was designed here, principally for the European market,' he explained. 'But the parent company is American and the car will initially be made there, so we are doing the shoot there. It can then be used for their advertising as well if they decide to, but we are allowed to use English artists. Robin Faulkner is well known on the Indi circuit so he is a good compromise. You *would* be available, I take it, Casey?'

'You bet I would!' Casey couldn't help the giggle that accompanied her swift comment. But she had no illusions. The audition might have fallen into her lap but she was far from getting the part. Collecting her bag when the interview was finally over she swiftly made her way through to the foyer of the building, nodding to the receptionist as she went through.

'Oh, Miss Taylor,' the girl called after her. 'Just a minute, I have something for you.' She handed Casey an envelope with her name on it. 'Tony asked me to give this to you.'

Slipping it into her pocket, she raced out of the building and made her way towards Tottenham Court Road and on to Warren Street tube station. She needed to rush now since she would be late at the pub and Bill, the landlord, would be furious. As it was she had to put on some make-up as the train jerked and shuddered its way towards Kentish Town. He would never tolerate her appearing with the fresh scrubbed look that Alexander Havilland had demanded. She looked about sixteen, she thought wryly as she grinned into her little mirror and changed her face to that of a sophisticated barmaid. Casey was a realist: Bill employed her for her looks and even badly paid bar jobs were hard to get. But the tips were good and, naturally enough with her looks, Casey always did well with those!

CHAPTER 2

Bill was mad. She was half an hour late, so apart from his threat to sack her if she let him down again she lost an hour's pay, and cursed Alexander Havilland anew. It was an exhausting seven-hour shift with only a scant twenty minutes break and she was almost on her knees as she hauled her weary body up the three flights of stairs to the flat at almost midnight.

Liz, her flatmate, was away on a modelling assignment so she had the flat to herself for a few days. It was a total tip, she had to admit as she walked in. Liz had left in a hurry that morning and it showed. Too tired to bother, Casey stumbled under what proved to be an almost cold shower to get rid of the disgusting smell the pub left in her hair and then fell into the bed she had left un-made in her own hurry to leave the flat that morning. Her mother would have had a fit at the chaos her daughter lived in, she thought guiltily, and re-solved to have a good clean-up in the morning. Casey actually enjoyed cleaning when she set her mind to it; there was too much of her mother in her not to.

While Casey worked behind the bar the lights burned late into the night in the top floor office of Havilland Gracey. Wreathed in smoke from the slim cigars that Ross was smoking, Alex stretched his arms above his head and locked his fingers together in a tired gesture.

'So, we're agreed then?' he asked the other two men. 'We'll show our respected clients Bridget, and that last girl?'

'Casey Taylor?' Ross nodded. 'Yes. Though I must say I prefer Casey to Bridget.'

'Hmm, in looks, certainly, she's beautiful.' Alex grimaced. 'However, she has a tongue that would neutralize acid given half a chance, and a fairly unsavoury background from the sound of it. Are you sure she's worth the risk, Ross?'

'Quite sure! So, OK, she's a stripper, we'll just not tell Kear that bit, and I don't suppose Casey would.'

'She's not a stripper, Ross,' Tony put in, rushing to Casey's defence. 'She refused outright when I asked her.'

'Probably very rudely, from my experience,' Alex said, drily.

'Firmly,' Tony corrected. 'She's a nice girl, Alex, and a very bright one, for a change.'

'You could have fooled me!' Alex was dismissive. 'But I wouldn't have sent her down to you if I hadn't thought her worth it. There's just far too much resting on this job to make a mistake, that's all! Decision made, then – I'm for home, it's been a long day.' He picked up the phone to alert his chauffeur waiting downstairs. 'And Tony . . .'

'Yes, Alex?' Tony was immediately wary.

'Don't ever let me catch you out like that again! Save the games for the pub – and out of office hours in future!'

'Sure thing, Boss!' Tony grinned in relief at having got off so lightly, and watched Alex gathering up his sleek calf-skin briefcase before he strode purposely from the room.

Alex leaned back wearily against the wall of the lift. It had been a long day since he had flown in from New York at seven that morning. He was indeed exhausted, having only slept fitfully on the plane during the overnight flight. He rubbed at eyes that felt gritty with tiredness and almost had to force himself across the foyer and outside where his patient chauffeur was waiting with his car.

'Sorry, William,' he groaned as he slid into the back seat of the dark blue Bentley. 'I'm bushed!'

'You work too hard, sir,' William reproved. He had known Alex for many years and was one of the few allowed the privilege of speaking his mind to him. 'I let Joan know we're on the way.'

Alex laughed and ran a hand through his dark hair. 'One of these days Joan *will* actually attempt to tuck me in with hot milk! I hope she hasn't got a huge meal ready. I'm not sure I could stay awake long enough to eat it!'

'It ought to be your wife looking after you, not your housekeeper, and you know it!' William said, sensibly. 'My Joannie gets real worried about you. Can't be natural, she says, living on your own like you do.'

'I have Miranda if I need companionship,' Alex argued, light-heartedly. He and William had this conversation frequently. His chauffeur's silence was enough to register William's disapproval of the current lady in Alex's life. Alex himself had doubts about his lack-lustre relationship with the exquisitely beautiful, but totally air-headed Miranda Bradbury. It was, he privately acknowledged, time he did something about Miranda before he got too far into the mire to get out. Miranda's father was an old friend of Alex's, and he was suddenly beginning to read far more into the friendship than Alex deemed wise. His life was his work – his precious company, the only thing that mattered to him these days.

He thought bitterly of the wife who had left him five years before amid furious accusations of Alex's neglect. Wendy had demanded far more than he was able to give in the early days of building the company up, when he and Paul had frequently worked twenty-hour days. Now they had achieved everything they had hoped for, but both their marriages had collapsed in the process. Paul, at least, had later re-married – his secretary at the

21

agency, much to Alex's amusement. But at least Paul was happy with Louise, and he had someone to go home to at night, unlike Alex.

Why, he wondered fitfully as William drove him sedately to his home just behind Kensington High Street, why did he keep on thinking about the startling young woman who had erupted into his life that afternoon? Why hadn't he simply had her thrown out of the building?

Instead, he had come up with the notion of sending her to Ross. OK, so she had the hair that Ross had demanded, and scrubbed of the layers of make-up she certainly had the looks – but why on earth did she disturb him so much? Beautiful women were ten a penny in his line of work, after all.

Alex was not even a man who needed constant female companionship. He was happy with his own company any rare evening he had free. In London, he read voraciously and kept up with movies and the theatre. In his country home he walked his labrador for miles across the Sussex countryside. He didn't need the complications women inevitably meant. Miranda, after all, filled the social obligations he had, a perfect and well-bred hostess, and he shuddered as he thought of the cocky young woman he had met that afternoon at the head of his dining table – giving his guests a piece of her mind more than likely!

And yet, despite his acid comments to Tony, he now knew she was an educated and seemingly intelligent creature – a BA in English Literature was not easily obtained, Alex knew that from bitter experience, having flunked his own degree course. So why the hell, he wondered, was she doing the next best job – in his eyes – to prostitution? Could she really be that desperate?

Still, he didn't doubt that she really would be the type to prefer starving to claiming dole money! Even he could recognize the hard pride in her eyes when she had said that. Those beautiful, almond-shaped eyes! He closed his own, and still saw those deep sea-green eyes flashing fury and defiance at him; sparkling deep, deep depths with thick dark lashes. Men had been lured to their doom by far less than that, he mused.

Not just her eyes either, he grinned suddenly to himself. A few more minutes alone in his office with her and he would have been very sorely tempted, he was certain. Her body, slender, yet full-breasted and long-legged – a classically beautiful example – was enough to tempt any normal man. Displayed even accidentally as it had been, it had been more than a temptation to him. He had recognized with some horror the stirring of his own body as the girl had struggled in his grip. Only ruthlessly applied control had prevented him from making a complete fool of himself!

Was he really getting so lonely he could be drawn to a girl like that? A Kissagram girl? Shuddering, he drew a hand through his thick, dark hair – he had come so close! And now, thanks to his stupidity, this girl was quite likely to be his constant companion for the next few weeks. Why on earth had he decided to produce the Keara commercial for the agency? He didn't have to do it. He freely admitted it had simply been nostalgia for his earlier days in the industry; now the very thought threatened his hard-won peace of mind. If the clients chose Casey Taylor, that month of filming wouldn't be the longed-for break from the monotony of his business life. He knew quite well it would be a long battle against his inner peace.

He didn't need that battle any more. After the drama of his life with Wendy, more than anything he wanted nothing to do with women, they were simply an aggravation he could do without. Even now the memories of the sulking, the screaming rows, the accusations, were enough to make him clench his fists in frustrated anger that he had let Wendy put him through so much before she had finally walked out. He had come so close to violence that dreadful day, and raged so bitterly after it, that he had firmly decided he never wanted that kind of trauma again. Since then he had rarely needed the comfort of a woman's body; if he had – even in these more cautious times – it had always been available. A privilege of his position, he realized ruefully, as William pulled up outside the white front door of the elegant Regency house he called home. A home totally free of Wendy's influence. He had sold their Mayfair flat within weeks of her departure and started afresh in the new Kensington house that he freely admitted was far too large for one man to live in.

His footsteps echoed into space as he strode across the marble hallway and mounted the curved wrought-iron banistered staircase. Alex took no notice of the dramatically lit hall. An expensive interior designer had simply presented him with an elegant, reasonably comfortable place to live in and he had accepted it as such. The truth was, that apart from sleeping and the occasional formal dinner party, he spent his social time in the kitchen with Joan and William. It was the only room in the house that felt truly warm with Joan's love of clutter. There, he tolerated the endless vases of flowers, family photographs, magazines, William's pipe and the frequent underfoot hazard of their two cats and his own black labrador, the ill-behaved offspring of his parents' dog. The other half of the basement contained state-of-the-art gym equipment but Alex rarely had the inclination to use it, preferring a fast game of squash to a lone work-out. He still had the physique to prove it, he thought with some satisfaction, as he threw off his clothes before going into his marble bathroom to take a welcome shower.

Alexander never really thought about his looks, they were of no real importance to him, but he was very careful of his personal fitness; in the toll-taking business he was in he needed to be, and he made very sure that he was able to out-pace many of his younger executives in the fitness stakes.

True to form, he had barely donned his towelling robe when Joan bustled in with a tray. Alex was an imposing and scary figure to his agency staff but in his home Joan more than ran the house – she ruled him as well as William. Having known him since he was a baby he was still 'Master Alex' to her. The only time she respected his privacy was on the rare occasions when he brought Miranda back to the house, mainly, he suspected, because Joan whole-heartedly disapproved of Miranda Bradbury as much as her husband did.

'No hot milk, Joannie?' he teased as she put the tray down.

'Waste of effort!' she sniffed. 'Nice cup of tea, few sandwiches, that's all. Them airlines don't serve proper tea!'

'Joannie! I *did* have lunch, *and* some supper today,' Alex protested, rubbing at his wet hair.

'Well, you look downright peaky to me, my lad! Too many late nights, that's your trouble!' Joan looked him up and down critically. 'You've lost weight, and your hair needs cutting.'

'You sound more like my mother every day!' Alex grumbled. 'Make an appointment with Trumpers for Saturday then.'

'I already did – early! You remember your parents are expecting you Saturday lunchtime?'

'Yes – yes I do! Penny phoned to remind me this morning.' Alex relaxed as Joan bustled around picking up his clothes. 'And just in case you thought I'd forgotten, Mary-Jo has sorted out their present.'

'You should be doing that yourself, not getting

some chit of a secretary to do it for you,' she chided.

'M-J has superb taste,' Alex defended, grinning. 'And I expect my sister had a hand in it too. Penny is nearly as adept as you are in telling me what to do! Now, leave those, Joannie, I am quite capable of putting my own clothes in the laundry basket, thank you.'

'Well, mind you do! Get some sleep, Alex love, that jet-lag can do funny things to you, you know – and you never seem to catch up with yourself, all these trips to America you keep doing. Can't be good for you!'

He *was* tired, but sleep wasn't on his mind. Once Joan had gone, he discarded the tea and wandered into his adjoining sitting room-cum-study and poured himself some brandy to take to bed with him. After the day he'd had, he needed it. There was a new thriller on his bedside table, one he'd looked forward to reading but somehow even that failed to grip him. The heroine had green eyes, he soon discovered and he found himself distracted again, shifting restlessly in his vast bed.

This was stupid, he told himself firmly. Tomorrow he would recommend Bridget to the clients, not Casey Taylor. They would listen and respect his choice.

And yet . . . And yet . . . She was something of a challenge!

Perhaps William was right. Perhaps he did need a wife – and children. Alex admittedly loved children, and they him. He was an adoring, and adored, uncle to his nieces and nephews, and to the children of his friends. Penny was relentless in her attempts to marry off her oldest brother again. Perhaps, finally, he would be a little more receptive to her efforts. He knew without even asking that there would be another of Penny's single and available friends lined up for him at her party for their parents' wedding anniversary on Saturday evening. After all, there weren't that many unattached millionaires around!

And yet . . . the last thing he wanted was more hassle in his life; a demanding wife and all the decisions that would need to be made where children were concerned. And certainly he would want to make those decisions, as his brothers and sister did. There would be no opting out and leaving it to someone else to take care of them in Alex's scheme of things. But a wife like Miranda would bore him within months, he was sure. Yet, even as he slipped finally into the dreamy state between sleeping and waking, the only woman who came into his mind had deep, deep sea-green eyes that held only contempt for him – and represented a challenge that he knew he had to resist at all costs, or his life would never be the same again.

CHAPTER 3

That same night a young man sat in a Sussex cinema, his whole being concentrated on the screen. Someone at the bank had teased him only that day about the actress he idolized being in the new film at the local cinema and he had hardly been able to concentrate on his work for the rest of the afternoon. Johnnie had been right, she was in the film. A small part it was true, but so significant he decided, and he had wanted to weep when her character died so tragically. To his surprise, he still had suspiciously wet eyes as the credits rolled down the screen. He sat on to watch them determinedly, despite the grumbles of those wanting to get past him anxious to get to the car park, or the burger bar. It was worth it just to read her name again.

Cassandra Taylor. He savoured it over and over as he finally made his way to his car. How beautiful she was! It had shocked him, and then embarrassingly turned him on to watch the leading man taking her clothes off so sensually, revealing her body for all to see. Surely, he thought, she couldn't be enjoying *that*! Yet she had seemed to be – hadn't she? Or was she just the superb actress he had always thought her to be? It hurt so much to see her in Brett Kennedy's arms when he wanted her in his own.

As children, they had lived in the same small town and he had adored her from a distance, even then. But she had always been part of a crowd – the girls from the high school had considered themselves the local elite, and Adrian was a year younger – and at the local comprehensive. The St Kilda girls only laughed derisively at him when he tried to be nice to them at the bus stop. Not Casey though, albeit from a distance, she had always smiled at his efforts to be friendly. But he had been a year younger and he never got anywhere with his overtures, and he was far too shy to try too hard. But now he was older, and he was still thinking about the pretty girl he used to know.

After seeing the film, more than ever he was determined to try and write to her and tell her how devoted he was to her, and wondered how he could find her. Tomorrow he would telephone the film company who had made the film, then buy all the film magazines he could find in the newsagents. Somehow he would get in contact with her, but it would be a while, he decided, before he would tell her who he was. First, he would woo her with letters – oh, what wonderful letters he could write to her – it was far safer that way, to begin with. Once he had found the courage to reveal himself, of course, she would write back to him, *then* he might reveal that he knew her of old. But first, first he would drop hints, try to rouse her curiosity.

Adrian Shawcross was twenty-six, the nice, clean and tidy kind of son any mother would be proud of, and Adrian's mother was just that. Her only son was a credit to her, everyone told her so. Tall, with neatly brushed, soft brown hair, he moved with a brisk confidence through the cinema crowds. Almost frighteningly intelligent, he spent his spare time engrossed in the hugely sophisticated computer operation he'd set up in his mother's spare bedroom and it was to this room that he retreated the moment he managed to disengage his mother's enquiries as to his evening. He was polite, as always, but she knew from his distracted manner that he had only one aim in mind.

'That dratted Internet!' she smiled, fondly. 'Always surfing, aren't you, love?'

'Cheaper than girls though, Mother,' he reminded her, returning one of her frequent comments. Mrs Shawcross dreaded the day her precious son decided to marry some bit of a girl. That Susan from the library had been phoning him a bit too often lately, she thought suddenly. Oh, she always made the excuse that Adrian was out, and he never knew about the calls, she made sure of that. Always out on his silly little cabin cruiser, or with his TA pals playing their war games, but she was happier when he was upstairs, surfing away, she decided. It was such a comfort to have him at home now her Len had gone. Not that Len had been much in the way of company. Quiet he had been, and Adrian took after him a bit, she had to admit. Never said a great deal, Adrian. Head always busy with his computer no doubt. Better that than mooning about over all those pictures of that girl he had pinned up in his room. It wasn't as if she was a famous film star or anything. Just some unknown actress, or model of some sort, but he had been almost demented when she had put some of the pictures in the bin one morning.

A good spring-clean, she had decided, and cleaned his room. The way he had raved at her about those few bits of pictures had terrified her for a few minutes. Since then he had cleaned his own room, and she never went into either his bedroom or her spare bedroom. They were Adrian's territory and he guarded his privacy fiercely. It was, after all, a small price for having him still living at home and looking after her.

Adrian carefully took off his neat, navy suit and discreetly striped blue tie, and in his comfortable shell suit he settled himself at his computer to download his messages on the Net. As his interests and expertise had grown his contacts were beginning to be world-wide and there were quite a few messages for him that evening. One even had news of his idol – an appearance in a mail order catalogue, according to one of his many fellow surfers. He would definitely have to send away for that one, he decided. It had certainly been a good day – for once!

CHAPTER 4

After a hard night's work Casey slept far later than she had intended and woke to the sound of the phone ringing. However hard up they were, Casey and Liz always kept their phone bill paid but this morning she cursed the instrument furiously as she rolled over and rubbed her eyes, childishly.

'Casey, it's Tony – Tony Sorensen, from Havilland Gracey.'

'Oh! What do *you* want?' Casey yawned.

'It's ten-thirty, Miss Taylor, are you still in bed? How could you be?'

'I worked late last night,' Casey snapped, never at her best if she was woken suddenly. 'Spit it out, Tony.'

'Fine way to talk to a man bringing you good news – well – goodish, anyway.'

'Such as . . .?' Casey sat up in a flurry of tumbled hair, shivering as her naked breasts met the chill morning air.

'Get yourself down here, girlie, the big boys want to look you over!'

'Not that damned Havilland again?'

'Among others! The Kear guys are dead keen to see you – twelve o'clock OK?'

'Twelve? Oh, Tony, I can't, I've got to work,' she wailed at him in consternation.

'Kissagram? Or the pub?' He laughed. 'Tell them you're taking the day off.'

'It's the pub, and if I don't turn up I'll get the sack, I can't afford it, Tony.'

'The hell you can't! You can't afford not to turn up here, Miss! Tell the pub they can forget the job, you can do better than that, I guarantee it. I'll help you find a job if you don't get this one, I promise you.'

'Oh yes? And the strings?' Casey had heard that kind of promise many times.

'None at all! Now, get yourself out of bed into a cab and over here for twelve o'clock, Casey Taylor.'

'Cab? Are you kidding? I can't afford a cab, I can't afford to eat at the moment.'

'Use the money I gave you yesterday, we'll replace it from petty cash.'

'What money?' she was puzzled.

'The envelope I left with reception, didn't you get it?'

'Oh, yes, but I was in such a rush, I forgot to open it,' Casey confessed.

'Then open it, ducky. You need it more than I do. See you later.'

Casey hung up and climbed out of bed, reaching for her bag to find the envelope she had stuffed into it the night before. In it was a twenty pound note and a slip of paper. '*Have a drink on me and forget that SOB!*' Well she had hardly had time to have a drink on anyone last night, let alone eat. She realized she was starving and, hastily pulling on her dressing gown, she went worriedly to put the kettle on. The dilemma of how to tell Bill she couldn't come in hung heavily. Finally, after a few mouthfuls of reviving caffeine she rang him. He was predictably livid.

'You're a good bar-maid, Casey, but not indispensable,' he warned her.

'I'm an actress, Bill, you know that,' she argued, not very hopefully. 'You *know* I have to go to auditions.'

'No more chances, Casey. I have a pub to run, and I need reliable staff. Come in today, or forget it!'

'I can't, Bill, I'm sorry.' She hated having to say it.

'Then that's it!'

'I'm sorry, Bill. I have to take the chance, don't you see?'

'I hope it's worth it, Casey.'

Well, that was that. She had burnt her boats. Casey shrugged, but she had done it now. She might as well go all out for the Kear job since she now had nothing to lose. A second coffee and she felt strong enough to raid Liz's wardrobe. Being a model, Liz had access to expensive clothes at bargain prices that luckily fitted Casey too and Casey happily took advantage of it. She quickly selected a black designer suit that showed off her figure to perfection with a short straight skirt and deeply vee-necked jacket. A sleek black body, sheer black tights – luckily she found an unladdered pair – and smart black suede high-heeled shoes completed the outfit and Casey was pleased with her reflection, for once.

Though she was never over confident of her looks, despite the jobs that came her way because of them, Casey was a stunning looking girl. The colour of autumn conkers, her hair, when loose, hung halfway to her waist, thickly wavy and shining with health. The almond-shaped sea-green eyes that had so mesmerized Alexander Havilland were bright with intelligence and often sparkling with mischief, below sweeping brows several shades darker than her hair. A balanced oval face with a neat straight nose and a wide curving mouth that smiled often, with a tiny mole just above the left corner. Casey had never made any attempt to have the mole removed – if famous models could have one, she reasoned, then so could she! Though slender for her long-legged height, her breasts were full and firm, giving her a body that could have given her plenty of the kind of work that showed it off. But she had always stead-fastly refused to do nude scenes in the past, only giving in on one major film that she still hoped would lead to better things.

Carefully, she made herself up with Liz's huge collection of make-up and, mindful of the day before, coiled her hair up into a high knot that could be unravelled easily. She was well aware of the effect that that simple gesture could have! By the time she had finished, she looked exactly what she was – a beautiful young woman, just a hint of sexiness but not blatantly so.

'Whore, indeed!' she grinned at her elegant reflection in the dusty mirror 'I'll teach you, Mr Havilland!' Then she looked around at the dishevelled room, even more so now she had tumbled clothes over Liz's bed as well as her own and she grimaced, ruefully. There would still be a few minutes before the cab she had grudgingly rung for arrived. Swiftly she hurled the clothes back into the wardrobe that they both shared and then straightened up her bed. The dirty dishes would have to wait, she dared not risk getting the precious suit spattered, but she swept up all the magazines into a neat pile and plumped up the cushions on the battered sofa. I'll worry about the rest later, she decided as the bell rang downstairs. It would be several days before Liz got back and it seemed likely she would have plenty of time to clean the flat after today. There really was no alternative but to ask Marty for more work, and she knew what that was likely to entail. But things were getting pretty desperate. All the money she had was her wages from the pub last night and the twenty pounds that Tony had given her. She prayed that he would do as he had offered and replace her cab fare from petty cash. It would be a Godsend as she could ill afford to throw away money on a cab fare.

The taxi driver did her morale good, however, whistling appreciatively at her as she got in. 'Where to, darlin'?' he grinned. Casey told him.

'My destiny, I hope,' she added, her fingers crossed.

'A job, eh? Nice bit of secretarial?'

'Not quite.'

'Classy lady like you deserves better than pounding a typewriter, I reckon. Ad agency ain't it?' Casey nodded. 'Yeah, I've heard of that Alex Havilland, done well he has. I drove him once when I was on the mini-cabs. Looked like a film star, real nice he was.'

Nice *film star* was not the description Casey would have favoured for the autocratic megalomaniac she had encountered! Handsome, maybe, she had to concede to that, but nice? Never in a million years as far as she was concerned!

The receptionist stared at her in slack-jawed amazement. 'Miss Taylor? You can't be! You're the Kissagram girl!'

''Fraid so! I'm in to see Tony Sorensen again, for real this time.'

'Not just Tony, Mr Havilland and Ross are with the Kear people waiting for you.' The receptionist reverted to her efficient self with difficulty. 'Take the lift to the sixth floor and Tony will meet you there. It's definitely top brass today.'

Nervously, Casey checked her make-up and hair in the mirrored panels as the lift sped upwards. So close now to the meeting and her heart was beginning to pound in trepidation as she stepped out of the lift to meet a grinning Tony.

'My word! Casey, my love, you'll knock 'em dead!' Tony stared almost as hard as the receptionist had done.

'I'm not your love, Tony Sorensen!' Casey rebuked with a grin. 'Behave yourself!'

'Do I have to? Wait till Robin Faulkner gets an eyeful of you, he'll wet himself!'

'I hope not, for his sake!' Casey couldn't help giggling, from sheer nervousness.

Laughing together they walked into the outer area of Alexander's spacious offices to be faced with the great man himself. 'About time!' Alex snapped as he stood in the doorway. 'Consolidating your conquest of yesterday, Miss Taylor?'

'Oh, get lost, you *gorilla*!' Casey turned on her heel – good job or not, she was not putting up with this! 'You don't miss an opportunity to put me down, do you?'

'Come back here this minute, young woman!' Alex whipped an arm out to grab at hers as she turned away. 'The Kear guys want to see you and that is exactly what they are going to do, whether you like it or not!'

'I've changed my mind! I don't want this job.' Casey snarled, equally belligerent.

'Liar! Like it or not you are going in there, and behaving like a lady, even if you aren't one. Now . . . smile!' His grip was like a vice on her wrist almost bruising the delicate skin that was pressed against her watch strap as he guided her firmly through the door to his office, followed by a shocked Tony. No-one had ever spoken to Alexander in Tony's presence as Casey had just done, and he was trembling with fear at just what might happen next, as he read the taut muscles in Alex's gripping hand on Casey's arm.

'Smile, damn you!' Alex hissed at her, as Casey glanced around the room. 'Gentlemen, Cassandra Taylor!'

'Casey!' Ross stood up to greet her with a friendly smile and a handshake. 'Do take a seat, honey.' He proffered a chair and Casey took care to sit carefully, legs demurely crossed. She was introduced to the three clients from Kear and then to the tall, blond man lounging against the window sill. 'Robin Faulkner.' Ross waved a friendly gesture at her as the man unfolded himself and sauntered across the room to her.

'Oh, yes!' he smiled, looking straight down at Casey's cleavage. 'This one I can do business with, to quote the great Iron Lady!' With an easy flick of his wrist he drew Casey to her feet. 'This is the one I want!'

'Take no notice of Romeo here,' Ross laughed. 'The Irish are all the same. I knew we should have made him wait outside.'

'And miss all the fun?' Robin was not easily diverted.

'So let's have a look at you, Cassandra.' James Wyatt, the elder of the three clients, interrupted rather sharply. 'Would you let your hair down please? It was just right on the video.'

It spoiled her elegant appearance but Casey pulled out the three or four pins she had placed so carefully and shook the red coil free in the graceful way she had planned, so that it cascaded down her back to murmurs of appreciation from her audience. It had been worth the little bit of careful planning.

'Could you take your jacket off too?' another man asked. Casey hesitated: the body under it was decent, but only just, and she wasn't wearing a bra.

'I . . . er . . .' she hesitated.

'Cassandra! Please do as you have been asked.' Alex put in, impatiently. 'We are not asking you to do anything you haven't done before.' They might just as well be, Casey thought, as she unbuttoned her jacket. In the short skirt and thin top she flashed a look at Alex that could kill and stood up tossing her hair back. To her surprise they were enthusiastic, asking her to walk up and down as Ross had asked her the day before. She felt incredibly vulnerable in the thin top and short skirt but, unknown to her, she was generating the exact kind of vulnerability they were looking for.

'Fine,' James Wyatt said at last. 'Would you wait outside please, Cassandra?' In relief, Casey picked up her jacket and followed the pretty secretary into an office adjacent to Alex's spacious suite.

'Coffee?' Mary-Jo asked and reached for the perculator she obviously kept hot.

'Mmm, yes please.' Casey put her jacket back on and re-coiled her hair . . . back in her outer skin she felt far more able to cope. 'Will they keep me long do you suppose?'

'Well, I've been waiting ages.' A girl with blonde highlighted hair looked up from the magazine she had been reading and scrutinized Casey thoroughly. 'They don't give a damn about keeping us hanging about.'

'Are you here for the Kear job, then?' Casey took the coffee Mary-Jo handed her and added sugar, to the intense disapproval of the blonde.

'Sure am! Nice little number it is too, and I must say that Robin Faulkner is dead dishy! He can share my bed any time he likes! I'm Bridget Sullivan, by the way.' The girl looked stunning and spoke with the careful enunciation that came from years of speech training. Stage school, no doubt, Casey decided, wearily. She could probably sing and dance as well as act, unlike Casey. Then she comforted herself – no one had actually asked if she could do either!

Casey smiled and, telling herself not to be so defeatist, introduced herself, needing to say little else then. Bridget was far too concerned about boasting how much work she had done for Havilland Gracey and how well she knew all the personnel connected with the Kear shoot, hinting strongly that since she so obviously had the job it was hardly worth Casey waiting. Behind her back, Mary-Jo lifted elegant eyebrows in apology and Casey surreptitiously smiled back. Bridget was a typical glamour type, and Casey just prayed the clients didn't see her in the same light; she would rather lose the job than be thought of in that vein!

Finally, just as she was thinking she could stand it no longer, Tony came out of the office grinning broadly. 'Casey, would you like to come back in? Bridget, I'm sorry, darling, another time maybe?'

Bridget was obviously furious at being kept hanging around for nothing and flounced out without another word. Tony and Mary-Jo exchanged grins. 'You owe me a fiver, M-J,' Tony reminded her. 'I'll collect it later. Come on, Casey, in you go, just don't blot your copybook again!'

'I'll try,' she promised wishing briefly she had been to the loo while she was waiting, before she braced herself and followed Tony back into Alex's office. The five men were clustered around the boardroom table sifting through her photgraphs.

'Join us for a glass of wine, Casey?' Ross offered, but Casey shook her head.

'Mineral water, please.' She needed a clear head for this one.

'Well, Cassandra.' The senior client was obviously the spokesman. 'We would like to offer you the job – four weeks' shoot, a contract for personal appearances with an exclusivity clause. Are you interested?'

'Yes, please!' Casey saw no point in playing hard to get – it was the job of a lifetime, Bridget had made that quite clear.

'Good girl! Well, we'll talk to your agent about fees, the important thing to concern you is that shooting starts in two weeks. You have a passport, I take it?' Casey nodded. 'Then you will need to spend the next two weeks with our stylist. There is a lot to do as you can imagine. Now, would you like to join us for dinner this evening? You, and Robin of course?' He nodded to Robin as he came back into the room from making a phone call.

Casey wondered with trepidation if that included Alex, then realized that dinner with the Kear clients would be a meal to remember and she could certainly do with that! So she accepted gracefully. 'We'll send a car for you at eight o'clock,' Tony told her as she stood to leave.

'Before you go, Cassandra, I'd like a word,' Alex rose, barring her way. 'It won't take a minute.' His smile was cold as he indicated her to follow him into another office. 'Sit down.' He waved her to a chair.

Sitting, she was at a disadvantage, her eyes on a level with his immaculately tailored dark grey suit. How flash, she thought suddenly: his white shirt was silk, echoed by the discreetly patterned red and grey expensive tie. Determined not to be beaten she crossed her legs carefully and met his hard dark eyes squarely. 'Mr Havilland?'

'Cassandra!' he challenged, perching on the edge of the desk, swinging one elegant leg as he balanced himself with the other.

'I prefer Casey.'

'Very well . . . Casey. Since you have been picked

45

for this job we need to discuss a few ground rules before this evening.'

'*Mr Havilland*, please be assured I do *know* which knife and fork to use and my table manners are quite adequate for the occasion!' Casey retorted, furious that he needed to even mention anything about her behaviour.

'I'm glad to hear it,' he said drily. 'However, it is more your tongue I'm concerned about, young woman. This evening I would prefer no mention of your present, rather unconventional, method of earning a living, if you wouldn't mind. Luckily yesterday you had so much rubbish on your face I doubt even your mother would have recognized you!'

'*I'm* not ashamed of it!' Casey blurted out, angrily. 'It's preferable to starving, I assure you!'

'Maybe! But Kear are *not* to know. The Keara girl must be way above that degrading level and you will have to learn to live with it. Do I make myself clear?'

'I have to pretend to be something I'm not, you mean?'

'You will simply be discreet! And carry on being so, understand?'

She nodded. 'I don't let people down, Mr Havilland!' Except, of course, Bill. She still felt very bad about that even if she had actually got the job she had taken the risk for. 'So you expect me to be exclusively available to Kear from today onwards?'

'Yes, we do, until after the shoot, then it will be

on a day-to-day basis and you will be free to do other *acting* work but not commercials. Is that a problem?' Only, she thought, if he expected her to eat and pay her rent at the end of the week as well!

'Er . . . no. I don't actually have any other work on my schedule, I'm afraid.'

'And definitely no more kissagrams! They are *right* out!'

'If you say so.' Casey's chin jerked up. 'Mr Havilland, I need this job though it galls me to admit it. I will be charm itself to your clients this evening and rest assured, I will arrive dressed correctly for the event.'

'So lack of legitimate work doesn't affect your wardrobe then?' he asked, sarcastically.

'Not when your flatmate is a model, no!' Casey returned and stood up to leave. 'Or I could, of course, wear my little green number!' Her eyes flashed with amusement at the appalled look on his handsome face.

'Don't even joke about it,' he snapped back as he swiftly recovered his composure. 'Wait!' He put a hand to his inside pocket and drew out a leather-covered cheque book. 'I realize things are tight financially.' Swiftly he scribbled out a cheque and handed it to her. 'This is a little unethical I know, since you have yet to sign a contract but . . . I will trust you to do so.'

The cheque from an exclusive bank was for five hundred pounds and Casey stared, first at the hastily scrawled cheque and then at him. She longed to refuse it but she needed it, and he was making her turn down any other work after all. 'I *will* pay you back,' she said, slowly and to her surprise discerned the faint glimmer of a smile on his lips.

'You bet your sweet life you will,' he said, firmly. 'I'm taking one *hell* of a risk over you, Cassandra – *Casey*. Let me down and I'll make sure you never forget it!'

'Is that a threat, Mr Havilland?'

'No, Casey.' His cool eyes levelled with hers. '*That* is a promise! Till this evening then? I look forward to seeing whatever your flatmate has to offer wardrobe-wise! We are dining at the Arbour, by the way.' So he *would* be there! Somehow Casey managed to stammer her thanks to him and walk out of his office with her dignity intact and, in relief, make for the ladies.

Newly composed and relaxed now her ordeal was over, she left the haven of the cloakroom and made her way down the corridor to the lifts, surprised then to be stopped by Ross coming towards her. 'Casey I'm glad I caught you,' he said. 'Come and have a sandwich with me? I'd like a chat with you about your agent.'

He whisked her through the building and out into Charlotte Street. 'On second thoughts,' he said, 'let's go to Luigi's. You aren't dressed for the sandwich bar.' Neither was he, since he was wearing designer suit – for Kear no doubt – she noticed as he bustled her to a table that the waiter immediately found for them. Ordering pasta and mineral water for both of them, he settled back with a smile. 'So, Casey, how does it feel to suddenly facing fame and fortune?'

'Am I?'

'You certainly are! This campaign is costing millions, the biggest Havilland Gracey have had for a while, that's why Alex is agency producer on it. You and he don't seem to be too friendly but he *is* an ace producer. His shoots run like clockwork, though he's as tight as hell about money!' Casey thought with fresh amusement about the cheque in her handbag.

'Millions!' She was aghast as she took the facts in.

'Yes, and I'm going to make sure you get paid properly! I don't like Jessie, she really is a lazy old cow! How firm is your contract with TSA?'

'Not very,' she admitted. 'I got the tour off my own bat because the director was a friend of a friend, I have nothing in writing because I just got passed on to TSA when my agent retired.'

'Not very helpful really. Look, Casey, I would like you to go and see Len Stafford, he handles quite a few top actors and I think he could do quite a lot for you.'

'Len Stafford? Are you joking?' Casey almost choked on a mouthful of linguini. Len was one of the top agents in London and she was well aware of his status.

'No, I'm not! I spoke to him just now and he would be happy to see you this afternoon. He can sort out taking you over from TSA. They really are a shoddy outfit, honey.'

'It's hard enough to get an agent at all when you have no real track record,' Casey reminded him.

'I'm aware of that,' he nodded. 'But I think you deserve a break and I think Len will give you that. He'll see you at three, OK?'

'Ross! This is fantastic! I can hardly believe it's all happening to me!' Casey stared at him. 'I was so desperate yesterday about everything – money, job, I was at the end of my tether.'

'So Tony said. Is it right you were in the building playing a strippagram?'

'Not stripping!' She was horrified. 'I made that quite clear when I started doing it. Marty is a bit of a shark but he was fine about it. The only time my top came off was when your precious boss manhandled me!'

'Alex did? I don't believe it!'

'He *was* pretty mad,' Casey grinned.

'That I can believe.' Ross grinned back. 'He does have a pretty short fuse, but you don't get to be a multi-millionaire by being nice.'

'You can say that again! He's the pits!'

'No, Casey. He's just tough, and he doesn't miss much,' Ross corrected. 'But he's not my actual boss. I'm employed by the production company. Terry Marsden is my producer for the production company; Alex is the agency producer on this shoot as well as being the owner.'

'So many people,' she sighed. 'I'll never get them all sorted out.'

'You will, and they won't all be on the shoot, don't worry,' he comforted 'The clients will drift in and out; you just smile at them. Alex will be around since he has made it his business to be available to us, but the only ones you will need to really know are the crew and they are all my own guys. And Robin of course, but then you've met him.'

'I like him,' Casey said. 'He's lovely.'

'Well he certainly likes you, the chemistry is great! I think you'll make a great pairing on camera. The TV public will love you, and not just TV, cinema too. Bang will go your private life, Casey. I hope your boyfriend won't mind too much.'

'I don't have a boyfriend,' Casey admitted. 'I haven't had one in ages.' And didn't want one, not since the last dismal experience.

'Then I suggest you keep that very quiet, honey; knowing our friend Robin he won't be able to keep his hands off you. Though, sadly I assure you, you're safe with me! I'm a married man with five kids!'

'Five!'

'We all make mistakes! Like Alex with his wife.'

'Oh, is he married?' Casey asked casually. 'I'm surprised he has the time.'

'Was! The bitch walked out on him a few years ago, blamed his work, his devotion to his business – anything but her own selfishness.' He waved for the bill. 'He was well rid of the two-timing cow if you ask me.'

'She must have had a good reason,' Casey ventured.

Marriage to Alex Havilland seemed to her a good enough reason to want out somehow.

'All she could see were pound signs,' Ross dismissed. 'Alex is far better off without her if you ask me. He's got a very classy lady now, Lord Bradbury's daughter, Miranda.'

'I wish her joy of him! Will she be there tonight?'

'Possibly, you never know with Alex.'

Casey rather hoped she would be, at least it might curb Alex's acerbic tongue where she was concerned. Mulling it over, she got into the cab Ross called for her and made her way to Len Stafford's office shaking with nerves at the thought of meeting him. But he was charming and delighted to see her.

'Ross is confident you have promise, Casey,' he said on greeting her. 'So let's find out, shall we?'

He went over all the work she had done, asked about what she wanted to achieve and then went through the Kear contract he had asked Havilland Gracey to fax to him. Casey gasped at the money they were offering her. 'Not enough, my dear,' Len said. 'Not nearly enough, leave it to me.'

'And TSA?'

'That too. You have never signed a contract with them?'

'No.'

'Then more fool them! There's no problem, my dear, I'll sort it out. Welcome to the fold, Casey.'

CHAPTER 5

The Arbour was one of London's top restaurants. Casey knew of its fantastic reputation from reading magazines, and dressed accordingly. Sleek and elegant in a white slip dress, one of a series she and Liz had made up in several differently coloured lengths of material they'd found in a Berwick Street theatrical fabric shop, cut from a pattern by a designer friend of Liz's. It was cut so well that there was no need for a bra, though she considered the problem for a few minutes, twisting this way and that trying to assess the need for one. Finally she decided to take a risk and went without, but selected a huge embroidered shawl that had belonged to her mother to wrap around her just in case she lost her nerve at the last minute! Letting her hair hang loose down her back, the sides caught up simply on her crown with a tortoise-shell slide, she deliberately made up her face to appear almost free of make-up with just the subtlest hint of lipstick; and the results pleased her for once as she gave a quick glance in the mirror before leaving the now tidy flat. Elated as she had been once she arrived home, her mother's training had still to come to the fore and she had spent some time with the battered vacuum cleaner and a duster before getting ready.

It *was* a beautiful restaurant, she discovered as she was conducted towards the Kear party gathered in the bar. Soft amber-washed walls and comfortable rosewood chairs grouped around low tables gave the bar a richly warm ambience and she relaxed a little more as she greeted the three men she had already met and was introduced to the two wives who had joined their husbands for the evening. Ross and Robin Faulkner were unacccompanied but just as she was seated and a drink was ordered for her, Alex strolled in with an exquisite and expensively dressed brunette on his arm.

'Ah-ha, the beautiful Miranda,' Ross murmured in Casey's ear. 'Alex will be on his best behaviour this evening, never fear.'

He was; urbane and charming to the clients and their wives, joking with Robin and displaying a prodigious knowledge of motor racing as they talked. Casey, he virtually ignored though she was frequently aware of his cool eyes on her, particularly when she talked to Robin, who swiftly seated himself next to her when they were finally conducted with great ceremony to their table.

Light-heartedly, Robin teased her life-story out of her, quite calmly monopolizing her attention. Needing to tread a very delicate path where the wives were concerned, Casey allowed him to do it,

54

knowing she was safe with his cheerful banter.

Robin was a complete charmer and had every woman in the party wrapped around his fingers within minutes, even Casey though she was loath to admit it! His hair was naturally blond, thick and wavy on his collar, and flopping forward frequently, his hazel eyes warm and friendly as he flirted cheerfully, despite the occasional frown that Alex flashed in his direction whenever Casey laughed at one of his more outrageous suggestions.

Seated on her other side and primed by a liberal application of alcohol, James Wyatt was in a good mood and patted Casey's arm possessively as coffee was served. 'We are delighted to have found you, Casey, dear,' he smiled at her. 'I'm sure the campaign is going to be a great success for you both.'

'Can't fail, can it?' Robin grinned. 'Casey's looks and my charm!' Robin had no false modesty!

'Plus a great deal of work on both your parts,' Alex put in, sharply putting him down. 'It's not all glitz and glamour you know, Robin, as you will soon find out.' This was obviously his first commercial, Casey realized.

'Neither is motor racing,' Robin returned, not at all put down. 'We have the glamorous side, yes, but we work very hard too! You should try driving a race car for several hours at a stretch with sweat pouring off you, not to mention being up half the night getting it ready sometimes. Silverstone at three o'clock in the morning can be a very cold and windy place, I assure you!'

'Well, now you have Kear sponsoring your next season you'll be spared that kind of hardship,' James pointed out. 'It will be our mechanics who stay up all night instead!'

'Thank goodness!' Robin sighed. 'I have better things to do with my nights,' he added quietly to Casey. 'Which reminds me, can I give you a lift home, Casey? I promise I have been drinking mineral water all evening.'

'No need, Robin,' Alex interrupted, firmly. 'I can order a cab for her.'

'But I'd like to,' Robin was equally firm. 'And Casey is quite agreeable. It's no trouble, Alex, save the cab fare!' he added, cheekily.

'Lexy, darling, let the children go if they want to.' It was the first time Miranda had openly acknowledged Casey all evening, though Casey had been aware of her eyes on her frequently. 'I'm sure they have *lots* of things in mind – don't be a spoilsport!'

Casey had nothing whatsoever in mind as far as Robin was concerned but the lightly drawled remark got her back up and her more wicked thoughts went into overdrive. Suddenly she made her mind up. 'I'll be fine with Robin,' she said, smiling sweetly at Alex's glowering face. 'And I promise not to lead him astray!'

'What a disappointment! Come on then, Cinderella. I'll see you home.' Robin caught her arm. 'Let's go.' Carelessly he made his farewells, waiting as Casey rose and made her own, more carefully, as she had been brought up to do.

'The office at ten,' Ross told her as he touched a kiss to her cheek. 'The stylist, Angie, is meeting you there.'

'Angie is amazing,' Robin said as he hustled her out. 'Looks like a gypsy but she's got great taste, I've got a knock-out set of clothes. You won't be able to resist me in them!' He led her to a gleaming red Lotus. 'Come on, now we've escaped the grown-ups, let's go dancing.'

'Oh, I don't know . . .' Casey hesitated.

'Casey! I'll behave, scout's honour!'

'Were you ever a boy scout?'

'Well . . . no! But I'll try and be one!'

'Oh . . . well . . . OK then, where are we going?'

'Somewhere dark, noisy and crowded where I can grope you because there's no other choice!' he promised with a wicked grin and Casey sighed inwardly. But she loved to dance and she took a chance for once, since it was hardly likely that Robin would push too hard when they had to work together in harmony for several weeks!

He was obviously well known in the smart basement disco and Casey relaxed, ready to let her hair down and enjoy herself. Robin proved to be an excellent dancer and made her laugh endlessly with his wicked impersonations of 'Lady' Miranda. 'What a vapid little wash-out *she* is,' he commented with a grin as Casey chided him on his more outrageous comments. 'Alex Havilland must be bedding her for Daddy's connections, that's all I can think of! He must be mad – or desperate!'

'But she's lovely to look at!' Casey protested.

'On the surface, possibly, but the head is air from ear to ear and there is nothing of her body-wise. You, on the other hand . . .!'

'Are you suggesting I'm fat?' Casey drew back as his arms encircled her slim waist.

'You're perfect and you know it! A lovely armful! Relax, Case, I won't bite – not yet anyway!' Casey gave in. She was having too good a time to argue.

However, suddenly it was three in the morning and she thought regretfully of her appointment with Ross and his stylist. But to her surprise Robin drove her home without arguing when she suggested it and did not even give her any hassle when they reached her street. He had to pull in and park a few car lengths from her door and she thought the worst when he leapt out to accompany her.

'I'm not asking you in,' Casey said, firmly. 'It's far too late.'

'Then I'll kiss you goodnight on the doorstep!' Robin swung her into his arms and before she could make any move to reject him, he kissed her. Not on her mouth as she had anticipated but on her cheek, chastely, and making her laugh at her own fears. In the street-light he saw her surprise and laughed back before he kissed her again, catching her mouth this time with a light unthreatening kiss.

'Got you!' he grinned. 'Ease up, Case, just a rehearsal,' he added as he released her. 'Shall we try and sneak dinner together this week, well away from Alex the Führer's eye?'

'Why do you call Alex the Führer?'

'He damned well behaves like one! He **even** warned me not to get too involved with you – **very** firmly hands off! Maybe the beautiful Miranda doesn't have the hold on him that she thinks she has!'

'Well I certainly don't fancy him!' Casey put her arms round his neck and kissed him back as lightly as he had done her. 'But let's keep this fairly business-like, Robin, I think it would be wiser.'

'For my sake or yours?' he countered.

'Just no hassles?'

'OK, bargain! But we'll still have fun on this job, no point unless we do! I'll call you about dinner, promise you'll come?'

'I'd like that. Goodnight, Robin.'

Musing on her new turn of fortune she slipped off her shoes and mounted the three flights of stairs up to the flat on weary legs. After weeks of uncertainty she had a fantastic job, one of the best agents in the business happy to take her on, and a glamorous racing driver begging her to date him. He was, she decided, far more suitable for the easy-going Liz than her, though. She was cautious, as always, where men where concerned – but worse things could happen than being thrown into Robin's amusing company for several weeks!

His comment about Alexander, however, both amused and alarmed her at first, though after second thoughts she was inclined to dismiss it. After all, in two days Alex had never been anything but arrogantly rude to her. He had noticed her looks, quite obviously, but his warning to Robin had surely been simply a professional worry to prevent her from getting into a state over him on location. It had certainly been known to happen between artistes thrown together on location, she had witnessed it herself many times. Little did Havilland know, she mused ruefully, that it would take a great deal for a man to affect Casey's heart. As far as the male sex were concerned that part of her was firmly off-limits.

Her heart had been broken fairly comprehensively in her first year at university by one of her lecturers whom she had afterwards discovered made a point of seducing the prettier of his students. Since then the species as a whole had been kept very firmly at bay. Casey's boyfriends soon learnt that it was a case of look, but don't touch, and Robin had been the first man to kiss her for many months, apart from Brett Kennedy on the film set – and that had hardly been a pleasant interlude, surrounded as they had been by dozens of technicians. Unhappy, and eventually frightened rigid, Casey had been persuaded by Brett and the director to do the scene naked and, though Brett had admittedly done the majority of the nudity, she still remembered the scene with embarrassment. But Brett had indeed been very understanding and she remembered him with gratitude.

'Keep your sense of fun, angel, concentrate on your lines at first,' he had advised as she had shivered in his arms and he had made her, and indeed the entire crew, laugh then with his jokes and his endless good humour. He had congratulated her afterwards and told her he wished he wasn't quite so firmly married! More encouragingly he had hinted at using her in another film of his own that he was trying to raise the capital for, but that had been eight or nine months ago. True, there had been a note from him to say he hadn't forgotten her when the film had opened in America but that was all and the urgency of keeping financially afloat had pushed him to the back of her mind until the note had come. But if her luck was really changing at last, she wondered sleepily if it would perhaps change for Brett too, and he would manage to get the funding for his project. She made a mental note to tell Len Stafford about it in the morning.

CHAPTER 6

Her first sight of the stylist the next day was hardly inspiring. Angie had bright red hair out of a bottle and an outfit consisting mostly of black studded leather and ripped denim. But she had been well briefed by the agency and certainly had Ross's trust in her ability. This meeting was run by Ross alone, thankfully Alex and the clients were nowhere to be seen, and Ross was comprehensive, and thorough. When Tommy the hairdresser joined them, to her surprise Ross knew exactly what he wanted to have done with her hair.

'Slightly shorter round the face,' he ruled. 'And lift the colour a few shades, more sun-streaked, I guess.'

'I've already booked her into Daniel's tomorrow,' Tommy confirmed. 'Sorry, Angie, it'll take time out of your schedule.'

Angie sighed. 'Typical! Well we'd better get going. I hope you've got comfortable shoes on, Casey.'

Casey looked down at the loafers she wore with

her own jeans. Time had been short that morning and she had taken a gamble by wearing jeans. She was, she reasoned sensibly, going out shopping and needed clothes she could slip in and out of easily, hence the jeans and the simple blue check shirt tucked into them. She was a professional. Her underwear was clean, and her bra fitted properly. 'And the rest,' she grinned. 'No clients today, Ross?'

'Not till Friday, honey,' Ross grinned. 'Then they will want a preview of everything you girls choose.'

'A private fashion show,' Angie grimaced. 'Show them fifty outfits and they'll only like ten, God help us!'

'Alex's decision,' Ross reminded her. 'Off you go girls, have fun!'

Angie, for all her bizarre appearance, was well known and respected in the fashion showrooms that she took Casey to and her experienced eye selected dresses at a bewildering speed. Overwhelmed by the stunning and expensive outfits she was being hauled in and out of, Casey left the decisions to her in the end, realizing she was in safe hands.

'You're a dream to dress,' Angie said, appreciatively as Casey complimented her on her taste during a much needed coffee break.

'Despite being a twelve top and a ten bottom?' Casey teased.

'Better than being the other way round,' Angie laughed. 'Cheer up, Casey, only a week or so more!'

If my feet can last that long!' Casey sighed. *Wrong Reason* was a breeze compared to this!'

'Funnily enough I went to see *Wrong Reason* last night,' Angie mused, as she cut her pastry into bite-sized pieces. 'You were great!'

'What little you see of me! A dead body most of the time!'

'Don't put yourself down all the time, Casey. I must say I envy you that sexy scene with Brett, and the bit at the beginning when you put the gambling chip down the front of your dress was knockout – a real teaser! You certainly seemed to get on with Brett, and he's not easy, I know.'

'He was great!' Casey defended. 'And he kept his hands to himself, which makes a change!'

'Married to Cheryl Hemingway he wouldn't have a chance to do anything else,' Angie commented drily. 'She's got him well under her thumb!'

'Rather like Alex Havilland and the honourable Miranda from what I've heard! What *is* that set-up? Do you know?' Casey asked casually. Angie seemed pretty clued up about the agency she worked for fairly frequently.

'Knowing Alex, I think he's just using Miranda,' Angie shrugged. 'He's a hard bastard underneath the glam looks. But she's besotted with him, poor girl.'

'So I noticed! Robin was quite scathing about how thick she was. *He* certainly didn't fall for the sweet baby act!'

'Trust Robin to call a spade a shovel! Has he tried

to get you into bed yet?' Angie giggled. 'He's going to be a handful on this shoot, I don't doubt!'

'Oh, I think he's manageable enough,' Casey shrugged. 'Don't forget, he hasn't done this kind of work before – a few days' shooting and he'll be too exhausted to try anything.'

'You hope! A libido like Rob's takes quite a bit of suppressing, especially when there are only four girls on the shoot.'

'Only four?'

'Yeah. You, me, Pearl the make-up girl and Donna, Ross's assistant-cum-everything. Pearl's a snotty bitch at the best of times, even Rob wouldn't get anywhere with her. So that leaves thee, and me, because Donna's newly married to the camera operator!'

'We'd better share keeping him at arm's length then,' Casey suggested. 'He's too much of a handful for me, certainly!'

'OK, we'll protect each other! This shoot could be fun after all, even if Alex Havilland is agency producer.'

'You don't like him either?'

Angie shrugged. 'Alex is incredibly good at running his company and that's where he should stay – in his boardroom – out of our hair! Oh, he's a great producer and the clients like him, but somehow you always get the feeling that he knows everything that goes on, especially on location – and that can be a real pain, I tell you!'

'Big Brother and all that?'

'And how! He runs a tight ship financially too. But he and Ross were very enthusiastic about you this morning; he likes you, Casey.'

Casey burst into astonished laughter. 'Well, if that's liking me, God only knows what disliking me is like! Robin calls him the Führer!'

'Good description! So what did he do to get your back up?'

'What didn't he do?' Casey laughed and filled her in on the way she had got the part. Angie roared with mirth.

'How on earth did you get away with calling him names like that?' she demanded, wiping her eyes. 'He must have had the shock of his life!'

'He did look stunned for a moment,' Casey admitted, rubbing reminiscently at the wrist Alex had gripped.' 'But he soon retaliated!'

'I bet he did! The whole company goes in fear of that man!'

'My dad taught me that respect has to be earned, not expected,' Casey said. 'And I certainly have no respect for a man who behaves like that to me!'

'Brave girl! Well, this shoot is certainly going to be different, I must say!'

'I may hate him personally, but he *has* given me the chance of a lifetime, and not just the Kear job. I am going to have to be nice to him from now on, much as it galls me.' Casey drained her cup. 'At last I feel I can get somewhere after, what, five years of bit parts and stultifyingly boring modelling. Ross sent me to Len Stafford and he is taking me on his books so I've now consolidated by having the best agent in London!'

'Oh boy! When luck turns, it really does it in spades, doesn't it?'

'It certainly does!'

For days, Casey was in a complete whirl of fittings, appointments and meetings. Her hair was cut and expertly highlighted with golden lights, her skin was treated and fussed over as Pearl took her share of Casey's time. A few sun-bed sessions turned her skin pale gold all over at Pearl's suggestion and by the time she arrived at Havilland Gracey to show off Angie's choice of dresses she felt like a completely new person.

It took two gruelling hours to display the dozens of outfits that Angie had put together. In make-up changed half a dozen times before Ross was satisfied, her hair brushed until it shone, she was grateful for Angie's good humour as she was hauled in and out of the beautiful dresses. The whole time she was becoming more aware of Alex's coolly assessing eyes on her every time she entered the room in a different outfit and he was beginning to unnerve her completely by the time they were nearly through.

James Wyatt approved three-quarters of the clothes to the two girls' intense delight. It made the hours of trudging around the showrooms worth while suddenly.

Casey's own particular favourite, Angie kept till

last. A soft cream chiffon evening dress with a filmy hood held in place by a halter neck front. Her back, now lightly tanned, was bare to the waist and her long legs were revealed in tantalizing glimpses when the long split in the side opened as she moved. There was a communal gasp from the assembled clients as she drifted across the room on high-heeled silver sandals.

'Knock-out!' Ross breathed at last. 'That is exactly right for the Grand Canyon kiss. Angie, you are a genius, girly!'

'Wait till you see my bills!' Angie grinned at him, happily reassured by their pleasure. Even Alex was smiling, albeit, reluctantly.

'Quite a transformation, Casey,' he said at last as Casey's eyes met his with a challenging stare. She was very aware of how much of the shape of her body was on display: the delicate dress left very little to the imagination. Yet apart from her back, cleverly, there was hardly any actual flesh showing. The look was subtly sensual as Angie had intended and, for once, Casey was totally sure of herself, and the effect she was having on the men around her. She paused, her eyes still on Alex, and remembered then the way the director had made her look at Brett in the casino scene.

Deliberately, she held his eyes and smiled, only to him. A slow, teasing smile flickering over a soft full mouth only lightly touched with lip gloss. Tantalizing, challenging him to retaliate and within seconds she recognized his confusion with childish glee. For a few triumphant moments Casey knew she had touched a raw nerve in the arrogant male leaning against the window sill. His composure shattered and to cover it he moved, reaching for the phone on his desk. 'I think a drink is called for,' he said. 'Gentlemen? Ladies, you agree?'

'Not in that frock!' Angie put in smartly. 'Excuse us!' She gestured to Casey to follow her and ushered her back to the room they were using as a changing room. 'My goodness, Casey! I have never seen Alex Havilland lose his cool – not ever. You completely floored him just now. It was – well – mind blowing! He'll never forgive you for that! You made him look an absolute fool for a second!'

'I hope I didn't overdo it.' Casey slid out of the dress, regretfully. 'I couldn't help it, it was such a challenge.' She giggled. 'He did look a bit stunned!'

'A bit!' Angie giggled in unison. 'He didn't know whether to hit you, or jump on you! God help you if he ever gets you alone.'

'He won't! Not if I can help it. Frankly he deserved it, he's put me through it a few times.'

'Don't play with fire, Casey,' Angie warned. 'And he is *definitely* fire – with a vengeance!'

Confused herself now, Casey shivered. As usual, she had leapt in feet first! Why on earth couldn't she curb her crazy instincts for once, especially where Alex was concerned, she wondered frantically as she changed back into her own black linen skirt and loose white top. Now she had to go back into the room and face him as well as the Kear clients; and if

Angie had seen what she had done, then they and Ross would have done so too. Issuing a blatant challenge like that went against any of the careful control she had always had over her emotions. Alex would probably think the worst of her – but then he did anyway, so what was she worrying about, she comforted herself finally.

'Have a large drink,' Angie advised, folding the scattered dresses into their zipped bags. 'And stick close to the clients, they at least are besotted with you!'

Gratefully, Casey followed her advice and strolled over to James and Ross to look over the scripts for the ten commercials that were finally ready. 'Lots for you to learn,' Ross said, handing Casey a glass of the mineral water he knew she favoured. 'The girl does the majority of the speaking in these new scripts and Robin has the action stuff. Each to his own talents!'

'Message for you, Casey.' Mary-Jo put her head round the door and caught her eye. 'Could you ring Len Stafford back?'

'Use my private office, Casey. It will be quieter,' Alex said, surprisingly, crossing the room to open the door for her. Angie grinned at her as she caught the look of trepidation on Casey's face and then gave her a wink of encouragement when Alex moved to speak to another of the clients who claimed his attention suddenly. Relieved to be left alone, Casey reached across to the phone on the birds-eye maple desk and punched in the number. 'Hi, Len? Casey Taylor. You were looking for me?'

'Yes, I was. Good news, Casey.' She listened with excitement as Len rustled papers at his end. 'I spoke to Brett Kennedy this morning, and he suggested I talk to a director friend of his who starts shooting at Pinewood in six weeks. He has just discovered his second lead is pregnant so she's out of it. Brett thought you would be perfect so Hal would like to see you at ten-thirty tomorrow.'

'Oh, Len! How wonderful!' Casey sat down on the edge of the desk and reached for Alex's notepad to write down the appointment details, hoping he wouldn't mind.

'That's not all! You also have to see the BBC on Tuesday about a new costume drama – starts in the autumn. You are on a roll, sweetheart, I can't believe Jessie Marks let you languish like that! Brett tells me he contacted her twice to no effect; you should sue the drunken old bag!'

'I can't believe all this! It's like winning the lottery.'

'No, ducky! I'm just a good agent, and that's all you really needed. Now, make sure you charm the pants off Hal Simmons tomorrow. Ring me when you get out, I'll be in my office Saturday or not.'

Casey scribbled the BBC details on the bottom of the sheet of paper and hung up in a daze, barely aware of her surroundings until Alex's cool voice broke into her reverie. 'Finished with my desk, Casey?' he enquired, reaching for a file Casey was half sitting on.

'Oh! Er . . . yes!' Embarrassed, Casey slid off the

71

desk and in doing so, dislodged a sheaf of papers. 'Oh hell! I'm sorry!'

They reached for them together, their hands meeting on the scattered papers until Casey jerked hers back swiftly, so anxious was she not to have any contact with him, her heart thumping suddenly, and her mouth was dry with fright.

'My goodness, Casey!' Alex sat back on his heels to collect up the papers swiftly. 'You do surprise me – not enough bottle to finish what you started?'

'What do you mean?' Casey stood up and backed away nervously. She knew perfectly well what he meant, and her blush said so.

'You know *exactly* what I mean, Cassandra.' He stood up too, within inches of her, trapping her against the edge of the desk. 'Unless your little act in there was *just* an act?'

'That's right, Mr Havilland!' Casey swallowed hard, horribly aware of the warmth of his body against hers. 'It was what the part demanded wasn't it? And I'm an actress, remember?'

'Just an actress?'

'Yes! An actress, purely and simply!' Bravely, she lifted her green eyes to his and met them squarely. 'Not a stripper, or a good-time girl, I wasn't brought up that way, Mr Havilland. My body belongs to me and I don't give it freely, whatever you think!'

'Why should I think that, Cassandra? And why should you need to try so hard to reassure me?'

'Because . . .' Casey struggled to move and found

she couldn't without rudely pushing him out of the way. 'Because, damn it, you always think the worst of me! Why the hell did you employ me, if you think that badly of me?'

'I merely pointed out your possibilities, that's all. The rest was down to Ross and the clients,' Alex said, coldly. 'My personal opinion has nothing whatsoever to do with it! I will, however, give you one piece of advice, Miss – as Angie says, don't play with fire, you really could get badly burnt!'

'You heard us!' Casey was horrified.

'I heard a little of your conversation, yes! Angie's voice carries further than she knows, since the windows of both rooms were open.' And he had been standing next to one of them, she realized in shock. 'I'm not the one who's confused, Cassandra, but I admit I'm very tempted to teach you a lesson you won't forget in a hurry!'

'*No!*' In a panic now, Casey brought her hands up to try and push at the hard muscled wall of his chest trying to make a space between them, to no avail. Alex caught her by her bent elbows, effectively pinioning her against him. '*Let go of me!*'

'Say please!' He held her firmly, his cold eyes amused now as he recognized her panic with a slight smile. Casey was not, after all, as cool as she made out!

'For heaven's sake! *Please* let go of me! There is such a thing as sexual harassment, you know!'

'And who would be harassing whom?' He was

73

openly laughing now, the light lines around his eyes and mouth more obvious as he did so. 'It might be worth it.'

'I'd rather die!'

'Such a melodramatic statement! Hardly worth dying I'd say. But . . .' She tensed under the hard fingers that held her arms captive and he felt it, before, with an amused shrug, he suddenly let her go. 'Go back to the others, Casey, and remember – like me, Robin Faulkner won't take too much teasing before he retaliates! Make sure you are ready for it, from either of us!'

'I have to go, it's late.' Casey moved rapidly now across the room, her heart thumping wildly.

'Casey, wait!' In trepidation she paused in the doorway. 'You forgot this.' He held out the note she had made and Casey was obliged to go back and get the precious scrap of paper. 'And Casey . . .'

'Yes?' She expected the worst, and got a surprise instead.

'My chauffeur is waiting downstairs, I'll call down and tell him to take you home. It's the least we can do since we made you late.'

'There's no need, really,' she protested, pushing the note into her skirt pocket.

'It would be my pleasure, Cassandra, I won't be needing him for a while.'

'Then, thank you,' Casey inclined her head, gracefully. 'I'd be delighted to accept.' It was as he had suggested, she decided, the least he could do, after the way he'd just treated her! She collected her scripts and making her farewells quickly before Alex came out of his office she went downstairs to the foyer. As Alex had said, the chauffeur was expecting her and came immediately to take her heavy model bag, though Casey was sure he winced when she gave him her address. Not many chauffeur-driven Bentleys went to her street, she decided with an internal smile.

It was a sleek and beautiful dark blue and she sank back into the blue leather upholstery with a sigh of pleasure. Alex Havilland definitely knew how to live, she decided, but then, she realized ruefully, he had certainly earned it over the last few years. Leaning her head back against the leather, she discerned the soft scent of aftershave that she had breathed in a few minutes earlier. It was light and faintly familiar – *Obsession*, she decided eventually, and smiled. It had always been a favourite of hers, both the male and female version of it.

Despite his earlier disapproving frown the chauffeur was all smiles when he courteously held the door open for her outside her flat, with a lofty disregard for the way he had double-parked and blocked the road. Casey swept out casually, as if she did it every day and was then childishly pleased to see her landlady peering through the immaculate net curtains that she fussed over constantly.

Giggling with delight, she raced up the stairs to find Liz was finally home, collapsed on the sofa with her feet up amongst a tangle of half unpacked bags. 'Liz – oh, Liz! The most wonderful job has come up!' Casey threw herself into the armchair and poured herself a glass of wine from the bottle Liz had just opened, evidently part of her duty-free allowance.

'So, darling, spill all! I guessed you must have something!' Liz smiled. 'Bill was very sour when I rang the pub to see if you were there.'

'I bet he was!' Casey giggled back and filled her in on the past week's events. 'It's like a dream come true, Lizzie!'

'Maybe with this job under your belt I can finally persuade you we could move to a flat with a bathroom of our own,' Liz said, delighted for Casey's sake. They were very close friends, and she had long felt that Casey deserved far better luck than she had had in the last few months.

'As long as I can manage not to upset Alex Havilland too much!' Casey reached over as the phone began to ring and picked it up. 'Robin, hi! Oh, I can't come out tonight, Liz is home, we need to catch up.'

'No problem! If she's as pretty as you, bring her – my brother is over from Dublin, well one of them anyway. We'll make a foursome.' Robin was quite adamant and Liz was immediately enthusiastic.

'I should look this guy over,' she said. 'If you're going to be off with him for four weeks. Tell him to take us somewhere where the food is expensive, and good – I'm starving!'

'I can't do *that*!' Casey had put her hand over the phone during their conversation but Robin had heard Liz's comment and was laughing as she went back to him.

'I know just the place – be ready to party, girls. Pick you up at eight!'

Casey was made up from the afternoon so she put her feet up and watched Liz get ready, chattering non-stop as she did so. Liz was tall, as Casey was, with a mass of dark curly hair and big brown eyes. Her fine bone structure, however, made her look far more delicate than Casey, though like most good models she had an iron constitution and enormous energy. It was obvious from the moment Robin set eyes on her that he was heavily smitten. Casey and his brother took one look and raised knowing eyebrows at each other.

'I'm Liam,' he said. 'We may as well get acquainted. Rob is still floating by the look of him – he'll never introduce us!'

'Can you blame me?' Robin hugged Casey in apology. 'Two beautiful women in the same room, it's more than a red-blooded male can cope with!'

'And nobody could accuse you of being anything but a red-blooded male!' Casey teased. 'He promised me he doesn't bite, Liz.'

'Not yet, and I have four weeks to get to know Casey. Remember, we've got all those sexy scenes to do.'

'Not so sexy when you are hungry, tired and fed-up,' Casey assured him. 'I know you're an ace driver, but have you *done* much acting, Rob?'

'He played Ophelia at school once,' Liam ratted on his blushing brother.

'And did Footlights at Cambridge,' Robin reminded him.

'Till you were thrown out of college!' Liam retaliated. 'The parents were well pleased with that!'

'Oh heavens, poor Kear!' Casey laughed. 'They labour to find two perfect stars to launch their car and what do they get? A stripper and a college drop-out!'

'You a stripper?' Liz stared. 'You *are* joking, I take it? What the *hell* has been going on?'

'It's a long story!' Casey laughed. 'I'll tell you over dinner.'

CHAPTER 7

Her cheerful mood carried her all through her very successful interview with Hal Simmons the next day. He seemed delighted with her, having had her talents apparently heavily sold to him by Brett Kennedy. The part was hers, he told her. He had seen *Wrong Reason* and he saw no need to screen test her since he was in a hurry.

'Wardrobe will be a problem since you are in the States for so long,' was his only worry. 'But if you can spare just one day before you go, our girl is very good, she can cope, I'm sure.'

'I will, somehow!' Casey thought of the punishing scedule that Havilland Gracey and Kear had planned for the next week, and knew that Alex would never let her have a free day. 'How about Sunday? Or an evening?'

'That bad, huh? You are in demand, Casey! Sunday then? We'll call you with a time later today. And when you get to LA, ring me, we'll have dinner.'

'Oh, well, I'm not sure . . .' Casey hesitated and Hal laughed.

'No casting couch, Casey! I'm a bit too elderly for that! Bring a chaperone, honey, if you'd feel better, but we need a longer chat than I have time for right now. I fly back to the States tomorrow and I have a lot to do before that.'

Casey had been about to say that Alex Havilland would be unlikely to allow her to disappear for the evening without very good reason, then decided that she was being paranoid about it. She had every right to go out in the evenings, she reasoned, as long as she wasn't needed for anything. 'I'm sure I won't need a chaperone, Hal,' she smiled. 'I'll look forward to it.'

'Maybe I'll invite Brett and Cheryl along as well. See you in LA, Casey.'

Despite his inexperience, Robin proved to be cheerfully competent during their frantic week of interviews and photographic sessions. He learnt quickly from Casey herself and also, Casey thought with amusement, from Liz as the two girls spent several riotous evenings with Liam and Robin.

'Lucky Alex knows nothing of this,' Robin said, as the two brothers dropped the girls off one evening.

'He's actually been quite polite for the last few days,' Casey commented, thankfully.

'The calm before the storm,' Robin shrugged. 'He's been too busy to notice what we're doing. Although officially, our social life is nothing to do with him.' He kissed Casey's cheek and bent towards Liz to give her a far more intimate farewell. 'Tomorrow?' he said, softly to her. Casey raised her eyebrows.

'It's our last evening till you get back,' Liz said, defensively, as the two girls went upstairs. 'Would you really mind if Rob and I went out alone tomorrow?'

'No, of course not! I do have to pack, after all! Don't tell me you are falling for Rob's patter?' she teased affectionately.

'A little!' Liz admitted, blushing. 'But he is rather nice, Casey.'

'He's an Irish rogue!' Casey warned. 'So be careful, Liz. I know he's lovely, but . . .'

'I think it's a bit late for warnings, Case,' Liz unlocked the door of the flat. 'And if he asks me, I shall stay late. Liam goes home in the morning. Anyway,' she added. 'Even Liam says he is more of a flirt than anything else.' Casey had to agree that Liam had stoutly defended his brother's reputation in between teasing him. The two brothers were close in age and friendship, frequently able to guess the other's thoughts, almost uncannily so at times.

'Well, as long as you're sure,' Casey allowed. If Robin had really fallen for Liz it would certainly make her life easier on location.

'I'm quite sure, Casey. I think I have finally found the man of my dreams.'

One half of Casey worried for her friend, the other half envied her, but she kept her feelings to herself and she happily wished her well. After all, the thought *had* occurred to her two weeks ago that Liz would like Robin!

Certainly on Saturday morning Robin seemed a little subdued, and very disinclined to flirt with anyone. Liz had crept into the flat at six-thirty with a satisfied smile and tumbled into bed just as Casey was thinking of getting up. Tactfully, Casey resisted teasing Robin as they checked in at Heathrow together and looked around for the rest of their small party. As most of the crew were already out in Los Angeles deep in preparation with Ross and Donna, only James Wyatt and his deputy were joining Robin and Casey on their flight, with Alex. But even after they had located James and Harry, Alex was nowhere to be seen. They were all seated in the first class section and the hostesses were beginning to look anxiously around for their missing passenger when Alex finally strode onto the plane.

He appeared entirely unruffled by the tardiness of his appearance and made no apology to anyone, simply nodded good morning to them all, settled into a seat behind Robin and Casey and opened his briefcase in search of papers.

Typical of his arrogance, thought Casey, as she unfolded the newspaper a hostess had just handed her. He would naturally expect the plane to wait for him, and judging by the way the hostesses were fussing around him, they probably would! Next to her, Robin yawned and leafed through the paperbacks they had bought at the airport bookstall.

'Tired?' Casey guessed. 'I thought you seemed a bit quiet! Last night too much for you, was it?'

'Last night was the best night of my life, Casey, bar none!' Robin sighed. 'I think I'm finally in love!'

'Well I *hope* it's the real thing! Because, Robin, if I have to pick up the pieces, your life won't be worth living, I warn you!'

'No, darling! This is the real thing! And a Catholic girl too: my mother will be over the moon! I can almost see the man in the white surplice on the horizon!'

'Oh heavens! It's only been a week, Rob! Are you that sure?'

'I certainly am! Have you never heard of love at first sight, Miss Cynical?'

'At first sight? No such thing, I'm afraid – not in my life anyway.'

'It'll happen, sooner or later,' he assured her and pushed the books into the pocket in front of him. 'I can't cope with these just now. I need sleep.' He settled back and Casey laughed.

'That good, huh?'

'That good!'

'Seen the papers, you two?' James turned around and held out his folded copy of the *Mail*. 'There's our first teaser ad, look.' Casey took it.

'I'm afraid my "lover" is out for the count,' she laughed. 'Oh, and quite the star too!' She studied the paper as the aircraft taxied and quite forgot her fear of taking off as she scanned the full page ad.

'Last year Robin Faulkner won the Formula Three championship, this year he has a new challenge!' There was a picture of Robin looking handsome in racing overalls standing by a car covered with a silk drape. It was one of the photographs that had been taken during the week and it had been explained to them that the ads would build up to the full scale campaign later on in the year. James had shown them the layouts in the office but it all looked so much more real in the newspaper. Casey suddenly began to feel frightened of the responsibilty that had been thrust on them. If *they* didn't get it right the campaign would fail, and millions would be wasted! But oblivious to it all, Robin slept on, relaxed and seeming surprisingly comfortable. Casey lowered his seat back once they were airborne and settled his head on the pillow supplied, her gentle gesture observed, unknown to her, from the seat behind.

She roused him to eat lunch and he quickly came back to life after a glass or two of wine and it was his turn to rib Casey. 'Have you noticed what the movie is?' he asked her, as Casey sipped at her own wine. 'A certain *Wrong Reason*?'

'Oh, no!' Casey shuddered. She could hardly believe bad luck could strike her again so soon. She was trapped in this flying prison amongst these people who would all be watching her naked in Brett's arms. True it was only a short scene but she could just imagine what sarcastic comments Alex would make. During that first dinner James had told her that he had seen the film and enjoyed it so she had no worries there, but Alex . . . He was something else altogether.

'I look forward to seeing the Führer's face when he sees you on that little screen,' Robin murmured in her ear.

'Have you seen the film?' Casey demanded and turned her attention to the lunch in front of her, to find she wasn't sure if she wanted it now.

'No, but in an hour or so I will have.'

'That's what I'm worried about!'

'Then hide in the lounge upstairs while they watch,' Robin suggested, helpfully. 'First class can be useful for having that little convenience.'

'Do you often travel first, then?' she asked.

'When my Pa is paying, yes,' Robin grinned. 'Don't worry, angel, Liz'll never want for anything – well, groceries, anyway. Among other things we own enough supermarkets to feed Ireland!'

He was casual about everything, so obviously the product of a wealthy upbringing, nothing would ever faze Robin. He had been born lucky, Casey mused, and whatever happened to him he would bounce back. Unlike her. Casey had lurched from one disaster to another for most of her twenty-seven years. From being bullied at school for her height, to her miserable experience with Colin Cooper at university that had almost ruined her exam results, followed then by the deaths of her parents within months of each other, life had never been easy for Casey. That her strength of character had carried her through it all without affecting her sweet nature had never occurred to her. Casey simply battled along as best she could, and always hoped for the best as far as life was concerned. Robin, she was certain, would have sat back and laughed if it had been his film that was showing, but she couldn't bear it. She did as he had suggested and fled to the privacy of the upstairs lounge the moment the film started. She took one of the paperbacks with her that Robin had selected but after only five minutes of relaxing, the glass of wine had overtaken her and she soon fell into a doze over it.

'Well, well.' An amused voice interrupted her solitude. 'Hiding from your fans? Or waiting for Robin to join you in the mile-high club?'

Casey didn't need to open her eyes to know who it was, but she did anyway, and glared. 'Trust you to come up with that stupid suggestion – I might have known it!'

'Is it so stupid?' Alex leaned against the bar, his hands thrust casually into his trouser pockets. He had shed both jacket and tie since he had boarded the plane and for the first time Casey was aware of the firm body and strong shoulders that had always been hidden by his immaculately tailored suits. At least today, she noted dispassionately, he was wearing a cotton shirt, and not the silk she had noticed before. Unbuttoned at the neck, the cuffs were folded back to reveal the dark hair of his muscular fore-arms, with just a hint of it visible at his throat. Standing, he dwarfed her and Casey shifted uncomfortably, pulling the folds of her soft muslin skirt around her. It was long and full, but her top was low-necked and suddenly feeling the penetration of his hard gaze she wished she'd kept her blazer on.

'You know darn well . . .! Oh, go away, Alex! Find someone else to taunt, I don't *want* to talk to you right now. Go back and watch the movie, for heaven's sake!'

'I've already seen it, Casey, and your seductive little contribution. Luckily James is quite happy about it, or we could have a problem.'

'Don't talk such rubbish, Alex!' Casey snapped. 'You're just out to wind me up and it won't wash! I told Ross all about that film anyway. Actually, I'm quite proud of it now, and it took all my courage to do it, frankly.'

'Courage? I doubt that.' He looked scornful. 'Certainly it didn't come over that way. You seemed very much at home to me, having quite a good time by the look of it.'

'I've had enough of this! Damn you!' Casey leapt up and sprang at him her hand connecting with his face with such speed he had no time to avoid her. She had finally been pushed too far, and boss or not, Alex had invaded her personal space. He was stunned, just for a second, as the impact of her hand stained his cheek, then his own hand shot up to catch hers, wrenching it behind her back as he used his free hand to jerk her hips hard against his.

'No one talks to me like that!' he hissed through

gritted teeth, his fury only too clear in his darkening eyes.

'Well, I will!'

'No, you won't!' She was hard up against him now, held firm, even closer than she had been that day in his office. 'And this time I *will* teach you a lesson! It might just make me feel a great deal better!' There was no chance to escape. His mouth came down, hard and raw on hers. It was *not* a lovers' kiss, nor was it meant to be. It was meant to punish – and it did, stopping her breath as the shock of his action stunned her. Trapped in arms of steel, the forceful and pitiless kiss went on and on, her head thrown painfully back as he pushed her against the side of her seat and she could do nothing to stop him.

Locked in their desperate embrace, neither of them heard the captain's announcement or saw the seat belt signs go on, and when the plane began to vibrate and shudder from turbulance they were taken completely by surprise. In one boneshaking lurch Alex lost his balance as Casey took the sudden opportunity to struggle to free herself and they both fell awkwardly to be thrown across the carpet up against the bar. For long agonized minutes his heavy body pinned hers to the floor, their arms and legs tangled together until Casey finally managed to wrench herself free.

'How dare you?' she demanded, breathing hard as she struggled to her feet. She longed to kick out at him since he was still on the floor, but it was more than even she dared do, however mad she was. 'You arrogant pig! I could sue you for that!'

'You could,' he agreed, calmly, his anger abated somewhat. 'But I don't think you will somehow.' He was right, he thought to himself, it did make him feel a great deal better!

Casey flung herself into her seat and ostentatiously fastened her seat belt as Alex pulled himself up with a lithe movement despite the tipping of the plane. 'The thought of spending a month with you is enough to turn my stomach!' she hissed at him, in impotent fury.

'It's not doing me much good either,' Alex drawled back. He went behind the bar and helped himself to brandy, raising an enquiring brow at her – his manners were still intact at least, she thought ruefully, but she shook her head scornfully. 'Please yourself!' Alex added, and dropped into another seat to pick up a newspaper, not bothering with a seat belt.

'I darn well will! And don't you forget it!' she snapped, and hoped against hope that the turbulance would throw him out of his seat, but of course it didn't. She was cheered to see a very dirty mark on his once immaculate white shirt, and even more delighted to note the still strong brand of her fingers on his cheek. She had definitely hit him hard!

Uncertainly, she ran her tongue over her dry, swollen lips; Alex had taken his toll too, she realized. She could even taste blood where his teeth had grazed her lower lip. Not wanting to draw attention to her mouth again, she swallowed hard and with a disdainful glare at him, reached for her bag to try and repair her shattered make-up.

The air crackled with animosity and Casey knew her hands were shaking as she struggled to hold her lipstick steady while she put it on. 'My, my! What *have* you two been doing?' Robin strolled up into the lounge with a disarming grin. 'You could freeze ice with the atmosphere in here!' Alex simply glared and returned to the newspaper. Casey laughed nervously.

'Don't be silly, Rob,' she chided. 'Would you get me a drink please, darling? Brandy, I think.' Robin did as she asked and was amused when she curved an arm around his neck to kiss him in thanks. Casey rarely kissed him voluntarily. 'Look cosy,' she whispered in his ear as he laughingly responded, playing her game enthusiastically until Alex got up abruptly, to stalk off downstairs.

'What the hell was all that about?' Robin demanded. 'Have you two been fighting again?'

'Of course!' Casey blushed. 'I'm afraid I just slapped his face.'

'So I guessed! You pack quite a punch too, by the look of him. What brought that on?'

'Oh, the usual nasty remarks on his part! The swine takes a delight in thinking the worst of me for some reason.' Casey shrugged and looked at her watch. 'Lord! There's still another four hours to go!'

'Another slug of brandy and we could have a kip,

or play chess perhaps? I never go anywhere without my little board.'

'Chess! You?'

'And why not?' he demanded. 'I do *have* a brain you know!'

'Then chess it is, but heaven knows, I haven't played it for years,' Casey confessed.

'Then I'll get the board. Alex will think we are up to no good in here but it serves him right.'

'I really don't care!'

'You should, Casey, he could be a dangerous enemy to a girl in your position.'

'Are you actually suggesting that I get into bed with Alexander Havilland then? To keep him sweet?' Casey asked, quietly. 'Because I rather think that's what he expects I do with every man I meet, including you.'

'It's hardly surprising, sweetheart. You're a very beautiful lady, he'd be a fool if he didn't want you.'

'Robin!' Casey put out a hand and gripped his arm. 'Please, look out for me! I think – Rob – I'm terrified of Alex!'

'Of Alex? Or his effect on you?'

'Both! I really do hate him!'

'Don't worry, Casey, I'll stick close by you.' He touched her cheek, gently. 'But there's a very thin line sometimes between hate and desire. You and Alex spark off each other every time you come close, and I don't think it's *all* hate on his part. He wants you, make no mistake about it! He just doesn't want to admit it.'

'Don't give me that playground philosophy, Faulkner!' Casey returned, with the glimmer of a grin. 'Alexander thinks I'm the worst sort of tramp and he's not going to change his attitude! Now, get your chess board before I hit you too!'

'The hierarchy of the playground is often the basis of life, Casey,' he warned.

'Not at my school!' she shot back.

'Funny school then.' Robin retreated and she leant back and sipped at her brandy. It burnt her sore mouth and she winced for a second until the spirit numbed it. She had scorned Robin's words but she knew deep down that he was right. Alex had intended revenge in his kiss, but he had achieved so much more. Now she was only too aware of him as a man – a flesh and blood male with strong sensual appetites under his cold exterior. Even during those few minutes in his arms she had felt the hard pulse of his desire for her and she shuddered inwardly. Alex was known to be ruthless in business – would he be the same with her if he decided he really did want her? She only hoped Robin would keep his word and take care of her. Alex was the last man in the world that she needed to get involved with!

But Robin kept his word. To him it was no hardship, and in truth, it amused him to let Alex think he and Casey were heavily involved. Now Liz was installed in his life he could relax with Casey and she was great fun to be with when she wasn't trying to keep him at arm's length. He now knew something of Casey's past disastrous love life from Liz and well understood her reticence, with either him or Alex.

He encouraged her to join the crew in the pool once they reached the hotel in Santa Monica, then wickedly pointed out that her white swimsuit would turn transparent in the water, to Casey's horror. The swimsuit was new, and she had been in such a hurry when she bought it that the thought hadn't occurred to her. 'Don't worry, they've all seen the film,' Ross comforted her, pushing the tactless Robin into the water. 'It was on *our* flight too!'

'In that case!' Casey leapt after Robin and proved herself to be the strongest swimmer in the pool. She had been taught to swim early in life by her father, in the cold water off the Sussex coast, out in all weathers and she was happy and confident in all water, though she still preferred the sea if given a choice. Robin, a strong swimmer himself, was impressed, then peeved when she beat him to the water-polo ball every time he went for it!

'Well, at least I beat you at chess,' he comforted himself as they climbed out of the pool.

'Only because I'm out of practice!' Casey was unrepentant. 'Wait till tomorrow, I'll show you!'

'According to Ross we won't have much time for that, unless it's the evening?'

'No – oh, Rob, I forgot. I spoke to Hal Simmons before I came down. Will you come with me to his house tomorrow for a barbeque? It'll be good,' she wheedled. '*The* Sarah Campbell is his next door neighbour and she's coming, as well as Brett Kennedy and his wife.'

'Good God! How could I refuse that kind of bribe? As long as I don't have to wear a tie, that is?'

'Hardly! The only problem is that Alex will think the worst, as usual.'

'Tell Ross where we're going, and why, then everything will be fine,' he advised. 'Alex may be in charge of the financial side but Ross is the director. I'm told he is actually in charge of the shoot.'

'I guess he is.' Casey cheered up. Robin was right. Over dinner Ross cheerfully told her her life was her own off the set, and to pass his regards to a few old friends at the meeting. Alex, she quickly noted, had not come down for dinner with them, neither had James Wyatt, so the atmosphere was totally relaxed.

'Dining à deux?' Robin gagged. 'How suitable!'

Casey went to bed with her body aching from laughing so much.

It was a horrible shock to be woken by an alarm call at five o'clock in the morning when her body was still on English time. They were filming in Rodeo Drive and Sunday was the only day they were allowed to do it. Groaning, she hauled herself out of bed and into the shower in a vain attempt to wake herself up. By the time Pearl and Tommy descended on her bringing coffee she was at least halfway awake, though hardly in the sunniest of tempers. Obediently she had washed her hair the night before for Tommy to style and she submitted to their cheerful ministrations in a total daze.

But by the time Alex and Ross appeared in her room – to her complete embarrassment at its chaotic state – she was fully made up, her hair in a complicated plait and dressed in the crisply pressed linen dress that Angie had deemed suitable.

'Nice', Alex declared. 'But can we try the black, Angie?' She was sure he was doing it just to show his power over her. Three times she changed dresses until Alex and then Ross were completely satisfied and she was back in the original dark green. Then she had to take it off again for the trip into Los Angeles! To be fair, the company had organized an air-conditioned trailer for them to use for changing and resting between shots, a vehicle that would stay with them for the entire shoot, they were grateful to discover from the driver. It was a hot dusty day and they were glad of it during the endless periods of hanging about while the crew set up.

'At least there's very little lighting to worry about today, they *always* hold things up,' Casey comforted Robin when he commented on the waiting around. 'I told you it would be boring, didn't I?'

'I'll get the chess board, then,' Robin countered.

Together they giggled over the game, completely relaxed until one or other were called in front of the camera. Casey found the work straightforward on her part, mostly a leisurely stroll along the street with a collection of shopping bags swinging from her fingers. Robin had the more difficult task, needing to stop at a very specific point, something he found very hard to do at first, particularly with the audience of curious sight-seers which built up around them as the day wore on.

'Everyone wants to be in movies in this town!' Ross sighed during a much needed break. 'And I've worked in the UK for so long, I'd forgotten just how hot it gets here. Still, we haven't done badly so far, hang on in there, kids.'

He was kind to Robin, knowing that Casey could easily cope, and Robin learnt quickly. Enough for them to finish in the time allocated to them in the street and drive back out to Santa Monica in a jubilant mood.

'You were great, Robin,' Casey encouraged later as they were driven out to Malibu by the assistant that Hal had sent to fetch them.

'I felt so stupid at first,' he confessed. 'I did so many takes, and you hardly seemed to do any!'

'It was really easy for me today,' she said. 'You'll have days like that too. Cheer up, Rob, think how many autographs you signed today. I didn't!'

'That's because I did an Indi season,' he laughed. 'They know me from that.'

Hal also recognized Robin from his Indi season and greeted him with enthusiasm, after kissing Casey with warm pleasure. 'Come out to the pool,' he invited. 'Drinks are all ready, I bet you could use one. Even *I* don't work on a Sunday very often. Brett and Cheryl are here already and Sarah will be over in a minute. Casey here says you're a fan of hers, Rob?'

'Isn't every male over the age of five?' Robin grinned.

'Better watch out for her husband, then,' Casey warned. 'He's even taller than you, and *very* protective, so I hear.'

'I don't blame him, I would be too!'

However, Robin was his usual charming self, to *all* the women at the party, wisely favouring them equally with his prodigious charm. The evening was as informal as Hal had said it would be and after her initial shyness had evaporated Casey found she was enjoying herself, despite her awe at meeting the star she had admired for several years. Sarah Campbell was alone at the party, since her husband was away, and she made a point of drawing Casey out. The beautiful English actress had lived in Malibu for several years but the Hollywood publicity system had managed to bypass her, even though she was one of the most successful actresses in the world. 'I don't let the hype bother me,' she told Casey with a smile. 'Never believe the newspapers, and live life the way you want to, not the way they think you should – it *does* work! They'll pursue *you* rotten once your ads go out, looking for an angle; just ignore it all!'

'Sound advice!' Hal added. 'It's only the wannabees who really look for publicity; this crafty madam drives a beaten-up old car that never gets cleaned and looks like a tramp when she goes shopping – I've seen her!'

'Rubbish, Hal! I just don't wear any make-up, that's usually enough!' Sarah laughed, tossing her blonde hair back. 'And I love that car, why should I bother to change it? It takes the kids' bikes and everything.'

'That, from a girl who earns what she does!' Robin said in wonder to Casey as he enthused over the party on the way back to Santa Monica.

'I guess she's right though,' Casey replied, thoughtfully. 'Her life would be a misery if she wasn't so careful with her privacy, I don't think I've ever *seen* a photo of her children.'

'They're cute though,' Robin said. 'She showed *me* a picture of them while you were talking to Hal, and the little girl particularly, is a cracker – she looks just like Sarah with dark hair.'

Taken aside by Hal part-way through the evening for a chat, Casey had a great deal more to think about than the party, and she was somewhat pre-occupied during the rest of the drive.

'Penny for them?' Robin enquired, when his conversation seemed to be getting nowhere.

'Sorry,' Casey said. 'I have a lot to think about.'

'Come and have a night-cap, and tell me?'

'No, no thanks, Rob, Hal was a bit heavy on the wine. I think I'll just take a walk outside for a few minutes, and let my head clear.'

'Shall I come with you?'

'No, I'll be fine.' She kissed his cheek almost absently. 'Thanks for coming, Rob, you were a great help.'

'I enjoyed it! It's not often one gets a chance to chat up one of the most knock-out women in the world, after all!'

'I'll tell Liz you said that!'

'If you did I'd have to tell Alex you fancied him rotten!'

'That serious?' Casey laughed, despite her worries and walked out to the floodlit garden of the hotel. It was cooler now and she breathed in the fresher air with a sigh of relief as she sank down onto one of the loungers by the pool.

'All alone, Cassandra?' The voice was familiar as its owner materialized out of the shadows and Casey groaned inwardly.

'Yes! And I'd like to stay that way. You don't own every minute of my time, Mr Havilland!'

'Ah, but I do, Cassandra, and you certainly shouldn't be out here alone at this time of night.' He moved to sit on the chair opposite her, taking no notice of her request to be left alone. For the first time she was seeing him casually dressed, in soft black chinos his black cotton shirt unfastened almost to the waist, revealing the mist of dark hair that she had guessed at the day before, and she shivered. He was the epitome of a sensual, male animal and she was alone with him, she realized, looking quickly around her. It was almost as if he'd been waiting for her. She wished now that she had agreed to Robin coming outside with her, but it was too late. Alex had no intention of letting her sit alone, his whole demeanour told her that, yet she was damned if she was going to give in and go back indoors just to please him.

'I'm quite safe, Alex,' she assured him. 'And I need to think.'

Alex leaned back casually. 'Problems?' he asked, quietly.

Casey stared at him. This was an Alex she didn't know: gentle, considerate and seemingly concerned, rather than sarcastic. 'Well, sort of,' she ventured, cautiously. 'I had supper tonight with Hal Simmons, in company with several other people including his wife,' she added hastily.

'And . . .' Alex prompted, casually.

'We had a talk about the film I'm going to do for him. And . . . well . . . the thought of it frightens me to death!'

'Why on earth should it?' he demanded. 'You don't appear to be the kind of lady who hesitates over anything! I have a bruised cheekbone to vouch for that!'

Casey stared at him in embarrassment. 'I'm sorry about that, Alex, really. I shouldn't have done it.'

'No,' Alex passed a thoughtful hand over his cheekbone. 'But then, I shouldn't have provoked you, so I suppose it was my fault, really.'

'Are you actually apologizing?' Casey rose to her feet in surprise.

'Yes, I suppose I am.' Alex rose too. 'I don't often.'

'I'd noticed!'

'Casey?' He seemed to stumble slightly over her

name as if he found it difficult to say. 'It's a lovely evening, come and walk on the beach with me? I won't talk if you want to think, but I could do with a stroll.'

Casey looked longingly across the road to the beach. The thought had occurred to her too, but regretfully she had decided that it certainly wasn't a safe thing to do. But with someone Alex's size beside her, it was a different story! Not that it was a *wise* thing to do! Robin would certainly taunt her unmercifully for taking such a chance when she had so freely admitted being terrified of Alex.

Apart from first thing that morning they had seen very little of Alexander Havilland. He had made sure everything was going well at the location and then disappeared for several hours. She knew his company had an office in Los Angeles as well as New York, and they all assumed he was taking care of some business or other. He had returned mid-afternoon and pronounced himself reasonably pleased with progress, only to then disappear again. So, it had been a relatively quiet day as far as he was concerned, and Casey for one, had been grateful.

But, wise or not, she smiled now and accepted his offer. 'Yes, I'd like that,' she said, slowly, and followed him along the path to the gate that led to the road. They walked along in silence on the moonlit beach once they had slipped their shoes off, and Casey took a childish delight in squeezing the cool sand between her toes as she walked. It was a while before Alex spoke at all and he made her jump slightly, lost as she was in a little dream of her own.

'So what *is* worrying you about this film,' he asked, casually. 'Too big a part to prepare, or not big enough?'

'Neither really.' Casey paused and gazed at the sea rippling around her bare feet, noticing then dispassionately that the bottoms of Alex's trousers were getting wet. 'It's the same old thing! He seems to think because I did that nude scene with Brett, that I'll do it again, and I'm not sure I want to.'

'Then tell him no.' It sounded simple to Alex, as indeed most things did, because he was in a position to make things simple.

'But if I did, I'd lose it, and it's a good part, Alex, a really good one.'

'I remember that you said on the plane you were nervous about that scene in *Wrong Reason*. You really were, then?' Casey gave a hollow laugh.

'I cried all morning! The director really shouted at me, and then . . . well . . . Brett persuaded me, and bless him, took a lot more of the scene on board himself. He realized just how scared I actually was. But it's hardly likely Karl Woodward will be the same as Brett – not many actors are.'

'No, I know Brett, he's OK.' Alex agreed. 'But, be comforted, Casey. After these commercials hit the air, you'll be big business and you'll have a great deal more control over your work than you have now, I promise.'

'Oh, I hope so!' Casey sighed. 'I might as well be

honest with you. I was at the end of my tether when I was offered this job with you, and because of that I have Len as an agent, which could be the help I need. I can't let him down by saying no to Hal.'

'So you'll do the scene just so that you don't let Len down?' he sounded scornful.

'Alex! You simply have no idea what it's like to be in the same situation as I am!' Casey returned, startled then to hear her voice rising uncontrollably. 'To struggle just to live, and not to give in to all those creeps offering you the money you need, and it was always to take my clothes off! I came so close to giving in to them, Alex, I came *so* close, and now Hal wants me to do the same, and because it's a Hollywood movie suddenly it's acceptable to everyone, even Len! Suddenly it's artistic and meaningful – when all they want is to sell a few more seats to dirty old men!'

'Casey, hush – don't cry,' Alex caught the shimmer of tears as she turned her face away, desperately dashing her hands at her eyes and suddenly he was reaching for her. They were completely alone on the empty beach and Casey was horrified to find she was really crying then. The soft wind cooled the tears on her cheeks as Alex, unbelievably, stroked her hair gently. 'Don't cry,' he said again. 'You don't have to worry about it any more. I'm glad you didn't give in to them – really glad. I misjudged you too, and I'm sorry.'

Startled, Casey straightened up from him with a

jerk at the genuine sympathy she detected in his voice, feeling the gentleness of his hand on her cheek as he brushed at her tears. 'Sorry?' she stammered. It was the second time he'd said it. 'Do you *know* the meaning of the word?'

'Yes, I do, Casey, surprising though it seems.' Oblivious of the waves washing around them he pulled her back towards him cupping his hands around her face. 'But for this . . . I'm *not* going to apologize!'

He bent his head, to gently touch his tongue to her lips and Casey shivered involuntarily at his sensual invasion. 'Open your mouth to me, Casey . . . I *need* to taste you,' he ordered, softly. And blindly Casey did so, her lips parting as his touched onto them, lightly at first, testing her stunned reaction until with a murmur of need he plunged deeper. The heady pleasure strengthened and Casey found herself clinging to him, her arms around his waist with no idea of how they got there. All she knew was that it felt right and that she wanted him to continue – and for long minutes he did. Beautifully, excitingly, sapping her will and her strength to repulse him.

When finally he relinquished her mouth and gently curved her head onto his shoulder with his hand, she gave a sigh of real regret. 'Now you can slap my face,' he said. 'I might deserve it! But I *still* won't apologize!' She heard the amusement in his voice and when she raised her confused eyes to his, he was smiling. The first real smile she had ever seen on his face, and in the moonlight he had a thoroughly wicked air of mischief about him.

'For a kiss?' She smiled herself now, relishing the unexpected warmth of his arms around her. 'I'll save the offer, Alex – I might need it at some time.'

'In that case . . .' he caught her fingers and lifted them to his lips, kissing them one by one. 'I might as well compound the transgression!'

'Alex . . .!' she tried to protest, but his lips came down on hers, his kiss strengthening as he bent over her. Neither noticed the sea washing around their feet, eroding the sand from around them until Alex's heels sank back unexpectedly and his balance went. Caught unawares he slipped and, held as tightly to his body as she was, Casey was dragged with him as he fell backwards into the sea. Alex landed inelegantly on his back and after a second or two of total shock he began to laugh.

Soaked and winded, Casey also began to see the funny side of it as Alex rolled her over, shaking with laughter. 'Do you make a habit of falling over? Because now I think I will slap you!' she told him, giggling as he finally managed to gain his feet and lift her back onto hers.

'Save it till we're dry, there's a good girl!' He grabbed her hand and turned her towards the lights of the road. They were both soaked through and Casey began to shiver in the cool wind. 'Come on, run, Casey! I don't want your getting pneumonia on my conscience!'

Together they raced across the sand to where they

had left their shoes. Retrieving the only dry item of clothing they had, they each stood looking at the other's bedraggled appearance and burst out laughing again. It was an expensive hotel and they both had to brave the reception area to collect their room keys.

'Heaven help us if any of the unit are in the foyer,' Alex grinned. 'I'm afraid both our reputations will suffer!'

'Since, according to you, mine couldn't get much worse, I shouldn't worry,' Casey said, tartly.

'I take it back,' he told her. 'For the moment, anyway! Come on, let's be brave!'

He strolled into reception calmly, as if it was normal for him to throw himself into the sea fully clothed at midnight and Casey did her best to look equally cool. Luckily no one from the unit was about, but they got some very old-fashioned looks from the receptionist as they dripped sea water onto the marble floor.

'I'm flying to New York in the morning,' Alex said as they went up in the mercifully empty lift. 'So I won't be around for a day or two, but I expect I'll be able to join you in Las Vegas.' And Casey wondered why that statement should suddenly make her feel bereft, instead of delighted, as it would have done an hour earlier.

'Well, at least there's no sea in Las Vegas, and it's relatively flat,' she ventured to point out. 'So I can stay dry, and on my feet for a day or two! Goodnight, Alex!'

He looked incredibly boyish as he ran his hand through his wet, tousled hair – hardly the arrogant millionaire Casey had come to know in the last couple of weeks. 'Goodnight, Casey,' he smiled and touched his lips to her forehead. 'Sleep well.'

Alex made straight for his bathroom and, stripping off his wet, salt-stained clothes, he stepped gratefully into the shower. He felt surprisingly chilled, his body sticky with salt, and the warmth revived him, bringing him back to reality. Briskly rubbing his hair dry, he stared at himself in the dresser mirror, and then thought long and hard about Casey Taylor.

For the first time in his well ordered private life, he had acted purely on a blind impulse; and he was astounded at how good that could feel and how wonderful Casey had felt in his arms for the few short minutes he had held her. Then he sank to the chair, in annoyance at himself and his stupidity. Casey was involved with Robin Faulkner, their every intimate action said so, and he cursed himself for being so blind. Casey had simply been teasing him – hadn't she? And yet . . . she had seemed so genuinely happy to respond to him. Was she really just a flirt and out for all she could get? Or was she really the innocent she told him she was?

With a sigh, Alex threw himself onto his bed and thumped the pillow in frustration. *He would find out.* He would find out the truth if it was the last thing he did. One thing was sure, he realized with amusement, as he vainly tried to settle into sleep, Casey wouldn't be joining Robin for the night in the state she'd been in when *he* left her, so he *had* effectively put a stop to that, for tonight anyway!

CHAPTER 8

After a fairly sleepless night herself, Casey was astonished halfway through the morning to be handed a delicate bouquet of white scented flowers by the grinning second assistant. 'You have an admirer already, Casey,' he told her. Hal Simmons, she thought immediately, but the card with them said simply, '*Hope there were no ill effects!*' and was signed AH.

Blushing, she pushed it into her tote bag and bent back to the mirror to finish tidying her make-up. It was even hotter that morning and despite frequent sprays of water her make-up was streaming off rapidly. It was barely midday and yet her scalp ached from all the frequent brushing out that Tommy had to do to counteract the whippy little breeze that constantly came off the sea. But she was professional and faced Ross and the crew with a cheerful smile during the gruelling afternoon. It was a long day, starting as they had at five, and finishing at seven in the evening. Casey slept all the way back to the hotel, oblivious to the world within seconds of getting into the car.

She cursed when her telephone rang just as she reached her room, half expecting it to be Alex and not knowing what to say to him. But it was Hal's breezy tones that echoed down the line. 'Casey, honey, why didn't you tell me that nude scene was a problem?' he demanded.

'How did you know that?' she responded, confused. 'I deliberately didn't tell you.'

'No, Casey, someone else did! No sweat, honey, we'll deal with it, don't worry. We'll wrap the sheets round you both. Karl is all for that. So don't worry that pretty little head of yours about it any more. Promise?'

'Oh, Hal!' Casey sank down on the bed, the relief only too obvious in her voice. 'Oh, thank you!'

'Don't thank me, thank your friend! And Casey . . . next time you don't want to do something like that, say so. Don't just grit your British teeth! It never looks right on screen if you're forcing yourself to do it.' Casey wished the director of *Wrong Reason* had had the same philosophy!

She almost sang as she showered and pulled on a dressing gown. Then she stopped. Who on earth had told Hal? Then she realized . . . Alex! He knew Brett, and Sarah Campbell, he must have somehow got to Hal on her behalf via one of them. But why? To save her pain? Or to safeguard Kear's investment? More likely the latter, she decided, cynically. Then her eyes caught the flowers sitting in a water jug on her dressing table and she smiled. Perhaps not? He was too much of a businessman not to expect something in return. That thought was enough to give her another difficult night!

By the end of the first week they were a tightly knit unit, English and American all very happily integrated. Ross was delighted with their progress and, though the shooting schedule was complex and packed, they were on target. The first two commercials were in the can and on their way back to London for the editor to cut, so when they flew to Las Vegas on Friday evening they all went out to dinner and then on to a floor show together, to celebrate.

'Two down, six to go!' Ross toasted. 'Day off tomorrow, guys, you can sleep in – most of this town does – the workers, anyway.'

They had been booked into a non-gambling hotel ten minutes' drive from the mind-blowing extravanganza of the Strip, and Casey realized the wisdom of it when she finally went to bed and it was relatively quiet. After roaring round all the sights with Robin, Donna and Ross, she was exhausted and ready to sleep the clock round, but Robin woke her at ten – to her fury.

'Can't waste time sleeping!' he argued. 'Get up, girl. I'll order breakfast from room service, shall I? How about a jaunt into town? I might even allow you to check out the shops, I need something for Lizzie.'

'Aren't you *ever* tired?' she moaned, heading for

111

the bathroom. 'Hell, Rob, I've got laundry to see to.'

'We'll find a laundromat somewhere, or leave it for the hotel to do,' Robin argued. 'You *don't* have to do your own washing, Casey! Let the company pay for that. Now, what do you want for breakfast?'

The phone rang while she was in the shower and Robin automatically answered it. He was laughing when she came out of the bathroom plaiting her hair with a practiced ease. 'That was Alex Havilland on the phone, he's on his way back from New York,' he told her. 'My, did *he* get a shock when I answered! I thought he'd blow a gasket!'

'It *is* ten-thirty in the morning,' Casey protested. 'Probably lunchtime in his sort of schedule.'

'Well, I did tell him that we were about to have breakfast together!'

'You wind-up merchant!' she accused, joining in his laughter, however. 'I suppose he thought the worst?'

Robin grinned, not at all abashed. 'Sure did!' Casey groaned inwardly. Just as Alex was beginning to thaw too. 'Anyway, his message was we are both on parade at eight. The financial director and the marketing director of Kear are jetting in to meet us.'

'Oh, hell! This is the downside of the job!' Casey complained.

'It's all right for you!' Robin attacked his breakfast with enthusiasm. 'I'll have to wear a dinner jacket, *and* a tie! You at least will be comfortable.'

112

'As long as dinner doesn't mean anything else, that's all!'

'With the clients? Dream on, sweetie! Alex will make sure of that. He's taking great care of his investment, never fear! Hey! Get your own! You said you didn't want bacon.' He tapped at her marauding fingers as she cheekily filched a piece of his.

Angie breezed by their patio and was easily persuaded to join their shopping expedition. She had already spotted a huge mall on her own meanderings the night before, and at least the Fashion Mall was cool, unlike the 110 degree temperature outside. 'And it gets worse! It's not midday yet!' Robin comforted. He had been to Las Vegas before.

With the temptation of designer boutiques, added to the novelty for the first time in her life of being able to spend money freely on clothes for herself, Casey found it a heady experience. However, long established habits were hard to shake off, and she still selected very carefully. Knowing she needed a suitable dress for dinner that evening, she enlisted Angie's help and was persuaded into a sleek, short black dress with a very complicated arrangement of rouleau straps to hold it up. The price made her wince, and hesitate for a few minutes, but Robin's wholehearted approval finally decided her.

'Wear the black suede shoes with it,' Angie suggested that evening as Casey dressed, and she then produced an exquisite silver barrette of her own to lift up one side of her hair. 'Knockout!' she decided.

'Tall!' Casey returned. In the three-inch heels she was inded taller than the two Kear directors so they were easily intimidated. Only Alex, devastatingly handsome in a white dinner jacket, topped her by several inches.

He was coolly polite at first, and then visibly amused as he watched the assured way Casey handled the two clients. They were important men, who paid the bills for the entire campaign and she knew Alex was watching and waiting for her to wrong-foot all the way through the meal. The food in the ultra chic restaurant was surprisingly good and as usual Casey did full justice to it, her eyes flickering occasionally to his, as if asking for reassurance.

When finally their guests decided to complete the night in a tour of the casinos, she made it an excuse to ask to leave them to it, but to her surprise Alex stood up too.

'I'll take Casey back to the hotel,' he said, firmly. 'I can see you would prefer to stay a while, Robin, and I have a few calls to make.'

'At this time?' Casey stared.

'It's eight o'clock in the morning in England,' Alex reminded her. 'Shall we go, Casey?' He brooked no argument, simply took her arm and guided her out of the restaurant. Naturally, a taxi seemed to materialize out of the air for him and he handed her into it politely.

'Sorry if I deprived you of Robin's company tonight,' he commented with a wry smile.

'I don't know what you're talking about,' Casey drew back into the corner of the spacious back seat.

'Oh, I think you do, Casey.'

'So you thought you'd do the honours, did you?' she demanded, sarcastically. 'Dream on, Alex! One kiss gives you no rights! The last time was the only time!'

'I shall merely escort you to your room, Casey, my dear.'

'And lock me in, I suppose?'

'Don't tempt me!'

She was about to retaliate sharply, but for once, her brain curbed her tongue. She remembered his intercession with Hal Simmons. 'I wouldn't dream of tempting you, Alex. Thank you for the flowers by the way, they were so pretty.'

'I'm just glad you didn't throw them in the bin! No ill effects then?'

'None at all, midnight swimming can be quite beneficial, I've found. Maybe we should do it again, Alex?' she added, cheekily.

'There's always the hotel pool?' he suggested. 'But it's not quite the same as the sea.'

'Then I'll wait!' she grinned at him, more comfortable now with him, until she discovered at reception that his room was right next to hers. He collected her key with his own and seemed to take it for granted that he should escort her to the door and open it for her. Firmly, Casey took the key from him, and found her fingers gripped in his as she did so.

'Goodnight, Casey.' He smiled down at her, aware suddenly of her unease. 'You did very well this evening, our clients liked you. You gave just enough, without flirting, which was very professionally done.'

'Praise indeed, coming from you,' she bit out, not quite sure if he really was praising her, or comparing her to a hardened escort girl.

Alex leaned against her doorway and took in the diverse emotions flickering in her expressive eyes. He wondered fleetingly if she knew just how much she gave away in the green pools gazing up at him? 'It was intended to be praise, Casey,' he said, softly. 'OK, so we didn't start too well, but . . . well at least meet me halfway?'

'Meaning?' Casey challenged.

'Meaning, you witch . . . I . . . Oh . . . go to bed, Casey, before I do something I'll regret!' He caught her up in his arms, kissing her almost violently before he turned swiftly away to his own room.

Breathing hard, Casey closed the door and dropped onto the sofa. Aware now that Alex was so close to her, she shivered as she hugged her knees defensively. Why, oh why, did he have this effect on her? Sleep was miles away as she mulled over her predicament and with a sigh she wandered around the room undressing in a desultory way, until she thought that perhaps a bath would help relax her nerves.

In typical Las Vegas style there was a jacuzzi bath

in a voile-curtained alcove of her bedroom and she decided to try it, sinking into the bubbles with a tiny bottle of champagne from her fridge. This was the kind of life she could get used to, she thought then, comparing her current situation with the grotty chipped bath and peeling paintwork of their shared Kentish Town bathroom. The landlady kept her own flat like a palace but her tenants' rooms were a different story.

She was half asleep by the time she reluctantly hauled herself out of the water and pausing only to wrap a towel around her body she tumbled into bed. Once the room was quiet she suddenly became aware of Alex on the other side of the wall. The headboards of the two beds were obviously back to back and she was horribly conscious of his restless movements so close to her. Hardly daring to breathe then, she puzzled as to why he was so restless. Was he, she wondered, disturbed by the same traumatic thoughts as she was? Or did he have other more important things to think about?

Yet, his teasing attitude on the way back from the restaurant and his passionate kiss after it confirmed to her that Robin had been right all along. Alex wanted her. She remembered her wild reaction to his kisses on the beach that night in Santa Monica and the comfort of his arms as he had held her, even the shock of rolling in cold sea water had been assuaged by his unexpected warmth, and his laughter. Lying still in the luxury of her huge bed she felt the aching tingle of the memory running through her body, as she too tossed restlessly then as she struggled unsuccessfully to subdue that ache.

CHAPTER 9

In the morning she was tired and wan-faced from her sleepless night, a fact bemoaned by Pearl as she struggled to cover up the damage, luckily, later than normal. Robin had been out with the camera crew since the crack of dawn but Casey wasn't needed until lunchtime, which gave her time to get herself together. It was even hotter out in the desert and they were all glad of the shelter of the air conditioned trailer. Casey lay on the divan in the dressing area with her hair in heated rollers, wearing the lightest wrap she could find, and endeavoured to catch up with her sleep.

'How can you sleep in those things?' Robin demanded, bouncing into the dressing room at lunchtime, still lively after a hot morning's work.

'Easily if you left me alone!' Casey groaned. 'Is it lunchtime already?'

'Fraid so!' Robin stripped off his damp shirt and went into the tiny bathroom to sluice himself down. 'It's hot as hell out there, and the hero car is playing up, I'll have to use the spare this afternoon, if they

119

can't fix it.' The unit worked with two cars which travelled in thier own trailer with two Kear mechanics and a devoted prop-man who spent his entire time polishing the cars. Casey had already irked him by getting fingermarks on his precious paintwork.

'My! You've certainly picked up advertising language quickly!' Casey laughed. 'Hero car indeed!'

'That's what Ross and the guys call it!' he defended. 'What's wrong with that?'

'You're showing off, that's what's wrong!'

'The hell I am! I've been working like a dog all morning while you've been lying around on your back!'

'I have not!' she protested. 'Here! Try one of these dragging your hair out by the roots!' She pulled a roller from her hair and gaily tried to twist it into his own curls amidst Robin's laughter and efforts to avoid her. They were laughing together, rolling on the divan when Alex walked into the van. He too, was hot and tired, weary of the Kear directors sniping at the unit's seemingly endless waste of time and money. Not stopping to think, he swung through the cabin and wrenched the two apart.

'What the hell do you think you're doing?' he roared at them. 'Anyone on the unit could have walked in here!'

'And they wouldn't have jumped to the same ridiculous conclusion you did!' Casey snapped, dragging her wrap together. 'We were just messing about, that's all!'

'And I never seduce ladies on an empty stomach!' Robin added, cheekily.

'Get dressed! Both of you, before those sons of bitches come waltzing in here!'

'Not PR again?' Robin groaned. 'We did that last night, till two o'clock in the morning in my case!'

'PR again, 'Alex confirmed, and grumbling, Robin dragged on a T-shirt. Casey simply ignored Alex and retied her wrap to march out into the cabin, rollers and all. He forced them through lunch with the clients and to his astonishment, the two men who had given him hell all morning melted completely when faced with Casey's charm.

They had thawed completely by the time Ross was ready for the afternoon's shooting. Since this involved helicopter shots of Robin and Casey driving at speed over a mile or so they were both enthusiastic about the work and the opportunity to zoom about over the desert in the helicopter while Ross checked the shots. Only Robin was uncomfortable and after testing the car he asked for the spare.

'I'd prefer you to use the same car,' protested the marketing director. 'It would mean reshooting some of the morning stuff, and that would waste both time and money. The spare would need time spent on the paintwork too.'

'It doesn't feel right,' Robin said. 'And certainly not at that speed. I just wish I could pin-point what it is.'

'Take it through just once more,' the finance

director suggested. 'We'll shoot in case it seems OK.'

Reluctantly, Robin agreed but he grumbled all the time Ross and the cameraman were setting up the shot. It involved the whole crew and they communicated with walkie-talkies since they were spread out over such a wide area. The desert road was a fairly rough track in places and the car threw up spectacular dust clouds whenever Robin increased speed.

'Looks great from up here!' Ross told them, watching the open topped car speeding along the track. 'Let's go for a shot. Happy, Rob?'

'Not really,' Robin admitted. 'But we'll try. OK, Casey?' She nodded, and lifted the receiver to her ear, waiting for Ross's signal. They were completely alone as Robin drove the car away from their motley collection of trucks, giggling over the inane comments the clients had made over lunch.

'Be careful, Rob, or I'll transmit this to the helicopter,' Casey grinned, wafting her finger over the transmit button.

'That would be poetic justice to the ignorant beggars! Hold on, sweetheart,' he added as he changed gear and accelerated up to the speed Ross wanted. They were over halfway through the shot when Robin swore violently as he detected again the vibration he had complained about earlier. Immediately, he decelerated but he was too late. The car was completely out of control even for an experienced driver like Robin. For a few agonizing seconds he fought to control the speeding vehicle, but the problem was compounded by the accelerator being stuck wide open, however hard he kicked at it in growing desperation.

'Get down, Casey! he roared at her. 'For God's sake get down!' There was a substantial roll-over bar around them but not enough to really protect them if the car turned over at speed. He finally slammed the car through the gears in a frantic effort to slow it and would have succeeded if the car had not slewed slightly sideways and hit a vicious rut to be sent into a bone-shattering skid.

Casey screamed in terror as Robin fought to hold it steady but nothing was going to prevent the inevitable as the spinning vehicle hit another rut and rolled over – not once, but twice, to finish on its side in the scrubby cactus-strewn soil, a good twenty yards from the roadway. For a few seconds Casey was numb and choking with dust, hardly knowing where she was as she fought the waves of sickness bearing down on her. Robin's whole weight was on top of her crushing her until he managed to wriggle free of his seat belt and thrust the buckled driver's door up and then open.

Reaching down he yanked at Casey's seat belt, struggling to calm her as she began to surface and realize she was trapped by the mangled and twisted belt. 'It's OK, Casey, I'll get you out, don't panic!' He worked frantically at the belt, aware all the time of petrol trickling from the back of the battered car and then, with relief, heard the noise of the helicopter landing near them.

Suddenly there was the welcome thud of several pairs of feet running towards them but it was Alex who got to them first. He assessed the situation in seconds and leant into the wreck alongside Robin. His movements were cool and assured and within moments the belt was free. 'Put your arms round my neck, Casey,' he demanded, grasping her by the waist, and as she numbly did as he asked, he dragged her upwards in one huge effort. With the realization that she was finally free of the terrifying wreckage, Casey clung unashamedly to Alex's neck, and long shudders of relief flowed through her. But even as Alex paused to check her for injuries, Robin grabbed his arm urgently and jerked his head to the car.

'Move Alex! Get her away from the car!' he warned and then Alex realized, and with Casey in his arms he began to run; sprinting across the rough ground to the helicopter as Robin summoned up the last of his strength to follow him. They had barely reached the ungainly machine when, with an enormous whoosh, the wrecked car exploded into a huge fireball, scorching their faces with its intensity, as they drew to halt in horrified silence to stare at it and realized just how close all three of them had been to absolute disaster. Robin's body ached with the punishment it had taken, particularly his arms from wrenching at the wheel, and he couldn't help the groan of pain when Ross and the cameraman helped him up. 'Jeeze!' he exclaimed, to cover it. 'I thought that was just a thing you see in movies! Casey? You OK?'

'I think so,' Casey got her breath back.

'Maybe, but we'll get you both back to Vegas to get checked out though.' Ross reassured Robin.

'I don't need a doctor,' Casey suddenly realized the vulnerable position she was in and tried to struggle free as Alex lifted her into the helicopter. 'I'm fine, just a bit shaken that's all. Put me *down*, Alex, you fool! Or *you'll* need a doctor for a hernia or something, I'm not exactly lightweight!'

'I'll be the judge of that!' Alex grinned in relief. 'Even though your evil tongue doesn't seem to have deserted you, a check-up is what you'll get, both of you! Ross, I'll go with them, Trevor and Ryan here can help you deal with the car.' His cold tone suggested exactly what he meant as he glared at the two Kear men before he swung into the helicopter and strapped himself into a seat.

There was no point in arguing with Alex, they both knew *that* by now, and as he pointed out, the insurance requirements had to be adhered to whether they liked it or not. Reluctantly, they submitted to being checked over thoroughly at the medical centre the pilot took them to, though Robin was still more concerned about his doubts being ignored than any possible injuries he might have had.

Dazed as she was, Casey was astonished at the way Alex took charge, demanding and getting immediate attention from the hospital staff with very little effort.

'The power of a Gold card!' Robin grinned at her as, finally cleared to go, they waited for the car Alex had summoned.

'The power of a handsome face, you mean!' Casey retorted, acidly. She hadn't missed the way a female doctor, and the nurses, had positively fawned over their all-powerful guardian. It also appalled her that she had not only noticed, but taken great exception to it!

'My darling girl! No American hospital takes account of a person over anything but his credit card, however pretty he is!' Robin assured her, rubbing ruefully at his bruised shoulder. 'Hell, this really does hurt! It's a hell of a way to get an afternoon off!'

'Afternoon? It's nearly four!' Casey pointed out.

'Time enough to loll in that disgusting fizzy bath in my room and iron out a few of these bruises,' Robin returned. 'Come and join me? We can hit the town later on with the guys.'

'Great! I could do with some fun for once,' Casey laughed.

'*Oh no you don't!*' Alex interrupted suddenly, his return unnoticed by either of the two conspirators. 'You were both told to rest this evening and that is *exactly* what you will do! In the hotel, *and* under my supervision!'

'Oh, for heaven's sake, Alex! Don't be so pompous!' Robin laughed, totally unabashed. 'We're fine, quite capable of looking after ourselves, you know!'

'Quite possibly,' Alex agreed. 'But tonight, you will do exactly as I say. You are both, I should remind you, in my employ, and it's in my interests to make sure you are fit for work – not to mention several million pounds' worth of campaign at stake if you were unable to do so! I could, of course, insist that you spend the night here in the hospital's care? Then I'd know you were in safe hands!'

'No way!' They both spoke in unison, horror written across both their faces and then, unexpectedly, Alex began to laugh.

'You have *both* been warned,' he said, firmly. 'Now, get in that car before I change my mind.'

'You really are being quite ridiculous, Alex,' Casey murmured, then winced as his hard hand gripped her arm.

'Get in, Casey,' he ordered, his laughter gone in seconds. Ruefully, Robin swung into the front, since Alex showed no sign of relinquishing his hold. Furious at his arrogance and the all too obvious power he was displaying Casey jerked her arm away from his. Pushing herself as far away from his body as she could possibly manage, she stared fixedly out of the window, seemingly fascinated by the other cars on the road.

Alex took no notice of her fury. 'I want your word, both of you, that you won't stir out of the hotel this evening, particularly since I have to be out for a while.'

'So *you* are allowed to hit the town?' Robin teased, turning from the front.

'I intend seeing those two cretins back onto their corporate jet to Detroit,' Alex said, grimly. 'Some fun – I don't think. Now do I have your word?'

'Sure!' Robin grinned. 'Cheer up, Case, a rest will do you good. He was unrelentingly cheerful, coaxing Casey out to the pool as Alex strode back out of reception. 'We'll lie around for a bit, then tell reception we don't want to be disturbed, then we can sneak out,' he said. 'Simple!'

'But we gave our word!' Casey protested. 'We can't!'

'What *can* he do?' Robin shrugged. 'Sack us? He's just playing God, it gives him his kicks, I suppose.' He ordered champagne to ease the aches and pains and after a glass or two she relaxed, and by the time a few of the crew joined them she felt quite recovered. Enough, anyway, to retaliate with gusto when they all offered to apply a soothing mixture that Pearl produced to her skin.

'My mum makes it and swears by it,' Pearl said as she handed it over, and Robin laughingly took charge of it.

'We'll put it on each other,' he suggested, wickedly. 'Casey, do you think we ought to ring Liz? I doubt she'd get to hear about this, but you never know, and if she did, she'd freak!'

'About you, or me?' Casey asked, but she rose immediately. The same thought had occurred to her too. 'Will she mind being woken up?'

'Course not!' Robin was amazed. 'I often ring her when I get back from location.'

'Golly, you are keen!'

'Told you I was! By the way, Liam tells me there's a flat come free in our block, it would be perfect for you and Liz to rent.'

'Perfect for you, you mean!' Casey retorted. 'But I suppose there's no harm in looking.'

Liz had not only looked, she had signed the rental agreement and paid the deposit. 'I move in next week,' she told an astonished Casey. 'It's too good an opportunity to miss. Just think, Casey, a bedroom and a bathroom each!'

'In that case, sold!' Casey was delighted.

'Thought it might be!' Liz chuckled. 'I can't wait to tell old Nellie Blanchard we're moving to Knightsbridge!'

'Maybe you should get together with Liam, Casey,' Robin suggested as he put the phone down. 'That would be really cosy.'

'Maybe,' Casey was non-committal, as she always was where men were concerned. Wearily she stretched out on Robin's bed, at least comfortable with him. 'Can you put some of Pearl's mixture on my shoulders?' she asked. 'They're really hurting now.'

'Sure, then you can do the same for me,' Robin decided. 'Pull your swimsuit down or it'll get greasy marks on it.'

Obediently Casey slid the straps down and lay on her stomach, sighing with relief as Robin skilfully applied the cool lotion. '*That* is bliss,' she sighed. 'You're missing your vocation, Robin, please –

don't stop!' She closed her eyes with pleasure and was almost asleep when a hard voice cut into their quiet fun with a whippingly cold effect that shocked them both.

'For goodness' sake, grow up, you two! Haven't you got the sense to close the door *before* you start fornicating?' Alex was leaning against the open patio door that led to the garden and pool area. Robin had automatically left it open to circulate the still humid air. Alex's fury seemed to vibrate through the quiet room and they both jumped guiltily as he strode in uninvited.

Robin, however, recovered quickly, and was not easily put down. 'Give over, Alex,' he said, casually. 'I'd have locked the door if I'd been really serious.' He tossed Casey her robe with an easy confidence as she sat up struggling to pull her swimsuit into place.

'Alex!' she protested. 'We were only messing around!'

'Like this morning I suppose?' Alex was in no mood to see reason. His iron grip snapped around her wrist again. 'Let's get a few things straight, miss. You've just had one hell of an accident, in which you were quite probably concussed, and you are meant to be resting, not rolling around a bed! I'll talk to you in a minute, Robin. Casey, come with me!'

He literally flung Casey into her robe and without another word simply dragged her out of the room and along the corridor to her own. 'How dare you!' Casey hissed at him as he paused at the door to reach into his trouser pocket. 'How *dare* you treat me like this?'

'I'll do as I think fit,' he snapped. 'And you will do as I say.'

Casey stared at the room card in his hand. 'That's my key!' she exclaimed in astonishment.

'You dropped it by the pool, I said I'd bring it back to you,' he shrugged. So – he *had* known she was in Robin's room! He operated the lock and pushed her inside. 'Now get into that bed, and stay there!' He slipped the key back into his pocket and flipped back the covers.

'No! Dammit!' Casey jerked away. 'I've had enough, Alex! I work for you, OK! That is all, you do *not* own me body and soul!'

'No? And Robin does I suppose?'

'The hell he does! Get it straight, Alex, once and for all. Robin is madly in love with my flatmate, Liz – not me!' Her angry eyes met his equally furious ones.

'So, what were you doing rolling around his bed with him?' he demanded, sarcastically. 'Two-timing your friend?'

'The hell I was! It was nothing – absolutely nothing! Ask Robin about Liz, he'll tell you! Now get out, Alex, I don't want to talk to you, or I'll say something I'll really regret!'

'I doubt you'll manage that! Just stay put, Casey, I'm warning you for the last time!' And with that he left her sitting fuming impotently on the edge of the bed. Furious, she beat at the pillows. How dare he?

131

she ranted at the empty room. Was the job really worth all this? For Alex Havilland to treat her like a minion, and ordering her about as if she was a naughty toddler.

The job would make her famous, she knew, but it couldn't be worth the misery and ignominy of this. Tears of fury and exasperation poured unchecked down her cheeks as she thumped repeatedly at the pillows, her heels drumming at the bed in frustration. All she achieved was an even more painful shoulder and, still sobbing with anger as well as pain, she admitted defeat and swallowed two of the pain-killers the hospital had provided.

When Alex returned a couple of hours later she was fast asleep, curled up on the bed, the T-shirt she was wearing rumpled up over her hips. Astonished by the strength of his reaction he swiftly bent to pull the loose sheet up over her. It was only then that he noticed the tear stains streaking her face. 'Casey! Oh, hell – Casey, are you in pain?' He was horrified. 'Is it me? What *have* I done to you?' He sat down on the edge of the bed and reached out for her involuntarily. She was soft and warm in his arms as he lifted her up against him and she felt so good! Gently, he brushed his lips against her forehead. 'I'm sorry, darling,' he whispered. 'I'm so sorry if I made you cry.'

Casey was sound asleep and yet she heard the soft voice deep within her subconscious. 'Alex?' Like his, her voice was barely a whisper, as if neither could quite understand what the other was doing. Alex was more likely to call her 'bitch' than 'darling', she reasoned groggily, but her eyelids fluttered open as he lifted her.

'It's OK, Casey,' he reassured. 'I've got you.'

'It's not . . .! No!' Casey jerked awake horrified to find herself in Alex's arms. Frantic, she tried to scramble away, only to find herself tangled in the sheets. 'I'm not available, Alex! I don't come as part of the package!'

Alex held her firmly. 'I never for a moment thought you did!' he retorted. 'I have always thought you were involved with Robin, I'm sorry, I really misjudged things.'

'And now you know the truth you feel free to jump on me, is that it? Get wise, Alexander. I'm not for you – I'm not your kind, I don't want you, I don't want anything to do with you!'

'No?' Alex smiled, calmly. 'Remember that night on the beach? You wanted me then, no problem. As I did you, and unlike you, I'm not afraid to admit it.' Abruptly, he lowered her back to the bed, his body holding hers down as he leant over her.

'A momentary lapse, that's all,' she retaliated, knowing miserably how wrong she was.

'Some lapse!' He caught her face in his hands, his grip preventing any movement from her. Then he kissed her, a deep, searching kiss, his tongue melding with hers and finally she gave way, allowing herself for a few wonderful moments the luxury of letting Alex wreak havoc on her senses. When he finally raised his head slightly she lay helpless, finding to her shock that her arms were tightly wrapped around his neck, and he felt the long shudder roll through her as she let them slip.

'No?' he asked, softly, for the second time.

'Bastard!' she hissed at him, still determined not to give in to him, even though unfortunately her body told him otherwise.

'I'm sure my parents would prove you wrong, my sweet!' Alex made no move to release her, instead his grip tightened. 'Let it happen, darling. Relax, I won't do anything you don't want me to, I promise.'

'Alex, I'm frightened,' she admitted, as he continued to press soft kisses to her neck and onto the fiercely beating pulse in her throat.

'You and me both!' With a sigh he pulled them both upright. 'I have *never* felt confused about anything, I've always known *exactly* where I'm going, and what I'm doing – but where *you* are concerned, I really don't know what the hell I'm doing any more.'

It seemed such an astonishing confession from so controlled a man that Casey stared, animosity forgotten. 'Over me?'

'Over you! Sleepless nights, the lot! Satisfied?' The dark eyes that met hers were warm now, almost twinkling with laughter, and she knew he was telling her the truth.

'I thought you hated me,' she whispered.

'I tried to, believe me! Look, I think we should talk. Are you up to coming out to dinner? If I stay here with you much longer, it won't be much good for either of us!'

'Yes . . . I guess so.'

'Then get dressed.' He laughed at her stricken face. 'Don't worry, we'll go somewhere quiet, you don't need to make a great effort. You look beautiful as you are, frankly.'

'Oh, sure! In a T-shirt!' she mocked, pulling it down to try and cover her thighs.

'Especially in a T-shirt!' he grinned. 'Just put on some jeans, not all restaurants in this town expect you to dress up.' Reluctantly, he let her go. 'I'll go and book somewhere. Will half-an-hour be enough?'

'I suppose so.' Bemused, Casey felt his lips brush hers again with a briefly electric effect. If only, she thought, ruefully, if only she had the courage to simply bolt! What in fact could he do?

Quite a lot, knowing Alex, she told herself and with a sigh she slid off the bed and headed for the bathroom. She took him at his word, however, did the sketchiest make-up possible and selected a pair of white jeans to tuck a pleated navy silk shirt into. With her hair swirled up on top of her head and high-heeled sandals on her feet she was well aware that she was almost six foot and, she guessed, only a couple of inches shorter than Alex was.

That will teach you, Mr Havilland, she grinned at the mirror. But he made no comment when he came to collect her, exactly on time, as she expected him to be.

'Nice perfume,' he commented instead, taking her arm. '*Obsession*, by any chance?'

Casey smiled. 'Your girlfriend use it too?' she teased.

'No, but I sometimes wear the masculine version.' Casey remembered the scent of it in his car and wondered then if it was why she had bought it in duty-free at Heathrow. How many men could recognize a perfume? she wondered, and smiled then at the effort he was obviously making to keep the conversation on an even keel as they compared their favourite scents and Alex told her amusing stories about doing a perfume commercial a few years back.

True to his promise, he took her to a relaxed but still up-market kind of bar/restaurant a little way off the Strip – a glorious over-the-top pastiche of a Western bar, and once Casey had ascertained that none of the crew were there she relaxed. Alex ordered wine for them and lifted his glass to her when it arrived. 'Truce?' he enquired, raising one dark eyebrow. 'For tonight, at least? I don't doubt that by tomorrow evening you'll be blaming me for something.'

'I do my best to keep out of your way, Alex,' she reminded him, tartly. 'It seems safer, quite frankly.'

'Now why should that be the case?' he asked with a silky innocence.

Casey busied herself with the huge menu. 'You know damn well why, Alex,' she said at last. 'I don't trust you!'

'Or yourself when we're together,' he pointed out, hitting the truth with his usual clarity, and noting her immediate blush with a spark of satisfaction. 'Why on earth are you fighting your feelings, Casey? Is it *so* difficult to admit you could be wrong about me?'

'What is there to admit?' At last, Casey raised her eyes to his. 'You gave me a job, Alex, when I needed one badly, and for that I'm grateful. But being grateful to you does *not* mean you have any other rights over me. I don't sell myself to anyone!'

'Is that what you think?' He was horrified. 'Casey, what on earth gave you that idea? I don't give a toss about the job! It's where you and I are going that concerns me.'

'I wasn't aware we were going anywhere!' She was confused.

'Oh! For heaven's sake!' He was exasperated. 'If you would only ease up on me for a moment!'

'If you would only stop behaving like a fascist dictator, I might!'

'Casey, this afternoon was one of the worst moments of my life,' he confessed. 'For a few minutes, until they got that chopper down and we didn't know what had happened to you, well to both of you, we thought the worst. I never want to go through that again – ever!'

Casey dropped the menu, forgetting all pretence of studying it. 'You mean it wasn't just the panic over the car?'

'To hell with the car!' He caught up her hands

and pressed them to his lips in a feverish gesture of possession, and as their eyes met she finally recognized the desire in his.

'Alex, are you suggesting we have an affair?' she asked, hardly able to believe she had the nerve to say it.

'I guess I am.' He smiled, and let his fingers caress hers, gentler now. 'At least, give things a chance to develop and stop fighting me?'

'Maybe . . .' she grinned back. 'Or maybe I like fighting?'

'Well . . . in that case . . .'

Fortunately for Casey the waiter approached at that moment and she took the opportunity to snatch her hand back. 'Oh, er . . . shrimp salad and ribs,' she rattled off, hardly bothering about what she was ordering. Alex ordered a steak and for a few minutes they were distracted by the complications of all the side order decisions the waiter needed.

'Golly,' Alex sighed, as he finally departed. 'You'd hardly believe it's a simple meal. Will you really eat all that? The ribs hardly look delicate.'

'I'm hungry,' Casey confessed, and suddenly she was. 'Garlic bread?' she queried, wickedly, remembering his order.

'One of the pleasures of sleeping alone,' Alex returned. 'Tonight, anyway. Tell me, are you suspicious of all men, or is it just me?'

'I'm not sure.' Casey considered. 'I had a bad experience with one man, I suppose it may have changed my outlook. But I'm more used to mixing with men than women. I was brought up and educated with boys, so I was never one for girly chats and stuff.'

'How come? Did you have lots of brothers?' He was intrigued.

'No, I was an only child. I went to Silverwood until I was eleven.'

'But that's a boys' school! A prep school!' He was astonished then.

Casey nodded. 'My dad taught English there, so the head's daughter and I were taught along with the boys. I did everything they did, played cricket even.'

'Cold showers too?' Alex remembered his prep school days with a grin.

'Not quite! But we did swim in the sea most summer mornings. Rosie avoided that like the plague but I got to quite enjoy it! I got a scholarship to a local girls' school after that.'

'So! You really *are* quite a bright lady? I know you have a degree.'

'I worked hard,' Casey defended. 'I had no choice. I got four straight As at A-level, my dad expected it.'

'Four As! My word!' he was impressed. 'But didn't you get teased? By the boys?'

'Not with him around!' Casey laughed. 'They didn't dare! Anyway I soon learnt to defend myself.'

'I'd noticed that!' Alex rubbed his cheek-bone in memory. 'Did you do boxing by any chance?'

'No, but I did try judo, and karate for a while.'

'I might have known it!' He shuddered. 'You swim well too, I notice, with your head down – like a real swimmer.'

'The way my father taught me,' she said. 'In the sea, I prefer that, more challenge somehow.'

He smiled. 'Then we do have *something* in common, after all. I have a house in Barbados, I swim far out into the bay there, sometimes even round to the next one, and it's over a mile.'

'A house in Barbados? *And* one in London?'

'I'm afraid so – and one in Sussex, not far from Chichester.'

'Heavens! Alex, you must be incredibly rich . . .!' Casey stared at him.

'I've worked very hard for it. And I have a very clever investment advisor.' He looked embarrassed suddenly. 'But Sussex *was* inherited from my godmother, I didn't buy that.'

'You don't have to make excuses to me about the way you live.' Casey looked up as the waiter put their first courses on the table. 'I *don't* judge other people by their possessions. Daddy was often scornful about the way the boys were spoilt with material things, a *sort* of socialist I suppose, though a closet one. He had to be. I have no real opinions on politics, I'm afraid.'

'No? A well educated young woman like you?'

'Does that make me more acceptable?' she challenged. 'Because I went to a private school for a while?'

'Of course it doesn't! Don't be an idiot, Casey, I

respect the fact that you worked hard at school, frankly. More than I probably did; I preferred the sports field to the classroom.'

'Well, *you* didn't need to,' she retorted.

'Now who sounds like a socialist?' he teased.

Casey took a mouthful of salad and chewed thoughtfully. 'I worked hard at school and you worked hard once you left,' she pointed out. 'Probably the best scenario considering where you are now – and where I am in comparison. I guess being able to write essays on the merits of Jane Austen and Charlotte Bronte doesn't count for much in the money-making world.'

'I noticed you had some fairly intelligent books on your bedside table.'

'Oh! And what else did you notice?' Her voice was noticeably cooler.

'That you sleep curled up like a baby,' he smiled. 'And you have a mole at the top of your thigh, right here!' He traced an intimate line with his fingertip.

'Alex!' She was blushing furiously now at the thought of Alex watching her as she slept, leaning over her, touching her. 'You . . . you had no right . . .!'

'Not to check up on you? Make sure you were OK? Of course I had! I was worried sick about you.'

'I'm perfectly fit, thank you,' Casey said. 'And on our next day off I'm going to hike down the Grand Canyon. Apparently you can easily do it in a day.'

'The hell you are! Casey, it's a nineteen-mile-or-so round trip down the Canyon. You can't be serious, all the guide books say it's dangerous to try that in a day, especially in this heat!'

'No, it's not – and I'm perfectly serious about it,' she retorted. 'It was something Dad always wanted to do and never managed it. Are you trying to forbid me, Alex?' Head on one side, she challenged him eye to eye.

'Would it do me any good?' he sighed. 'But OK Casey, if you must go – I'll do the walk with you. It would be quite a challenge for me too. It's the only way I'd let you do it, my girl, so it's that or nothing!'

'You don't let up, do you?' said Casey. 'We were supposed to have a truce.'

'If walking down the Canyon with you isn't a truce, I don't know what is!' Alex finished his bread and wiped the butter from the tips of his fingers. 'We've rearranged the schedule thanks to the accident. We've decided to do the double car shots in Phoenix instead of Nevada and change the rest days into travel days for the trucks. So we'll go to the Canyon on Friday if you like. Unless you'd rather spend the day in LA shopping?'

'No way! You can back out if you want to, but I'm not.'

He sighed heavily. 'Why on earth didn't I make them choose Bridget? The most exercise that one takes is waving her hands to get her nail polish dry.'

'Yes. And you wouldn't have had to try so hard to get Bridget into your bed, would you? I certainly don't come easily!'

'Don't challenge me with that, Casey,' he warned, laughing. 'Not in the middle of a restaurant!'

Casey blushed again, suddenly realizing what she'd said. 'I didn't mean . . . oh, Alex . . . I didn't mean that . . . I meant . . .'

He was really laughing then. 'You mean I have to work hard to win you? So be it, Casey. If that's what you want, that's what you'll get!'

Casey grinned at him and then looked down at her newly arrived plate. 'I think I might skip dessert,' she murmured.

'Don't change the subject,' he demanded. 'Is it what you really want? To be wooed?'

'Don't most women? Your steak will get cold, Alex!'

Mostly because Alex didn't think she could finish it she enjoyed every mouthful of her dinner and demolished ribs, salad, plus a huge baked potato and sour cream, to his complete astonishment. 'There are several restaurants I know that would love you!' he commented as the waiter finally removed their plates.

'I'm afraid I've always had a healthy appetite,' Casey confessed. 'My mum's fault, I guess. She was always cooking, and she made me eat everything!'

'You were fond of your parents, weren't you?' he guessed.

'Very! I suppose it was because I was an only child, and born quite late.' She bit her lip. 'I still miss them. Mum would have been so proud of this job. She used to love watching me in school plays.'

'I'm the eldest of four,' Alex said. 'I've got two brothers and a sister.'

'Don't tell me . . . boarding school, ponies and a house in the country? An old rectory, I suppose?'

'There's your socialist bit coming out again,' he protested.

'I'm right though, aren't I?'

'No, actually, you aren't! It was a farmhouse, still is in fact – and if you must know, since we're baring our souls, I hated boarding school. Well, prep, anyway. I used to cry in the bathroom when my parents left me.'

'I don't believe it! You?'

'Yes, me!'

'Some of the boys did at Silverwood. My mum used to take them back to the house and make them cocoa,' Casey remembered.

'In that case, I wish I'd gone to Silverwood!' Alex smiled. 'How do you feel now? We could dance in the other bar if you're up to it?'

'I'm fine.' She hesitated then, realizing what dancing with Alex might mean. 'Unless it's line dancing? I'm not sure I can cope with that.'

'No, I think it's ordinary-type dancing,' he assured her. 'Shall we give it a try?'

The music was slow country and western, and he immediately drew her into his arms, barely moving on the crowded dance floor. Wearing jeans as she was, her limbs were far closer to his than if she'd been wearing a dress and she was horribly aware of the hard pressure of his thighs against hers, his warmth, and the steady beat of his heart against her breasts. Even as his hands moved caressingly over her back she shivered, and wished she'd worn a bra. It had been so hot earlier that she hadn't bothered and now Alex was discovering it for himself as he pressed her against him. Slowly, and against her better judgement, she began to relax in his arms and Alex gave a sigh of pleasure as he gradually rested his cheek against hers.

'Better than fighting?' he murmured in her ear.

'Mmm, I suppose so.' She was wrapped tightly in his arms, every inch of her body touching his, and her traitorous body was loving every minute of it. She was dreadfully aware that her nipples were peaking against his chest – and that Alex knew it, just from the way he moved erotically against her. His fingers moved from her back up over the nape of her neck to curve round to her chin tilting it up to him.

Kissing Alex was totally unlike kissing anyone else, she decided then, as his mouth claimed hers. There in the middle of the dance floor she forgot everything, except the man who held her and the lips on hers, invading her very soul, it seemed at that moment.

'Well, well! Who'd have thought it?' Alex and Casey jerked apart in horror as Ross and Donna drew level with them on the dance floor, and Ross's jokey comment broke into their reverie. 'Oh, carry on, guys!' Ross added, grinning. 'Nice to see Alex has such devotion to duty!'

'Cut it out, Ross!' Alex snapped. 'Heaven help us – is everyone else here?'

'No, relax! I just brought Donna for a drink after all her hard work tonight,' Ross shrugged. 'The mob are down on the Strip somewhere, spending their overtime.'

'Thank goodness for that!' Alex looked relieved. 'Come and join us, then.'

Casey was astonished that she could feel so cheated as they left the bar and returned to the cosy booth she and Alex had eaten in. Suddenly it was a party and Ross and Donna made it fun, but even so, a small part of her longed still to be alone with Alex. This time, instead of sitting opposite her as he had done earlier, he sat next to her, his arm placed casually along the top of the seat; a silent demonstration of his claim on her. He was reluctant to let her dance with Ross when he asked her but Casey calmly over-ruled him, getting up happily, leaving Alex with Donna.

'This is definitely one for the record books,' Ross teased. 'I'm sorry we interrupted you two. I had no idea.'

'Neither had I,' Casey admitted. 'Until this evening. Alex is not the easiest person to fathom out.'

'*That* is the understatement of the century,' Ross said. 'Take care, Casey, he's been very hurt in the past.'

'Alex?' Casey stared at him. 'Don't be stupid, Ross! How could anyone hurt Alex? He's one very tough customer!'

'I told you about his wife a while back? Try the word *Wendy* in his ear, and watch his reaction!' Ross frowned. 'Alex is a hard man, in business, yes. As for the rest – well, he has great depths, and he keeps things hidden deep inside him. I guess you've learnt there's a gentler side to him?'

'I suppose I have,' Casey sighed, remembering his persuasive kisses. 'I like him, Ross, I really do, but, well . . . he's just so different from anyone I've ever met.'

'Take your time, sweetie,' Ross advised. 'Alex won't push you into anything you don't want, he's far too cautious.'

'Don't worry, Ross,' Casey smiled. 'He won't get anything from me that I'm not willing to give.'

'I rather think our Mr Havilland may well have a battle on his hands.'

'I hope so, Ross,' Casey grinned. 'I really hope so! I don't give in easily.'

'This I must see! Come on, I'll take you back to him before he comes looking for you.' He guided her back to their table and within minutes Alex was suggesting that he take Casey back to the hotel.

'I'm sorry,' he apologized as he hailed a cab. 'But I just want to be alone with you.'

'Not in bed though, Alex,' she warned.

'No, Casey, not tonight,' he said. 'I did promise, and I don't go back on my promises.'

147

Why, she wondered, did she feel so disappointed at his words? He sat apart from her in the car, talking only of trivial matters, casual even as he had been earlier; until they reached her room door. Then he took her key card from her to unlock the door, pulling her inside before she had a chance to argue. 'Don't panic, sweetheart,' he said. 'Since we were interrupted earlier, I'd simply like to finish kissing you, is that allowed? As part of the wooing process?'

Her bag dropped from her nerveless fingers as he drew her into his arms. Neither of them had turned on the lights as they had entered the room and the bright moonlight glowed on Casey's hair as he looked down at her. 'I want you, Cassandra, and I mean to have you, sooner or later,' he told her simply. 'You'd better get used to the idea.' Gently, he teased her lips apart until she was melting in his arms. Only then did he lift her onto the sofa, all the time letting his lips wreak havoc on hers until Casey was clinging to him, her fingers almost knotted in his hair as she twisted herself against him. His hands went to her breasts as they had longed to do all evening, and he cradled their full, warm weight through the silk of her shirt before, with an impatient gesture, he pulled at the buttons to release them to his sensual touch.

So this was what he meant by *kissing*, she thought mistily, as his warm mouth suckled at each throbbing tip in turn until she couldn't think at all and simply collapsed into his arms, his name on her feverish lips. If, at that moment, Alex had lifted her into the bed nearby she would have agreed without even thinking – but he didn't. It was as if all he wanted to demonstrate to her was her need for him, because suddenly he drew back, appearing totally controlled, but inside he struggled desperately to rein back his own raging desire to forget his promise and throw her onto the bed.

'I'm going, Casey,' he groaned, as he eased his weight from her body. 'Before I break my word! Will you really be OK on your own?'

'I'll survive, Alex. And if I need help I'll bang on the wall.' Casey tried to hide her frustration. 'But before you go . . .' She reached up and curled her arms around his neck. 'This is for me.' Her lips were tentative at first, just touching his until Alex took the initiative and, scooping her up, he kissed her. A deeply erotic kiss that Casey made the most of, prolonging it until they were both gasping for air.

'Don't *do* this to me, Casey,' he warned as he finally stood up, and pulled her shirt fronts together, hiding the temptation of her naked breasts.

'Maybe it's my turn to do the wooing?' she grinned back at him.

'Do I get the impression you are trying to confuse me?'

'Could be! Goodnight, Alex!'

Laughing now, he left her with a light kiss and, sighing with some regret, Casey switched on the bedside light. Then she stared. On the bedside table was a delicate bouquet of pale yellow rosebuds and baby's breath. Shaking, she reached for the envelope perched on top and pulled the card from it. She half expected it to be from the crew, or Ross but the card said 'Round One to me!' How on earth had Alex managed it? she wondered as she fingered the card. He had, after all, barely left her side all evening, apart from the brief minutes she'd danced with Ross. He must have seized the chance then and ordered the flowers by phone, she assumed.

Their scent drifted over her as she lay in bed a few minutes later. Alex was indeed wooing her, determinedly, and despite her bold words to Ross, she couldn't wait for Round Two!

CHAPTER 10

In the next few days Casey was left in no doubt that Alexander was paying court to her, and neither were the astonished crew. On location very little passed unnoticed by a closely integrated group and theirs was no exception. That Alex stayed with the unit instead of disappearing back to Los Angeles or New York as he had been doing was enough in itself to make them wonder. Just that he and Casey appeared to have given up arguing was certainly enough to alert them that something different was going on – to some regrets – their pithy fights had often enlivened a boring afternoon! Love affairs on location were nothing new, they happened frequently and Casey was well aware of that. She was just not used to them happening to her!

Even though Alex demonstrated his intentions by taking her off to dinner every evening she assumed that it could well be just a fleeting thing. After all, what would a man with Alex's connections really want with a girl from the sticks like her? Well educated, it was true, but no pedigree to speak of

– no knighted captain of industry for a father, no exalted friends scattered around the globe when she needed a favour, as Alex had.

And yet, he now seemed relaxed and comfortable with her and to her astonishment she found herself looking to him for approval after a shot. They had been shooting for almost three weeks and suddenly she was glowing at the camera when Alex was standing behind it. Ross positively crowed at the quality of the rushes. Though the original emphasis had meant to be on Robin, now Casey was quite simply stealing it from him and Alex seemed delighted. He knew from the viewing reports coming back from London and Detroit just how pleased the company were with their discovery. Casey *was* going to be a star after this, he knew instinctively.

He stunned her by chartering a plane to fly them both to Flagstaff, the nearest town they could get accommodation at short notice. A month ago she had hated Alex, Casey mused, yet now she was actually enjoying being alone with him in the luxurious jet as they flew the short distance between Las Vegas and Flagstaff. The crew were driving, and shooting on the way with Robin to try and make up some of the lost shots, but Alex saw no reason to make the long hot drive if they didn't have to.

'It will give us the time to take your great trip,' he suggested to Casey when she objected to the elitism of a private plane. 'Besides which, I want to be alone with you for a while!'

'Mile high fetish again?' Casey raised her eyebrows.

'Neither high enough, nor enough time!' Alex returned swiftly. 'For me, anyway!'

Casey blushed as she absorbed the impact of his suggestion and turned her head to the window to avoid his eyes. Alex leaned over and turned her swivel chair towards him. 'I have something for you, Casey, close your eyes.' Grateful that she could avoid looking at him, she did so, and found her fingers being wrapped around a small package.

'Just wooing,' Alex said, softly. 'Don't worry.'

Gingerly, Casey unwrapped the myriad pretty ribbons and gazed in astonishment at the delicate diamond and sapphire flower pendant that nestled in the glossy box. 'Alex . . . I can't!' she gasped. 'It's far too valuable!'

'Rubbish!' Alex took the pendant from her suddenly useless fingers. 'Bend your head.' Obediently she did so and he slipped the chain catch back together before he gently tilted her head up again and kissed her.

'Alex! It's beautiful and I love it.' She tried again. 'But you don't have to buy me – I'm *not* for sale!'

'I'm not trying to buy you, simply to please you. He shrugged. 'The same as the toy bear the other night, and you liked that.'

'A teddy in the casino is one thing, expensive necklaces are quite another,' she objected.

'Darling girl, wait for the shower of teddies, then,

if you prefer them! I love buying things for you, simply because you *don't* expect them!'

'Alex! You *are* impossible!' Casey tried to look stern. 'No more gifts, promise me? No flowers, no teddies – nothing!'

Alex simply laughed and pulled her into his lap. Any other girl, Miranda included, would have bitten his hand off for the valuable necklace he had just placed around Casey's neck. 'My beautiful Cinderella! You really *are* quite a little Puritan under that alluring exterior, aren't you? But *I'll* promise nothing,' he said. 'Just wear that for me? You can always tell people it's paste, if it bothers you!'

'I probably will do, I'd be too embarrassed to say anything else! My Aunt Mary would be terribly shocked.' Casey wrapped her arms round his neck. 'Thank you though, Alex.' After a week of his constant company Casey was a great deal more relaxed with Alexander, almost – she knew – to the point of trusting him. Certainly Alex had respected her wishes over most things. When he touched her she ignited, finding satisfaction in the lightest touch, but he wisely never over-stepped the boundaries she set, and perversely, Casey had begun to wonder if he was being too much of a gentleman!

As Ross had wisely pointed out, there was a great deal more to Alex than the tough business-like exterior and now she was discovering for herself the thoughtful yet sensual man under the façade. He was cheerfully determined to spoil her, his whole attitude announced as he returned her kisses, and Casey finally let it go in the heady experience of being in his arms.

Even its most loyal residents could never call Flagstaff a beautiful town but after the glitz and hype of Las Vegas Casey found it quite a relief. 'Much more like real America,' she told Alex as they reached the hotel.

'Including the freight line,' Alex grimaced at the line just across from the hotel as a procession of huge trucks began rattling past. 'I think the office may have slipped up, for once.'

'Including the freight,' Casey nodded, dreaming slightly over the evocative names emblazened on the trucks. It seemed rather like every pop song was being paraded in front of her. 'Why do American place-names sound better in songs than British ones?' she mused, thoughtfully.

'Oh, I don't know.' Alex considered for a moment. What about those songs about London or the Tyne?'

'I've never heard songs about either of them.'

Alex sighed. 'You make me feel *very* old sometimes! Let's go for a swim when we've registered, I could certainly do with it.'

It felt rather like taking an illicit holiday, she decided as later they lay by the pool and drank beer, and really quite wicked! She admitted to being tired, but then, near the end of an intensive shooting programme, that was inevitable. They had lost rest days, thanks to the accident, and they were all a little weary, even Alex.

'I don't normally drink beer,' Casey confessed. 'But this is nice.'

'You don't seem to drink much at all,' he commented, stretching out his long legs in front of him, relishing the unusual luxury of doing absolutely nothing.

'Working in a bar for any length of time can put you off for life!' Casey said, drily. 'I like the odd glass of wine, especially the kind *you* buy, but I can live without it. I've had to. Wine has not exactly been a priority recently.'

'That bad, huh?'

'It has been at times. Sometimes the tips for serving a drink have made all the difference between meeting the rent and not! It may seem odd to you, Alex, but that's what it's like in the big wide world sometimes!'

'Not any more, Cinderella! I promise you, the Keara ads will see to that.' Or he would, Alex added silently to himself.

'Len Stafford is also doing quite a lot,' Casey smiled. 'I've got the BBC part I went for, did I tell you?' The very thought of financial security was incredibly cheering after the last year of penury. 'I just pray that you're right, and it goes on that way.'

'I'm always right! Haven't you noticed?'

'Too damn sure of yourself you mean!' Casey reached for her glass and found her hand caught in his, instead. Slowly, he tip-toed his fingers up her arm raising goose-bumps on her skin, despite the heat. She could hardly believe that such a simple gesture could affect her so much! But then, looking at Alex, clad in minute black swimming trunks, she could see exactly why!

It was the first time she had seen him so lightly clad. He had never joined them in the swimming pools of the various hotels they had stayed in, and on location he had probably been the only one to wear trousers and a shirt, albeit light ones, all the time, despite the heat. She had begun to wonder, but there was no doubt that his tanned and trimly muscular body was actually superbly made. The brief, black trunks clung smoothly to his slim hips, and just the right amount of dark hair furred his chest, arrowing intriguingly into his trunks and sleeking his long legs. It was hard not to stare, and she found herself suddenly wanting to touch him; to wrench her hand from his and stroke it over the soft hair on his chest.

But somehow, she found the strength to pull away and stand up. 'I have to change – rinse my hair,' she stammered.

'Stop making excuses,' he grinned, lazily. 'We'll eat in the hotel, shall we?' he added. 'It saves trying to find a good restaurant in a strange town. The bar, at eight?'

'Not coming to get me?' Casey moved carefully out of range.

'I think the bar is safer! We're more likely to eat

that way, and we need an early night, I intend to leave here at four-thirty.'

'You must be joking! That's earlier than filming!'

'If we want to get down in the coolest part of the day, we need to,' he said. 'And it's at least two hours to the Canyon from here.'

Despite that threat it was hard to sleep when she went to bed. She was alone with Alex several hundred miles away from the rest of the crew, and though they had separate rooms she felt very vulnerable. She sat up in bed with Alex's goodnight kisses still tingling against her mouth, and hugged her knees as she considered her predicament. She finally had to admit to herself that she *was* in love, *and* with the most unsuitable man she could have found! However much she had tried to deny it to herself she knew it was true, and all her worst fears told her that he would end up breaking her heart just as Colin had done.

With trembling fingers she touched the pendant around her neck and began to cry. Sad tears this time, not the temper of a few days ago. Somehow, she had to get through the next day – and night – alone with Alex until they were safely back amongst the crew. There were, after all, only a few more days before they all returned to London. Then Alex would be swept back into his own busy life, and into the beautiful Miranda's clutches again, and she would be safe.

So why then – if it was what she wanted – did the thought of it make her want to cry all the more?

She was pale and hollow-eyed when Alex met her in reception next morning and he looked her up and down with some concern. 'Casey, you don't have to do this, you know,' he insisted.

'Yes I do!' She looked at him with newly defiant green eyes. 'I'm never at my best first thing in the morning, that's all!' And certainly not after a night spent worrying about her relationship with him, she decided, ruefully!

Alex was thoughtful as he tossed their bags into the hire car he'd taken delivery of the night before. As always, he was well organized with the help of his Los Angeles office, despite the fact that his staff thought he had taken leave of his senses! His secretary had even managed to book rooms at the Canyon for that evening so at least they were spared the long drive back to Flagstaff. He insisted that Casey rubbed liberal quantities of sun cream onto her exposed skin during their drive, which seemed all the more bizarre to her since it was barely light, and not that warm. In fact the air was still positively chilly as they reached Grand Canyon Park a little after six. With little traffic on the roads he had felt able to take a few chances with the speed limits and they made very good time.

'Look,' he said, suddenly, pulling into the side of the road a few minutes after entering Grand Canyon Park. 'There's the Canyon.'

Casey could hardly believe it. In a flurry of movement she was out of the car and standing spell-bound mesmerized by the stunning view of rock formations spread out in front of her. Reds and blues, gold and silver, the strata of thousands of years were spread around them with the soft swirls of bluish early morning mist still eddying through the endlessly twisting valleys.

'Two hundred and seventeen miles long,' Alex said, as they watched the colours changing even as they stood there. Casey shivered in the cool air and he immediately wrapped his arms around her to warm her.

'Dad would have loved to see this,' she said, wistfully.

'There's nowhere quite like it,' Alex agreed. 'Still want to go right down?'

'You bet I do! More than ever!' Casey wriggled out of his arms and turned back to the car. 'Let's get on with it!'

'It was worth a try,' Alex sighed. 'I must be crazy!'

'Don't be silly, Alex,' she grinned at him. 'After the crash, what else could go wrong?'

'Don't even think about it!'

He found the car park nearest to the start of Bright Angel trail and handed her one of the rucksacks he'd acquired from the Flagstaff hotel.

'You really do think of everything,' she marvelled inspecting the well packed contents – mineral water, bandaids, snacks, even a baseball hat!

'I take advice,' he said, drily. 'One of us has to! Come on then.'

Even at that time in the morning there were a few

people strolling around the paths as they made their way to the top of the trail. Four or five feet wide, and starting by the side of a log-cabin style house perched over the very edge it seemed, the track wound and hair-pinned its way through the pine and scrub to disappear way below.

'My goodness! There's no rail!' Casey gasped. 'Nothing to catch you!'

'That would take a hell of a lot of fencing,' Alex commented. 'Stay nearer the rock, you'll soon get used to it.' He held out a hand to her and for a few minutes she took it. In fact it hardly felt like walking downhill as the path wound so much, the drop was very gradual and her attention was quickly taken up by the astonishing amount of wildlife around them.

She squealed with delight as a mountain goat leapt out in front of them to disappear into the bushes and they were both wildly curious about the different birds they could see, and neither could recognize. All the time the colours around them changed as the daylight grew stronger and the early morning sun began to highlight the pinnacles of rock around them. Streams and sudden springs of gushing water made the air surprisingly noisy – often they had to shout to make each other hear above the noise.

She was confident now, sometimes striding ahead, sometimes letting Alex lead her, for the odd moments savouring the light brush of his arm as he helped her over a rough patch. Despite his disapproval of her brief shorts and skimpy vest top, he too wore shorts, and well used trainers. Alex Havilland was no desk-bound businessman, she soon discovered as they descended the winding trail. He was fit – astonishingly so – probably more than she was, and Casey walked miles most weeks. They walked together easily now, exchanging their views on life in general and unwittingly got to know each other far better as they talked.

Alex insisted they paused at the Indian Gardens rest stop and, though she would never have suggested it, Casey was glad of the opportunity to flop out on the grass with a can of Coke. It was already getting warm and Alex eyed the continuing trail with a certain amount of respect.

'Do you want to carry on?' he asked, hopeful of a change of heart.

'Absolutely!' Whatever happened, Casey was determined to make him go the distance, even if she was also beginning to feel somewhat daunted at the thought of the climb back up.

'Then I may need some encouragement,' he teased, holding out his arms.

'Liar!' Casey grinned, tossing back her heavy plait, and ignoring his gesture. 'I take back all I said about you, Alexander. You're a lot fitter than I gave you credit for, you obviously take a lot of exercise!'

'I always have done.' He smiled back at her as she hugged her bare knees to her chest. 'At school it was atheletics in the summer and rugby in the winter, now I walk the dog and play squash twice a week.'

'I'm surprised you find the time.'

'I can always find the time for the things I want to do,' he said, quietly. 'Haven't you noticed?'

'You are certainly pretty determined.' Casey fingered the pendant, still hanging round her neck because she was nervous of leaving it in an empty car all day.

'Some people say ruthless,' he shrugged. 'But I prefer determined. It's how we built the company up. Paul is the same, though he prefers the quieter methods. I'm the front man, the one who goes out to get the business in – he runs it. We're a good team, together.'

'Successful,' she agreed.

'I had a lot to prove.' Alex lifted her plait in his fingers and played idly with the end wisp caught with a red ribbon. 'We gambled a fortune, borrowed in part from my Pa. It had to succeed.'

'And it certainly did!'

'Thank goodness! I'd never have forgiven myself if we hadn't.' He shuddered at the very thought, remembering just how close to the brink they had come in the early days before the clients had begun to flock to them. Wendy had complained bitterly at the sudden financial restrictions and life at home had been a nightmare for several years before she had finally consoled herself elsewhere. Since then he had felt himself to be cold – had in fact frequently been accused of being unfeeling, and yet now all he felt was warmth and pure tenderness as he fingered the soft length of vivid hair in his hands. 'Casey?' he said, softly.

Their eyes locked, challenged and he held her gaze for long moments before he leant forward and touched her lips with his. Then he laughed and drew back, the words he'd wanted to say drying in his throat. Time for those later, he told himself. 'Put your hat on,' he told her instead. 'It's getting hot, already.'

'You too?' Casey jammed her baseball cap on and swiftly rubbed another layer of sun-screen on the exposed skin of her neck. 'Happy now?'

Alex produced a somewhat battered cotton hat from his rucksack and Casey smiled. Without his customary expensive suits, and his muscular frame clad in old denim shorts and a T-shirt, far from being diminished, Alex was a man who exuded an incredible sexuality. His hand on her arm, as they began making their way along the path again, was bringing the now familiar goose-bumps to her skin again, especially when he stroked his thumb over the sensitive flesh inside her elbow. He was deliberately teasing her, reminding her of every encounter they had had together, and Casey gritted her teeth, equally determined not to let him get to her. She concentrated grimly on the stunning and ever-changing scenery around them, craning eagerly for a first glimpse of the river below them.

Finally, they were above it as it swirled and eddied muddy brown water amongst the boulders along the Canyon and she gave an involuntary cry of terror at the sight of the flimsy bridge they had to cross, though it was still almost a mile away. 'It looks terribly wobbly!' she commented, nervously.

'Can't be,' Alex said, sensibly. 'The mules cross it every day, after all.'

'I suppose so.' Casey still looked doubtful. 'I suppose you're right.'

The bridge swung high over the river but of course Alex was right, it was perfectly safe and once on it she forgot to be nervous. They could see so much more of the Canyon from the middle of the bridge and both stared up with awe at the multi-coloured layers of rocks that towered above them. 'See the track?' Alex pointed it out. 'It's a long way back up!'

'We'll make it,' Casey laughed. 'We haven't got much alternative, have we?'

''Fraid not!'

On the last mile now they joined another young couple on the walk to Phantom Ranch, cheerfully exchanging cameras to take photographs as mementoes of their achievement. Casey had been surprised that Alex had thought to bring one, and laughed nervously as the American girl told her to cuddle up to her boyfriend! That would be a picture to surprise Miranda with, she thought with wry amusement!

'I have never *ever* met a woman who can look as slim as you and eat so much!' Alex marvelled when they had finally finished an enormous late breakfast, and Casey decided she had to have one last blueberry muffin.

'It's a long walk, and we got up so early. I was starving,' she defended, aware that he was laughing at her.

'Don't worry,' he assured her. 'I'm delighted to pander to one appetite, even if I can't assuage the other yet!'

Casey blushed furiously at the way he said 'yet'. 'Let's – let's take a look at the river?' she suggested, quickly. 'I want to collect a pebble for Daddy.'

'A stone? Whatever for?' He was puzzled.

'For his grave,' Casey said, solemnly. 'I know it's not really allowed, but I want to do it for him.'

'I guess it's as good a reason as any! OK, let's go and find one.'

They still had a fair walk from the greenly wooded area around Phantom Ranch to where the river ran through the main Canyon. It was incredibly hot and humid on the Canyon floor and they were both sweating hard as they reached the river so they were delighted with the excuse to dip their hands and feet into it. Casey took her time in finding the perfect pebble beside the river, leaning down to trail her fingers in the water between the rocks, turning pebbles over and discarding them in her careful search. Fascinated, Alex knelt beside her, offering various stones for her approval.

This means a lot to you, doesn't it?' he asked as Casey sat back on her heels to look more carefully.

'Yes, it does. It was such a dream of his to come here. Oh – look Alex – that one!' She leant over and reached for the special pebble she wanted and promptly over-balanced, tipping forward into the pool with a shriek.

'Idiot! But at least it wasn't my fault this time!' Alex scooped her up still clutching the precious stone. 'Why that one?' he demanded, in exasperation. 'Of all the rocks down here?'

'It's just right,' Casey said, undeterred as he reached for his rucksack and pulled out a spare T-shirt to dry her face and hair. Her own vest top was soaked, moulding itself to her breasts, and amused, she followed his eyes. 'It'll soon dry,' she grinned.

'Put this on,' he suggested.

'Instead?' she raised an eyebrow.

'I meant on top – far safer for me!'

'Too hot. Look the other way then, Alex Havilland. It will do you good to suffer!' And suffer he did for the first mile or so back along the river and over the bridge. She teased him relentlessly by staying a few steps ahead of him. Alex had certainly shed his sophisticated autocratic self along with his suit. He was as relaxed and carefree as she was and teased back cheerfully. For a while she forgot that they were climbing upwards and that her legs were beginning to ache ferociously.

The temperature was in the thirties by then and her vest was wet with perspiration now, trickling unpleasantly between her breasts and dampening her back. She was wild with envy when Alex finally stripped off his own T-shirt. Crossly, she threw him the tube of sun-screen he had made her apply.

'Heed your own advice, Mr Havilland,' she told him. They made it an excuse to rest for a few minutes while Alex smoothed the cream on his chest and shoulders.

'You'll have to do my back, I can't reach,' he said, apologetically. 'But I'm afraid I'm a bit sticky.'

'So am I.' Casey had never felt so unattractive in her life as she did then, with dirt-streaked clothes and hair, her face shiny with sweat. Alex didn't seem to notice, he was just as grubby and sticky as she was. His back muscles bunched and tensed under her fingers as she spread the cream and saw with some surprise how his fists clenched at her smooth touch.

'Casey!' He turned back to her as she carefully capped the tube and then he noticed the line of mules coming down the track towards them. He moved her back against the rock wall out of harm's way, his arm loosely about her shoulders as the line of riders passed. Some of the cheerfully exchanged banter with Casey and Alex, others looked simply terrified, especially when the foot-sure mules tried to reach that little bit further for tastier morsels as they ambled along.

'I think I prefer walking to that method of travelling,' Casey shuddered as the last rider disappeared along the track. 'They look so high up on those things, I had no idea mules were so big!'

Alex laughed. 'Oh, I think they're safe enough, those mules go up and down this track every day, remember?' He offered her a drink from his water bottle to save getting hers out, then took a long draught himself. 'There's still plenty,' he assured her since they had re-filled them at a water tap en-route. 'Hold out your hands,' he suggested. He tipped water into her cupped hands and Casey gratefully splashed it over her face. 'Better?'

'Mmm,' Casey licked absently at a stray drop of water on her top lip, making him shudder at the innocent gesture.

'Casey!' He pulled her hard up against him, stroking his thumb over the fullness of her lips. 'Casey – tonight – one room – or two?'

Casey met his dark eyes and read the desire in them. 'I . . . er . . . I think . . . one, Alex. Heaven help me!' They had been building up to this for days and she finally bowed to the inevitable. Lifting her face to his, she kissed him.

Gently, Alex smoothed her damp hair away from her forehead. 'Do you have any idea at all how much I want you?' he asked, huskily.

'Even in this state?'

'Perhaps even more so!' He ran his hands down from her waist to her hips. 'And I intend to get you in the same state in my bed, I promise you!' He felt her shivering in his arms and he hugged her tightly. 'However, we still have a few more miles to go and I, for one, would certainly prefer to have a bath, and a shave, before I touch you! So I shall just have to be patient for a while.'

CHAPTER 11

It still didn't make the climb any easier. Casey's calves and knees were beginning to ache relentlessly and an hour later, to her horror she felt the horrible sharp pain of cramp in her left leg. With a cry of defeat she subsided onto the grass clutching at her leg in agony. For once, she gave way to Alex without arguing, as without hesitating or listening to her agonized cries of 'don't touch it!' he knelt in front of her and grasping her calf in firm hands he briskly massaged the cramped limb as she yelled with the pain.

When, finally, it subsided enough for her to be able to stand on it, she was ashamed to find tears of pain added to the dirt on her face. 'Cramp is agony. I know,' Alex sympathized. 'I get it playing squash sometimes. I'm sorry if I hurt you, but it's only way to shift it.'

'I know,' she nodded. 'It just hurt so much for a moment or two.'

'Lean on me for a while,' he offered. 'Don't play tough, Casey – I want to help.' She hated being so weak but she had no choice, her leg still hurt badly. She only made the last mile with Alex's supporting arm tight around her waist, and gave a huge sigh of relief when they finally reached the top of the trail and the terrace full of sight-seers. 'We did it!' Alex grinned at her. 'I had my doubts, but . . .! Well done, my darling!'

'Only thanks to you, Alex,' she admitted, truthfully.

'You couldn't help cramp, angel! But now for a bath, and a very large drink,' he decided, firmly. 'Then maybe we'll watch the sunset. It can be pretty spectacular.'

'I doubt I'll be awake!' Casey grinned.

'That would be just my luck!' he sighed. 'Come on then, just a few more yards to the car.'

In embarrassment, Casey frantically brushed out her hair and did a swift repair job to her face before they found the hotel Alex's office had booked for them. She left Alex to deal with registering, too tired to do more than follow the porter with their luggage.

Naturally enough, Alex had acquired one of the best rooms in the busy hotel, its wide balcony opening onto a stunning view of the Canyon in the late afternoon sunshine. They both stood spellbound for a moment until Alex pulled himself together enough to tip the porter. As the door closed behind him they met each other's eyes. both feeling rather awkward now, with the huge bed between them. Alex turned, uncomfortably, and then opened the French windows onto the balcony.

'You take the bathroom first, Casey,' he suggested, quietly. 'In the meantime, I'll order some drinks, because I for one could do with a large scotch!'

'Thanks,' she said, grateful that he had smoothed the awkwardness over. 'I could certainly do with a bath.'

Take your time,' he replied, reaching for the phone. 'Just don't go to sleep in it! Or would you like me to bring a drink in for you to keep you awake?'

'No!' Casey said, more sharply than she meant to, and she realized it. 'No – I didn't mean . . . Alex, I won't be too long.'

Her hands were still trembling, however, as she closed the bathroom door and started to run the bath. She had, after all agreed to this – to sharing a room – and ultimately a bed with Alex Havilland. She had agreed to his confident request because, despite her misgivings, she also wanted him as badly as he evidently wanted her. Her throbbing body told her that all too obviously as she slid into the warm water and with relief she found the button that operated the jacuzzi. She had become used to using them over the last few weeks. It eased her aching legs and back enormously and finally she found the physical strength to wash her hair, before she worked up the courage to wrap herself in a large bath towel and saunter back into the bedroom, with her wet hair hanging down her back as if she hadn't a care in the world.

She needn't have worried. Alex was sprawled comfortably in an armchair, whisky glass in hand and showed no sign of wanting to claim her at all! He was probably just as tired as she was, she thought in relief. 'Bathroom's free,' she told him, sinking down onto the armchair facing the long dressing table and reaching casually for the hair-dryer.

'I was almost asleep,' he admitted, ruefully, standing up and stretching his aching limbs. 'There's champagne for you. Since you wouldn't let me in, I kept it cool for you!' He put the glass of wine in front of her on the dressing table, but he made no attempt to touch her as he turned away. She made a real effort to dry her thick hair and then gave up and shook it free to dry naturally. She was desperately tired. A quick nap, she decided, just while Alex was in the bathroom. For a moment she tipped her head, listening to the reassuring sounds of his movements swishing the water around in the bath. Only then did she move across to the wide bed and tossing the gaily coloured Indian spread aside, she flopped out onto the crisp sheets, and was asleep in seconds.

She woke with a start to find the room bathed in the red gold light of the most incredible sunset. Mesmerized, she sat up and stared at the show clearly visible from the bed, obviously placed for the purpose. The Canyon was a daze of reds and touched with bronze, changing in every second she gazed at it. Alex had opened the balcony doors when they had first come into the room so she had the full benefit of the view her father had always wanted to see, and never had.

'I made it, Daddy,' she said, softly. 'I made it! Thanks to Alex – Alex! Where . . .?'

Then she realized! Wearing only a brief towel around his hips, Alex was fast asleep on the other side of the bed. He seemed deeply asleep, his breathing slow and even, as he lay on his side facing her, his head cradled in the curve of his arm. For blissful minutes she gave herself over to the precarious pleasure of simply looking at him. In the last twenty-four hours she had become aware of his powerfully muscular build, now she carefully took in the smooth texture of his tanned skin against the hair-roughened texture of his chest. The faint blue shadow of stubble had gone from his chin – he had certainly honoured his promise to shave, she thought, with amusement. It had, after all, been a slightly unusual thing for the normally immaculate Alex to look unshaven, but then they had left incredibly early that morning.

Greatly daring now, she leant on one elbow and gently stroked the dark hair on his chest as she had longed to do the day before. It felt soft and sensual beneath her fingertips and with a growing pleasure she explored further, curving them lightly over the flat male nipples, astonished then, to find them hardening under her touch.

Startled, she jerked her hand back and to her

horror she heard him laugh. A low, husky laugh as his own hands reached out for her. He was *certainly* not asleep. His dark eyes were open and sharply in focus as they met her startled ones. 'Don't stop,' he said, softly. 'It was just getting interesting!' His fingers curled determinedly over her wrists and pulled her hands back to his chest as she would have attempted to draw back in confusion.

'Relax, Casey – let go – relax for me,' he persuaded, gently. 'I've wanted you for so long, my darling.' One by one he kissed her clenched fingers until they opened under his gentle lips and he began to feel the tension ease from her body. Only then did he lift his other hand to tangle his fingers in the thickness of her hair to pull her over him and bring her lips down to his.

His mouth was gentle and tender and he felt his way with care as he teased her lips apart with his, until with a groan of frustration he curled his tongue into the velvety recesses of her mouth the instant her lips parted to cry out. In only minutes her arms were clasped tightly around his neck and he gloried briefly in the new sensation of the soft pressure of her bared breasts against his chest as the towel she'd been wearing slipped down. Swiftly, he jerked it away completely and Casey shivered involuntarily as her naked limbs met the warmth of his, when he tossed his own brief covering onto the floor. His skin was like silk, his back smooth and unblemished under her fingers; yet there was hard muscle under the silk, muscle that flexed and tensed as he moved to roll her over so that he could press the length of his body over hers.

'Mine!' he murmured as he moved erotically against her, making her writhe with pleasure, despite the agonizing feeling she still had that somehow she should be resisting. 'Oh, hell!' He had a sudden terrible thought. 'I should have asked you this before! I should protect you!'

'Alex – it's OK – it's safe, I promise.' Casey almost smiled at his sudden indecision, and his concern for her, though she was too embarrassed to openly admit she took the Pill.

Alex breathed a blissful sigh of relief. He didn't want any barriers between them, selfishly, he knew, but the relief was enormous. 'I want this to be so good for you,' he added, his voice heavy with emotion. 'Let go, darling, don't be frightened of me.'

'I'm not,' she lied, struggling to sound matter-of-fact – she was hardly a virgin, after all! 'Why should I be afraid of you, Alex?'

'No reason at all – not now. I think perhaps it could even be the other way round!'

She smiled, but her body was trembling with nerves as slowly and deliberately he began to kiss his way down the length of her neck before he found the tempting fullness of her breasts. She couldn't help the soft cry of pleasure as he drew first one nipple then the other into his mouth, his tongue swirling around the hardening tip; Casey thought dreamily then that she had never known such sweet sensual bliss as that which Alex was creating in her heated body.

In control now, he stroked, he kissed, erotically, yet with a tenderness that surprised and delighted her, until finally she was almost demented with wanting him, and any underlying resistance simply melted away. Her thighs parted easily against his persuasive fingers, making her moan softly. It was a gentle invasion at first, until he found the tiny pressure point he was searching for and she couldn't stop her anguished cry of sensual pleasure as his clever fingers worked their magic on the damply yielding flesh.

'Alex! Oh . . .!' He slid down her writhing body and his lips joined his exploration, making her hips lurch upwards as the sensation hit her. She was so close to tipping over the edge into orgasm, yet somehow she fought not to. It seemed too soon. Multiple orgasm had never played a part in her love-making with Colin and she had no real idea that it could happen to her. Alex felt her inner muscles convulse under his hands and realized what she was trying to do.

'No . . . let it happen, Casey,' he whispered, persuasively. 'I *want* to hear you cry out – again and again, don't hold back!' He renewed the erotic pressure and Casey was finally beyond holding anything back. Her entire body shook with the force of the climax that rushed through her and despite all the effort she made not to, she couldn't help the second frantic cry that burst from her.

In a frenzy she jerked against him, feeling his manhood hard and hot against her thigh; and then the only place she wanted it was inside her. With a sudden flash of desperation she reached down, her hands suddenly as swift and expert as his. Alex gave a groan of capitulation as her hand closed around him, moving the hard velvety flesh in a gentle rhythm. He swore furiously and then gave in, thrusting her hands away to part her thighs and drive himself hard inside her, finally assuaging the ache that his exploring hands had caused. For a moment or so he paused, fighting for some control, desperate not to have it end too soon. He knew how close he was.

Casey felt his tension in the pulse that beat so frantically in his chest as he jerked his head up. 'Alex . . . I want you!' she whispered. 'Love me . . . please, love me, Alex.'

Alex gave a sigh of release, and gathering himself, he began to move again in hard thrusts that seemed to find the very depths of her soul. Slowly at first, then gathering a momentum he could do nothing about as Casey wrapped her legs about him, her movement matching his. He realized then that he had truly forgotten what it was like to make love with a responsive partner. Casey gave herself with the generous warmth he had come to know – indeed respect – and her frantic cries as she recognized the new orgasm he brought her to triggered his own. He collapsed into her arms, as breathless as she was, and for a few minutes neither had the strength to move as they fought to breathe normally again. Finally, he found the energy to roll onto his side, smiling softly at the girl in his arms. 'Did I love you?' he asked, enigmatically, 'as you wanted to be loved?'

Casey smiled back. 'Oh . . . yes, Alex! In every way! It was fantastic!'

'And for me!' he sighed with satisfaction. 'It's been a long time since I've made love to anyone.'

'Me too,' Casey admitted. 'I haven't felt the need for it, either.'

He laughed. 'Yet we probably both thought the worst of each other! I was so convinced you were sleeping with Robin.'

Casey sat up and ran her fingers through her damp tangled hair, wincing with pain as she found out how knotted it was. 'It isn't fair! Because of the way I look everyone thinks I've had dozens of men! And I haven't!'

'You've been hurt,' Alex commented, quietly. 'And that situation I know all about. Forget the T-shirt, I have the hand-knitted sweater in that department!' He brushed his mouth gently over hers. 'I won't hurt you, Casey. That I will promise you.'

But you will, Casey thought, sadly. You'll go back to Miranda, the perfect hostess, your ideal partner, and I *won't* be the other woman – no way! However, now she smiled, hiding her fears outwardly by occupying herself in trying to untangle her hair.

'Let me help,' he suggested and, fetching a brush

from the dressing table, he knelt behind her and began to patiently brush out all the knots until her hair hung smoothly and glossily down her back. It was a simple, yet stunningly erotic gesture – they were both still naked and just the touch of his hands on her bare shoulders as he eased the passage of the brush was enough to make her melt inside.

'This,' said Alex, as he put the brush down and slid his hands through the smooth length of her hair 'was almost my undoing that day in my office! I'm still not sure how I kept my hands off you!'

'You were horrible to me that day,' she objected, distracted then as he used the twist of hair to lower her back across his thighs into the curve of his arm.

'Only because I was fighting not to look a complete fool!' he confessed, ruefully. 'What I actually wanted was to do what I'm doing now.' He bent his head back to her breasts, suckling with a devastating pressure – not gentle now – his desire was still far too strong to be gentle. Her back arched automatically as he held her, lifting her breasts up to his hungry mouth.

'Alex – oh Alex!' she moaned, raking her fingers through his dark hair to press his lips down. Alex couldn't help himself, his body ached anew as hers ground helplessly against him. Firmly, he rolled her over so that she was above him, encouraging her to kneel astride him as he explored. Casey laughed with uninhibited joy, and grasping his hands each side of his head so that he was trapped, she took the initiative as he joined in her laughter.

'My prisoner this time!' she told him, in delight at his apparent surrender, and began to move herself devastatingly. But it was mere seconds, before Alex took control back, wrenching his hands free to sieze her by her waist moving her as he needed and Casey forgot everything but the man giving her such wild erotic pleasure. With a groan of capitulation she instinctively threw her body back to achieve a greater penetration, letting the length of her hair sweep his legs and sobbed out her wonder in the climax he finally invoked.

'I've never met anyone like you, Cassandra!' he gasped as finally they lay wrapped together exhausted and gloriously satisfied. Casey snuggled blissfully into his arms and savoured every moment of his attention as he gently stroked her hair back from her face. It was tangled again, but she didn't care now.

'It feels so good, Alex,' she replied. 'I'm glad we stopped quarrelling.'

'I don't somehow think we'll do that for long!' He grinned boyishly at her, relaxed and almost playful now. 'However, how about food? Because I, for one, am starving!' Raising himself reluctantly from her he reached across for the room-service menu. 'Let's have supper here, in bed? Saves getting dressed.'

He ordered steak sandwiches at her suggestion and more champagne as Casey fled to the bathroom, horrified at the idea of a waiter finding them naked. The tumbled bed alone told its own story. 'They won't care! Don't be such a baby!' Alex chided, striding into the bathroom to find her pulling clothes out of her bag. 'Come and take a shower with me?' Refusing to take no for an answer, he tossed the shirt and jeans back onto the floor and lifting her into his arms he carried her into the huge shower cubicle.

'Hold your hair out of the way,' he ordered, thoughtfully and she immediately obeyed him, to her complete surprise. There was, however, a clever reason for his suggestion. It left him free to let his soapy hands roam her body without hindrance. Casey squealed with delight and her hair tumbled and got wet all too quickly.

'This is crazy!' she giggled. 'I can't believe I'm letting you do this!'

Alex finally turned the shower off and reached for a couple of towels. 'Have you never showered with your lover before?'

'No, Alex, I'm glad to say I haven't.' She wrapped herself securely in the towel and found another for her damp hair. It would need drying for a second time, she thought, ruefully aware still of the shoot and keeping it in good condition.

'Tell me?' he suggested.

'About past lovers? There's very little to tell – one man really – not very interesting, anyway.'

'Only one?' He stared at her.

'One! I learnt my lesson about men from that, Alex. I learnt not to trust any of them and so far I've been proved right!'

Towelling himself briskly, Alex took in her harsh statement in some shock.

'Casey, I'll prove to you that statement is complete rubbish!' he said, vehemently.

'I doubt it, Mr Havilland.' Casey finally found her blue silk dressing gown and put it on, despite his amused look. 'And I for one, am not going to face a waiter in just a towel!'

'It could be a waitress?' he joked, but though he wandered back into the bedroom teasingly slowly, and very naked, he finally donned a towelling robe when he realized just as the waiter knocked on the door that she was truly horrified at the thought of being caught almost naked. 'I love to see you blush, my darling,' he confessed after the waiter finally left. 'You do it so innocently!'

Casey suddenly found she was blushing furiously again and began setting out everything he had ordered, to hide her confusion. 'Alex, actually I *am* quite inexperienced,' she told him. 'Colin really ruined things for me.'

'Colin?' Alex held a chair out for her at the small table and poured champagne. 'Tell me about him?'

Reluctantly, Casey took the chair and sipped at her wine. Just thinking of Colin was enough to curb her usually robust appetite. 'He was a lecturer at college. I met him during my first Rag week, and . . . well . . . we had a thing for a while,' she shrugged. 'He really was a bastard – I found out too late, that's all. He apparently specialized in picking out new girl students for his entertainment, and if they were inexperienced and a virgin as I was, so much the better!'

Alex shuddered at the resignation in her tone. 'And there hasn't been anyone since?' he asked, in astonishment.

Casey shook her head. 'No, not really. When someone tells you to your face that you're useless in bed, it does put you off trying with anyone else.'

'In that case, he was covering up for his own inadequacies,' Alex decided, firmly. 'There is absolutely nothing at all wrong with you, darling, I assure you! Though I quite definitely owe you an apology, I just assumed you were a lot more experienced than you were. I'd have been a lot more . . . well . . . gentle, if I'd known.'

'Because I don't look innocent?' Casey was bitter. 'Because I'm not some simpering little thing?' Like Miranda, she wanted to add.

'No, simply because you exude self-confidence,' he argued. 'And you have to admit you can look after yourself.'

'I've had to, especially the last few years! OK, so I probably couldn't play Juliet or Ophelia, but I feel like them inside!'

'Maybe, but you would be perfect for Beatrice, or Katherine, and you'd certainly make a wonderful Rosalind.'

Casey laughed. 'I played Rosalind at school once.'

'Lucky Orlando! Though personally I would prefer to play Petruchio to your Katherine!' Alex suggested, wickedly. 'It might be the only time I'd win with you! However, I should have guessed that night in Santa Monica that you weren't as you seemed. You really *were* upset about that scene, weren't you?'

'Yes, I was.' Casey remembered then. 'Alex, did *you* speak to Hal about it?'

'Yes, I'm afraid to say I did, do you mind too much?'

'No, not really, not now,' she admitted. 'I was curious that's all. Hal said he knew *of* you, but that he'd never met you, I wondered . . .?'

Alex fiddled with the stem of his glass. 'I don't know him,' he said. 'But I know Sarah Campbell, and her husband is an old friend. I've known Nick for years, he ran a production company in London and we used to work together a lot. In fact, when Nick and Sarah were still very much "illegal" – when Nick was still married to Diana – he used to borrow a cottage I had on Dartmoor, for weekends. I knew Hal lived next door to them in Malibu so first I asked Sarah's advice and then I approached Hal. I'm afraid I did pull a bit of rank with him over Kear. I told him they wouldn't like it.'

'Well, thank heaven for Kear!' Casey said.

'Thank heaven for Kear, for several reasons,' he grinned at her, boyishly pushing his hands through his tousled hair. '*And* for Sarah's expert advice. She went through exactly the same kind of misgivings about nude scenes as you on her first film, Casey. She hated it, and she knew immediately how you felt.'

'But she still *does* nude scenes.'

'Usually only when Nick is directing,' Alex

pointed out. 'She trusts him, but no one else.' He smiled. 'We *all* thought that marriage was doomed, but I have to admit it's become one of the love stories of Hollywood. They are the only couple I know who live for each other, and actually *worship* their kids!'

'Robin said Sarah talked of nothing else at the barbecue,' Casey remembered.

'That sounds like Sarah!' Alex laughed. 'When I first met Nick, he had one teenage daughter and didn't want any more children. Now he's, well, in his forties I suppose, with two more little ones and he adores them, even changes nappies like an expert, I've seen him do it.'

'He does?' Casey could hardly believe her ears. Nick Grey hardly seemed the domestic type from what she had heard about him in the business.

'Certainly! He changed for the better when he married Sarah. He's *always* been a hands-on father with Sam and Abby. Sarah may be sixteen years younger than him, but she has a wise head on those beautiful shoulders. Nick is very lucky to have found her.' He sounded almost wistful as he spoke of his friend's successful marriage, and Casey reached for his hand in sympathy.

'There *are* successful marriages around, Alex,' she said. 'My parents had one, my aunt and uncle *still* have one, and your own parents are still married, aren't they?'

'Hmm, hardly bliss though! My mother thrives on crisis, and if she hasn't got one, she invents one!

Pa slinks off to the golf club at every available moment!' Alex grinned. 'My brothers and I all play pretty well, we used to go with him!'

'So that's your solution,' Casey returned. 'Get married and play golf!'

'The solution is not to bother at all,' Alex said, wryly. 'Change the subject, Casey, we're getting morbid!' He reached across the table and pulled at the sash of her dressing gown to reveal her lissom body. 'Come back to bed, darling, I'm feeling neglected.'

'Neglected! Alex Havilland, I think you must be a sex fiend!'

'I could easily turn into one! Try me?' Laughing now, Alex scooped her up and carried her back to the bed, efficient as always in pausing to make sure their champagne was within reach before he joined her. Despite his threat he was tender now, his kisses subtly persuasive on her newly sensitized skin and Casey almost wanted to weep with love for him as he touched her so gently. In that moment she offered up a prayer of thanks that she had finally given in to him.

CHAPTER 12

Casey woke with a start to bright daylight and she jerked upwards in shock. Alex lay peacefully asleep face down, his arm buried under the pillow. 'Alex! Alex! It's late!' she cried frantically, shaking at him.

Alex stirred, and then reluctantly opened his eyes. 'Take it easy,' he groaned. 'The unit won't be here until lunchtime, I made darned sure of that! We have plenty of time for a leisurely breakfast, even a swim if we want it.'

'Do you manipulate everything?' Casey got up, and pulled on her dressing gown.

'Yep! Come back to bed for a while, Casey – please?'

Never at her best in the morning, as Alex already knew from the set, Casey ignored his plea and made for the bathroom, and he wisely let her go. When she finally went back to the bedroom feeling more comfortable once she had washed her face and cleaned her teeth, she found Alex still lying in bed, on his back now with his arms folded behind his head, and completely at ease.

'I'll – I'll make some coffee, shall I?' Casey suddenly felt embarrassed at their intimate situation, particularly as she knew Alex would laugh if she told him. Without waiting for his assent, she busied herself with the coffee percolator provided by the hotel.

'Shall we order breakfast in here?' Alex asked. 'Or would you prefer the restaurant?'

'The restaurant!' Casey said, firmly. At least there she would keep her clothes on and Alex wouldn't be able to touch her. She desperately needed to get herself together before she had to face the knowing looks of the crew.

'Spoilsport!' Alex grinned. 'But I could get used to this.' He pushed himself up against the pillows as Casey handed him a cup of coffee, black and strong, as she knew he liked it. 'It beats Joannie, any day.'

'Joannie?' Casey stared at him. This was a new name to her.

'My housekeeper!' He laughed at her horrified face. 'Sixty if she's a day and when she gets going her tongue would make yours sound like Mother Teresa's!'

'An elderly housekeeper bringing you coffee! You do surprise me! Not some glamorous young thing? Like Miranda?'

'Miranda would never manage such things as making coffee – at any time! Casey, Miranda and I are friends, nothing more. I don't sleep with her, and I never have!' He shrugged, dismissing the idea. 'Frankly, kissing Miranda is like trying to get a

189

reaction from a snowball! She is happy to act as my hostess when I need her, but as far as anything else is concerned, forget it.' Casey was fairly certain that Miranda didn't think that way, but the words cheered her more than a little. 'Joannie loathes her, anyway,' he added, as if that was the deciding factor.

'And that matters?'

'Does to her! Anyway, Joan is a very good judge of character, though it galls me to say so!'

'She adores *you*, I take it?' Casey asked, sarcastically.

'Joan has known me since I was two,' Alex admitted. 'So I probably allow her a little more leeway than anyone else. I wonder what she'll think of you? You met her husband by the way, my chauffeur. He rather liked you, I gather.'

Casey curled up on the bed hugging her knees as she sipped her own coffee. 'Cosy set-up,' she commented.

'It suits me now. Wendy – my ex-wife – hated Joan – and Joan her, so for a while she and William went back to work for my parents. Wendy resented their familiarity, more than anything.'

'Alex, did you love your wife?' Casey asked, diffidently.

Alex met her eyes squarely, barely surprised by her straightforward question. It was what he had come to expect from Casey. 'Yes, I did, for a long time very much indeed. I would have taken her back even after she left me. I was married, and to me that

190

meant a lifetime commitment, not one to be broken just because things hit a rough patch. It will take a great deal to persuade me to take that step again, believe me!'

Was he warning her? That however good things were between them it was merely sex? It would be natural enough for someone in Alex's position after all. He obviously envied his friend's happy marriage, but he seemed to feel unable to try and emulate it? Ross had said he had been badly hurt. How sad, she thought then, that it had soured him so much. Yet, he was already surmising what his trusted housekeeper would think of *her*!

'I'm not so keen on the marriage bit myself,' she said, as casually as she could manage. 'Especially now that I seem to have a real chance in my career at last.' Was there, she wondered, just the hint of relief in the momentary frown that flickered on his face before he laughed?

'Wise girl! Now *come here*! Before I die of neglect!'

They were almost the last guests to eat breakfast in the cosy restaurant but no one seemed to mind. Their waitress chatted cheerfully and poured endless coffee for them as they lingered over their meal. Alex was relaxed and amiable as she had never seen him before, reaching for her hand as they rose to leave. 'We need to walk this off,' he suggested. 'Come on.'

'Not down the Canyon again!' She recoiled in mock horror. 'I've done that!'

He laughed at her sudden apprehension. 'No, no, just a stroll. There are lots of trails around the Rim. We can happily occupy ourselves until the unit are due.'

It was cooler and pleasant under the trees and an easy walk. Alex stopped frequently to kiss her as if having discovered her, he couldn't bear to let her go for too long without imprinting his presence on her.

Finally, they paused at a rustic bench with the endlessly fascinating views of the Canyon stretching away to the horizon. Alex leant back, his long legs, clad in soft cream chinos, stretched out before him. 'Casey?' he touched her cheek gently with the back of his hand.

'Hmm?' Casey was too content to move.

'When we finish here, would you like to come to Barbados with me for a few days?'

She smiled. 'To your decadent third home?'

'Yes! Oh, why do I always have to explain myself to you?' He was almost irate. 'You make me feel ashamed of being wealthy! Dammit, Casey, I have earned every penny, believe me!'

'I'm sure you have!' Had he taken Miranda to Barbados? she wondered.

'Well? Will you swallow your principles and come with me?' He stroked persuasively, his fingers on her lips now. 'The house is high above its own cove, we can swim naked in the bay if we want to. It's so private, no one will know we're there, except Dora, of course.'

'*Another* housekeeper?' she mocked, cheerfully.

'No, more a caretaker, I suppose,' he defended. 'She only comes in the mornings to tidy up. I often use it as a stopover to recharge my batteries after I've been to one of the American offices.'

Hooked now, Casey thought longingly of having a few days of Alex's undiluted company – and the bliss of his love-making. Quite definitely he was under her skin in a way she could never have dreamt of a few weeks before. 'Well, yes, Alex. I guess I could spare you a few days,' she said at last. 'Now Hal's film starts a little later than he planned.'

Alex groaned with relief, sure that she had been going to turn him down. 'We'll have a great time, I promise. I'll do my best to convert you to my capitalist ways!'

After the last few weeks it wouldn't actually take that much to convert her, Casey thought, but it was the next few days that concerned her more. 'Alex, while we're here . . .' she hesitated. 'I need to have my own room, not share yours, you know.'

'Maybe, for appearance's sake,' he agreed. 'But I have no intention of spending the nights alone, my darling, not any more. And – no, I don't really care what the unit think, and neither should you. We are both single remember, and free to do exactly as we please.'

Casey shivered. Alex seemed quite happy to flaunt their new relationship to the unit – happy, even proud. But then, she acknowleged, ruefully, Alex had achieved everything he had set out to achieve. And she had fallen for it, hook, line and sinker! Her fingers went instinctively to the pendant she had automatically put around her neck that morning, to please Alex, she realized then, and Alex noticed the gesture, following then with his own fingers to curve them into the hollow of her throat.

'I can't quite believe this is me,' he confessed, his voice husky with need. 'I want you so badly, all the time.'

'But with a late night shoot, you have a long time to wait!' Casey reminded him as his arms closed around her.

'Not so long!' Alex glanced at his watch over her shoulder. 'The boys won't be here for an hour or so! I can't wait until tonight,' he repeated. 'Let's go back to the hotel! Or here, perhaps?'

'Alex!' She was horrified.

'The hotel then, my prudish darling!' He smiled. 'Shame, I rather like the idea of making love to you under the trees! In Barbados we certainly will – and on the beach in the moonlight.'

'Somewhat gritty!' Casey said, practically.

'We'll take a blanket or something,' Alex promised, wickedly. 'Come on, we're wasting time!'

It was getting harder all the time to resist him she mused, recognizing the way her own body responded to his sensual suggestion. Despite making love that morning she was as eager as he was once they reached the sanctuary of their room. Unlike his autocratic business persona, Alex made love in a totally easy, unselfish way, taking pleasure from skilfully satisfying her, before succumbing to his own need. How unlike Colin he was in that respect, she thought gratefully, realizing that even though they had made love many times, her body showed and felt no trace of it beyond a pleasurable ache. A night in Colin's bed on the other hand had often left her bruised and sore for days afterwards. She suspected that Alex had been right, as he usually was: Colin had certainly *not* been the great lover he had made himself out to be.

Just one glance at her was enough for Robin to know exactly what had taken place in the unit's absence. 'Ho, ho!' he grinned at her. 'Alexander has done more than walk down the Canyon with you, I know!'

'Rubbish!' denied Casey, quickly – far too quickly, she realized as Robin yelled with disbelieving laughter. 'It's far too exhausting a trip to think of anything else.'

'Tell that to the birds, sweetheart. You have satisfaction oozing from every pore! What did I tell you about Alex?'

Casey blushed then, since it was exactly how she felt. 'Robin, don't tell Liz, will you?' she begged. 'She'll laugh herself silly.'

'I won't need to,' he said. 'She'll only have to look – as I did. Alex looks the same, frankly.' Casey sank down onto the banquette and swore.

'Is it so obvious?'

Robin leant over and hugged her. 'Does it matter? Just as long as you don't get hurt in the process, but from what I've heard from the others the last day or two, Alex is not the casual type.'

'He *has* got Miranda Bradbury though,' Casey said.

'Not for much longer, if he's got any sense,' Robin assured her, lifting up the pendant to examine it more carefully. 'Wow! This *is* real! When do you get the ring to match it?'

'Robin! Don't be silly!' she laughed. 'I'm hardly the type to marry Alex Havilland – come on! Keep your fantasies for yourself and Liz. I'll be your bridesmaid instead.'

'And why shouldn't you be good enough for the mighty Mr H?' Robin demanded with a grin. 'Case, you're good enough for anyone you set your heart on, remember that. You didn't get so carried away you forgot about precautions I hope? That might just be the one way to frighten him off!'

'Leave it out, Faulkner. Does Alex look stupid?' Casey laughed, remembering Alex's diffident question and his delight in discovering she was on the Pill.

'He'd look pretty stupid if he got you pregnant,' Robin said, sensibly.

'Pregnant!' Casey stared at him, suddenly envisaging Alex's child in her arms, and Robin quickly caught the panic-stricken look in her eyes that she couldn't hide.

'Don't tell me you forgot?'

'No, of course not!' Casey turned away as Angie bounced into the trailer with their clothes over her arm. Only that morning Alex had reminded her to take her Pill, after all. She would have been astonished had she realized that Alex himself had been surprisingly reluctant to remind her.

'Forget what?' Angie asked.

'Nothing,' Casey said and picking up her dress she went into the dressing area, firmly closing the door on their questions.

Because they had a time limit on the sunset they had to work fast. Having seen the location only once, Ross was up against it but he still found the time to make sure Robin and Casey were comfortable with what they were expected to do. Being a popular tourist spot meant that crowds of on-lookers quickly gathered, making Robin more nervous than usual when he was required to do more than just drive a car.

Behind the wheel he was a master, confident and expert; required to act he often needed a great deal of encouragement, usually from Casey. 'It's just a kiss, Robin,' she cajoled. 'Hardly a problem for you, surely?'

Robin fidgeted with the immaculate white dinner jacket he was wearing. 'Not normally, no,' he admitted. 'But with Alex watching your every move, I'm afraid to touch you! Especially in that dress, there's so little of it!'

'Oh, heavens! Is that all?' Casey almost choked with laughter. 'Forget Alex. We have to do the take

– if Ross misses the sunset because we can't get it right he'll be the one to explode, not just Alex.'

Her cream chiffon dress was the one she had worn when she gave Alex such a shock to his composure that day early in their relationship, and he felt the same deep ache as he watched her walk through the moves with Robin and Ross. The chiffon moved fluidly around her long limbs and curved over the full breasts his hands and mouth were now so familiar with, and he knew just how much he wanted to whisk her away from Robin. Yet he knew he wasn't being fair to either Casey or Robin, they had a job to do, and they were doing it, as he himself had dictated. So he bit back his displeasure and made himself useful, concentrating on helping the first assistant in keeping the crowd of on-lookers way back behind the camera.

It surprised him to realize just how proud he felt when he heard people in the crowd discussing how pretty Casey was. She was beautiful, he recognized, and she was *his*; but still a complete professional, guiding Robin through the rehearsal until Ross called for a take and Robin then took the initiative, kissing her with abandon as Ross had instructed.

'Cracking shot,' Ross enthused. 'I'm happy with that! Alex?'

Alex looked at his watch and back up to the still brilliant sky. 'Let's have one more try before you go for the reverse,' he instructed. 'I'd feel safer, and we just have time.' For all his misgivings, the job had to come first, and there had been just a tiny element of doubt in his mind about the angle Casey had turned her body in the final second. Above all, Alex was a perfectionist.

'Mmm, I'm getting the hang of this!' Robin grinned.

'Behave yourself!' Casey told him, and glanced across to Alex. Standing amongst a small group he was a good head taller than any of the men around him and easy to pick out in the crowd, laughing to her, he blew her a kiss and was rewarded with a warm smile that lit her face.

'Now do that for me,' Ross told her, 'and we really will have the goods!'

'Honeybun, that man really *is* in love with you,' Robin bent close to her ear to whisper to her.

'Ross?'

'No, idiot! Alexander – the great – Havilland! How are the mighty fallen. I don't think it will be long before you get that ring!'

'Oh, it will! Concentrate, Robin, for goodness' sake!'

Robin concentrated.

CHAPTER 13

Much later she thought about Robin's comment as she lay wrapped in Alex's arms. Alex had told her how jealous he had been watching Robin kiss her. He'd told her she was beautiful – that he wanted her, everything except that he loved her. Perversely it was all she wanted to hear even if his soft cries of pleasure were proof enough. Naturally Alex had won over their sleeping arrangements. Casey's room held her clothes for the shoot. Casey herself was firmly installed in his bed. There was absolutely no point in arguing with him, she was well aware of that and she simply gave in. The entire unit knew exactly what was happening anyway and Alex left them in no doubt. He had simply curved an arm around Casey's shoulders after a few drinks with them and said, 'Well, we're off to bed, see you in the morning.'

Casey paled visibly amid the laughter and affectionate ribbing, aimed mostly at her. They were all slightly too much in awe of Alex to tease him, though it was obvious they all respected him.

'There, I told you they wouldn't be embarrassed,' Alex said, as they walked across to their room.

'You didn't exactly give them a chance to be,' Casey grumbled. 'Just announced you were sleeping with me! Not exactly subtle, Alex! I'm just labelled as your crumpet!'

'Hardly!' Alex swept her into his arms. '*You* are a beautiful, sexy lady – and yes, I want to take you to bed. I've been longing to do this since two o'clock this afternoon. But more importantly, I recognize you are also a very bright lady, and so do the crew. They know you're sure about what you're doing, whether it's with me or anyone else, so don't delude yourself about being mere mistress material, I want you for everything about you, and no one else!'

Casey clung to his neck as he swung her up and onto the bed. 'Do you really, Alex?'

'Yes, darling, I do! I don't have time for empty-headed women, I never have had.'

So Miranda must have something else going for her, Casey thought miserably, much later as Alex's arms held her close to him as he slept. But then she realized, she held the trump card. She was the one in his arms, where he professed Miranda had never been; she was the one who had made him writhe with sensual delight at her touch; and if she truly wanted him – she had a week to win him, or get him out of her system. It would be far the wiser thing to forget about him, her common sense told her that, unfortunately her body was telling her otherwise.

Sighing, she turned, and murmuring in his sleep,

Alex buried his face in her hair. 'Casey, darling Casey,' he whispered softly.

'It's OK, it's OK,' she soothed, afraid that if he woke he would move away – the bed was certainly wide enough. But Alex had no intention of moving. He was perfectly content where he was, it seemed, and still fast asleep. 'I'm here,' she said, quietly to the sleeping figure. 'And I'm not beaten yet! To hell with you, Miranda!'

In the darkness, Alex smiled to himself. They were his sentiments entirely.

There was precious little time for romance in the last few days of the shoot. The next days were spent frantically catching up on all the double car shots they had been unable to do, and picking up the odd shots that had been missed out for other reasons. Then they packed up to drive down to Phoenix to shoot the set pieces on a skid pad Kear owned. In desert temperatures approaching thirty degrees, they were all exhausted and bad-tempered by the time Ross called it a wrap. Casey simply threw off her filming clothes and tumbled onto the bed in the trailer. 'I'm going to sleep all the way to Phoenix,' she groaned.

'Some people sleep at night,' Robin pointed out. 'Come on, guys, let's set up a poker school to pass the time.'

'In that case I'm glad I'm out of it,' Casey said. 'You lot are far too good at poker.'

'Not travelling with Alexander then?' Angie

asked, as she produced the cards and began shuffling them expertly.

'Sleep holds more appeal at the moment,' Casey grinned. 'He and Ross will talk business the entire way, they won't miss me.'

'Bet he will! Don't worry, sweetheart, we'll wake you up in time to tuck him in,' Robin told her. 'At least you'll have some energy by then!'

'Can it, Faulkner!' Casey hurled a cushion at him. 'I'm shattered from that driving alone!'

'Sunshine, that was easy driving today, wait until you get on that skid pad!'

'Don't!' Casey groaned anew and pulled the blanket over her head. 'I don't even want to think about that.'

Ross had offered her a stunt driver if she felt unsure, but with Robin's assurance that he could easily teach her enough to cope with the shots required Casey had turned the offer down. Now she was beginning to worry, knowing just how much it would cost if they wrecked another car. Not that either Alex or Ross seemed to worry overmuch. Ross had laughed. 'It's the last day of the shoot, don't worry about it. Robin seems confident enough you can do it,' he told her. 'And you were spot on today.'

It was after midnight before they arrived in Phoenix and even Alex was tired as he greeted the weary crew. Having the fastest car, he, Ross and Donna had been almost an hour ahead of everyone else. Donna had taken the opportunity of efficiently booking everyone in, a task they all hated, so she could simply hand out keys to them as they arrived. Alex swept Casey off the moment she stumbled down the steps of the trailer, half asleep and rubbing her tired eyes.

'Alex, no,' she protested, wearily. 'I'm tired.'

'I know, darling.' He led her purposefully across the lawns of the hotel and up some outdoor stairs to a suite on the first floor. 'Tonight, I'll pamper you, but that's all.' Pausing, he closed the door and then reached for her. 'Casey, there's more to a relationship than sex, so much more. Can't you see that?'

'I want to – oh, I want to.' Casey drooped in his arms. 'But I've only seen the other kind of relationship, Alex. It's hard.'

'Yes, but not impossible. Remember, I'm ten years older than you, and I've been married.' He sighed. 'Maybe I know too much about the caring side, and not enough about the romantic side.'

'I think you do just great on all sides,' Casey reassured him. 'Sorry if I sounded snappy, Alex, but I really am tired and hungry, and I desperately want a bath.'

'All sorted!' Alex waved at coffee and sandwiches on a tray. 'And I ran a bath for you before I came over to meet you.'

'Are you clairvoyant?' she marvelled.

'No, I just kept in touch with your driver by phone! Now, come and be pampered, my love.' Pampering, she discovered, meant Alex joining her in the bath and massaging her aching limbs with soapy hands until her tiredness melted away.

'Better now?' he enquired, as Casey sat in bed eating the cherry tomatoes from the salad that surrounded the huge platter of sandwiches she had cheerfully demolished.

'Wonderful!' She sighed contentedly. 'I rather think you know exactly how to get to me.'

'I hope so – it means a lot to me, Casey, being with you, like this.' He moved the tray from the bed and switched off the lamp. 'Go to sleep, angel, we really do have an early start.' He was almost too considerate, she thought, sleepily as she curled her back against his chest spoon-fashion, remembering how Colin would have demanded her attention whatever the time. Then she felt Alex laughing. 'But we'll make up for it in Barbados, never fear! I can only be patient for so long with this temptation so close.' He curved an arm round her, settling her close and Casey, knowing he meant it, simply closed her eyes. Finally she was beginning to learn how to trust Alexander Havilland, as well as love him.

Trusting Robin was another matter! After watching him take Ross through the required moves on the skid pad she began to have more than second thoughts – they were more like third or fourth ones! Ross was definitely a pale shade of green when he stepped from the practice car supplied by the local dealer.

'Ready, Case?' Robin slid gracefully out of his seat for her to take his place.

'You don't have to do this, Casey,' Alex said, worriedly. 'We can get the stunt girl in for you.'

'No, I'll be fine.' Casey got into the car and fastened her seat belt as Robin got in beside her.

'It's a piece of cake!' Robin assured her. 'Let's go!' Behind the wheel he was serious, and a complete contrast to his day-to-day personality. In no time Casey had grasped the finer points of spinning the car on the slippery surface and learnt not to slam her foot instinctively on the brake. Robin took her carefully through the sequence several times until he was sure of her competence. 'Let's try it with the two cars now,' he nodded at Ross. 'No problem, she's OK! Attagirl!'

Finally she was judged safe enough to drive the new Keara through the same moves and though she had new quavers of fear on stepping into it she was quickly on top of it. Robin relayed instructions through her headpiece as Ross instructed him, stopping frequently to play the shots back on the video to check them until they had it lined up perfectly. Only then did they shoot.

It was mid-afternoon by then and in her thin silk dress Casey was sticking to the leather seats. She had cursed them all the way through filming. With the top off the car the air-conditioning was not much use and she grew hotter and more uncomfortable as the time went on. Yet, no way would she complain, she stuck doggedly to her task as if her life depended on it, earning the respect of the whole crew.

'Imagine Bridget doing this?' Ross grinned at Alex and Donna as Robin and Casey tried out another movement before the helicopter took off again to shoot.

'Not for one minute!' Donna laughed. 'She would have had hysterics by eight o'clock this morning!'

'And the shoot wouldn't have been quite the same for someone else either,' Ross said, with a wink at Alex.

'Might have been less traumatic, though,' Alex commented, wryly.

'So, maybe it's time you found a worthy adversary, for a change,' Ross said, seriously. 'And you must admit, Casey is never dull!'

'That is an understatement!' Alex said, remembering the sweet hours of the previous few nights. 'But I am glad we chose her.'

'So are Kear! James Wyatt was almost hysterical with delight when I spoke to him this morning.'

'Thank God!' Alex sighed. 'I've been pitching for the rest of their account for the last few weeks. It would be quite a coup to wrest the full account from Porters.'

'The Monopolies Commission will be investigating Havilland Gracey soon if you go on at this rate,' Ross said. 'But keep it up, Alex, I need the work. School fees go up again in September.'

'I don't think you need worry about that!' Alex clapped his old friend on the back. 'Cheer up, Ross, party-time tonight, and you'll be back home with the mob again tomorrow.'

'And ready to leave again on Monday, no doubt!' Ross replied with a rueful smile. 'I sometimes wonder how Carolyn copes with them all, especially when I'm away so often.'

'What rubbish! A nicer bunch of kids I've yet to meet!' There was a note of regret suddenly in Alex's voice and Ross gave him a surprised look.

'Don't tell me *you* are getting the urge to push a pram! Well, well!'

Alex shrugged. 'I'm not getting any younger, Ross. Maybe I should think about it.'

'With your devotion to work it might be hard to find the time,' Ross commented. 'Having a family would certainly cut down a bit of your gypsy lifestyle.'

'I have to say *that* is certainly losing its appeal. I think this is the first time in two years I've been in the same country for a whole month, and I have to admit I rather like it.'

'But still jetting between LA, New York and Detroit,' Ross pointed out, grinning. 'Forget it, Alex, you'd suffocate if you didn't have the next deal to think about!'

But would he? Alex pondered the thought seriously as Ross swung back into the helicopter and waved for it to take off. In the last ten years, from nowhere, he had created a huge and successful company and he had a sudden feeling that Ross could be right. He *had* become addicted to the constant exhilaration, the buzz, that running it gave him. He would be thirty-eight on his next birthday – not so long away now – was it really time to change direction? Do something else? Writing perhaps? Enough overtures from publishers had been made in his direction after all.

He was beginning to be weary of it all – the last month had shown him that, and the happiest moments had been in the last few days – and nights. Even just thinking about the wildly erotic nights then made his body stir with need. And, he thought ruefully, all due to the siren with red gold hair spinning the car in front of him. Beautiful seductive Casey, with the power to drive him crazy if he let her; and it was all too easy to let her!

'Dammit!' he cursed, slamming his fist against the fence post he was leaning on, and turning away from the cars as he willed his heated body to behave. It was a crazy situation to be in. He was, after all, an experienced, mature man, not a raw, untried schoolboy. Maybe . . . in Barbados being together would just solve the problem and allow him to think straight again. He smiled fleetingly then with anticipation; in less than twenty-four hours they would be installed on the island he loved so much. It was the one place in the world where he could do exactly as he pleased and what he wanted to do was make love to Casey Taylor until they were both replete, and then the problem would be resolved, one way or another.

He was pensive during the dinner he and Ross gave for the unit that evening, longing to simply whisk

Casey away right there and then, instead of watching her (in her democratic way) dancing with as many of the male members of the crew as she could. He would have preferred not to go on to the disco at all with the celebrating group, but they had all overruled him with good-natured banter until he'd given in and joined them.

'They all like you, Alex,' Casey told him as they finally danced together. 'You should mix with the units more, it makes you more – well – approachable, I suppose.'

'Still trying to turn me into a socialist, Casey?'

'No, a human being!' she retorted, a little tartly. 'You're a truly nice man, Alex Havilland, when you let it show!'

'I run a hard-nosed business,' he reminded her. 'I can't afford to be too easy going.'

She took the initiative for once and looping her arms round his neck, she kissed him. 'You could, my love, just a bit more of the time, it wouldn't hurt.'

'Your love?' He smiled, gently against her mouth. 'Am I your love?'

Casey stiffened and he felt it under his sensitive fingers around her waist. 'A figure of speech,' she excused. 'Oh . . . well . . . maybe . . . a little bit!'

'Mmm, I think it really is time we left, don't you? So that I can persuade you the rest of the way?'

'So that you can play with the car they gave me?' she teased. The unit, thanks to Angie's shopping prowess, had found a radio-controlled Kear car for both Casey and Robin as a farewell gift that had touched them both.

'I'd rather play with its owner,' he said. 'Much, much rather!'

CHAPTER 14

Impatient to reach his destination Alex chartered a plane to fly them to Barbados from Phoenix. Casey almost expected it, she realized in shock as they boarded the luxurious jet at Phoenix airport.

'We have seven hours or so of travelling time,' Alex told her. 'So we might as well be comfortable.' Casey took him at his word and reclined her seat so that she could sleep almost the minute they were airborne.

'Well I missed so much sleep last night,' she said. 'And we woke up at the crack of dawn.'

'Since you insisted on partying with the unit so late, it was hardly surprising,' Alex said, drily. 'But I will allow you to sleep now – it's in my interests, after all!' He tucked a blanket over her and dropped a light kiss on her forehead before he opened his briefcase for the endless paperwork that seemed to dominate his life. Even on holiday it seemed impossible for him to stop working, she thought, wonderingly. But when she woke the briefcase was gone and Alex was leaning back in his seat.

'No briefcase?' she murmured.

'All done,' he promised. 'For the next four days I'm all yours – as you are mine! Look,' he added, as the plane began to bank. 'You can just see the island.'

Casey leant forward, excited now, and Alex straightened her seat before he began to point out familiar landmarks. He had been coming to the island since he was a small child so it was like home to him.

'My great-grandparents built the house during the twenties,' he told Casey. 'Then it passed to my grandparents and then eventually to my parents. I bought it from them when they decided to buy a house nearer home – in Portugal. I couldn't bear the thought of anyone else living there.' Casey thought of the pain of parting with her parents' home even though it had only been rented from the school. All Alex had needed to do to save his home was to write a cheque. But she had learnt to swallow her more acid comments on his wealth.

'Luckily,' she said, blandly.

Alex raised amused eyebrows but he too decided not to comment. The plane was turning now on its final descent and they could just see the runway below them.

'It's so green,' Casey said in surprise.

'We have quite a lot of rain here,' Alex explained. 'Certainly between August and November, it can rain for days.'

She laughed. 'Just like home, then!'

'Not quite. But we do drive on the left, and have red ER pillar boxes.'

'We?'

'I feel at home here,' he admitted. 'I do come quite often.' Which explained his deep tan.

'There was me thinking you had naturally dark skin,' Casey grinned. 'And all the time it's because you rush here to sun-bathe!'

'I've always had this kind of skin-tone,' he defended. 'And I rarely lie in the sun, I just tan easily, I'm afraid. I don't normally have the time, even here.'

'You will this time, though, won't you? You promised me.'

'Yes, I did indeed!'

'And I shall make you keep to it! Oh, Alex, just look at the ships!' They were passing over the deep water harbour which was solid with elegant cruise ships and yachts, white and gleaming in the sun. It was a beautiful sight and Casey took it all in with pleasure as they came in over the south coast beaches.

Their landing was smooth and uneventful, to Casey's relief, Alex guiding her then through customs and out into the airy arrivals hall open to the fresh breeze. Expecting his usual luxurious mode of transport she was astonished to be led out to a dusty Range Rover, parked in the car park.

'Dora's husband brings it down for me,' he laughed at her surprised face. 'Did you expect a Bentley? Or, heaven forbid on these roads, my Ferrari?'

'You have a *Ferrari*?'

'Sorry, angel! I have to confess I do, not here though. This car is part of life here, lots of people have them.'

'How long till we get there?' Casey lifted the last bag in helpfully.

Alex shrugged. 'Forty minutes or so; it's quicker now there's a ring road around Bridgetown. We'll be having tea by the pool in an hour.'

He drove the Range Rover as expertly as she had seen him drive the various high-powered hire cars he'd had in America, reaching out occasionally to touch her when he had to slow down for one of the overcrowded local buses or a horse and cart. Casey finally began to feel as if she really was on holiday, full of questions and comments as Alex drove between fields of sugar cane, ripening in the afternoon sun.

His home was simply beautiful, basking in a huge flower-filled garden. Bold bright flowers the like of which Casey had never seen in her life. A gracious colonial-style house with a central pillared portico flanked by two wings, facing west towards the sea and surrounded by mature trees. Tamarind, frangipani, and the cabbage palms she had been seeing all the way from the airport.

'Alex! It's not a house, it's a mansion!' she gasped as Alex pulled up and tooted the horn to alert his house-keeper.

'Not compared with some of the houses along the coast,' he said as a beaming lady bustled out to meet them. 'They really *are* palatial! Come and meet Dora.'

The cheerful housekeeper talked non-stop as she organized them briskly and in no time they were settled by the turquoise swimming pool with Alex's idea of tea – huge rum punches and a plateful of wonderful pastries.

'I'm going to get enormous!' Casey grumbled, good-naturedly. 'Is it in my contract – getting fat?' She had pulled on her white swimsuit, knowing Alex liked it and it showed every sleek line of her body.

'I'll get you a membership of my health club if it proves necessary,' he promised. 'You may need it after Dora's fantastic cooking, even I put on weight here.'

'Doesn't look like it,' Casey said, glancing at the hard muscles of his very flat stomach, well displayed by the brief trunks he was wearing.

'I swim it off,' he smiled. 'And go sailing and scuba diving or wind-surfing.'

'I've never tried that,' Casey said.

'Then I'll teach you – if we can find the time, or the energy,' he offered. 'Now, Dora has gone home, so let's swim, but first . . .!' He reached for the straps of her swimsuit and lifting her to her feet he eased it down. 'You won't need this!'

They swam naked together in the warm pool, and afterwards, Alex carried her through the peaceful house to his cool, elegant, canopied bed and made love to her as the sun slipped down over the sea in a huge blaze of red glory, reminding her of the first time – only days before.

She smiled as they walked along the beach next evening their bare feet swishing in the warm water that lapped gently onto the sand. 'Remember the walk we took in Santa Monica?' she asked.

'And we both ended up soaking wet?' he smiled too. 'You had a silk top on that went completely transparent, I wanted so much to rip it off!'

'Oh, no!' She was horrified. 'Why didn't you tell me?'

'That I wanted to tear it to shreds?'

'No! That it was transparent!'

'And spoil my pleasure? You weren't even wearing a bra, I seem to remember.'

'Alex Havilland! I thought you were such a sober upright man too!'

'Who frightened the hell out of you?'

Casey kicked at the silky white sand. 'Well, sometimes, I suppose you did, but now I think that perhaps it's the other way around!'

'You could well be right!' he sighed, gently. 'Certainly you are having the kind of effect on me that I last had in my teens, pure unadulterated lust!'

'Didn't you feel that for your wife?'

He hesitated for a moment. 'No – no it wasn't quite that kind of love. Wendy was – is – quite beautiful, dark and elegant. I worshipped her, but there was never any real depth to our love-making.

217

She always held something back, somehow. I realize that now. Not like you.'

'Am I so different, then?'

'Different from any other woman I've ever known, my darling, so very different.' He paused and turned her, brushing the loose hair from her forehead as the sea breeze lifted it. 'I've never been as happy in my life as I have been the last few days. I just wish we could stay here longer. Damn that wretched TV show, I wish I'd never agreed to do it.'

'Well, you hadn't met me then,' she said.

'My green-eyed witch,' he whispered. 'I should have run a mile from you! Instead . . .!' He couldn't wait until they reached the house, instead, he took her hand and led her back up the beach to the dry sand before he tumbled her onto it.

It felt as if they had been lovers for ever as the days went by all too quickly. Plainly ready to indulge every fantasy either of them had ever had, Alex turned it into a magic world for both of them. He was true to his word about making love to her in the garden, as well as the beach, surrounded by the overwhelming night-time scent of the white trumpet flowers. They sailed his little catamaran along the coast giving them access to otherwise unreachable little coves, went scuba diving in calm clear waters and laughed till they cried when he spent a hilarious afternoon trying to teach her to wind-surf.

Loving the island as he did, he wanted to show it to her, and drove the Range Rover on one outside trip. Down to Bridgetown, then back past Holetown and up the track to the top of Mount Hillaby to show her the spectacular view from the top. Casey began to see not just the sugar cane, the colourfully painted houses and the children playing around them but the poverty and seemingly happy simplicity with which the local people lived.

Alex mostly opted to eat Dora's wonderful cooking at home and scorned the expensive European or American-styled restaurants. He made an exception in taking her to the local rum shop owned by Dora's brother and, apart from the lethal rum drinks she had become accustomed to, fed her on Oscar's speciality. 'Flying fish!' he told her with a grin. Casey grimaced, but it turned out to be delicious, rather like small herring cooked in spices.

But on their last evening he surprised her, suggesting she dressed up for dinner, as they lay by the pool. 'I booked a table at Sandy Lane,' he explained, casually. 'It will be safe enough: since we are leaving tomorrow, there will be no time to take up any invitation, and once I appear in there the grapevine will work overtime I'm afraid.'

Dressing up meant Alex finally putting on a pair of trousers, elegant pale linen ones, and a thick cream silk shirt instead of the variety of rather disreputable shorts he had worn all week. 'I hardly recognized you!' Casey told him, laughing as she came down to the loggia where he was pouring drinks. Overlooking the garden it was Alex's favourite area of the house with the scent of flowers drifting across and the night-time sounds of the tree frogs' piping whistle echoing across the garden. Casey had shrieked out in shock on finding one in her shower with her, but she had soon got used to the tiny creatures.

Now she sat on the long wicker chair arranging her black dress carefully and thought sadly how she would miss them. 'CNN say it's raining in London,' she commented, dipping her finger into the champagne and sucking it. 'I just watched it.'

'We'll come back, Casey,' Alex said. 'Soon, I hope.' Her face was in shadow but he still saw the flash of delight in her eyes. 'Why don't you leave some clothes here, then you won't have to bring too much?'

'I've hardly worn anything since I've been here,' she laughed. 'And if I have, you've taken it off!'

'Isn't that half the fun of getting dressed?' He reached for a sprig of pink hibiscus growing against a column of the loggia and tucked it carefully behind her ear. 'There, now you're completely dressed. Shall we go?'

True to his prophesy they met several of his friends in the hotel bar and they finally shared dinner with another couple who apparently lived a few houses away from Alex. They were wildly curious about Casey as Alex had known his friends would be, but again he made no secret of their relationship.

'Well, well, Alexander, there we were beginning to think you were gay!' the wife teased him as they walked through to the restaurant, rather piqued at not knowing he had been around.

'Definitely not!' Alex returned. 'Eh, Casey?'

Casey blushed crimson, making them all laugh. 'I guess not!' she managed, wishing they'd stayed at the villa as the waiter fussed around them. Both Alex and the Sandersons were well known to the hotel staff.

'So, little lady, you're an actress I hear,' Julian Sanderson smiled at Casey. 'What would I have seen you in?'

Casey shrugged. People always asked the same embarrassing question, and if she didn't give them a show they knew, they automatically thought she was lying about her job. She was honest though, as always. 'Very little I should think. I'm afraid I'm not famous, Julian, I've mostly done TV, and only in England. Just one feature that you might get to see, a film called *Wrong Reason*.'

'We'll look out for it, then,' he said. 'But I don't suppose you'll be saying that for long, not with Alexander here helping out.' Casey stared, stunned, but for once Alex was quicker to reply.

'No fear of that, Julian,' he said, firmly. 'Casey is her own person. I wouldn't dare interfere in her career, her agent is the one who guides that, not me.'

'Met your match at last then, Alex?' Clare Sanderson smiled at Casey. 'How *did* you manage to hook the most eligible man on the island, Casey?'

'Stop teasing her, Clare,' Alex put in. 'I'm no more eligible than the next man, and if anything *I've* done the pursuing, not Casey. Now, come on, tell me the latest island gossip.' Clare was good at that – and amusing; despite her earlier misgivings Casey began to warm to her. Alex was clearly fond of the couple and once they relaxed with her, she began to realize why, by the time they left.

'Clare's a bit miffed not to be able to marry me off to someone of *her* choice,' Alex laughed. 'My sister is as bad.'

'Poor you! Too rich and deservedly under siege for it! I don't know how you survive with all these women throwing themselves at you!'

'You, madam, are going the right way about getting thoroughly chastised!' Alex's eyes were dark with mischief as they met hers.

'Oh yeah?' Full of confidence, not to mention rather a lot of Chardonnay, she reached for the straps of her dress and slid them down to display her breasts and make him draw in his breath with a sharp hiss.

'Casey! For Pete's sake! We'll get arrested!'

'Really?' Casey's eyes drifted down in a casual exploration of her naked breasts, wriggling as she then slid her hands down to lift her dress above her thighs. Alex was driving considerably faster, thankful that they were only half a mile from the house. He finally hurled the car through the gates, driven almost to a frenzy as she deliberately teased him, the dress a narrow strip around her hips by the time he jerked the car to a halt by the front portico.

'You witch! You'll pay for that!' Torn between

raging desire and fury at being outwitted, he was out of the car and gloriously out of control when he grabbed her to bear her indoors in triumph. Casey shrieked as he threw her to a rug in the hall, ripping off the remains of her dress and the brief silk pants in one go. He didn't wait to undress himself, simply wrenched his clothing aside and plunged into her as Casey writhed and squirmed under him, crying his name out into the echoing marble hall.

Hot and hard, goaded beyond endurance, Alex thrust blindly, his full weight pinning her down until all too quickly for both of them, he reared up with a groan of release before he collapsed down onto her, trembling in her arms.

'Darling, I'm so sorry,' he murmured, finally dragging himself off her. 'I can't *believe* how I lose control with you.' His face was flushed from exertion his hair mussed where her hands had raked through it, his silk shirt torn where he had dragged at it in his efforts to pull it off before he'd given up, and she knew for once she had won.

'I teased you, Alex,' she confessed. 'I *wanted* you to lose control.'

Alex pulled his clothing back into place and retrieved her dress from the floor but he refused to give it back to her. 'My turn to be boss,' he said, more steadily now, but as he reached for his shoes Casey leapt up and ran through the house towards the pool, her cascading hair her only covering. Racing after her, Alex found her floating languidly in the centre of the floodlit pool and laughing wickedly. This time he did pause to strip off his clothes before he dived after her and he caught her easily. Casey was going nowhere. They surfaced in the shallow end, gasping for breath and Alex caught her by her shoulders pinning her against him as water streamed from them both.

'I love you, Casey!' he shouted. 'Dear Lord! I really do love you!'

CHAPTER 15

Heathrow in July was cold and wet and they both shivered as they followed William out to the Bentley parked, naturally, right by the entrance. 'Welcome home!' Alex grimaced as Casey pulled her jacket tighter around her. 'We'll go back to the house first, William, then you can take Miss Taylor home after lunch.'

'Alex . . . I said . . .!' Casey protested.

'Freshen up – have lunch first,' Alex said, and promptly closed the partition between them and a grinning William. 'I have to do this wretched TV thing this evening. I need you!'

'You are perfectly capable of doing that on your own,' Casey retorted, leaning back. 'It's just an excuse,'

'So . . . I need an excuse now? Listen, I'll do the show, then we'll go down to Sussex for the rest of the weekend to make up for having to come back early, shall we?'

'Are you asking me? Or telling me?'

'Asking, you silly girl! I've learnt my lesson on that one, I think!'

'Good! Then I'll come. But I must go home and see Liz first,' she smiled. 'I have the wine. It's something we always do.'

'OK, I'll pick you up at six-thirty, but we'll have lunch before you *actually* go home?'

'Fine,' Casey closed her eyes. 'Frankly, it is nice to be back, Alex. I do like London, hot, cold or wet.'

'I must admit, I'm beginning to want to stay in Barbados more and more. It's so comfortable, somehow.'

Alex's whole life was comfortable, Casey thought then. No struggling with luggage and finding the tube station after a long flight. Porters materialized for him from nowhere, his chauffeur was waiting, and he didn't even have to walk to the car park. Whisked to work closeted in his Bentley, his every need taken care of by his devoted staff, Alex indeed lived a very privileged life – and it would certainly be very easy to get used to sharing it as she knew she had done in the last few days. At the airport she had been hugely embarrassed to be swept past tired mothers struggling with several small children and luggage, yet a small part of her thoroughly enjoyed the luxury of the car and the chauffeur.

Alex's Kensington home was as luxurious as his Barbados house and despite her resolve to appear laid back about it she *was* impressed. 'William will see to the luggage,' Alex said, casually. 'Come on, a drink before lunch.' Casey followed him up the stairs to the drawing room, her eyes rounded with astonishment at the lavish house. Alex laughed. 'My pension fund,' he teased her. 'I can always sell it if times get hard!' He pushed open the drawing room door just as Joan came down the stairs, her eyes curious as they swept over Casey.

'Alex, you have a visitor . . .'

Alex swore quietly, expecting his sister, but it wasn't Penny who rose to greet him – it was Miranda. Upset and tearful, she hurled herself across the room into his arms. 'Oh, Alex – Alex! I'm so glad you're back! I have to talk to you – I'm going to have a baby – I don't know . . . Oh!' She jerked to a choked halt as she realized a horrified Casey was standing behind Alex. 'Lexy! What's *she* doing here?' she demanded.

'Casey!' Alex stammered, his arms hampered by the clinging Miranda. 'Just give me a minute – it's not what you think . . .!'

'*You lying* swine!' Casey spat out the words before she could stop herself.

'Casey! No!' Alex cried as Casey turned away. 'Wait . . .!'

'*Get lost!*' Casey couldn't bear to hear any more. With a moan of sheer panic she turned and fled down the stairs towards the still open front door. William had brought her cases in first and she grabbed at her own bags in near hysterics. Her film clothes she left; luckily her own clothes bags weren't so heavy and she swung them reasonably easily down the shallow steps.

'Miss Taylor!' William looked up with concern as

Casey ran across the front garden into the street. 'Can I help?'

'No!' Casey waved frantically at a mercifully free cab. For once luck was on her side where taxis were concerned and it stopped. She hurled her bags into it, not waiting for the driver to help her, and rattled off the address of the new flat, desperate to get moving before Alex came after her. If indeed he was going to – he had appeared far too concerned with Miranda to worry.

Fuming and shaking with temper she struggled to pull herself together, hating Alex, hating Miranda, and more importantly, herself for being so stupid. Alex had lied to her all along! Not only had he been sleeping with Miranda, he had fathered her child, yet he had seemed totally uncaring about her when he had spoken of her just days ago.

'Carlton Court, Miss,' the driver cut in to her tumbled thoughts. Casey jumped slightly and fumbled for her purse, praying she had enough English money in it. There was just enough. She thrust it at the driver and ran into the foyer hauling her bags with her. She knew the block vaguely, having visited Robin and Liam and, aware that the flat was on the third floor, she made her way to the lift. All the way up to the third floor, she had fought to keep the tears at bay but they were streaming as she looked around her for number thirty. She didn't have a key so all she could do was pray that Liz was there. She had been expecting her to arrive back that morning but it was later than Casey had expected to be.

However Liz was in, racing to the door, excited to show her friend their new home, and was horrified as Casey fell into the flat in floods of tears.

'Casey! Oh, heavens! What on earth's the matter?' she demanded, hugging Casey in astonishment. Both Liam and Robin came rushing into the hall and it was Liam who came to the rescue.

'Tea, I think, Lizzy,' he said, as Robin collected her bags and closed the door.

Slowly and painfully Casey gulped out the minimum of the details of the last few days and the trauma of the last few minutes. 'He lied to me!' she sobbed into Liam's sweater. 'He said he loved me and all the time he was lying to me!'

'No, Casey, I'm sure that's not true.' Robin knelt in front of her and offered a surprisingly clean handkerchief. 'Alex loves you, I'd bet a fortune on it. Shouldn't you at least give him a chance to explain?'

The only thing I would give that two-timing pig is a kick where it hurts!' Casey snapped. 'Oh hell! I've been such a fool to let him get to me like that!'

'You're no fool, Casey,' Robin said, firmly.

'Dry your eyes, sweetie,' Liam persuaded. 'And we'll decide how to cheer you up.'

'We'll take her home with us!' Robin suggested. 'I'm sure we can get a flight; a trip to Cork would be great, and Liz could meet the Mammy.'

'Cork! Robin, I've just got off an eight-hour flight,' Casey objected.

'So? Another hour won't hurt! We can have a great time!'

'*And* I have to see Hal Simmons on Tuesday.'

'Then fly back on Monday. Come on, Casey, come with us?' Liam hugged her and reached to dry her tears. 'Let Alex stew for a bit – he's bound to come looking for you.'

'He can't,' Casey gulped. 'He doesn't know where I live now, the agency only have the Kentish Town address.'

'He'd *soon* find you,' Robin said. 'Go tidy up, honeybun. I'll book the flights.'

Liz proudly showed Casey the pretty pink and white bedroom and bathroom that were now hers. 'Heavens! It's like a dream come true,' Casey cried, as Liz opened spacious wardrobes and she viewed the comfortable-looking double bed. It would have been nice to bring Alex here, she thought wistfully then, and began to cry again, despite her efforts to stop.

'Casey, don't, darling!' Liz begged. 'He's obviously not worth it.'

Casey dropped onto the bed. 'He is though, Lizzie, I promise you! At least I thought he was.'

'Well I can't agree on that score,' Liz said. 'Not if he can get you into this state! Look, five minutes and lunch will be ready – and before you say a word, I've been cooking all morning and you'll damn well eat it.'

Casey thought guiltily of Alex's plans for lunch and made a successful effort to pull herself together. She explored her new bathroom and hurriedly hung up the dresses from her suitcase in the roomy white lacquered wardrobes, then found the possessions that Liz had brought from Kentish Town for her. At last, she thought, she could collect her parents' bequests to her from her aunt's garage and install them in her own home. Pictures, her mother's embroideries, and the delicate inlaid table her father had made years before. It cheered her as nothing else could do, and she was almost smiling as she joined the other three.

'OK, I've got four seats on the five o'clock flight – we'll have enough time to pack and stuff,' Robin put the phone down. 'And Ma is delighted.'

'I'll bet!' Liam grinned. 'Shall we really confuse her and introduce Casey as my girl?'

'No way!' Casey vetoed. 'Haven't I got enough problems?'

'It would serve Mr Havilland right,' Liam grinned wickedly.

'No deal, Liam. Just keep me awake long enough to get there.'

They were all a little on edge for fear that Alex would arrive and demand to see her, but there was no sign of him by the time they retraced Casey's steps to Heathrow. By six o'clock they were landing at Cork airport and being met by an excited Jan Faulkner. She was engulfed by the two boys hugging her before she turned to the girls. 'You have to be Elizabeth,' she guessed correctly. 'Welcome to Ireland, dear – and Casey, you must be *so* tired. Come along now – see to those bags, boys.'

'Yes, ma'am,' Liam obediently swung the cases into the car and shepherded the girls into it. 'Let's get Casey home, before she drops!'

Casey tried to take notice of the green and beautiful countryside as Jan drove, talking non-stop as she did so. After the dry heat of the desert and the more recent palm trees and sugar cane of Barbados, Cork was a total and lovely contrast. The hedgerows were vibrant with wild fuchsias and roses, but she was too tired and miserable to take much on board. Even the Faulkners' house, a gracious Georgian mansion of softly mellow stone, failed to merit much more than a cursory glance as Jan swung the car up the long gravelled drive.

From the window of the room she was shown to she could see the sea, a grey cold sea that day, unlike the turquoise of the Caribbean that washed the beach alongside Alex's house.

Alex! She should be with Alex now, not here in Ireland, however welcoming the Faulkners were to their unexpected visitors. And they did welcome her, so much that it was impossible not to cheer up as the evening progressed. The food at dinner was delicious and she managed to do full justice to it despite her misgivings.

'All from our farm,' Jan told the girls. 'Including the beef – you'll be glad to know!'

Edward Faulkner joined them halfway through the meal, held up, he explained apologetically, by the traffic from Dublin where his main offices were located, and where Liam normally lived and worked.

'Get a helicopter, Dad,' Robin told him. 'You know it would make sense.'

'Possibly,' Edward grimaced. 'But I happen to prefer the power of the accelerator under *my* foot, not a pilot's!' It was obvious where the two blond boys got their looks and height from. Though Edward was taller than both of them, he still had the thick, though now paler, blond hair that Robin and Liam had, unusual for Irish men. They were evidently a close family full of familiar in-jokes with each other and drawing Liz into the group with an easy acceptance. Liz would be happy with Robin, Casey knew.

How well things had turned out for her in so short a time! And despite her own misery she was delighted for her friend. Liz had had as many ups and downs in her personal life as Casey had, which was why the two girls were such strong friends. Brought up in a series of foster homes, Liz had fought hard to make something of herself, and though she would never be a top flight model she worked steadily, far more so than Casey did. 'Young mums and catalogues,' she always laughed when asked about her job, but she was professional, utterly reliable, and clients always warmed to her, as the Faulkner parents were doing at that moment.

But however glad Casey was for her she felt out of it – tired, aching, and longing for Alex. She wished with all her heart now that she had not let them persuade her to leave, and had stayed in London to face him. He would at least have wanted to explain, surely? Or would he have simply walked away feeling that the only right thing to do was to marry the mother of his coming child, even if it was Casey that he loved?

She refused Liz's offer to share her room, knowing how much she wanted to be with Robin. 'I'll see you in the morning,' she told Liz, firmly. 'I'll be fine.'

'We'll go riding first thing,' Liam suggested. 'So I'll get you up bright and early, Miss.'

'Not if you know her first thing you won't,' Robin joked. 'She's a nightmare!'

Robin and Liam did their best to entertain her and she was ever grateful to them both. Apart from their obligatory attendance at Mass which Liz also went to, Casey was not left to her own devices for long. They rode on the Faulkner land most of the morning and had seafood for lunch in a tiny bar miles from anywhere. For a while she even forgot about Alex in the sunshine and warmth of those two days. But Hal Simmons was expecting her and with a reluctant feeling she packed her bag again and Liam drove her to the airport for an early afternoon flight.

'You know you always have me as a friend, don't you, Casey?' he said as he hugged her at the departure gates.

'Yes, thank you, Liam, I do,' Casey hugged him back.

'I'll be over in a few days, we'll go out,' he promised.

'It's a deal! Thanks, Liam.'

CHAPTER 16

The flight was late in and they had to stack before they were finally allowed to land. Casey grumbled to herself but she had very little else to do, and no Bentley this time to whisk her off to the flat. 'The underground for you, girly,' she told herself, firmly. The old ways of economy were still very much with her, she realized with a smile. Would she ever change, despite all the efforts the Faulkner brothers were making? Somehow she doubted it!

She was still smiling at the thought as she strolled towards the exit, looking quickly around for the entrance to the tube station and it was then that she saw him . . .

He was angry. Every muscle in his well-dressed, taut body told her that in one glance as he strode through the crowd towards her. Panic-stricken, she turned to run but her passage was obstructed by a couple with several children and two trolleys of luggage. As she tried to skirt them Alex caught up with her, grabbing one arm in his iron grip, her bag in the other.

'Where the hell have you been?' he demanded, furiously. 'I've been tearing London apart looking for you!'

'Get lost, Alex! Let go of me!' Casey tried to shake herself loose. 'Get back to your girlfriend,' she hissed. 'And leave me alone!'

'Oh no, my girl, not without some explanation! Come on . . .' He tried, without success, to pull her towards the exit. 'I left the car outside.'

'No way!' Casey struggled, miserably aware that people were pausing and looking at them. A couple as attractive as Casey and Alex were unusual enough, but quarrelling in public they were enough to create quite a stir.

'Is this man bothering you, Miss?' A burly security man shouldered his way through the crowd towards them and Casey met his eyes with gratitude.

'Yes, he most certainly is!' She finally jerked her arm free from an astonished Alex's hand and grabbed at the bag he'd dropped in the struggle.

'Do you know him?' the guard asked as he grimly inserted himself between her and a fuming Alex.

'I've never met him before in my life!' she fibbed, crossing her fingers as she did so. 'It's OK, though, just make sure he doesn't follow me, that's all!'

'We'll do more than that!' he said as a colleague joined them and he grabbed a protesting Alex's arm a little more firmly. 'Just come with me "sir", we need to cool down somewhat! Jock, you escort the lady out.'

'You don't understand!' Alex protested, struggling again but horribly aware now of the attention they were attracting. 'I have to talk to her! Look, my name is Alexander Havilland, of Havilland Gracey.'

'I don't care if you're the king of England! You have no right to molest this young lady.'

'I'm an actress,' Casey said, bolder now. 'It happens all the time! Men seem to think they have the right to talk to me. Please don't worry, let him go,' she added to the security man.

'You –', Alex was speechless, beside himself with fury when the security man hustled him away from her to comments of approval from onlookers as the two men grappled with each other.

'A girl's not safe in broad daylight these days,' a woman said, in disgust.

'Nice-looking man like that, too!' her companion agreed. 'He shouldn't *need* to accost strangers.'

Alex, knowing when to give in gracefully, stopped struggling and simply watched furiously as the security man escorted Casey out of the arrivals door. 'Right, Sir, let's just straighten a few things out!' the guard said.

'Surely that's not necessary?' Alex argued. 'I left my car on a yellow line.'

'Tough! You just added to your troubles! Now, would you like to come with me?' There was no arguing without another scene ensuing. Being man-handled like a common thief was enough in one day for Alexander Havilland!

Frantic to escape, Casey opted for a taxi, all the

time fearful of Alex coming after her. 'I don't want him charged with anything,' she insisted. 'It was a misunderstanding, that's all.'

'We'll deal with him,' her guardian said, grimly. 'He did resist my mate, after all. Don't worry, Miss, we'll take care of it. He'll probably just get a warning.'

The thought of Alexander being reprimanded by a police sergeant or two made Casey grin for a moment, but as she sank back into the taxi she had earlier decided not to take, she broke into a cold sweat and cursed her impetuous tongue. Why, oh why, had she done such a stupid thing?

Her only hope was that Alex didn't know where she lived. But it was a vain hope. If he had known she was flying in from Cork, he would surely be only too aware of her new address. She would go out, she decided, as she let herself into the flat. Go somewhere – a movie – or out to eat, maybe even go and see Bill to make amends. He had, after all, sent a message of congratulations to her, via Liz.

For the first time she could look at the flat properly, and she loved it. She knew now that it was part of the Faulkner property portfolio – a manoeuvre on Robin and Liam's part to get them both out of the squalor of Kentish Town, and Casey was delighted. They would never have been able to afford it otherwise even with her increased earnings.

'Good enough for a lifestyle magazine!' she told herself, gleefully. 'I'll teach you, Alex Havilland. Who needs you?'

Casey did. She sank down on the navy, linen-covered sofa and burst into the tears that had never been that far away despite her resolve. With no one else around to stop them the flood of tears completely engulfed her and she simply sobbed until she was exhausted, calling Alex every bad name she could think of. At first she was impervious to the doorbell ringing continuously. Finally the strident noise broke through her misery and she knew without doubt that Alex had found her.

'Casey! Casey, let me in!' he demanded through the front door and reluctantly she trailed through the flat, wiping her eyes ineffectually with the back of her hand. She had barely opened the door before he had flung himself through it, slamming it behind him. If he had been angry at the airport, he was practically *incandescent* with rage now.

'You crazy woman!' he yelled at her. 'What in hell did you think you were playing at?' He grabbed at her as she turned to try and flee for cover and his fingers bit deep into her trembling shoulders, as he held her, clearly trying to control his rage.

'Alex! Let go of me!' she protested.

'Let go? I'm going to *strangle* you, make no mistake about that! Have you any idea what your infantile act put me through in that damned airport?'

'Goodness me, Alex,' she taunted. 'Did you actually have to mix with the great unwashed? How awful for you!'

'Mix! I was thrown into a cell until I could prove who I was! And in the meantime my car was towed away!'

'So? No doubt you just waved your wad of credit cards?' She was still scathing even as she struggled to free herself. This was not the sensual game they had played in Barbados. Alex was angry, and she began to feel real fear under her bravado. He was frightening her, and he meant to.

'If I'd had them with me I *might* have done, but I'd left my wallet in the car by mistake,' he snarled. 'I had very little cash in my pocket and no means of identifying myself whatsoever.'

'Oh dear! No money to hide behind! Welcome to the real world, Alexander Havilland.' Even in her panic she couldn't help being amused by the thought of Alex finally being caught out. 'You deserve every damn thing they did to you! Now let me go – and get out of here! I don't want anything more to do with you!'

'Tough! We are going to talk, and you are going to listen!'

'The hell I am!' Casey kicked out suddenly, making him gasp with agony as her high heel found his shin. She had spent her early years with boys and she knew how to fight – and fight dirty if she had to. Now she used every trick she knew, kicking harder, and scratching, as she fought to escape his relentless grip and he fought equally hard to subdue her. Even for an angry man of his strength it was an effort and it took him several painful minutes before he finally threw himself over her on the sofa, grabbing both her hands in one of his.

'I've never hurt a woman in my life,' he gasped, breathless from the effort of holding her down. 'But, by heaven, I'm coming very close to it now!'

'That's just about your style, bully-boy tactics!' she spat at him. 'Just try anything else, Alex, and I'll sue you for assault I swear I will!'

His breathing a little more even, Alex jerked a leg over her still kicking ones; finally he had her under control. 'Assault is the last thing on my mind,' he assured her. 'But make no mistake, if I wanted you I would take you, and you *wouldn't* cry wolf. I know you too well, Casey. Now, if I let you go, will you try not to behave like the hellcat you've proved yourself to be?'

'I hate you!' she retaliated, furious at the ignominious position she had ended up in. 'You're a liar and a hypocrite!'

'The hell I am!' Cautiously he let go of her hands and realized his mistake as she immediately took the opportunity to swing her fists at his face. She missed, because Alex reacted in time and grabbed them back again.

'*Enough*!' he roared at her. 'I'll damn well tie you to the chair if I have to! Now, *ease up*, Casey.' His suit jacket had come off in their struggle and she felt the heat of his body through the fine cotton of his shirt. Despite her humiliation she was furious to find her breasts peaking spontaneously as his chest pressed against them. 'You see?' Alex laughed with cold triumph and smoothed his free hand over the hardening crests. 'You want me, Casey, admit it. Maybe making love to you *isn't* such a bad idea, after all – it might calm you down a bit.'

'Don't you *dare* touch me!' Casey twisted her head aside but Alex had control now. Leisurely, he bent his head to hers and took her mouth in a cold hard kiss, his teeth grinding at the soft flesh of her lips until she opened them to protest. He was relentless and determined now, and despite her resolve she found she was reacting to the hard thrust of his tongue as he found his target and the kiss gentled a little. She heard the low moan that somehow emanated from the back of her throat and she hated herself for it. She couldn't help it – she wanted him still.

When Alex finally released her mouth she found her arms around his neck, with no idea of how they'd got there, and then she was astonished as he abruptly pushed her away slightly. 'Alex – aren't you . . .?' she was bewildered.

'Going to make love to you? Isn't that the normal thing after such a kiss?' Alex loosened his tie and undid the top buttons of his shirt, meeting her eyes with a stony glare. 'No, I'm not – if I did I'd probably hurt you, and despite what I said, I don't *really* want to do that.

'Though it would serve you right, after that first kick,' he said standing up painfully. 'Lord, I could do with a drink, do you have anything?'

Casey looked around vaguely. 'There's some

Bourbon I brought back with me, over there.' Alex preferred scotch but he was in no mood to quibble. He poured two drinks and brought one back to her as he took a reviving mouthful of his. Only then did he take a really good look at her.

'You've been crying,' he accused.

'So? I was upset with you harassing me, and you know why!' She sipped at the neat whisky, grimacing as it stung the back of her throat, and then put it down. Alex reached over and with one finger holding her chin he smoothed his thumb over her swollen eyelids.

'You were upset because Miranda was there when we got home. OK, I accept that, but why just take off to who knew where, without a word?'

'Alex, are you *so* insensitive?' Casey stared at him. 'She's having *your* baby and you're still pursuing *me*. Of course I ran; the further away the better as far as I was concerned.'

'Thank goodness the Faulkners only live in Ireland, then,' Alex said, drily. 'Let's get one thing absolutely straight, Casey. Yes, Miranda *is* pregnant, but it's nothing to do with me! I had no idea that was what you thought! I told you the truth about her, I thought you believed me! She came to me because she knew I would help her with her father, and I feel I owe her that much. Miranda being Miranda, her trust fund is very important, and she was frantic about what he'd do when she told him, especially who the father was.'

'Not *you*?'

'No, silly girl! Her father's assistant, I believe.'
He sighed wearily. 'I managed to straighten it out,
but it took all weekend. George was, predictably,
furious. Talk about Victorian father!'

'It's hardly a great sin in this day and age,' Casey
said.

'Maybe not to us, but to George it is. His
daughter is supposed to be above that sort of
thing, and Charles, though useful to him, is hardly
the kind of son-in-law he had in mind! I'm afraid *he*
did rather want a marriage between Miranda and
me, but I bow to no one's wishes, as you've
probably noticed!'

'I never thought I'd end up feeling sorry for
Miranda,' Casey said, softly.

'Only for yourself by the look of you,' he replied.
'Now, tell me you hate me . . . look me straight in
the eye and tell me.'

Casey met his eyes but the words wouldn't come
from her stricken throat. 'Alex . . . I . . .!'

'You can't, can you?' he demanded. 'Casey, *I love
you*, I love you to the point I can't think straight. I
even walked out of a board meeting when M-J
found out you were coming back from Cork.'

'You did?' She was horrified, it was so unlike the
efficient Alex.

'And then ended up having to phone my assistant
MD and ask him to come and bail me out! *You* are
going to pay for that whether I love you or not! If
Kear get to know of that little fracas we're both in
deep trouble. It was the only reason I didn't make

any more fuss. I could certainly have made you leave with me if that gorilla hadn't come to your rescue. I'd have carried you out if I hadn't had to worry about Kear. As it is we have some damage limitation to consider.'

'So, what do you suggest?' Casey was immediately wary.

Alex considered, while he let his hands smooth over her hair in a newly gentle gesture. 'We'll go out,' he decided. 'I have tickets for David Mackenzie's new musical that opens tonight. The press will be out in force – ideal!'

'Alex! I look a total mess! I'm going nowhere with you, I'll never be ready in time! It's almost seven now!'

'Oh, yes, you are! You owe me that much.' Alex jerked her to her feet and checked his watch. 'You have ten minutes to get dressed, then we'll go back to my place so that I can change and then I expect you to play sweetness and light for the cameras.'

'Just like that?'

'Exactly like that!' He bent his head and this time he kissed her gently. 'I'm in love with you, Cassandra, learn to live with it.'

'I don't have to, Alex.'

'Oh, but you do, sweetheart. After all, you love me too, don't you?' His arms were tight around her now unresisting body.

She did love him, she knew without doubt now, but as with the evening on the island, she couldn't tell him, however fervent his own declaration was.

She had chickened out then and she did so now. To admit her feelings would make her far too vulnerable. 'It's too soon, Alex, much too soon,' she agonized. 'We hardly know each other.'

'We know every inch of each other,' Alex corrected.

'Sexually . . . yes,' she allowed. 'And making love with you is the most wonderful thing in the world . . . but . . .'

'There's always a *but* with you, isn't there?' he sighed. 'However, I shall go on telling you until you finally accept it! Now, much as I'd like to take you to bed – since you've finally stopped spitting – we *are* going out.'

'I've nothing to wear!'

'Don't give me that old excuse!' he laughed. 'Wear the black strappy thing you bought in Las Vegas. *I'm* intrigued by that one, so the press will be too – and don't tell me it needs ironing because I know damn well it doesn't. It's Lycra.'

'Do you miss anything?'

'No, I'm an advertising man, I can't afford to! Now, *get dressed*!'

He stood over her while she pulled on the black dress and found tights and shoes. 'I look awful!' she moaned, sinking down in front of her new dressing table, unable to find any make-up except the bag she'd taken to Cork with her. Alex looked down at the complicated arrangement of straps that held the dress together – just.

'You look very sexy, and very desirable,' he told

her. 'Lipstick and mascara is all you really need.'

'The hell it is!' Casey glared at her image, and reached wearily for her make-up bag. 'You'll just have to wait, Alex.'

By the time she'd finished, even she was surprised, and Alex gave her an 'I told you so' look as he ran a hand over the curves he knew so well. 'You forgot the pendant.' He held it up having found it in her make-up bag and made her put it on. 'There's still something missing . . .' With a smile he reached into his jacket pocket. 'You have pierced ears, right?'

From his fingertips dangled sapphire and diamond ear-rings in the flower shapes that matched her pendant. They were, to put it bluntly, spectacular and Casey gasped in astonishment. She was well aware that no one would mistake the beautiful jewels for anything but the real thing. 'Put them on, Casey,' he told her and smiled as, numbly, she did so. 'Now the *world* will know you're mine,' he said, in triumph.

'Possessions! That's all this is about, isn't it, Alex?' Casey reached to snatch at the ear-rings, only to find Alex's hands covering hers, stopping her. 'Your need to possess me?'

'No, it darn well isn't!' Alex roared at her in frustration. 'Those are meant as an expression of my . . . love . . . I've had them since Las Vegas if you must know, just waiting for an opportunity to give them to you, and you are going to wear them, like it or not! You got used to the pendant, didn't you?'

Wear them she did. Bitterly resentful of the role he made her play, she nevertheless played it as demanded by the actress she was. She sailed through the phalanx of photographers in the theatre foyer leaving Alex to skilfully parry their inevitable questions. As he had anticipated, the rumours of their fracas at Heathrow *had* been leaked to the press.

'A lovers' tiff, that's all,' he said, airily. 'We've made it up now.' He curved an arm around Casey's shoulders to hold her closer to him. There was no mistaking the warmth in his eyes as he looked at her.

'You're the Keara girl, aren't you?' one of them asked Casey. 'Mixing business with pleasure, Alex?'

'Do you blame me?' Alex grinned.

'So, you two are an item?'

'You could say that,' Alex tightened his grip to stifle Casey's instinctive gesture of fury. 'Come on, darling – if you will excuse us, gentlemen?'

'That should get us nicely into the gossip columns tomorrow,' he said, with some satisfaction.

'Did you really need to say all that?' Casey grumbled.

'If we are to salvage the situation, yes. Kear will forgive a lovers' argument, after all we *are* human! But *you* throwing a paddy in a public place for no real reason, that's a different story.'

'I *did* have a real reason!' she protested.

'No, you didn't! Casey, for the next eleven months you are going to *have* to watch your tongue, hard though it may seem. You simply have to consider Kear every minute of your life. Image is everything to that particular company!'

'And being known as your girlfriend is part of it?' she asked, sarcastically.

'Not really, that bit is mostly for my benefit! It really just means hands off, to anyone else!' he admitted.

'This is just a ploy, isn't it?' she demanded. 'Just because Miranda has someone else, you can't bear the thought that you might look as if you've been ditched.'

'Don't be so ridiculous!' He sounded so genuinely astonished that she relaxed at once. 'I was thoroughly relieved about Miranda if you must know. She *needs* someone like Charles, who will worship her in the way she wants.'

'And you don't?'

He laughed and kissed the tip of her nose. 'Rest assured, Cassandra, I only worship at *your* beautiful feet! Would I have forgiven you for this afternoon, otherwise?'

'Was it *so* bad?'

'Let's say I've had better afternoons. I should be locking you up with just bread and water, not fêting you with champagne and diamonds!'

'I didn't *want* the diamonds, Alex,' she reminded him.

'Nevertheless, I want you to wear them and you look stunning in them.' With her hair worn in an unswept style, at his command, the jewels were highlighted, and noticed, by the majority of the people Alex deliberately acknowledged as they took their seats.

Fabulous as the show was, she barely saw it. Written by David Mackenzie as a comeback vehicle for his talented wife, it had all the trademarks of a successful show and Francesca Wade revelled in the opportunity offered to her. Casey had long admired her and, like everyone else in the audience, had been horrified by the accident that had almost crippled Francesca a year before. Ordinarily she would have been engrossed by the show, but all her confused mind could think of was Alex, calmly sitting beside her, devastating in his black dinner jacket. He was everything a woman could want, and yet she was still wary about her own feelings for him.

As if he sensed her turmoil he reached for her hand and held it against the warmth of his black-clad thigh in a possessive gesture, just as every move that evening had been. He was enjoying this, she thought then, he was actively enjoying her discomfort, and with a hiss of annoyance she snatched her hand back.

'We'll go to the party for a while?' he suggested as the final applause thundered through the theatre.

'More PR?' she asked, sarcastically.

'No, Miss Suspicious, I just think you might enjoy it! David does give pretty spectacular after-show parties.'

He was right, the party was mind-blowingly extravagant. A huge Battersea warehouse had been turned into a fairground, complete with rides and sideshows, even the food was fairground orientated. 'I don't believe it!' Casey stared. It was all way outside her experience.

'Told you!' Alex curved an arm around her. 'Come and meet David and Francesca.'

'And then the dodgems!' Casey bubbled with enthusiasm as Alex groaned. 'I love those!'

'I might have known it!' But he was good natured about escorting her on the rides she wanted to try, only drawing the line at eating candy floss.

'And hot dogs! Oh, and pizza – my two favourites!'

'Pizza?' Alex shuddered. 'It looks a bit messy.'

'Don't you like pizza?' She stared at him.

'I don't really know, I don't think I've ever eaten it.'

'Never eaten *pizza*? Where have you *been* all your life?'

'I prefer other foods, that's all. Is it a crime?'

'No . . .' Casey smiled. 'I just forgot that you live in a different world to the rest of us.' Weekend homes, holiday homes, chauffeurs, housekeepers – she wondered if Alex had ever travelled on a tube train in his entire sheltered life!

'So, if I eat pizza what will it prove?' He picked up a piece and took a mouthful, then cursed as it splattered on his jacket. Casey giggled and cleaned it off as best she could with his handkerchief. A simple intimate gesture, and Alex looked down gripping her hands, his eyes intense. 'Let's go!' he said, urgently.

He had told William to go home after he had delivered them to the party so they got a taxi back to Knightsbridge, Alex paying it off at the entrance to her flats. 'We really are going to talk,' he said, firmly when she queried it. 'Now you've calmed down somewhat.'

'Alex, I'm not sure I want you to stay tonight,' she demurred. 'I need time to think.'

'Yes, I know, darling, I think we both do.' He took her keys from her trembling fingers in his polite way and opened the door for them.

'Coffee, then?' Casey moved uncertainly towards the kitchen. 'Oh, heavens, I don't know where anything is!'

They made it together and Alex shed his jacket as they settled in the living room. 'This is nice,' He looked around in approval at the dark blue sofas complemented by blue and yellow striped curtains and soft yellow-washed walls. 'I didn't have time to see it earlier, I was too busy protecting myself!'

'A vast improvement on Kentish Town,' Casey commented, drily. 'You wouldn't have approved of that, Alexander. It really was a total slum.'

'You have a very distorted view of my opinions,' Alex argued.

'Which rather makes my point,' Casey replied. 'OK, you know my body as well as I know yours, but we really know nothing else about each other, our feelings about life, politics, religion . . . everything.'

'I certainly know your politics!' Alex sipped at his

coffee. 'Darling, learning about each other is what being a couple is all about, it doesn't have to be all in the same week.'

'*Are* we a couple?'

'I hope so. I want us to be, Casey.'

'Alex, it's a brave idea.' Casey reached for some mail addressed to her that Liz had left on the coffee table and began to open it. 'But what would your family think of me, for instance? I'm hardly from the same class as Miranda.'

'Thank goodness! Anyway, let *me* be the judge of that! Frankly, I'm sure they'd love you as I do. Casey? What's the matter?' She was staring in shock at the letter in her hand, the second one she had opened.

'Nothing.' She screwed the letter up. 'Just some crank, I suppose.'

'A prolific crank!' He picked up a couple more. 'These look as if they are all from the same person.'

'Luckily they were sent to Kentish Town.' Casey looked relieved. 'He obviously doesn't know I've moved.'

Alex scanned the contents quickly. '*This* one was sent to the agency first,' he said, wincing slightly at the tone of the letter. The writer was quite definitely a little strange, to say the least, openly declaring his desire for a woman he had obviously never met, in sickeningly explicit terms. But the last thing he wanted to do was frighten Casey. Casually, he too, screwed the paper up. 'It's harmless enough,' he lied. 'You're right, he's just a crank, throw them in the bin. We'll filter them out if any more come to the office.' Swiftly, he tossed it into the waste paper bin. 'Frankly, there are far more important things for us to discuss.' For a tall man he could move incredibly quickly and now he did, kneeling in front of her, to press his lips on her hands as they lay in her lap.

'Let's start again,' he suggested. 'Right from the beginning. I'll learn your way of doing things, if you'll learn mine, and difficult though it will be, I'll go home at night for a while if that's what you want?'

'I don't know what I want.' Casey leant back relishing the heat of his lips against her hands. 'I know that I want to make my own way, I don't want your help, Alex.' She thought ruefully of Julian Sanderson's comments in the restaurant.

'None at all?'

'No, Alex. I have to make it on my own. It's important to me. *I don't want to be like Francesca!* She's so talented and beautiful, yet all people said tonight was how lucky she was that David gave her the show – not that she deserved the part because she's so good! You chose me for the Keara girl, that's enough. What I do with that is up to me.'

Alex pulled her into his arms. 'I wasn't wholly instrumental in choosing you for Kear, the clients and Ross did that. But I won't interfere, if that's what you want. Len will guide you perfectly well, I don't doubt.'

She was immediately suspicious. 'Did you tell Ross to send me to Len?'

'No, I didn't. Ross thought of it first. Len is a good friend of his, so you see, it's not just me who wants to help you.' He kissed her gently, almost regretfully. 'For the first time in my life I've found a woman who isn't concerned for what I can give her. Even after this afternoon, I want to keep you, Casey.'

Casey lifted her face to his. 'I was crying when I got back here because I thought I'd lost you,' she confessed.

'You will *never* do that,' he said, firmly. 'And sooner or later you'll realize it. Though this afternoon was quite a shock, believe me. I've never felt so helpless in my life.'

'Having to do what other people told you? It must have been a surprise!'

'It made me realize I'm not quite so important as I thought I was,' he confessed, shamefacedly.

'Well, *that* won't do you any harm!'

'*You* are a cruel woman!'

'No, I'm an honest one . . . because . . . I . . . care for you, Alex.'

'At last! An admission! And having got that out of you, I shall go.' This time his kiss was long and tender, as if he was loath to let her go, and Casey's resolve almost crumbled under the sweet pressure of his mouth.

'Old showbiz maxim,' he said, softly as he withdrew. 'Leave 'em wanting more!'

* * *

It was a warm night and he decided to walk the reasonable distance between Casey's flat and his home. After his anguished weekend, life had suddenly taken on an entirely different aspect and he was whistling as he strode along, tie off and his jacket over one shoulder. For the first time in many years, despite his denials, re-marriage was beginning to have quite an appeal to him. Life with Casey would certainly never be dull, that was certain. She was wary of him, and he knew quite well that she didn't trust him, he only wished he knew why. But he was determined that he would find out the real reason for her distrust and put her right, sooner or later – and he could wait. After all, he had no option if he wanted her – and he did.

CHAPTER 17

Adrian Shawcross bought a newspaper every morning before he caught the 8.15 bus to the bank. He never took his car to work, he was always too worried about getting it damaged in the car park – or worse, stolen. He treated his car as he treated his boat, with reverence, and lavished great care on both, polishing and cleaning obsessively. They were a part of his regular weekend routine and it never varied. Likewise with the newspaper: he always bought the same one, and always read it in the same order, checking first if there were any advertising pictures of Casey Taylor, and then turning to the sports pages. The news in between was always left untouched.

Today though, his attention was caught by the front page. A full-length photograph dominated it. Casey – his Casey – in the arms of another man. A dark-haired, good-looking man, wealthy too. He recognized Alexander Havilland's name, even as the dark gremlins of jealousy gripped his innards. The arrogance of the man! To lay claim to *his* girl!

Every dream he had was woven around the girl in the photograph. She was smiling up at him, lovingly – or was she? He wondered hopefully. *His* Casey wouldn't go out with a man just because he was rich, he was sure of that.

Then he looked harder, noticing the jewels in her ears, and round her neck. If she liked jewellery, that was wonderful! The millionaire might be able to buy them for her, but then so could he now that he had all the credit cards organized! It was useful working in a bank sometimes! What kind of jewels would she like? he wondered as he continued to study the picture.

'Seen the papers, Adrian?' Ruth, one of the counter clerks looked up as he walked into the bank. 'Your little film star has got herself a rich boyfriend, and a new job! You'd better find another bird to fancy! She'll be way out of your league now.'

'No, I won't!' Adrian straightened his immaculate tie. 'Casey and I are old friends, we're in touch all the time; he means nothing to her, I know.'

'Oh, yeah! And James Bond will be cruising in here today to claim my favours!' Ruth laughed. 'Get real, Shawcross! Stick to Susan at the library, she's much more your league. Casey Taylor is just a wild dream!'

But she was Adrian's dream. He dreamt all morning as he sat at his computer and went out at lunchtime to buy all the newspapers he could find with any tiny piece about Casey in them. He found plenty about her and discovered that the man who displayed her so arrogantly on his arm was only her employer.

So that was the reason! He could forgive her that; she did have a living to earn after all. In her world they called it PR, didn't they? And from what he then read about Alexander Havilland it was a part of the job he excelled in. Long a revered figure in the media, his choice of girlfriend was a source of endless fascination for the tabloid press and this unknown beauty sent their curiosity into overdrive, particularly on a day when hard news was non-existent.

In the process Alex had cleverly promoted Kear, putting a name to the girl whose shadowy image was beginning to appear in the Robin Faulkner car ads. A name, but nothing more; the hacks were left to fathom out the rest for themselves.

Adrian knew of course. He hugged the knowledge to himself, and wondered fleetingly if the papers would be interested in hearing about Casey. Then he decided no, he would be better keeping her to himself! Tomorrow he would go out and use his newly acquired credit cards to buy her something really beautiful. A bracelet perhaps. He would go to London to get it – he was due some time off, after all – and then maybe he would deliver it in person. He'd get flowers too. He would compete – and he would win against the handsome self-assured man who thought he owned her. He would soon find out that he didn't. Casey belonged to Adrian Shawcross . . . and no one else!

* * *

Alex himself was under no such illusion that Casey was his. Casey had made it plain that she wanted no help from him, and after the ear-rings, no more expensive gifts. She was furious when the bracelet and a bouquet of flowers were handed to Liz for her by the block's porter as she walked through the foyer, and she took Alex to task the moment he arrived to take her out that evening.

'Hold on, Casey,' he countered as she hurled the offending bracelet at him. 'This is nothing to do with me, I promise. Firstly, I would never buy orchids, they're appallingly tacky, and secondly, if I bought a gold bracelet it would be from Cartier, or Asprey; certainly not from this shop,' he said, pointing to the name on the box. 'They may be in Bond Street but they are not *my* kind of store.' The disdain in his voice told her he was telling the truth.

'Then who . . .?' It was still an expensive item, whether Alex was scathing or not.

'Did you ask the porter where they came from?' Alex demanded, sensibly.

Liz phoned down to the porter. 'He said our old landlady had dropped them off,' she reported.

'Then phone *her* and ask her how she came by them,' Alex said. 'Was there nothing with them? No note, a card, anything?'

Casey flipped through the flowers and finally did find a card. 'From your devoted admirer' was all it said.

Alex fingered the card and a niggling worry began

to form. 'This is the same handwriting as those letters the other day,' he said. 'I'm almost certain of it. Maybe we should take this a little more seriously.'

'What can we do, Alex, if we don't know who he is?' Casey was exasperated.

'Well, you could send this back to the store,' he suggested. 'They might have some record of who bought it and they can return it to him. Leave it to me, I'll get someone from the office to do it. They might even find out who it was, then we can quietly warn them off.'

Liz put down the phone. 'All she knows is that a young man came with them. Tidy and polite, she said, but a bit put out to find we weren't there. Thank goodness, she thought she'd better not give him our new address. I've asked her not to give it to anyone, just in case.'

'Wise girl!' Alex approved. 'Now, throw those disgusting things into the bin and forget about it. I'll deal with the bracelet tomorrow.'

He got his own way over the restaurant that evening because Liz and Robin were coming too, and Robin had the same expensive taste in restaurants as Alex had. But over the next few weeks he began to discover just how different Casey's way of life was from his own, and how much she had had to struggle.

Bill had put him right on that score on an evening when Casey and Liz had decided to pay him a visit at the pub. Despite their acrimonious parting, Bill was delighted to see them and produced a bottle of champagne. 'On the house, girlie,' he announced. 'It's not every day we get a celebrity visiting!'

'Celebrity?' Casey laughed. 'Bill! This is me – your ex-barmaid! Remember?'

'Best barmaid I ever had! And now you have to go and get famous! I'll expect a signed photo for the bar, at the very least.'

'I'll make sure you get one,' Alex promised as Casey blushed. Later when he went back to the bar Bill left him in no doubt of his affection.

'Cracking girl she is,' he told Alex. 'She deserves to make it, the way she's worked. Three-fifty an hour I paid her, and she worked like a Trojan for it.'

'Three pounds fifty!' Alex was appalled, it was a pittance in his eyes, and he resolved there and then that Casey would never again suffer that kind of indignity.

'Standard rate,' Bill shrugged. 'She won't have that problem now, I hope.'

'Not if I can help it!' Alex followed his eyes to where Casey was greeting a crowd of regulars with hugs of delight.

'You really her fella?' Bill asked, suspiciously. 'Like the papers say?'

'I'm working on it, Bill,' Alex sighed. 'But she's a stubborn cuss sometimes, she suspects every simple gesture.'

'Tell me about it! There's more than one regular in here who's learnt that the hard way!' said Bill. 'She's got a better left-hook than most men! I didn't

263

need a bouncer when Casey was here!' Alex smiled, ruefully. There were still parts of him that ached from Casey's fists after their fight. 'That's my girl!' Bill added, laughing as he realized that even the powerful Alex was not immune. 'You take care of her now.'

Easier said than done. And the more he learnt of Casey's life the more respect he had for her. He also discovered that there were other restaurants than the Arbour and his select favourites. He learnt about *her* favourite pizza parlour, and Chinese food eaten from cartons at the kitchen table, and drinking beer and wine that were certainly not the vintages he was used to. He learnt about buses and walking in London parks, which art galleries let you in free, and how to acquire good seats in the theatre cheaply. Casey was also appalled to find he rarely set foot in a supermarket and had no idea of the price of food, unless it was part of a campaign of course!

'I run a major company,' he protested when she taxed him on it. 'I don't have time for shopping. Joan buys stuff for the house, and M-J does everything else.'

'*Your secretary buys your clothes!*' she almost burst with indignation. 'That is the most *sexist* thing I've ever heard! How do you get away with that?'

'M-J doesn't mind, and anyway she has better taste than me. It's only shirts, ties, that sort of thing, my tailor does the rest.'

'Well, make sure M-J finds you some jeans for

Saturday, I am *not* going to Wembley Stadium with you in a suit!'

'I *do* wear jeans in London, my love, as you well know!' He sighed. 'I just can't believe I let you talk me into going to a pop concert! Can't I get a box for it?'

'No you can't! Half the fun is being in the crowd,' Casey told him, firmly. 'So is going on the tube with everyone else.' However, he did draw the line at that. William dropped them off and collected them. But in the end he stood amongst the vast crowd with Casey held tightly against him for fear of losing her in the crush; laughed and sang the encores with everyone else, and admitted afterwards that he wouldn't have missed it for anything.

William was horrified, reporting the outrageous goings-on back to Joan. 'Nonsense!' Joan said wisely as he sputtered out his tale. 'Do him good! That silly little chit Miranda would never have got him out like that! Young Casey knows what she's about, that's for sure. Have you ever heard him sing in the shower before?'

'Surprised he's got the energy!' William said, grumpily, reaching for his pipe.

'Leave him be, William. Can't you see she's making him happy?' For all his busy, fulfilling life, it was the first time in years that she had seen Alex so cheerful, and her romantic heart prayed hopefully that it would only get better for him.

* * *

Somehow he kept his promise to Casey, kissing her goodnight and keeping his distance, though he found it increasingly hard to leave her. He longed for the sexual freedom they'd had in Barbados, but to be fair he knew she was working incredibly hard on the Hal Simmons film, as well as the growing Kear commitments. The campaign was proving to be an immense success, to Alex's relief and delight. Casey was a hit with both Press and public alike, and because Kear insisted her interviews were kept to a minimum it only added to their intense curiosity – as had been intended right from the beginning by an astute James Wyatt!

Much as Alex needed her, Casey was grateful for any chance she got for rest in the hectic weeks that followed. Certainly there was no time for another trip out to Barbados, for either of them, to his constant regret.

He finally broke his self-imposed denial the Saturday evening she fell asleep in his arms on the sofa from sheer exhaustion. It was late, Joan and William had long gone down to their own little flat, so they were alone in his part of the house. For a while he let her sleep, curled up against him, her abundant fall of hair soft against his cheek; then finally he lifted her up and carried her through to his bedroom. Even as he gently put her down on the bed she opened her eyes, smiling as she realized what he was doing.

'It's Sunday tomorrow,' he said, softly. 'You aren't working.'

'Alex, I thought you'd never give in again,' she whispered.

'I've wanted to, so many times!' He undressed her as quickly and eagerly as he undressed himself, and sank into her with an urgent passion that made them both cry out with a joint relief that they had finally given in to their needs. 'I won't do without you again!' he told her when at last they had satisfied every possible desire they could have imagined. Casey lay contentedly in the curve of his arm twisting tiny curls in the damp dark hair on his chest. Once she had been almost afraid to touch him there, now it was an intimate gesture that she knew Alex loved.

'Next weekend I'll take you to Sussex,' he suggested, sleepily. 'We can take the pebble to your father's grave if you'd like to?'

'And perhaps collect some of my parents' things from Uncle John?'

He laughed. 'We'll need the Bentley, then?'

'No.' Casey rolled on top of him. 'The Ferrari will do, so that it's just us.'

'Which reminds me – I forgot to tell you. Kear are arranging for you to have a car, from next week. You'll be able to drive yourself down to see your aunt and uncle soon.'

'Is that such a good idea? I live in the middle of London, after all, I don't really need a car.'

'They'd prefer it if you arrived at presentations in a Kear, though not the Keara itself yet! *We* thought you'd like the independence.'

She stiffened immediately. '*You* thought?'

'James Wyatt did, actually, so just do as you're told and accept gracefully!' he told her firmly. 'Now, my darling, do you really think I can sleep, with you wriggling around on me like that?'

She wriggled a bit more – and got exactly what she was aiming for!

CHAPTER 18

Playing the leading part in a film was a totally new experience for Casey. She was cosseted and fussed over this time; no longer was she ordered around or bullied as she had been on *Wrong Reason*. Karl Woodward was a serious, thoughtful actor who prepared his work carefully and in doing so taught her to do the same. In their action sequences he was superb, preferring to attempt many of the stunts himself, so Casey elected to do the same even though she did end up with far more bruises than he did. She cursed the fact that Karl could protect his legs by having padding hidden by his trousers whereas she wore a skirt, so couldn't.

Only in their love scenes did they experience difficulty and Hal soon realized it. He wisely began slipping them in when they least expected them and Casey soon discovered she was more comfortable with them than Karl was. Karl liked her, she knew. He had, after all, been consulted on Hal's choice and had approved her, and he was just as reticent with his other co-star. Paula Fry knew him well and consoled Casey when she worried about it.

'He's a closet queen, darling,' she laughed. 'He's just the same with me, don't worry about it!'

'Gay! He can't be!' Casey was astonished. 'He's been married!'

'Heavens above, darling! Which gooseberry bush did you climb out from under? Most of them are!' Paula reached for a hairbrush and began to tidy her hair. 'It's a smoke screen, that's all. Wouldn't do for a macho star like Karl to have it known that he prefers boys, now, would it? Pity really, he's got the cutest bum when Hal can persuade him to show it! Nearly as neat as Brett Kennedy's, but you know all about that!'

Casey joined in her laughter. 'Brett certainly didn't seem to mind,' she commented.

'Why should he? He works damned hard to keep that gorgeous body in shape. As far as Karl is concerned, honey, just treat him like the big kid he is. He *does* genuinely like women, he just doesn't like sleeping with them! Mind you, I sympathize over this afternoon's script! It's a bit vague to say the least! Talk about Hal hoping something will develop!'

'Well, at least we've got all our clothes on!' Casey flipped through her now dog-eared script and checked her lines again. She was paranoid about making sure she was word perfect before she walked on set.

'Package for you, Miss Taylor.' The runner appeared in the open doorway.

'More flowers from that cracking boyfriend of yours?' Paula teased.

'Doubt it! He's picking me up this afternoon.' Casey handled the flowers with some distaste. These were not from Alex, she knew, they were the fourth bouquet to come from her unknown admirer, though, strangely, he had now progressed to signing himself 'A'. The return of the bracelet had provoked a bitter response followed almost immediately by several letters apologizing for his outburst and redeclaring his love. This time, Alex suggested she keep the letters, 'just in case' but Casey dismissed the suggestion in horror. Somehow, she couldn't bear to keep them in the flat. Finally, Alex calmed her down and put them in a file in his own office, beginning to worry more as each new letter arrived. He made light of them to Casey, but he could detect a slightly more sinister note in each one, and he worried continually that the man would find out Casey's address.

She gave the bouquet of orchids to her dresser and deliberately put the thing out of her mind. The afternoon's work was far more important than some silly young fan, she decided as she went to discuss the scene with Karl and Hal. It was a simple scene – a kiss interrupted by the appearance of the other woman – and the writer had purposely left it rather vague, so that they could interpret it any way they thought fit. They rehearsed several different ideas in the drawing room set, which Hal dismissed almost the moment he saw them. It wasn't until

Casey sat down idly at the grand piano to amuse herself while the lighting was changed yet again for another try, that inspiration came.

'That's pretty,' Karl commented, pausing behind her, his hand on her shoulder as she played a Strauss waltz. Casey smiled up at him as the long remembered melody from her piano lessons rippled from her fingers.

'Got it!' Hal exclaimed as he watched them. Skilfully he built up the simple gesture into a full-blown love scene. 'Clever girl!' Karl added, thoroughly relieved that the impasse had been sorted. 'Let's go for it, Hal, it feels good.'

'I won't quarrel with that!' Hal nodded. 'Make-up checks please, stand-by studio!' There was a slight buzz of noise as the shooting bell sounded but Casey and Karl were too involved in the scene to worry about visitors to the set. They were frequent enough since Hal was a well known and popular figure in the business. It was only when Hal called, 'Cut! Save the red!' that they looked up to find there was a reverent silence as Hal's two visitors moved across the studio.

'Well, well! The divine Sarah Campbell!' Karl smiled. 'We are honoured!' Casey followed his welcoming smile and watched the progress of the lovely actress as she picked her way gracefully over the tangled cables towards them, her arm curled possessively into that of her tall dark-haired husband. Nick Grey was a director renowned world-wide for his talent and they were both revered by the entire industry. Sarah was one of the few female stars who could open a film with her name, and certainly at the moment, the only English one who could claim that.

Returning Karl's welcome, Sarah turned her sparkling hazel eyes to Casey. 'Darling, remember me? We met at Hal's house?' Remember her! How could anyone forget meeting Sarah Campbell? Casey thought, helplessly tongue-tied. She stammered in confusion as Sarah drew her handsome husband forward. 'Casey, meet my husband, Nick. There, you see darling, what did I tell you? Casey would be perfect to play my sister!'

Nick Grey smiled at Casey. 'I've heard a lot about you, Casey, from Brett and Hal.'

'And me,' Sarah put in. 'Look we won't get underfoot now, we'll see you later. I believe Alex is bringing you to supper with us tonight.' She gave a grimace at Casey's astonished face. 'Of course! He forgot to tell you! Typical Alex!'

'He didn't tell me where, just to some friends,' Casey found her voice at last, and her manners. 'Thank you, I'll look forward to it.'

'Not if you knew my wife's cooking you wouldn't!' Nick smiled affectionately at his blonde wife.

'Oh, don't worry, Casey, we'll barbecue again,' Sarah said, totally unconcerned. 'Alex is good at that!'

'Alex is?' Casey stared at her. In all the time she had known Alex he had only ever managed to make coffee or tea, and that had always been at her suggestion, more to tease him than anything else.

'Sure! He loves playing with the barbecue!' Sarah grinned. 'Till later, Casey.'

'I'll kill him!' Casey muttered as the two left the studio.

'Nick Grey?' Karl stared. 'He's just paid you the biggest compliment possible.'

'No! Not Nick, Alex, for not telling me where we're going tonight.'

'Probably didn't want to panic you, they're a formidable couple those two.'

'Alex knows them well, I believe.'

'Then make the most of it, sweetie,' Karl advised. She was immediately suspicious of Alex, even though Karl pointed out that it had been Brett and Hal that Sarah had mentioned. Alex, however, was more concerned about the flowers, and a call from Liz to say that a letter had arrived correctly addressed to the flat.

'This is getting serious,' he told Casey as he drove her to the Greys' Richmond home. 'I think we should consult the police.'

'Oh, don't be so melodramatic, Alex,' she protested. 'They'll laugh at you. It's a few letters and some flowers, that's all. Leave it – we have all weekend to enjoy ourselves, don't let's spoil it.' She leant into the back of the car to hug Griff, his black labrador. 'And you, you villain, will have to behave yourself!'

'Shame I had to bring him,' Alex said. 'But Joan deserves a break from him.'

'Of *course* you had to bring him!' Casey had loved Alex's dog from the outset. She had never been allowed one of her own as a child.

'I guess Nick and Sarah's kids would be disappointed if I didn't have him with me,' Alex allowed. 'He even lets Abby ride on his back, probably because she gives him stacks of biscuits.'

'How old are they?'

'Sam's six, and Abby is just over two, she's my goddaughter, little terror! You'll love her, she's the cutest thing on two legs.' His voice softened as he spoke of the child he patently adored. 'Sam's cute too,' he added, quickly. 'He's bright as can be, but Abby is – well – my Abby. Look, there's the house, hang onto Griff or he'll be out of the car the second I open the door.'

It was a gracious three-storey Georgian house set in its own huge and well-tended garden, It suggested butlers and maids, but it was Sarah herself who opened the door, casual in jeans and T-shirt. 'Nick's on bath duty, it's Nanny's night off,' she laughed. 'He'll be down in a minute, come on through.' She led them through a cheerful yellow hallway to a huge airy kitchen-breakfast room with its French windows still open to the sunny garden.

'Oh, it's lovely!' Casey cried. 'So cosy!'

'Thank goodness!' said Sarah. 'I can't bear tarted-up tidy places.' Tidy it certainly wasn't. There were toys everywhere in glorious chaos. 'Alex, be a darling and open this, will you?' she added, holding out a bottle of Chablis. Alex was obviously quite at home amongst the clutter, pouring wine while Sarah tossed a salad together and gossiped merrily about mutual friends until a noisy clatter from the hall indicated that bathtime was over.

'Alex! Alex!' Both children tumbled squealing into Alex's outstretched arms in an obviously familiar routine, as he let them search his pockets for the toys and chocolate buttons they knew were hidden there. He hugged Sam, a handsome, dark-haired little boy, and played cars with him, but it was Abby who claimed his full attention, climbing onto his lap to hang round his neck with chubby arms.

'You get her over-excited before bedtime, Havilland, and *you* get the job of putting her into it!' Sarah warned, as she attempted to clear some of the mess.

'My pleasure! Isn't it, Abby?' Alex tickled and played with Abby, before he romped merrily with both children on the floor. It was a totally new Alex that Casey saw that evening, playing endless childish games with them. She soon forgot the almost godlike status Nick and Sarah had wherever they went. At home they were simply parents, clearly devoted to each other and great fun to be with.

Amid much teasing from Sarah, and eventually from Casey as well, Nick and Alex barbecued steaks once the children had been put protesting into their beds. Casey found it very easy to relax with them, and without realizing it, her natural warmth came to the fore, endearing her to both of them.

'I knew Alex would find someone really nice, sooner or later,' Sarah told her as they left to drive to Sussex. 'I'm really glad to meet you again, Casey. See you soon?'

'I hope so,' Casey meant it and not just from a work point of view. Nick had seemingly endorsed his wife's idea on casting her and had finally convinced Casey that Alex had had no hand in it. Sitting beside him as the Ferrari ate up the miles she sat back and realized that with Nick's film added to the list she had a full year of very profitable work booked. It was a heady feeling, after the years of uncertainty.

'Nice evening?' Alex asked, as she smiled reflectively.

'Great! I quite forgot to be nervous of them,' she admitted.

'So I should hope! You have no reason to be frightened of meeting anyone, Casey.'

'Most people I'm not, not any more, but they *are* rather different, you must admit.'

'Not when you've known them as long as I have,' Alex said. 'We became really close friends when they went public over their affair – after Sam was born. Nick came to me for advice on the PR side of it. Do you remember that?'

'Just slightly! It was all the papers talked about for weeks. No wonder they quit England! They were really persecuted. It was all very unfair, especially when all they did was fall in love with each other!'

'Sarah still hates the British press for that, it's the only thing I've ever seen her worked up about. She guards those children against them like a tigress.'

'I remember Hal laughing about the way she outwits the photographers when we met at his party.'

'I adore her,' he admitted, honestly. 'And her daughter! Success has done her no harm at all, thank goodness. And Nick thinks the world of her.'

'My father was a bit like that with my mother,' Casey said, reflectively. 'They were totally devoted to each other.'

'*My* parents seem to thrive on a good fierce argument once a week, always have done,' Alex grinned. 'How would you feel about having lunch with them on Sunday?'

'Your parents?'

'Why not? I'll be meeting your family tomorrow after all.'

'Well . . . if you're sure?' She was still doubtful. It seemed such a definite step, and where Alex was concerned she was still anything but definite.

'Yes, I am! I'll ring them in the morning.'

Alex charmed her aunt and uncle with consummate ease as they collected some of her possessions from the garage of the pretty cottage they lived in, only twenty miles or so from Alex's own, lovely, tile-hung Sussex farmhouse. They had already been to add the pebble to her father's grave and Casey had been near to tears as they arrived at the cottage, but the feeling was soon gone as Alex gently coaxed her back to her usual happy self.

She was cheerful as they paused to walk the dog through woods, halfway home, running ahead with Griff as Alex locked the car, laughing as he ran along the track to join her. Sweeping her into his arms, he then demanded the kisses he had been denied all afternoon. He looked almost boyish in jeans and a sweatshirt, and Casey suddenly felt her heart flip as he swung her around, her feet high off the ground.

'Alex?' She leant back in his arms revelling in the warmth in his eyes. 'I love you! I really do love you.' Finally, she could manage to say it without embarrassment.

'Then marry me, Casey darling. Let's get married?' he said, softly. 'I need you so much, and I *hate* living apart from you. I want to wake up next to you every day, not just at weekends.'

'Marriage?' Casey stared at him. It was the last thing she expected. 'Are you serious?'

'I've never been more serious in my life, darling.' Alex cupped her face in his hands. 'I want to marry you, live with you – have children with you – everything!'

Her knees felt as if they were going to buckle and she clung desperately to him just to stay upright. Sensing it, Alex turned to seat them both on a fallen tree trunk. 'Think about it, Casey – if you have to,' he said, gently.

'No, I don't have to think about it.' If she had

time to think about it she knew quite well her courage would desert her, and common sense would kick in. 'I *will* marry you, Alex, I can't think of anything I want more, but . . .'

'But what?' A sudden fear clutched at his heart. He knew too much about Casey's 'buts'!

'Can we wait just a little? I won't be thought of as marrying you for your money!'

'I don't care what anyone else thinks!' Alex said, firmly. 'I just want you to be my wife! I've thought long and hard about this, Casey, it's not just a spur of the moment decision. Look . . .' He fished in his jeans pocket. 'I even bought this, days ago. I've been carrying it around just waiting for the right moment to ask you.' Reaching for her hand, he slid the sparkling diamond ring onto her finger. 'I don't mind waiting a little while, but will you wear this for me?'

'Oh, Alex!' With a cry of delight she twisted her hand this way and that, admiring the beautiful gem on her finger. 'It's so perfect.' The square cut diamond was simple and yet totally flawless.

'As you are, Casey, for me.' Gently, he brushed his lips over hers. 'I love you so very much. Will you let me tell my family tomorrow?'

'You planned all this! To time it with a visit to them!' Casey jerked away from him.

'Not specifically, I promise. There's no way I can be sure enough of you to plan anything! All I know is that I want to marry you, more than anything in the world.'

'I'm afraid, Alex,' she admitted. 'I just *don't* want to be seen as a gold-digger. I've no real idea of how to cope with your way of living, that's why I wanted you to see how we lived.'

'And haven't I proved to you that I understand that?' he demanded. 'OK, I may never have had the hard times you've had, but I've had to battle for the life I have now.'

'From a position of strength though,' she pointed out.

'And now it's all there to lavish on you,' he said. 'So as a newly engaged couple, where shall we start? Dinner out tonight?'

'Well . . . since we don't have to worry about saving up for a house – or two,' Casey grinned. 'I suppose you could afford to take me out, but first, perhaps we'd better find Griff. He must be miles away by now!'

Alex cursed. He had completely forgotten about the dog and he was nowhere in sight. They spent the next half-hour calling and searching until eventually a soaking wet, green-weed-bedraggled dog bounced up to them shaking himself joyfully all over them.

'So much for a romantic proposal!' Alex laughed as he clipped the lead onto the wet dog. 'Trust him to find a damned pond!'

'He was probably hot, poor baby,' Casey defended. Sighing, Alex turned back towards the car.

'You even defend my dog more than you defend me! I shall make you pay for that, later! *And* you can wash all that green gunge off him if you love him so much!'

Casey began to laugh. 'Not to mention the car!' But Alex was in such a happy mood he was quite prepared to overlook muddy paw-marks on the leather upholstery; and indulge later in a playful, almost hysterical session of trying to bath a completely uncooperative dog.

Alex sat back on his heels, thoroughly soaked as Casey towelled the complaining dog dry. 'I thought bathing Abby and Sam was messy enough. I bet he doesn't play Joan up like this! Put him in the kitchen, he'll dry off by the Aga, we have better things to do.'

'Well at least he'll be clean and lovely to visit your parents.'

'You must be joking!' Alex grinned. 'He'll be in the lake with the other dogs five minutes after we get there!'

She was totally panic-stricken at the thought of meeting his parents, despite his reassurances. It didn't help that they were incredibly late getting out of bed, reluctant to share their private happiness with anyone, until Alex finally knew they couldn't delay any longer. 'I wish I hadn't thought of going there now,' he grumbled, as Casey struggled to find something respectable to wear. It wasn't an occasion she had packed for. 'Don't worry about that bit of it,' he added, pulling on a pair of his favourite cream chinos. 'They'll be so glad to see that ring on your finger, they won't notice what else you're wearing!'

'I just hope you're right! Everything is creased!'

'Sweetheart, it's my Mama and Pa, not royalty,' he protested. 'They won't eat you! My mother will probably cry all over you with relief!'

Three months ago, Alex had been a terrifying figure; now, despite all her denials, she was wearing his engagement ring and committed to marrying him. Liz, she thought ruefully, would wet herself with laughing when she told her. But she pushed her doubt aside as Alex skimmed the car along the half mile drive of his parents' home a little later, and shivered with fright.

'Some farmhouse!' she spluttered gazing in awe at the huge silver-timbered manor house that faced them.

'It was, once,' Alex said, casually, tooting the horn as the dogs rushed at the familiar car. 'Brace yourself, my darling.' He was so proud of her and so loving that Casey began to feel almost sure of herself. They met astonishment, disbelief and, as Alex had predicted, tears from his mother. Until she pulled herself together and got organized.

'Champagne first, Henry!' she cried. 'I must ring Penny to come over. Alexander! You'll be the death of me!' She bustled around them in a frenzy until both Alex and Casey burst out laughing in sheer relief.

'Mother! We're engaged, we're going to get married, *that's all*! Now calm down!' Alex told her. 'And no, I'm not sure when, so don't even ask. We're just enjoying the novelty at the moment.'

But to Lady Havilland everything had to be done properly. 'Of course it will have to go into *The Times*, Alex. It would be expected,' she enthused over lunch. 'And Casey should get on with arranging the wedding. You *have* to think about it all.'

'Stop right there!' Alex ordered. 'Mother, we may just slope off to Barbados to get married, so stop getting excited. Church is *out*, I'm divorced, remember? And, officially, I'm the guilty party! Penny, back me up, for heaven's sake!'

'Leave them alone, Mother.' Penny lifted her glass. 'Welcome to the family, Casey.' By the time they left, the Havillands knew all about Casey and, being Casey, she had been refreshingly honest with them, endearing her to them all the more.

'Casey has a week of Kear commitments,' Alex finally excused them. 'We need to get back so that she can get organized.'

'I'd almost forgotten that,' Casey said. 'In all that excitement.'

'I hadn't,' Alex said. 'I can't afford to. I just hate the thought of handing you over to Tony Sorensen and James Wyatt for a week.'

'I'll phone every night,' she promised.

'Don't worry, angel, I'll be phoning you!'

He took her pile of treasures up to the flat and was greeted by an anxious Liz. 'There are two more letters and a package,' she told Alex, worriedly. 'All addressed here.'

'Then just throw them,' Casey said. 'I'm not at all

interested! Look, Lizzie!' She held out her ring, to shrieks from Liz.

'You sneaky pair! What brought this on?'

'A sudden attack of courage!' Alex put down the hastily packed boxes and picked up the letters. 'Casey, I think you should open them, in case there's a clue to this guy.'

'You do it!' Casey shuddered. 'I couldn't bear to!'

Alex was glad he had. The tone of the letters was certainly changing. Though still anonymous, the writer was getting bolder, more forceful, and angry that she was still seeing Alex. Venom poured from the pages as he took her to task for, as he saw it, her treachery to her true love. This time the package contained black silk lingerie, expensive and erotic.

'Oh, dear heavens! It's disgusting!' Casey stared at the scraps of lace and silk.

'At least it's new!' Liz said, in relief. She had had other friends harassed by admirers who had not been so lucky.

'Alex!' Casey looked at the envelope, realizing for the first time that it had been correctly addressed. 'What if he comes here?'

That had occurred to Alex too. 'You're away next week, don't worry, we'll get some security sorted out in the flat, and I'll speak to the porter. If there is any sort of problem Liz can move in with Robin, and you can come to Edwardes Square.'

'Oh no! I'm not being driven out of the first really nice home I've ever had by some pervert!' Casey almost stamped her foot. 'We aren't married yet,

Alex, and you are *not* going to tell me what to do!'

'OK, for now,' he acquiesced. 'But if he gets any more threatening, *you* are moving out, and there is *no* arguing.'

'Alex is right, Casey.' Liz, surprisingly backed him up.

'It's a kid, no more,' Casey said, firmly. 'With silly ideas.'

'Casey, he's no kid,' Alex said. 'No kid could afford thousand pound bracelets.'

'What?'

'It's true! When M-J took it back to that store, though they wouldn't tell her who bought it, she did find out the price.'

'And these aren't exactly chain-store knickers,' Liz turned the lingerie over, assessing the quality with a practised eye.

'I just wish he'd sent an address, then at least I could write and tell him I'm not interested,' Casey shrugged.

'That would defeat his purpose,' Alex said. 'I don't mind admitting; I'm getting a bit worried.'

'Alex, I'll be fine, and as you say, I'm away all next week and so is Liz.'

'Well wait until he reads the announcement of your engagement; it doesn't sound as if he'll like it very much,' Liz added.

'Hell! Alex, perhaps we'd better not do anything for a week or so,' Casey worried.

'Oh no!' Alex was quite firm. 'For one thing my family would never forgive me, and for another, I'm not hiding my love for you from *anyone*, least of all some creep!'

'Cheers!' said Liz. 'At least you're together on that! She'll be careful, Alex. I promise.'

'I seriously expect you both to be careful,' Alex said. 'But in the meantime I will get some professional advice. I think it's necessary.'

Casey disagreed, but she had more sense than to argue with Alex now. After all, he had her safety at heart. She watched him slip the offending items into an envelope – anything to have them out of the flat, out of her life, and silently she handed him the spare key to the flat for the security firm he had in mind.

'I guess you're right about security,' she told him, quietly. 'But I will *not* let him spoil things for me. I'm sure I can cope.'

'Of all the women I know, I would bet on that!' Alex bent to kiss her. 'But until we know what, or who, you are dealing with, you are going to be looked after. Let's just hope he gets bored with it, or finds someone else to worship, because I'm not sharing my wife with anyone!'

'Wife-to-be!' Casey corrected.

'Not for very long! Have fun next week, sweetheart, I'll call you every evening, I promise.'

CHAPTER 19

He did too. In Paris, Geneva and Rome there was a call each evening and she was astonished to find herself waiting impatiently for it. Every minute of the day was taken up as she and Robin introduced the car to dealers and journalists from half a dozen different countries. The commercials, of course, had been launched weeks before, world-wide with a huge blast of publicity, and they were known wherever they went, a daunting experience for Casey, having spent most of her life in relative obscurity. Ross had done a fabulous job on the cutting and they were quite stunning visually – like mini-films, she thought in amazement when she first saw them – and a roaring success with public and trade alike.

Suddenly the taxi drivers all knew her, and travelling on the tube became a lot more of a hazard as people began to stare at her. Few approached her directly, but to her surprise, she began to find that the fame she had longed for could actually feel distinctly uncomfortable. Finally she started to use the car Kear had provided for her. She was beginning to realize Sarah Campbell had been right in her advice as she read some of the more lurid press reports that James passed on to them. Robin, of course, simply laughed, and told her not to worry and that at least she had Alex to protect her from now on.

Kear had spared no expense, the parties were lavish and exhausting, but James Wyatt became increasingly delighted at the way the two handled themselves. 'I had no idea your French was so good, Casey,' he told her as the reception in a chateau just outside Vichy drew to a close.

Casey shrugged. 'A-level, that's all. And waitressing in a couple of French restaurants one summer vacation.'

'I think we chose extremely well! It's prob . . .' But Casey wasn't listening. Across the room, one man stood head and shoulders above the others around him and Casey simply flew into the arms he held out to her.

'Alex! You didn't say you were coming!' she cried into his chest as he hugged her.

'No, I decided to surprise you, darling.' He looked down at her bare hand. 'Why aren't you wearing your ring?'

'I am!' Casey lifted the gold chain from around her neck. 'It's here, safely.'

'Well I'd rather it was on your finger! It's official now, it was in *The Times* yesterday, so I guess every paper will have picked it up by now. We won't get any peace for a while, I'm afraid.' He slipped it back where it belonged and smiled. 'James and Robin know, so why shouldn't everyone else here?'

'Now you're here, no reason at all.' Casey smiled back. 'But I expect Tony will get a shock, I wouldn't let Robin tell him!'

'Well, since it's all his fault . . .' They both looked up and across at Tony's astonished face as he took in the sight of his normally supercool and correct boss with Casey held tightly in his arms. 'Let's go and surprise him. I shall enjoy this – he's always so sure he can put one over on me! If he wasn't such a good creative director I'd have fired him years ago!'

He took her off to dinner in Vichy and they relished the unexpected time together, strolling around the elegant boutiques surrounding the brilliantly lit Parc des Sources before they went to eat in a restaurant built out over the lake. To Casey's surprise, her French was actually better than Alex's; she joked easily in the shops with assistants as she bought perfume for Liz, and then drew back in shock at the price of a beautiful pair of white, beaded and embroidered shoes that she tried on. '*Four hundred pounds*!' she translated. '*On another planet*!'

Alex shrugged; it meant nothing to him, she realized in horror. 'They'd make wonderful wedding shoes,' he suggested. 'Let me buy them, Casey?'

'They do suit Madame's feet,' the assistant said. 'So elegant!'

'We'll take them!' Alex said, dropping his credit card on the counter.

'Do I get the idea you are pressuring me about a wedding now?' she asked as they left the shop to walk towards the lake.

'I wouldn't dream of pressuring you! But . . .'

'I have three months for the BBC,' Casey reminded him. 'After I finish Hal's film that is, and then Nick Grey's film. Next summer perhaps?'

'I was thinking more of Christmas,' Alex said, casually. 'We could go to Barbados then, for a honeymoon. Or of course, there's nothing to stop us getting married before that, even if you can't get away. October, perhaps?'

'October! Alex! That's only six weeks away!'

'Why not October? You have the shoes, Cinderella. How long does it *take* to buy a wedding dress?'

'And do the rest,' she reminded him.

'Leave that to me – just tell me where you want to get married, and what you want.'

'I'm not sure what I want, though I did always promise Aunt Mary that I'd get married from their house, after my parents died.'

'Then that's what we'll do,' he smiled. 'It's not so far from my house so it gives me a start. How would a wedding at Penswood Castle sound?'

'Penswood? Alex, it's beautiful! I did a shoot there once. But do they *do* weddings there?'

'Guy Penswood had it licensed when the law was changed a while back, no problems there. So – October?'

Casey took a sip of wine. 'A bull-dozer has nothing on you, has it? What *have* I let myself in for?'

Alex raised his glass to her, smiling. 'Being loved to distraction for the rest of your life? Is that enough?'

'I think it would be enough for most women,' she smiled back. 'I do love you, Alex.'

'Then October it is – and it can't come soon enough for me!'

'Good grief, Cassandra!' Liz stared at her. 'When you decide to do something, you do it! You *were* going to make him wait!'

'I don't seem to be able to make any rational decisions these days,' Casey excused. 'Blame Alex!'

'Well he's certainly made some here,' Liz waved an arm around the flat. 'New locks, video camera, alarm buttons, the lot! It's like Fort Knox!'

'We're safe from intruders, then?'

'Hmm, but not from these.' Liz held out three letters from the pile she was sorting.

Casey swore but this time she opened them herself. 'I think he must read *The Times*,' she said. Her tone was light but Liz only had to look at her face to know the truth. 'They're worse, aren't they?' she asked, quietly. Casey held them out to her.

'Yes,' she replied. 'I'm afraid they are, he sounds almost crazy.' The original love-letters were now angry, at her 'betrayal' of his love, fury pouring from every line, and threatening both her, and him, if she didn't give up Alexander Havilland forthwith.

'Alex is right,' Liz frowned. 'We *should* tell the police. These are definitely threatening violence now. There are laws about this kind of thing now.'

'Not many — I doubt they'd take this seriously.'

'Try telling Alex that!'

'No, don't! He'll only fuss! Hell, Liz, we've got enough security to save the world from danger and in six weeks I suppose I'll be moving to Edwardes Square with Alex anyway. I just wish you could come too!'

'Oh, yes! I'm sure Alex would love that! Anyway, I'm going to move in with Robin until we get married.'

'Both of us married! Heavens, who would have thought it six months ago?'

'Of either of us?'

'I'm still not sure,' Casey admitted. 'Oh, I love Alex, don't get me wrong. I'm just frightened of letting him down. He's so *grand*! He even had lunch with the Queen the other day, and didn't even think to mention it! Mary-Jo told me, quite by chance.'

'Don't be so stupid, Cassandra Taylor! He's very lucky to have you! And don't you forget it! Now stop behaving like a Cinderella who has just met her prince!'

'But I feel rather like that! Even the newspapers are saying it,' Casey moaned.

'Remember what Sarah told you about the press?' Liz grinned. 'I thought you were tougher than that!'

'I rather think I'm going to need to be,' Casey sighed. 'I must be mad, Liz.'

'No, you're in love with him, I should know all the signs by now! Go with the flow, darling, and let Alex do it all. I'm sure he'll do it beautifully.'

Alex was as good as his word. He took care of all the wedding arrangements with the help of his well organized secretary. In what limited time she had, Casey flew around London looking for a wedding dress, to no avail – until Sarah Campbell stepped in to offer her help, sweeping her off to a designer she frequently used herself.

'Marco is a fabulous designer,' she said. 'And he'll be discreet, which is what both you and Alex want.' Liz greeted the news with enthusiasm, having worked for Marco Ferranti in the past, and kicked herself for not thinking of him before. Both girls liked him and fittings became a party especially when Sarah came too. Casey found herself turning more and more to her as the weeks passed. It was even Sarah who accompanied Casey's aunt to a boutique in Richmond to buy an outfit for the wedding, when Casey herself couldn't go. After years of practice she was a master at going unnoticed in public and Mary Taylor had no idea who her charming advisor really was until Casey told her afterwards. Sarah loved all the conspiracy to keep the plans from the Press and bubbled with good ideas and wicked suggestions whenever they met.

It was Sarah too, who wisely advised Liz and Alex

to hide the increasingly vindictive letters that arrived almost daily now for Casey. 'She has enough to worry about,' she told Alex sympathetically. 'I've been lucky I suppose, but I do know other people who've had the same thing happen and it's very unpleasant. Don't worry though, Liz,' she added. 'At least he doesn't phone every five minutes. It's usually just words, most of these people haven't got the bottle for anything else, thank goodness!' She giggled. 'I did have one though, who sent me dozens of bars of expensive soap every week, for months!'

'Soap!' Liz joined in the laughter. 'What on earth did you do with it?'

'With all our houses it was quite useful! Look, are you sure Casey won't move into Edwardes Square? Or even out to Richmond with us?'

'Not a chance!' Alex groaned. 'We've all tried!'

Casey felt relief that the letters seemed to have stopped but even the combined efforts of Alex and Liz couldn't completely prevent the bouquets of orchids and the odd parcel filtering through. She knew now, and threw them away unopened, her main thoughts occupied with the coming wedding and Alex – she happily embraced his suggestion that they look at a house in Richmond on the edge of the Park and not far from Sarah and Nick.

'Ideal location to bring up a family,' he told her, casually, the day he came up with the idea, and took her to see it. 'Much healthier place to live than the middle of London, I'll sell Edwardes Square and we'll live out here.'

'Oh, yes?' Casey raised an eyebrow. 'Just so you and Nick can slope off more easily to play golf you mean? I remember what you said about your father!'

'I rather think *I'll* have more exciting things to do than play golf!' he grinned. 'It's more so that you have friends nearby. I know you like Sarah, as she likes you, and after all, Liz will soon be travelling with Robin now he's going into Formula One, you'll need someone to gossip with! Frankly, now that Sarah and Nick are planning to spend more time here, I'd like to see more of them too. But only if you like the house, naturally!'

The trouble was, she *did* like the huge and elegant Regency house, with its wrought ironwork balconies and the rambling tree-filled garden. It would be the first home she had ever had that actually belonged to her, and wasn't rented, and the thought thrilled her. 'Won't it mean travelling for longer to get to your office?' she asked, casually, trying not to betray just how much she wanted it.

'I'm working on cutting down on the office,' he admitted. 'Paul feels the same, that maybe we should let some new, younger blood have their heads; you never know, it could be good for business!'

He would tell her no more, and she had to bite back her curiosity; when Alex decided not to say any more she knew quite well there was no persuading him to change his mind! She gave in over the house, as she frequently did over most of Alex's suggestions, and agreed that it was a good idea to buy it.

She just knew that, even with her doubts about the wisdom of marrying him, she loved him more each day as she began to realize just how much he loved and wanted her.

Slowly, she was growing more confident of her place in his life, happily acting as his hostess at the increasingly frequent dinner parties he held at Edwardes Square, and to Alex's delight, endearing herself to his many friends and acquintances with a frightening ease. He laughed to himself as he recalled his horror-struck thoughts at their first meeting and, indeed, once or twice he felt somewhat shamefaced about thinking such a thing. But it was more than he dared to confess to Casey!

CHAPTER 20

But even the night before the wedding she still harboured some niggling doubts, sitting up with Liz in her aunt's lavender-scented spare room worrying endlessly about what she was about to do. It still seemed far too sudden and somewhat bewildering.

'Stop it, Casey!' Liz said, finally. 'Just think that by this time tomorrow you'll be Alex's wife! You *know* you're as crazy about him as he is about you, any fool can see that! What *is* the problem?'

'Nothing – nothing at all.' Casey hugged her knees. 'I guess I just can't believe I can be so lucky as to find a man like Alex! I've never been lucky like that before – in anything!'

'Then it's time you were.' Liz stretched out, luxuriously. 'That was quite a party he threw for you – heaven knows how the wedding will better it.'

'Knowing Alex, I'm sure it will,' Casey said softly. 'He was so sweet having fireworks tonight, I told him just once that I loved them, and tonight was like the fourth of July and bonfire night all rolled into one!'

'Wonderful! And I thought your Uncle John would burst with pride when Sarah kissed him!'

'Oh, Lizzie! I wish it had been Daddy, that's all,' Casey sighed.

'I know, darling,' Liz frowned. 'But at least you *have* your uncle.'

'I'm sorry, Liz, I'm being silly, I know. I have them both,' Casey said. 'And they're so proud of me.' She stood up and smoothed her hands over the slender column of bias-cut creamy-white silk that Marco had made for her. 'Do you think Alex will like this?'

'Course he will! Though I dare say he'll prefer taking it off!' Liz grinned wickedly. 'Now for goodness' sake, leave it alone, or you'll end up snagging it, you're so nervy! Get some sleep, girl!'

She slept in the end but fitfully, and it seemed no time at all before her aunt was cheerfully banging on the door with a breakfast tray. 'I can't eat all that!' Casey protested as her stomach revolted at the mere thought of it.

'Since when have you not wanted to eat?' Mary demanded, memories of Casey's healthy childhood appetite fresh in her mind.

'Since I decided to get married!' Casey swallowed some coffee and made a futile effort at some cereal.

'You eat, my girl!' Mary ordered. 'Lunch will seem a long way off soon, and we don't want a bride with a rumbling tum, do we?'

Casey looked at the tray. 'I'll be sick.'

'Give over!' Mary leant over and hugged her.

'Now do try, dear.' To please her aunt, and a worried Liz, she made an effort and managed to make a fair stab at the tray before they set to on her make-up and hair. They had both refused the offer of a hair-stylist and make-up artist, preferring to do it themselves. Casey wanted the time alone with Liz to giggle and lark around together for the last time simply as girlfriends.

'We'll soon both be married ladies,' Liz said, pushing one last pin into the silvery wreath that held the veil on Casey's torrent of chestnut hair. 'Shall we have a bet on who's going to have a baby first?'

'Definitely you'll be first!' Casey laughed. 'I have a film to do before I can think about babies. Alex knows we have to wait for that; after all, it's for his friend.'

'Doesn't he want children?'

'Yes – oh, yes! That's why he bought the house in Richmond! He wants lots, I know!'

'Ouch!'

Casey grinned. 'I used to think that. It scared the hell out of me just thinking about having babies, but Sarah – well – she makes it sound such fun, being a mum, I mean!'

'Her kids are *lovely*,' Liz agreed. 'And *so* well behaved.'

'Perhaps that's why Alex likes them so much. There – will I do?'

'You'll more than do, and you know it! You look beautiful.'

Casey smiled and stood up to let the folds of silk drop into place over the embroidered slippers that Alex had bought her. He had been right, they *were* wonderful wedding shoes. 'You too, darling,' she said. 'Robin will fall at your feet in admiration.' Liz was not exactly a bridesmaid, declaring herself far too old for that sort of thing, but they had compromised on a simple and short pale-blue dress that echoed the classic lines of Casey's own.

'Casey, Liz! Ten minutes!' Mary called up the stairs. 'Come and have a drink, if you can keep it off your dresses.' They laughed together and made a toast to Casey's parents. It was deliberately low-key as Casey intended it to be. 'No Press, no fussy security, no bridesmaids, just a quiet friendly wedding,' she demanded, silencing Alex's mother and Penny into submission, since Alex agreed wholeheartedly with her.

Consequently, Liz drove Casey's aunt and herself to Penswood in Casey's Kear, the only gesture she was prepared to make to her sponsor. 'My wedding is my own affair,' she declared. 'Nothing to do with Kear whatsoever!'

With a new confidence Casey kept her own car waiting as she had a swift last-minute conversation with Alex on the house phone. 'Casey! We'll be late,' her uncle reminded her as time ticked past.

'Brides are always late,' she laughed. 'I love you, Alex – see you at the altar, just don't move till I get there!'

Their driver was young and uncommunicative as

he drove. The partition between them and him remained firmly closed all the way, to their surprise.

The one and only time Casey had been a bridesmaid she had remembered their driver being full of chat all the way to the church. She had just assumed he would be as happy as she was, somehow. 'Strange,' she commented, after musing on it for a few minutes. 'This isn't the way to Penswood, surely? It's on the Chichester road.'

John leant forward and tried to open the partition but it wouldn't budge. Impatiently he rapped hard on the glass to attract the driver's attention, but to their surprise he ignored them. 'This is ridiculous!' John declared. 'What's the matter with the young idiot? He's going miles out of his way!' Casey began to get worried, they were already late and getting later by the minute. Getting lost would only add to the problem and she rather regretted the last-minute phone call taking up time. Still, she could hardly have known the driver didn't know the route properly! John, however, was thoroughly alarmed and even more so when the car swung off the road and into woodland. The track was bumpy and narrow and they stared at each other in horror as the trees thickened around them.

'Oh no!' Casey gasped. 'What on earth is he doing?'

John tried to open the partition again and then attempted to open the door of the moving car. It didn't budge. 'Child locks,' he realized out loud. 'We're locked in! What is he playing at?' Casey gripped his arm in terror as the car suddenly slowed and pulled into a flat area alongside the track. A solitary car was parked in the tiny parking area, a shiny dark blue Escort. Within seconds the driver was out of his seat and wrenching open the back door.

'You! Get out!' he ordered Casey's uncle. John, an ex-policeman, recognized the power of the automatic pistol in his hand and knew they had no chance against it. But with an agonized look at Casey he still hesitated for a moment, until Casey whispered, despairingly. 'Do as he says, Uncle John.'

'She's right!' The driver waved the gun menacingly, quite firmly in control.

'Don't touch him!' Casey, unbidden, scrambled after her uncle. He was, after all, in his seventies, and not in particularly robust health. 'Just tell us what you want! Is it my ring? Because you'll be disappointed if it is! I don't have it.' She had given it to Alex the night before, so that he could replace it after the wedding.

'I don't want your ring, Cassandra.' The man's voice was coolly menacing. 'I want you – get into that car.' He indicated the Escort with a brief movement of his head and Casey stepped back, clutching at John's arm. 'No, not him, just you.' There were two of them to his one, but he had the gun and from the look on his face he would quite happily use it. Why, she wondered desperately, were there no other visitors to the wood? Sussex was normally teeming with tourists all the time. The driver had chosen his spot well.

'DO IT!' he snarled at her, sensing her hesitation. 'I don't want to hurt either of you, but I will!'

Casey gripped John's hand, fiercely. 'Tell Alex – tell Alex – I . . .' she tried, but the driver yanked her away from him hurling her towards the car. Hampered by her long skirt she stumbled and fell awkwardly and, even as John automatically went to help her, the driver swung the gun at his temple, crashing it down on the fragile elderly bones. With a hoarse moan, John collapsed at his feet in an unconscious heap as Casey struggled to her feet almost hysterical with shock. 'You said you wouldn't hurt him!' she cried in panic.

The driver shrugged. 'He'll live! Now, do as you're told, unless you want me to do the same to you?'

'The hell I will!' Casey was on her own now and felt able to fight, but in a long clinging dress and with a veil hampering her vision she was no match for a fit and determined man. With seemingly little effort he bundled her into the boot of the Escort and forced her hands behind her back into handcuffs, before he dragged her veil off to tie it tightly around her mouth as an effective, if very painful, gag. The net cut into her mouth as she tried desperately to yell, but it cut off her screams completely as he slammed down the boot lid shutting her off from light and a last sight of her stricken uncle.

It took the driver only a few minutes to haul John's unconscious body into the grey Rolls and shut the door on him. With any luck, he thought hopefully, it would be hours if not days before he was found – if at all in this isolated spot. Adrian had chosen carefully, he had worked the whole thing out very methodically, as was his way, knowing this was his one and only chance to get to Casey Taylor. There was nothing, he thought as he drove, that he had left to chance. The number plates on his car had been changed; he preferred to use his own, shuddering at the thought of driving a hire car anyone *dirty* could have driven; he had persuaded his mother to take a few days away at her sister's home in Scarborough, and he had made provision for a few weeks away as far as the bank were concerned. His wallet was stuffed with money, and credit cards in several different names, all courtesy of the bank. He had even studied a pile of sex manuals at some length. Susan from the library had been some help there, he had to admit – and not just in providing books. Sex was not something that had been part of Adrian's life before, but now, in his meticulous preparations, he wanted to be sure that he was getting everything right. He was going to pull it all off – and to hell with the cynical Ruth at the bank. Casey Taylor was going to end up as *his* wife, not married to that flashy advertising fellow with the smarmy smile!

He was actually humming as he backed the Escort out onto the track and turned it round to retrace his route back to the main road. It had been far more difficult to work out the best place to put his cabin cruiser so that he wouldn't be cut off from it by the tide, but even that had worked out for him. This was obviously all meant to be, he told himself gleefully, as he drove. In an hour the boat would be reachable in the dinghy he had hidden in the tiny inlet where he had moored the boat, he would just choose his time to row Casey out to it. He had of course assumed she would be compliant about it, grateful even that he had rescued her from her dreadful fate. It had astonished him that she had been so angry, but then maybe it had just been shock? She would come round, she would understand, eventually, he told himself. He still couldn't believe how easy it had been.

With her hands firmly secured behind her back Casey had absolutely no way of protecting herself from being thrown about by the fast moving car. Her shoulders and head were repeatedly hammered against the sides or the floor as she struggled in vain to protect herself. At first she was just desperate about John, then her own dire predicament began to sink in as the minutes passed.

She should be saying her vows to Alex at this moment, not being driven in the opposite direction by an obvious maniac! And she began to panic then. What on earth would he do to her, especially when she was so trussed up and helpless? Alex would be frantic by now, she thought, desperately. Would he think she had run away – changed her mind? She had, after all, voiced her doubts more than once! But John would tell him, she was sure.

However, John was, at best unconscious, at worst dead. He wouldn't be able to tell Alex anything for hours. Maybe he would never be able to tell him even if he was found quickly. The thought of that finally made the tears of frustration and fear trickle relentlessly from her eyes. They ran unchecked down her cheeks, soaking into the silk that choked her mouth, blinding her with their intensity. The dark metal box of the cramped boot was airless and hot, heavy with fumes of some sort – the exhaust she guessed. It began to make her feel light-headed, almost woozy and she had to fight then just to stay awake as the car bounced along.

'Stay awake!' she told herself firmly. 'Don't go to sleep!' But her head was heavy and there was no focus in her tear-bleary eyes. Slowly, relentlessly, she could feel herself sliding closer to oblivion. Despite the gag she tried to cry out. It was Alex she wanted – Alex would come and get her, Alex would find her – somehow!

It was her last coherent thought before she blacked out completely.

Alex was almost beside himself with worry after an hour had passed and Casey had not arrived. The journey should have taken no more than fifteen minutes – twenty at the outside. Frantic, he paced the floor of the reception area, his agitation growing by the minute.

'Alex! Calm down,' Nick Grey tried to reassure him. 'Maybe it's just a breakdown, or something.'

'Then they'd phone, surely,' Alex cried. 'Nick, something's happened to her! I'm sure it has, we have to do something!'

'I'll call the car company,' Nick offered. 'They must be in contact with the driver. Have you the number?'

Alex shook his head. 'Mary must have it – they booked it, they insisted on doing it,' he said. 'The company boss is an old friend of John's.'

'Alex? What's happening?' Liz came out into the hall. 'Everyone is getting anxious.'

'We just don't know,' Nick said. He told her what little they did know and Liz ran back to tactfully get the phone number from a bewildered Mary.

Nick was equally bewildered as he put down the phone after making the call. 'There's no reply on the driver's radio,' he said, anxiously. 'It appears to be switched off. All they know is that he went off in good time and that he is one of their regulars – they made sure of that.'

'And we know he was waiting when we left the house,' Liz put in.

'I'm going to ring the police,' Nick said. 'Just in case there's been an accident; it does seems the likeliest explanation. Liz, would you try and explain things to the others? Get them a drink or something?'

Their high-profile names were enough to guarantee instant reaction from the local police. Within ten minutes a call confirmed that no accident had been reported, making the situation even more worrying to the two men, and Nick finally gathered himself together demanding more action, as he realized that Alex was in too much of a state to try. 'Something is definitely wrong,' he said, looking anxiously at Alex's stricken face. 'We need someone down here – NOW!'

Five minutes later two reassuringly efficient detectives arrived, with a promise of more on their way. 'We thought it might be wiser in the circumstances, to come in smaller numbers,' the senior detective explained. 'I'm Detective Inspector Booker, Chris Booker.'

'Bruce Johnson,' the younger man introduced himself. 'Detective Sergeant. Is there somewhere we can talk in private?'

Guy Penswood, who had joined the two worried men, nodded, and led them to a small study just off the hall. 'Use this room, as long as you need it,' he said. He was an old school friend of Alex, and touched his arm sympathetically. 'Bear up, Alex,' he added. 'It's bound to be something quite simple.'

Alex shook his head, numbly. 'Something has happened to her! I know it! She was on her way here, I spoke to her just as she left. I would have known if anything was wrong with her. I need action, and now! We have to search for that car as soon as possible!'

'A helicopter?' Nick put in quickly. 'That would be the quickest way. Do you have one?'

'Not at the moment, Sir, though we could get one quite quickly,' Inspector Booker frowned.

'*Nightingales*!' Alex and Nick said it together. It was a company they both frequently used in film work, and Nick reached for the phone. 'I can have at least two of them within the hour, I'm sure,' he said, and dialled, glad for something to do while Alex and Liz filled the two detectives in with as much information as they had. They were intelligent, and thorough, so that even the distracted Alex had to admire their expertise. They were quickly on the phone themselves, giving orders and liaising efficiently with the helicopter Nick had managed to call in, with the promise of another being with them inside the hour.

Even as the helicopters began their search, Chris Booker took the phone call that set many more alarms ringing. 'I'm afraid they have just found the car driver,' he said, as he put the phone down. 'The man has been dead for a couple of hours, since at least eleven o'clock.'

'But he was at the house at eleven-fifteen,' Liz said, puzzled.

'No, Miss, it was certainly *not* him,' Chris looked sympathetically at Alex. 'Whoever drove your fiancee, Mr Havilland, he didn't work for the car hire company. Have you any idea who might have a reason to do this? Miss Taylor is an actress, I believe? I have to ask this, difficult though it is, but, I take it there's no way it could be a practical joke or anything simple like that?'

'Good God, man!' Alex almost exploded. 'Do you think *anyone* I know would do something like that? On her wedding day?'

'It's more than their lives would be worth!' Nick agreed.

'Alex!' Liz jerked up from her chair. 'The letters! That man! Didn't you say they were mostly posted in this sort of area?'

'Oh, hell!' Alex stared at her. 'Liz! You're right! I forgot about those.' With a shudder he remembered the violent threats in the sinister prose. 'He said she would never have the chance to get married! And she laughed it off!'

'These letters, Sir,' Chris Booker interrupted. 'Do you still have them? Or any of them?'

'Yes, in my office,' Alex said. 'I can have them brought down here.'

'Very discreetly, and as soon as possible!' Chris frowned. 'We can get a psychologist to examine them, just in case there's any clue to the writer. In the meantime, let's hope those boys in the chopper turn something up – and soon!'

Alex made the call to Mary-Jo and then sank down into a chair with his head in his hands as he recalled more of the contents of the letters, particularly the ones Casey hadn't seen. He cursed himself for not being more vigilant, and letting her talk him out of going to the police when he wanted to. She had been so determined not to let the man spoil her wedding day, and now it appeared very much as if he had done just that! The mere thought of Casey in the hands of that deranged writer almost unhinged him. If he had already killed a man, what could he do to Casey?

'Alex, darling.' Sarah had come in unnoticed, but she had overheard most of the conversation, and she quickly bent to wrap her arms round him in a sympathetic hug. 'There's no real evidence that man has taken Casey, not yet!'

The two policemen's eyes glazed slightly as they recognized the girl trying to comfort the distraught man. 'I'm afraid it does seem a distinct possibility, Miss,' Bruce Johnson said.

'Alex,' Nick joined his wife. 'I'll go and sort out the guests – I think we'd better tell them there's a problem.'

'Yes, yes,' Alex tried to pull himself together. 'Fetch Mary, we shall have to tell her the truth, after all it's her husband – and her niece, who are missing. But for heaven's sake, try and get Penny to take my parents home, I can't face Mother's hysterics at the moment.'

Betwen them, Guy and Nick dealt with the bewildered guests, and a few minutes later a weeping Mary joined Alex and the two policemen. Her description of the car driver confirmed that it had not been driven by the company driver. 'It's just so cruel and unneccessary!' she said, sadly. Typically the warm-hearted Mary thought first of all of the dead driver's family, since she knew the company owner and had been told that his son-in-law would be doing the honours for them.

'We can't do much more here,' Alex decided. 'We'll go back to the house, set up some kind of head-quarters there. At least we'd be safer from the Press at home.'

He had finally pulled himself together, in the face of Mary's courage, and took charge then, his naturally commanding nature coming to his rescue. Within hours, he had the letters in his hands to give to the police, and Mary-Jo at their disposal. Fax machines and extra mobile telephones were produced within minutes it seemed, and if he had been allowed to he would have been out searching himself, Nick was sure; only the police assurance that he was more use to them at the house kept him in one place. As the loyal friend he was, Nick elected to stay with Alex, and only after it was realized that it was going to be a long wait did Sarah wisely decide to take the children home. Nick hated the thought of her driving alone, but she convinced him finally that Alex needed him most and that he should stay in Sussex.

'I'll call the security firm to keep the Press away if it seems necessary,' she promised Nick, as she kissed him goodbye. 'Don't worry, darling, I've got two other adults in the house, and no one would get to us past Isabelle and Donald! Besides, I promised to do the Carnegie show tonight, I'll have to go, but I'll come back as soon as I've done the show. The kids will be fine with Issy.'

'You could cancel,' Nick worried. 'It would be safer in the circumstances.'

'Don't worry, I'm the soul of discretion! Anyway it would look far worse if I cancelled, I'm not *known* for letting anyone down after all.' She was right, they knew. 'They'll find her, Alex darling, I'm sure of it!'

Alex hugged her. 'I hope so! Oh, God, I hope so!'

CHAPTER 21

Adrian couldn't quite believe how his luck held as he parked his car under the trees that almost overgrew the tiny inlet where he had left his boat. The tide was perfect, he noted with satisfaction as he dragged his dinghy from where he had hidden it under the branches, and swiftly attached the outboard motor he had kept in the back seat of the car.

He got a shock when he opened the boot and found his prisoner unconscious in a huddled heap. For a few horrified seconds he thought she was dead – as dead as Billy had been, He hadn't really meant to shoot him, it had been Billy's fault for getting cold feet at the last minute, after all. But Casey wasn't dead as Billy was; his nervous fingers found a pulse in her throat and with a sigh of relief he set to to lift her out of the boot and into the dinghy. She was a dead weight and he struggled, fit as he was. But adrenalin, and panic at being seen, helped him and he finally reached the boat, covering her with a blanket before he started the outboard. Even *that* finicky thing managed to behave according to plan, for once.

The priority in his mind was to get her onto the boat and hidden before he moved the boat. His aim was to keep on the move until such time as Casey accepted that she was his, and joined his adventure. He dreamed of marriage to her; eventually he told himself Casey would want to marry him. He was proud of himself – having rescued her from the clutches of that man – he even saw himself as a hero!

But, for the moment, he had to keep her hidden and guard against her being seen as he transferred her onto the boat. Breathing hard, he battled to lift the deadweight up into the boat and finally almost dragged her to the tiny cabin in the stern to lift her onto the built-in bunk that almost filled the small space. Even though she was still unconscious he left the handcuffs on – just in case – but with a certain amount of concern he untied the veil gag from her mouth. Her head fell back, her tangled hair spilling over his hands and he paused, wanting desperately to touch her.

Then he noticed as he lifted her legs onto the bunk that her shoes were missing and he cursed. If they *had* dropped off in the Escort he would be easily traced as the owner, changed number plates or not. He toyed with the idea of going back to the car and checking, then he realized how time-consuming that would be and he dismissed it. She could easily have lost them before she was put into his car. The sensible thing was to get moving, away from the car park, out into the river and eventually out to the channel – and France. The tide wouldn't wait, after all. Carefully he shut the door and, after quickly changing his grey suit for jeans and a sweater, he went to start the engine.

Casey felt herself gradually rising as if from a thick fog, blinking rapidly, then struggling to focus in the dimly lit cabin. Her head ached miserably, and she felt sick in the hot dry air. There was a distinct sound of engines throbbing under her and suddenly the drifting smell of something pungent. It was different from the car exhaust, and then as she roused herself she recognized the distinctive smell of diesel.

With a supreme effort she dragged herself up into a sitting position, using her bound hands to steady herself. One tiny porthole was her only clue as she realized in horror that she was on a boat. Somehow, she managed to manoeuvre herself up against the porthole, only to discover that it was dark outside. Even if she had been wearing a watch she couldn't have looked at it with her hands pinioned as they were. There was no way of knowing just how long she had been shut in this small dark place. It was airless and hot from the engines, she thought wildly.

'The car driver!' She remembered then – about John, about Alex. Was John really dead? What would Alex do to find her? What could he do if she was out in the middle of the sea? It would be the last place he would look. He would try though, she was sure about that. But in the meantime what would happen to her?

She soon found out. A short time later she heard

the engines stop and the anchor chain rattle down. Within minutes the door to her prison opened and the car driver appeared in the doorway. Instinctively she recoiled but he only laughed at her gesture.

'It's all right, Casey,' he said, reaching out to pull her to her feet. 'I'm glad to see you are awake at last. Come and have some supper, you'll soon feel better.'

'I don't want supper!' Casey spat at him. 'I want to get out of here! I want to go home! I should be getting married today!'

'But, Casey . . .' a frown passed over the thin pale face. 'This is your home now, here with me.'

'The hell it is!' Casey returned angrily as he pulled her across the cockpit and into a larger cabin forward.

'In a few days you'll be perfectly at home,' Adrian told her calmly as he went behind her to unfasten the handcuffs.

'Never!' There was no sign of his gun and the second her hands were free she went for him, her nails visibly raking lines on his face before he threw her down onto the floor. She banged her already throbbing head heavily as she went down and it knocked all the fight from her for a few seconds. Just enough time for him to shackle her hands to a rail at the edge of another bunk before he let go of her.

'You will do exactly as I say, Casey,' he said, coolly. 'You have no choice! Now, let's take off that dress, shall we? You don't need it any more, I have much prettier things for you to wear – for me.'

'No way!' Casey said, defiantly. Adrian smiled. The feeling of power that washed over him was beginning to make him feel really good – strong and invincible. At last he was someone, not the little boy his mother thought he was, or the meek and mild clerk from the bank that Ruth laughed at. This beautiful woman was his – in his power – and at last he could do exactly as he wanted with her, everything in fact that he had dreamed of doing as he had sat at his computer at the bank. Suddenly there was a knife in his hand, a long, glintingly sharp knife, and she recoiled in new fear. He grabbed at the front of the now pitifully stained and torn dress, and with one slash of the knife, thousands of pounds' worth of couture fell in shreds to the floor. Screaming with terror, she huddled back onto the bunk but Adrian dragged her forward, his eyes fixed on her breasts, barely concealed by the delicate lace wedding bra she still wore. The beautiful lingerie had been bought for Alex's benefit, not for this pervert, she thought hysterically as she struggled unsuccessfully to cover herself by bending her knees up.

'Better,' he commented, and then flicked the knife at the tiny bow that held the bra together at the front. It gave way immediately, releasing her breasts to his hungry eyes.

'No!' she screamed in fury and humiliation as he gazed long and hard, as if he'd never seen a naked woman before. He was gloating, actually gloating over his prize, reaching to touch her trembling skin, and in spite of her resolve she began to cry again. Silent, desperate tears running down her face, and soaking into her tumbling hair.

'Casey?' He paused in his tentative exploration of her upper body as he felt her shaking with fear. 'I don't want to hurt you, my dearest one. You could be a lot more comfortable, you know.' He touched the curve of her bare thigh and she immediately flinched away.

'Let me go!' she spat at him. 'I'll never give in to you! Never!'

'Oh, but you will, Casey,' he said, menacingly. 'You see, I have this.' He picked up the revolver, left carefully within reach. 'And I could use it any time I like. I'm trained to use it, you know, I've spent years learning how to use a gun.'

'You're crazy if you think you can get away with this,' Casey stammered, trying in vain to draw her body away from the hot hands roaming freely over it.

'But I already have, Casey,' he pointed out. 'You are here with me. We have transport, and I have money – a great deal of money. We can go anywhere, be together – see the world if you want to.'

'I don't want to see the world with you – I want to go home – to Alex!'

'*No!*' Adrian ignited at the sound of his hated rival's name. He jerked out his free hand and dragged her towards him so close that she could feel his hot breath on her face. 'You will never *ever* see him again! You're mine now, Casey – mine! I'd kill you before I'd let you go back to him!' The gun was at her throat and she froze as she felt the steel cold against her skin. Very slowly, he drew it down her trembling almost naked body, circling her breasts and then pressing it threateningly into her navel. She held her breath when he began to tease it at the edge of the lace pants, lifting them away from her skin with the point of the barrel before he slid it along the length of her thigh. Adrian was almost beside himself at the thought of his own cleverness in inventing this kind of sexual torture. This wasn't in any of the sex manuals he had read, and he was delighted to have thought it up. 'Remember what I promised to do to you, Casey? In my letters?'

'Letters?' The realization hit her then. '*You* wrote all those letters? And sent the flowers and stuff?' She realized then just what she was up against! Alex and Liz had declared the writer to be crazy – and now she knew all too well that he was!

'Yes, I wrote them, and I meant every word in them.'

'I didn't read them!' she declared, defiantly. 'I threw them away, all of them so you're wasting your time, whoever you are!'

'You don't remember me, then?' he asked finally, as he digested her angry words while he still held the gun firmly against her thigh.

'No, why the hell should I?'

'My name is Adrian – Adrian Shawcross,' he told her, searching her face for a sign, any sign that it meant something, but Casey's face was blank. 'We used to go to school together.'

'So did a million other kids!' Casey was scornful. 'You mean I'm supposed to *recognize* you? After – what – ten, fifteen years? Dream on, buster!' She literally laughed in his face. To hell with all the stories of hostages making friends with their captors, she thought, defiantly. This hostage was going to fight, every inch of the way.

'I'll make you remember,' he promised her as he started to move the gun once more against her skin. 'And soon you won't want anyone but me.'

He was going to rape her, in that instant she knew – and at that point she braced herself, to fight as she had never fought before.

The first break came in late evening, when one of the helicopters Nick had hastily summoned finally discovered the whereabouts of the grey Rolls. Car-based searchers were soon on the spot, guided by the pilot. 'They've found John Taylor in the car,' Chris Booker relayed to Alex and Nick with a relieved sigh. 'He's a bit woozy, but they say he'll be OK. Johnson here will get you over to the hospital, Mrs Taylor.'

'I'll come with you, Mary,' Nick offered, cheered at last by the sudden joy on Mary's tired and tear-stained face. In the last few hours Nick had been a tower of quiet strength to both Alex and Mary. A decisive man, used to working under stress, he seemed able to make decisions that Alex, for all his normal efficiency, seemed unable to bring himself to do. Though Nick himself was quick to realize that if it had been Sarah who was missing, he would be in the same frantic state as Alex had been for most of the evening.

'Alex, if they've found John, they'll soon find Casey,' Mary comforted him as Alex hugged her.

'Of course they will.' Alex tried to sound reassured. 'Go to John, Mary. He needs you right now.'

As he needed Casey, to hold her and know that she was safe. He remembered a casual comment Nick had once made about buying their Palm Springs house for Sarah and then nearly losing her, and he shuddered. It had seemed such a joke at the time, and now suddenly it was true for him too. He *had* lost her. Alex Havilland was not normally the praying kind, but he prayed now, long and hard as he paced the old oak floorboards of his sitting room while the policemen came and went. He couldn't eat or sleep, he kept going on coffee and nerves, despite Joan's efforts to get him to do both.

It was the middle of the night, soon after Nick had returned from the hospital, having left Mary with a recovering John, that a squad car arrived and after a rapid conference Bruce Johnson came hurrying in to Alex. 'Mr Havilland? Do you recognize these?' In his hand, encased in a polythene bag, were a pair of cream embroidered silk shoes.

Alex went white. 'Yes – yes – I do. They're Casey's. I bought them for her! Where . . .?'

'Mr Taylor mentioned a blue Escort when he came round,' Bruce grinned. 'And being an ex-copper he even remembered most of the number plate. False as it turned out, but . . . we were lucky with the car. One of the most popular cars around – and the lads found it! The shoes were nearby. At least one was, the other was in the boot. It was tucked away by the river. I would guess our man had a boat waiting. We are wasting our time looking for her on land.'

'A boat! There must be thousands in this area!' Alex was appalled. 'It will be like looking for a grain of sand on a beach! She could be anywhere even if we knew where to look, and we don't even know what kind of boat to look for!'

'Not necessarily.' Bruce gave a weary smile. 'This man is not quite as careful and precise as our psychologist friend thinks he is. The car is not listed as stolen, so there's a good chance he used his own, the idiot. We are checking the engine numbers now; the registration is false but that is more likely to be correct.'

'He'd be crazy to do that!' Alex said. 'Surely?'

'Alex, we aren't dealing with a normal guy,' Nick picked up a handful of letters. 'These prove that. And the more careless he is, the better for us.'

'Or the more dangerous for Casey!' Alex collapsed into an armchair, his head in his hands, his despair raw and deep.

'It rather depends on Casey,' Bruce looked just as worried as Alex. After many hours with the two men he felt as involved as they were, and the thought of such a beautiful girl in the hands of an obviously unstable kidnapper was terrifying him now.

'Casey will fight him,' Alex said, grimly. 'It wouldn't occur to her to do anything else!' And it would be the worst thing she could do.

Bruce shuddered.

CHAPTER 22

It hurt too much to cry. Casey lay very still on the bunk where Adrian had pushed her, after dragging her back into the tiny rear cabin and locking the door firmly. Every bone and muscle in her body seemed to have suffered damage from his savage kicks and punches when she had steadfastly resisted his attempts to invade her body. At least, she thought, in relief, she had fought that off successfully – for the time being, though there was no doubt in her mind that he would try again. Thankfully, he had not bothered to tie her hands again; obviously he had considered that she was past resisting by then.

With only a thin blanket to cover her now naked body Casey shivered in the unheated cabin and tried in vain to huddle under it. She was shaking with cold and really hungry now, with a throat hoarse from screaming at the man she was convinced was mad. It was many hours since Mary had persuaded her to eat breakfast; a brief glance through the tiny porthole told her it was now daylight. They were anchored way out somewhere, well away from other boats. She was so fuzzy she could hardly work out what day it was, Thursday? Friday? She finally realized it was actually Friday. She would have been missing almost a full day, Alex would be going frantic, she knew. She rolled over with difficulty onto her side, trying to ease the pain in her ribs, sure that at least one was broken, it was so painful to breathe, and thought longingly of Alex. Ironically, he had chartered a yacht in Monte Carlo for a few days over the weekend, as a short honeymoon since she had such a tight work schedule. She should be with him, sailing in the warm Mediterranean, not in some cold, grotty little cruiser just off Chichester somewhere – if that was actually where she was – she really had no idea. And if she hadn't, what chance had Alex got? The realization finally brought the tears again and she cursed herself for being so weak. Casey rarely cried, and now she seemed to be doing nothing but sob her heart out.

'Casey?' Suddenly Adrian was standing by the bunk. She had been so immersed in her misery that she hadn't heard him come in. Raising her head, her first instinct was to tell him firmly where to go, but something stopped her. Wisdom at last? 'Please, Casey, come into the cabin and have something to eat?' He touched her bare arm. 'I'm truly sorry I hurt you, it's really the last thing I wanted to do, you know.'

'Oh? Really?' Casey struggled to sit up and pull the blanket around her at the same time – no mean feat when every movement hurt. She stared in amazement at the gentle tone in his voice. This, from a man who had beaten her almost senseless only a few hours before!

'Yes.' He went to help her off the bunk and she shook him away violently. 'Come on, I have some clothes for you and hot coffee ready.' Just the thought of coffee was enough to make her bite back her more forthright comments. Very slowly, she followed him across into the main cabin and sank down onto the edge of the banquette, still hugging the blanket round her, kanga-style.

'I need a bathroom,' she stammered, hesitantly. 'Is there one?'

'Of course!' Adrian was proud of his boat, and the tiny basin and loo were immaculate as indeed was the rest of the boat, she noted with some relief. 'It's here.' He opened a door in the corner and to her gratitude allowed her to shut it behind her. For a moment or two she simply stared at her white bruised face in horror before she managed to wash some of the tears and grime from it, and use the loo, struggling with the pump arrangement but only too grateful for it. There was even a brand new toothbrush set out for her on the tiny shelf, with a comb at the side of it. Why she needed to bother she couldn't think, but it made her feel slightly better to rinse the foul taste from her mouth and wash what she could of the man's touch from her body. Her hair was past redemption and she didn't bother much with that, merely passed the comb over it.

Adrian was standing by the bunk when she finally emerged, holding an armful of clothes. 'I bought these for you,' he told her proudly. 'I'm sure they'll fit, but if they don't, well, 'I'll get you something else in Deauville, they have very smart shops there.'

'Deauville? You're not serious?' Casey stared at him.

'Of course.' Adrian said, surprised she should query it. 'I often take the boat over to France, it's quite sea-worthy you know.'

'I'm sure it is! But . . .' She hesitated, and realized it would be fatal to argue. 'Er . . . where are these clothes, then? I'm freezing!'

He handed her a skirt and a brief T-shirt-type top, totally unsuitable for the fairly cool morning and she looked at it in some distaste. 'I really need a sweater,' she demurred, carefully. 'Can't I have one of yours?' It disgusted her to think of wearing his clothes, but there seemed little alternative.

'Try those first,' he said, and reluctantly she slid into the skirt and tiny pants he gave her. There was no bra, she was resigned to that, and in the skimpy top she knew her breasts were almost fully visible, but at least he had thought of underwear, though his idea of her size was a little on the optimistic side. She almost grabbed at the blue wool sweater he finally produced from an overhead locker, and dragged it over her head. It at least covered her, almost to the hem of the skirt which *just* about covered her hips. The effort of simply putting them all on was enough for her in her weak state and she sank back onto the banquette clutching at her ribs with a moan of pain.

'Here, have some coffee. Do you really hurt, Casey? I have some aspirin in the cupboard.' Adrian looked at her in concern and Casey suddenly realized he actually looked quite worried. Now was the time to get to his weak side. She took the pills he offered, careful to check what they were before she swallowed them, however, then gulped at the coffee. Even without the sugar she liked it was heaven, and she cradled it in her cold hands to warm herself as she watched him make toast on the tiny grill. He was meticulous in everything he did, wiping up the crumbs he had made even before he put the bread under the grill; spreading butter carefully for her before he handed her a plate.

'Adrian?' she tried, once he had finished and sat across the table from her, unnervingly watching her eat. 'I think maybe we should talk, don't you? I mean – what do you really intend to do with me?'

'I intend to marry you, Casey.' Adrian looked at her in surprise. 'I thought that was obvious!'

'Not to me!' Casey finished the toast and sipped at the last of her coffee. 'I think it may have slipped your mind that I was about to marry the man I'm in love with, Adrian. I'm not free to marry you.'

'No! Forget it!' Adrian stood up, suddenly menacing again as he leant over her. 'I've given up everything for you! I even had to kill for you!

I'm not giving up now! I have nothing to lose, so I'm going for broke, and *you* are coming with me!'

'What do you mean, kill for me?' Casey stared, trying to hide her fear at his statement.

'The driver of your car,' Adrian smiled. 'My friend, Billy. He started to get stroppy, I had to show him I meant business, I couldn't let him pull the plug when I'd gone so far, could I?'

'Oh, no!' Casey shook with terror. A man had died – for her! She felt sick as she stared at him, her disgust apparent, she couldn't have hidden it even if she'd wanted to. The man was completely evil! He was even proud of what he'd done, she was sure.

'So you see, Casey, I have no choice, we have to go on, because I can't go back.' Adrian got up. 'I think I'd better get the boat under way, don't you? Now, are you going to be a good girl? Or am I going to have to tie you up again? I don't want to, but I will!'

'No, please don't!' Casey shuddered. 'I'll stay down here. I won't move.' There was nowhere she could go, it was apparent they were far from land, she couldn't swim that kind of distance, particularly in water that was hourly growing ever more choppy. She was uneasily aware that a storm was brewing and although she was a fairly good sailor, she had distinct doubts when she thought of Adrian controlling the fairly small boat. Satisfied that she meant it, Adrian went out on deck and left her huddled on the bunk.

Finally alone in the cabin, she looked around and

spotted another blanket rolled up in a corner of the bunk. It was still cold and she pulled it gratefully around her, conscious now of the engines running. He would be too busy steering the boat she reasoned, he would leave her alone at least while he was doing that, and with a sigh she curled up on the bunk and tried to get some sleep. She was too tired and sore to do much else. Adrian had finally succeeded in subduing her spirit, though to Casey it meant she was trying to conserve what strength she had left, waiting for his next attack. He had been almost kind in the last half-hour or so, but she wondered desperately how long that would last before he tried again to rape her. Would she be so lucky next time? He had openly admitted killing someone he had called a friend; why should he hesitate to kill her, once he had got what he wanted from her?

With a soft moan she twisted at the ear-rings of softly gleaming pearls that Alex had given her the night before the wedding. Amazingly, Adrian hadn't seemed to notice she was wearing them, but since they were a gift from Alex he would hate them when he realized they were there. She hated the thought of taking them off, but somehow she knew she had to save them and within seconds she had slipped them under the mattress for safety. Adrian was quite likely to throw them overboard if he got into another rage.

'Alex, oh, Alex!' She couldn't stop crying again. 'I love you, Alex, why didn't I tell you more often?'

She had always held back from the declaration, just the briefest little statement had passed her lips when embarrassed into it. It was such a hard thing to say somehow, and yet she knew quite well that she adored Alex. She just found it impossible to tell him, and now it was too late. He might never know how she really felt. All she had done was criticize his background, and ridicule his wealth, belittling anything he had tried to do for her, or give her, all in the very real fear of being overwhelmed. She had been so unfair in letting her own precious pride take precedence over her feelings for Alex, and now she regretted it, knowing at last that whatever he had done was because he loved her and for no other reason.

Alex would now be using all those hard-earned resources he possessed to help find her, she realized with sudden hope. Even while she tried to sleep the thought came to her: if she ever got out of this mess she would tell him how much she really loved him, it would be the first thing she would tell him, just to make sure he knew before anything else. For the moment all she could do was pray, and do her best to get through the day without provoking Adrian into more violence. If she really put her mind to it she was sure she could do it!

The growing storm was her saviour in that respect. Adrian battled the cruiser out into open sea around the Isle of Wight and realized his mistake at once. All day he struggled to keep his course but the small craft was simply not up to it. By late afternoon, to his fury, he finally had to drop anchor just outside a small harbour and pray that he wouldn't be noticed in the confusion of other small boats running for cover from the deluge. Casey had obediently stayed in the cabin, half asleep on the bunk where he had left her, and seemingly oblivious to the storm, or him. *She* deemed it wiser to avoid any contact with him, but the enforced stop meant he was back in her company as the evening drew in. The wind seemed to grow more threatening, howling around the boat tossing it about so relentlessly that she was sure it would jerk free of the straining anchor chain sooner or later.

Luckily for them both, Adrian was actually a good and seasoned sailor and often took the boat out into the Channel, as he had indeed boasted. He knew he only had to shelter for the duration of the storm before he could make a run for the French coast and, though he resented the interruption to his plans, he resigned himself to the delay. Casey looked up, her eyes bleak, as he came back down into the cabin after making everything as secure as he could.

'A little storm,' he said, quietly. 'We'll be fine, don't worry, Casey. Would you like something to eat now? I'll cook for you, I'd like that. I've been looking forward to looking after you, you know. Do you realize you will never have to do a thing for yourself from now on? I'm here to do it all for you.'

'Yes, I am hungry,' Casey said. It was far from the truth, but she had quickly latched on to his words. If he was cooking or trying to look after her, he was far less likely to be able to touch her. If he wanted to demean himself to look after her, then why shouldn't she think of things for him to do? The trouble was, there was precious little he could do, in the confines of a small boat. She demanded the most complicated of the things he offered to cook for her and though, even when they were finally prepared she had very little appetite for the meal, she forced herself to make a fair effort at it, just to spin out the time. Adrian was convinced that she was weakening, and even though the boat was tipping alarmingly, he reached across the bunk she had curled up on to touch her. Casey flinched without even realizing it, and then shivered with horror at what she'd done.

'Adrian,' she said, softly, pleadingly, 'the storm is getting worse, don't you think you should check eveything is OK?' Reluctantly, Adrian went to check outside, returning soaked through to the fuggy warmth of the cabin. 'Oh, heavens, you're soaked!' Casey tried to sound motherly. 'Shouldn't you get dry?' To her horror he suddenly turned on her.

'Don't you dare tell me what to do!' he roared at her. 'I don't need you telling me what to do! You *aren't* my mother!'

'I'm sorry.' Casey tried to look suitably distressed. 'I was concerned, that's all.' She couldn't have said a wiser thing. Adrian seemed to melt in front of her.

'Were you really?' He stripped off his wet shirt, but to her relief, he pulled a sweater over his damp chest. He was thin in his body, but even in her panic she could see he had a formidable wiry strength. 'I said you'd start to get used to me, Casey. I knew it! We can have *such* a good life together!'

In your dreams, Casey thought, desperately. But her sense of survival was beginning to kick in. 'I'm a realist, Adrian,' she said, carefully. 'Tell me, what do you plan?'

She sat frozen with fear at the crazy plans and dreams Adrian poured out to her, while the boat rocked and groaned on its flimsy anchor chain. He lived in a frightening fantasy world, she recognized, as the time passed, but she had finally realized that her life hinged on making him believe that he had made her believe him. He actually gloried in the fact that he had killed Billy for her. Making the final great sacrifice, he told her, gloatingly, and she shuddered anew at what he could do to her if he so chose. The gun and the knife were still very much in evidence, as he talked. Occasionally he played with one or another, as if he was giving himself new courage to use them. It became a desperate game then, to keep his mind occupied and away from the evil toys in his hands. 'Adrian, I think we should try and sleep,' she finally tried to suggest. 'We are going to need all our energy in the morning to sail this.'

'I want to sleep next to you, Casey,' he pleaded. 'I want to feel you!'

'No!' She couldn't help the sharp retort even

though she regretted it the moment it was out. 'It . . . it's far too soon, Adrian!' she tried.

'No!' Adrian grabbed at her. 'I *am* going to sleep next to you!' He twisted both her wrists together, and before she could even cry out to stop him she found the handcuffs he had used earlier snapped tightly around her wrists again. True they were pinioned in front of her so she could if neccessary use them as a weapon but she was to all intents and purposes, a prisoner again and she bitterly regretted her hasty words.

'Adrian?' she pleaded. 'Please don't.'

'I like it!' He stood over her, rocking slightly as the boat tossed. 'I like having you at my mercy, it makes it far more fun, just like in the films, really.'

'Whatever films do you watch?' she demanded, visions of him sitting up late at night watching porn films filtering through her panicking head.

'Oh, the usual ones!' He ran his hands along her bare thighs, revealed by the flimsy skirt he had given her to wear. 'Soon, Casey, when this wretched storm is over, you and I are going to do really beautiful things together, I promise you.'

Casey gritted her teeth as his exploration became bolder and more intrusive. It was more than she dared do now to fight back. She shut her eyes and let him touch her, all the while holding her body rigid and unresponsive. He would get no pleasure from his mauling, *that* she silently promised herself . . . and him.

CHAPTER 23

Mrs Shawcross sighed wearily as she crossed the square from the station to the bus-stop that afternoon. She knew it had been a mistake to go and visit her sister. She and Vera had never got on, she had only gone because Adrian had been so keen on the idea. But thirty-six hours, and she had been ready to strangle her, so she had made her excuses and taken the first train home. Now she found she had an hour to wait for a bus. Crossly, she made her way to the little supermarket; she might just as well get a few bits in, Adrian was off on that boat of his, she knew, so for once she could indulge in the kind of food she liked instead of the fancy stuff he wanted. Smiling with anticipation, she didn't see her friend Maisie until she bumped into her in the doorway, and found herself agreeing to going to the nearby cafe for a cup of tea. Well, Adrian was away, so there was nothing to rush home for, was there, she reasoned, and ordered some doughnuts too.

Maisie was full of wonderful gossip and the time flew by. Before she realized it she had missed the bus and had to wait for the next one, so Maisie suggested that instead they hung on and waited for the bingo to start at the Mecca. That agreed, she settled back to continue her story. Maisie often did part-time waitressing at Penswood Castle, and she was full of the wedding that had been cancelled at the last moment the day before. 'Bride just didn't turn up!' she laughed. 'There was chaos! Police and everything! They think she's been kidnapped, though Lord Guy said *we* weren't to tell anyone in case the Press got hold of it. We all got a grilling from the cops though! Just like a police drama it was!'

'Who was she then?' Mrs Shawcross was totally immersed in Maisie's tale. 'Anyone famous?' Penswood was renowned for celebrity weddings, mostly because Guy Penswood had so many glitzy friends.

'Not sure, actress I think . . . That Keara girl. You know, the advert for the sports car? It's on TV all the time these days.'

Mrs Shawcross knew only too well. 'My Adrian is nuts about that girl,' she confided in Maisie. 'Collects everything about her, has done for years. Used to go to school on the bus with her – so he says! Daft if you ask me! He worships the girl, has loads of her pictures in his room. Even writes to her regularly, though he doesn't know I know!'

'Sure it isn't Adrian who took her away, then?' Maisie laughed.

'Don't be soft!' Mrs Shawcross laughed back. 'Our Adrian's off on his boat to France, he said.

Won't be back for a few weeks. He's owed holiday from the bank after all. He never normally takes all his allowance, too devoted to his work.'

'Or worried he might lose it!'

'No, not my Adrian, he's far too valuable to the bank!'

'They all say that, until they get made redundant!' Maisie laughed. 'Come on, dear, let's get moving or we'll miss the opening game.'

Later that same evening Maisie mentioned her conversation to her policeman husband, just casually, but to her astonishment he almost leapt from his armchair. He had heard the discussions at the police station during the day. Seconds later, it seemed, she was in the car and being raced into the police station. It felt quite weird being grilled by the Detective Inspector that her husband thought of as God, and she was bewildered by the speed of it all.

Chris Booker was delighted with the uniform sergeant. 'It may be nothing,' he admitted. 'But, on the other hand, it could be just the break we've been waiting for.'

Within minutes a squad car was on its way to the Shawcross home and Chris and a woman constable were on the doorstep. Mrs Shawcross, with her in-built reverence for the police, was only too pleased to help, but at a loss to know how Adrian's whereabouts could be of any interest to them. 'Yes,' she said, 'he has a boat, he's out on it at this very moment, gone to France, he said.' She looked totally perplexed at Chris Booker.

'It may be nothing, Mrs Shawcross,' Chris said. 'But could we take a look at your son's room?'

'I suppose there's no harm in it,' she looked worried. 'But you won't touch anything, will you?'

'We'll try not to,' Chris promised, and followed her up the stairs to the immaculate rooms where Adrian kept his computer equipment, and the enormous collection of Casey's photographs. He stared in astonishment as he viewed the wall of pictures all depicting the girl he had been searching for for the last thirty-six hours. When he tapped into the computer he found even more references to her. Her address, her phone number, almost a complete dossier on her work right down to her personal appearences for the Keara. This guy knew more about Casey Taylor that Casey herself did! He was certain of that! How on earth had he collected it all?

Chris was fascinated and appalled at the same time. This was someone's life displayed on a computer as if it was a simple form to be filled in, and the majority of it must have been collected illegally, he realized then. Sifting through the piles of neatly written notes, he began to discover then just how Adrian had collected them, in his nightly trawls of computer networks. There didn't seem to be a computer he hadn't hacked into, he thought, in fascination. Banks, the Inland Revenue, even doctors' files. The man was a genius with the computer network! And all for information on one woman! He felt sick at the thought of the damage one man could do if he had turned his energy and thought processes to anything else. And something else hit him as he stared at the notes. *The handwriting was familiar!* He had been staring at it for the last thirty-six hours!

The police psychologist had been right after all. The writer of those letters had been obsessional to the point of lunacy to have done all this in such detail. Shaking with sudden fear over his discovery, he went back downstairs to the innocent-looking woman dispensing tea to the woman PC. 'Mrs Shawcross, do you by any chance know the name of your son's boat?' he asked, casually.

'Why, bless you, of course I do.' Mrs Shawcross beamed at him. '*The Lady C*, he calls it. After some Lady Chatterley he said.'

Or Cassandra, Chris thought, worriedly. 'Thanks,' he said, briefly. 'Sorry to have bothered you, but we thought your son might perhaps know something about this lady who is missing. We'd just like a word with him, that's all. If he contacts you, would you let us know?'

'Course I will.' Mrs Shawcross looked puzzled. 'But my Adrian wouldn't have anything to do with something like that, he's such a nice honest boy, anyone will tell you that.'

But the manager at the Western Bank told a different story. The lights were still burning at the bank as Chris Booker drove past and on instinct he called in. It was highly irregular but the manager was pleased to see him. He knew Chris, as everyone knew everyone else in such a small town.

'Funny you should turn up tonight,' he said as he let him in. 'I would have called you in the morning. One of our employees seems to have been a bit naughty with the bank's money. We've just been doing a bit of checking.'

'*How* naughty?' Chris drew out his notebook. 'It wouldn't be a man named Shawcross, would it?'

'How on earth did you know that?' The manager was astonished.

'A long story,' Chris sighed. 'I'd better take some details.'

An hour later, overwhelmed by facts about computers and the bank's detailed way of transmitting money, Chris sat in his office barking orders into the phone. He had gone almost two days now without sleep, as had several members of his team, but pure adrenalin kept them all going, as indeed it had Alexander Havilland.

Alex! He had forgotten him in the excitement of his investigation. Swiftly he reached for the phone again. 'Mr Havilland?' He tried not to sound too confident. This could be another false alarm after all, and they had had several of those! 'I may just have come up with a name for your letter writer. I'm coming right over.'

Alex shook his head in bewilderment; the name meant nothing to him, or to Liz. But Chris Booker was on a high. Convinced by the sheer volume of evidence in Adrian Shawcross's computer, he knew he was on to something. If indeed Casey Taylor had been abducted by someone who wanted her, rather than ransom money, his bet was on this man!

'We have to get those helicopters back out, the moment it's light enough,' he told Alex. 'And I'll get some others in, the coastguards have been alerted, and the Channel shipping. We are doing all we can, believe me!'

'We'll get them out now,' Alex declared, in agitation. No way could he bear to wait until dawn. 'They have night sights don't they?'

Alex paced the floor, for hours it seemed, as news of the search became at once optimistic, then the hope was dashed again when alerts were found to be false. Nick found another company of his film contacts in Southampton and persuaded them to join the sea-search for the dark blue cabin cruiser called *Lady C*. The whole world was looking for Casey it seemed, and he felt so helpless just waiting. Their problem was that it was such a huge area, even Chris admitted that they were in real trouble. They could be anywhere between Chichester and the Channel Islands by then and they really hadn't a clue where to start. One boat frankly looked very much like another from the air, after all.

'Let's face it, he could just be sitting amongst a million other boats in Chichester harbour,' Bruce said. 'Or have slipped up into the Hamble; we'd never find him then. I have to admit he's a tricky one.' Alex came closest to complete despair then.

Unshaven and dishevelled from his second day of the search he was at the end of his tether, yet still coming up with new ways of speeding up the search. He and Nick had co-opted every single company and security firm they knew to supplement the police's considerable resources, not always to their gratitude but still useful in some ways because it gave Alex hope that he was doing something – anything – to help things along.

It was two o'clock in the morning when a coast-guard station reported yet another sighting of a dark blue cruiser seemingly anchored just outside a small Isle of Wight harbour. At first they were cautious but as the light grew stronger the optimism grew with it. A helicopter confirmed that indeed the boat was blue, the right size and though they couldn't read the name yet it certainly seemed more hopeful.

'We might just be onto something,' Bruce said, his voice husky with tiredness after only a couple of hours' snatched sleep. 'I can't promise anything, but I think we might just go out and take a look at this one. I don't want to scare him into a panic, so I might just send a local guy to take a quiet look, though even *that* is pretty dodgy in this weather. There's no one moving at all at the moment.'

'The hell with worrying about a bit of wind! They must go! And I'm coming too,' Alex demanded, leaping up.

'Alex! That's hardly wise!' Nick tried. 'Let the police handle it, it could be nothing after all.'

'But it *could* be Casey! I'm going, Nick! I *have* to

be there, just in case it *is* her. We'll go in the chopper, it can take off from here, surely? The weather isn't too bad for that!' Alex was adamant and Chris recognized immediately that there was no arguing with him. Alex didn't run a major company by giving way to people.

'I *will* take you with me, Alex, once we've decided it's worth a try,' he agreed. 'But on the condition that it's my show! I'm in charge, and what *I* say *goes*!' He, of all of them, recognized the anguish that Alex had gone through in the last forty-eight hours. He had little doubt that Alex would do his own thing, and that if he didn't take him, Alex would find some way to be there. 'I think perhaps you'd better come too, Nick,' he offered. He had come to respect Nick's quiet strength, as they all had, and he knew the strong influence Nick could use to calm Alex, when necessary. They waited an anguished hour while a local unmarked patrol boat slipped out of the harbour and checked the name of the dark-blue boat.

'It's the *Lady C*, all right!' Chris was exultant. 'The daft sod didn't even have the sense to paint the name over! Our lads are keeping him under obs; he won't get away now!'

Within minutes they were in a police helicopter as it battled through the unforgiving wind. It was on the brink of being unflyable but somehow they made it out to the Isle of Wight in one piece. Ironically it was a place where Alex had spent many happy sea-side holidays as a child; now he would never again be able to think of it in a friendly way. Warmly clad in the jerseys and water-proof jackets that Alex kept at the house for use when sailing his own thirty-foot sailing boat, he and Nick craned their necks for a view of the harbour, but wisely the pilot kept well inland as he carefully put the bucketing craft down on a sports field close to the small village. A police car was waiting for the party, backed up by another helicopter carrying a small army it seemed, to an astonished Alex.

'The guy has killed once,' Chris said, chillingly. 'I have armed back-up. This is not going to be easy, Alex. If you really would prefer not to be there I *will* understand.'

'*I'm coming*!' Alex almost shouted. 'If Casey is on that boat, I'm going to be there!' He and Nick were given bullet-proof jackets to wear, increasing the tension of the moment as Chris and Bruce donned theirs too. As the morning light filtered across the sea they boarded a sleek and fast cruiser, and followed by its twin they slipped unnoticed out of the harbour, into the teeth of the wind – and out to Casey's rescue, they hoped and prayed as the boats tossed and manoeuvred through the choppy sea.

CHAPTER 24

Casey woke from her fitful sleep to find Adrian's body still hard and hot against hers, as indeed it had been all night. Her own limbs were an agony of stiffness and pain from the previous punishment he had inflicted and there was little life in her pinioned wrists as she struggled to sit up and drag what was left of her flimsy clothes back down over her body. Only the slightest of movements, yet it woke the light sleeper at her side as she winced with pain. 'The wind seems to have dropped slightly,' Adrian said as he glanced out of the tiny porthole. 'I think we can get under way at last.' It sounded just as bad to Casey and she shuddered, then she looked again at the porthole as Adrian moved across the cabin. She could just see a small cruiser – *and it had people aboard* – it could be her chance at last to attract attention.

'Leave it just a little longer,' she pleaded. 'I'm not a particularly good sailor, Adrian.' Adrian wasn't to know that she was lying, after all.

'Well, we'll have some breakfast first,' he conceded, coming back to the bunk.

'Please, unfasten my wrists, won't you, Adrian?' Casey tried, holding her hands out to him. 'Then I can help you.'

'I don't need help to cook, I told you.' Adrian looked down at her. 'Stay right there, Casey.'

'At least let me get some fresh air,' Casey pleaded. 'I feel as if I've been stuck in here for weeks instead of days; it will help me feel less queasy, I'm sure.'

'Only for a moment.' Adrian was doubtful, then he realized that in this weather there was hardly likely to be anyone else around.

Pulling the sweater down as much as she could as protection against the chilling wind, Casey followed him into the tiny mid-section of the boat that held the steering gear. Her eyes were alert for the boat she had seen and she hadn't been mistaken. It was quite close, and getting closer all the time. However her hands were still fastened in the hand-cuffs as Adrian had declined to remove them; she had no way of attracting the attention of the wickedly fast-looking motor boat and she felt a chill of disappointment as it suddenly veered away. There was nothing she could do except watch it go. Adrian saw it too, through narrowed suspicious eyes, and he turned suddenly to try and push her back into the cabin.

She turned back on him, with the frustrating thought of help being so close to hand and leaving her in Adrian's clutches again. She had no hands to help her but she had legs, and she used them, kicking out suddenly and strongly, screaming out as she had never screamed in her life for the boat to come back and help her. Cursing and swearing, Adrian launched himself at her, doing his utmost to hurl her back down into the cabin, but Casey forestalled him, slamming the door shut with her foot as she sent him sprawling again.

'Help me! Oh help me!' she screamed anew at the boat, and it was turning, coming back to them, men on the deck were waving to her and suddenly she heard the blissful reassurance of a voice over a loud-hailer. '*This is the police! Surrender Casey to us — right now!*'

Adrian recovered his feet and his wits at the same moment and the gun she had thought to be back in the cabin was suddenly in his hands. Casey heard the sickening click of the safety catch being taken off. 'He's got a gun!' she screamed at the policemen, only a few yards away she thought, knowing they were in the same danger as she was. The boat was still tipping about badly, so much so that it was difficult to keep her feet but somehow she clung on to the flimsy rail as Adrian tried to haul her away, back against him to use her as a shield.

'I won't give her up!' he shouted in frenzy. 'I'd rather die first!'

'Don't be a crazy fool!' Chris Booker stepped forward on the deck of the power boat they had requisitioned. 'Let her go, *now*!'

The gun was at Casey's neck as he bent her forward and her head was at an almost impossible angle as she struggled to get away from him yet still clinging to the rail as a life-line. If he got her below decks she knew frantically that she would have no chance. He would harm her, she was sure; however much he declared his love for her, he wouldn't allow Alex to have her back. His hand was twisting her arm until she was in absolute agony and she screamed in pain, she couldn't help it. It was too much for Alex to stand back and watch; he moved forward instinctively and she finally saw him, screaming his name in her agony and relief as she recognized the tall dark man whose cry of anguish splintered the air, echoing over the wind and lashing rain.

'*You'll never have her!*' Adrian recognized him too, and it was all too much for him. With a howl of fury, he pushed at Casey, and in that split second she took her chance and kicked out backwards, and devastatingly – upwards. His legs were braced against the rocking of the boat and slightly apart. With a force she hardly knew she had, her heel caught him between his spread legs and with a howl of agony he buckled and slumped to the deck. It was her only chance and she had no time to think about what she was doing – all she wanted was to get away from Adrian and back to Alex. She drew a deep breath and simply jumped. One swing was enough to hurl herself over the rail into the swirling, heaving water. Sobbing with pain, Adrian rolled momentarily back behind the shelter of his wheel-house as Casey tumbled head-first into the black icy cold water. Her head went under and she felt herself sinking down and realized that without her hands to save herself she was in real trouble. Her mouth and lungs filled with icy sea-water as she plunged down helplessly, kicking out wildly to try and limit the distance, but inevitably, panic set in almost immediately.

Alex didn't hesitate. Throwing off his shoes, and the heavy protection he had only half-fastened – unknown to Chris – he simply leapt into the heaving sea, to strike out towards the spot where Casey had disappeared. Several of the policemen followed him but he was precious seconds ahead of them. In moments, his frantic hands had caught at the fabric of her sweater and, fighting for breath, he dragged her upwards towards the precious air she was gasping for. They broke the surface, their lungs bursting with the need for air and Adrian saw them first.

'*NO!*' He shrieked his protest out into the wind and levelled the pistol at the two battling with the waves as the water swept them away from the two boats that were closing in on him. At first, Alex barely felt the bullets entering his shoulder, and then his upper back, as he fought to get a firm hold on Casey as she slipped in his grasp. It seemed an age before the realization of the new danger hit them both, as Alex suddenly weakened, and as other swimmers closed around them, Casey became aware of other shots and Alex's grip slackening.

'Casey!' He groaned in her ear, as her pinioned hands gripped in panic at his sweater, while he fought to keep her against him. 'I've got you!' he assured her, fighting the new sensation of pain and nausea in his body as he numbly realized something was amiss. With all his remaining efforts he kicked out, using the phenomenal strength in his legs to drag her towards the dinghy being launched from the rear of the cruiser, as shots resounded all round them.

'*I want the bastard alive!*' she heard Chris roar out, his own gun poised and ready as Adrian disappeared into the cabin of the boat. But at that moment her only concern was Alex as she felt the heat of his blood welling out of him against her back, while despite the pain, and barely conscious, he still gripped her ferociously, doggedly keeping her afloat until the men reached them, battling in the swell.

'He's hit!' she cried as Bruce Johnson reached her to take her as gently as he could from a rapidly weakening Alex. 'He's bleeding! Oh, please help him!'

'I've got you both!' Bruce gripped Casey with one hand and grabbed at Alex with the other, before another swimmer took Casey and dragged her up onto the deck of the power boat away from Alex.

'Alex!' Forgetting her own desperate state, Casey turned back to Bruce, as he carefully lifted Alex into the dinghy on the blind side of Adrian's boat with the help of the two men in it. Alex was unconscious and bleeding ferociously by the time they achieved it and Casey was frantic, beating at the hands that tried to peel her away from the rail and her only contact with him.

'Casey, let them handle him! They know what they're doing,' someone pleaded, and Casey reeled back as she realized in shock that it was Nick Grey who was holding her in his arms.

'Nick!' She fell against him and sobbed out her anguish into his jacket. 'Alex! He's hurt! He shot him!'

'There's a doctor on board,' Nick soothed her. 'Let him do what he needs to do, Casey. We need to look after you for a while.' He carried her down into the blissful warmth of the cabin and handed her over to the ministrations of a young policewoman. Mindlessly, Casey allowed them to cut the handcuffs off her numb wrists before she was undressed and dried to be wrapped in someone's dry clothing, a track suit and thick woolly sweater before she came back to life and began screaming for Alex.

Nick joined her and wrapped an arm round her. 'They've taken him off by helicopter,' he said. 'He'll be at the hospital by now. Don't worry, Casey. He'll be fine, they are doing everything they can.' He sounded the epitome of reassurance but the brief glimpse he had had of Alex before the helicopter had whisked him away had been far from encouraging. However, he was the only familiar anchor Casey had amongst total strangers, after an ordeal that would have floored most women, and he drew on his considerable reserves of optimism to buoy her up for the new nightmare she had been plunged into.

The boat they were on had been ordered back to the harbour, to get Casey away from any recurring danger. Adrian was still holed up in the cabin of *Lady C* and Chris Booker wanted her well away. He was determined that Adrian Shawcross was going to come out alive to face the punishment his actions surely deserved. With a gritty resolve, he was going to stick it out to the bitter end, now he knew Casey was safe, though Alex was another matter. He cursed the fact that Alex had stripped off the bulky flak jacket, but he understood why. It had been the action of a man saving the woman he loved, above all else. He threw a quick prayer up for him and began to concentrate again on the evil piece of slime who had brought about the whole distressing episode. '*I'll get him*,' he muttered as he strode to the rail again. '*I'll get him if it's the last thing I do!*'

By the time Casey and Nick made it to the hospital in Southampton Alex had been away whisked into the operating theatre. Casey refused any help for herself, clinging resolutely to Nick and Bruce Johnson as they waited for news in a small office put at their disposal. 'Casey, at least let them check you over,' Nick asked, finally, as he detected a definite slackening of Casey's strength.

'No! Not until I *know* Alex is safe!' Casey was mutinous, her mouth set in a firm line of dissent. It was an attitude Nick knew only too well from Sarah and he sighed.

'Casey!' He gripped her arm tightly. 'Alex wouldn't like to think that after all you've gone through you weren't getting the treatment you need. Please, let the doctor look at you, and let her decide if you're OK or not!'

Reluctantly, Casey let the doctor check her out and at Nick's instigation she was finally put to bed in a little room on her own. Her ribs were still very sore, but to her relief were not broken as she had thought they might be. She was given a shot of something to make her sleep, much against her better judgement, but with the promise from Nick that he would wait, and come to her the moment he knew what was happening to Alex. In a haze of the drug and sheer exhaustion she slept, guarded throughout by the young policewoman, though she knew nothing of it, until she woke in the late afternoon.

'Alex?' was the first word that came from her parched mouth.

'He's OK, Casey.' Nick was still there, as he had promised. 'You can go and see him quite soon.' She gave them no peace until she could get dressed, in the clothes that Liz had brought to the hospital, and Nick took her up to the Intensive Care Unit where Alex was being treated. Casey quailed at the terrifying equipment that surrounded him as he lay on the high bed. He was as white as the sheet that covered him from the waist down; but his normally tanned skin had a distinctly grey tinge where it wasn't covered with the huge white dressings. She stared in horror at the tubes and wires attached to him, even breathing for him.

His mother was sitting beside him, his limp hand clutched in hers, but when she saw Casey, she got up and went to give her a reassuring hug. 'It looks worse than it is, Casey,' she said, gently as Casey's features convulsed with shock. 'They've given him something for the pain, so he's pretty woozy, but he's going to be fine, they promised me.' Alex had been in deep shock, and had lost a great deal of blood during the journey to the hospital so it had been touch and go at times during the long night she had endured at her son's bedside. But she knew just how much Casey herself had gone through, and her main thought was for her at that moment, now she knew Alex was safe.

Casey slid into the chair she had vacated, knowing that her weak legs wouldn't hold her up much longer and clutched at Alex's seemingly lifeless hand spread on the sheet. To her delight, he seemed to know immediately that she was there. For a moment he opened pain-hazed eyes and looked at her, with such love that her heart couldn't take it. She simply burst into tears of relief. They fell onto his hand and then onto his chest as she bent over him, and he felt them dampen his skin.

'Don't cry, baby,' he whispered, agonizingly slowly. 'I need you . . . don't go?'

'I'm not going anywhere!' Casey declared, firmly. 'I'm staying right here!'

And stay there she did. Nothing and no one could

move her. Mary came and sat with her for a while, to tell her that John was recovering in a ward downstairs, and later both Chris and Bruce stopped by to check on them. 'In your own time, Casey,' Chris told her. 'I need to talk to you, as you obviously know, but it can wait a little while.'

'That man . . .' Casey shuddered. 'Have you . . .?'

'We have him in custody,' Chris said, grimly. 'He put up quite a fight but we got him in the end. He's inside for life, Casey. Have no doubt about that, he'll never bother you again.'

'I'll never forgive him for what he's done to Alex! Never!' Chris stared at her. Adrian Shawcross had put the girl in front of him through two days and nights of torment, but her only thoughts and desire for vengeance were because Alex Havilland had been hurt.

'You must love Alex very much,' he said, softly.

'I do, Chris,' Casey said, simply. 'He's my entire world. If anything had happened to him – I couldn't live.'

She had thought Alex was asleep, but as Chris withdrew, Alex opened his eyes. They were almost his normal colour, dark and sharply focusing at last. 'I never thought I'd hear you say that,' he murmured, still finding it difficult to talk, several days after the long and complicated surgery that had saved his life. The bullet that had done the most damage had managed to bypass vital organs but there was still a great deal of damage that needed time to repair and he was desperately weak from the enormous loss of blood.

'I meant it, Alex.' Casey leant her face blissfully against his hand, only too happy to hear him talk after watching him lie in a sedated state for hours. 'I meant every word of it, and I'll never stop telling you from now on. I adore you! On that boat I thought I'd never get to see you again or tell you the truth about how much I love you, and I regretted that so much.'

'I shall keep on making you tell me, for the rest of our lives,' Alex whispered, gripping her hand. It was the only movement he was capable of at that moment. 'Oh damn these wretched drips! I want to hold you!'

'Patience, darling,' Casey smiled at his impotent fury. 'For once you *have* to behave, *and* do as you're told! It will do you good.'

'The only thing that will do me good is holding you in my arms,' he told her, grimly.

'That can be arranged – and soon – if you promise to behave!' Casey laid her cheek against his good shoulder and pressed her lips to the warm flesh. 'Get some rest, Alex, I'll be here.'

He was peaceful when she was there, and restless when she wasn't. With great difficulty, Nick finally persuaded her to get some rest herself, while Alex's mother or Penny took over and then Casey found she had to relive the whole distressing abduction when Chris needed to interview her at length, and she couldn't put it off any longer.

But it was with Alex that she had the greatest difficulty in talking about the past few days. Even as

Alex gradually recovered enough to be moved to a room of his own and then was allowed out of bed for an hour or two each day, she found she couldn't tell him even any small detail of what had happened on the boat with Adrian. It made her feel all the more guilty, and yet even when Chris, and the therapist he called in to help when he talked to her, assured her that it wasn't her fault, she still felt the most enormous remorse over eveything. She sent the therapist away. Alex had been hurt, and it was her fault, she knew it, and nothing any of them could say would refute that fact. Even Alex himself couldn't get through to her. He felt his own regret that he had ignored Chris's advice and cast off the bullet-proof vest, but at least he freely admitted that it had been down to him, and no one else.

Over the weeks that followed he learnt a little from Chris and Bruce about what had happened but Casey had seemingly cut the whole event from her mind. Alex worried, but Chris Booker, their self-appointed guardian, told him not to. 'You have to concentrate on getting well,' he told him. 'Let Casey go back to work, and deal with it in her own way. She's tough, seemingly she has her own way to deal with it, she'll get through it, one way or another.'

It didn't help that the Press dogged her every footstep, to the point that both Alex and Nick worried about her, and Chris Booker finally found an ex-policewoman to act as bodyguard after things got completely out of hand in a frenzied chase from location back to Alex's home. Moira was a big and briskly friendly woman, and a great comfort once Casey got used to having her around, acting as surrogate mother, secretary and dresser all in one. The BBC unit she was working with teased her endlessly about her 'minder', but Moira took it all in good part, threatening to take them all on if they didn't stop. They were all a bit too daunted to try though – much to Casey's amusement! At least, she thought with relief, when they were teasing her about Moira they forgot to treat her like some sort of invalid, as they were inclined to do a lot of the time. She hated that more than anything, and for the first time in her life she longed for a filming stint to be over, so that she could simply stay at home and care for Alex.

She had quickly got into the routine of living in Edwardes Square and adored the loyal Joan and William as they soon did her. It was bliss to be able to run round the corner to Kensington High Street if she wanted to shop, even if she had to wait for Moira to go with her. After just one disastrous foray she had realized the wisdom of having her escort, when she had tried to walk the dog in Kensington Gardens on her own.

Alex loathed the enforced idleness that his weak state dictated once he was allowed out of hospital and back home into Joan's care. It was a boring and frustrating time for a normally busy man. The new house was full of decorators, and no way could they move in yet, since he insisted he wanted it to be perfect for Casey. But at least consulting with the decorating company kept his active mind occupied for a short while, Casey thought in desperation after yet another spat over his fury at his inactivity. He could barely manage a full day out of bed for weeks, as he fought his way back to a semblance of normal health. When Casey finally snapped, and proposed that he stopped fretting, and went back into the office for an hour or two a day, he was delighted at first, until trying it sapped his precarious energy to the point where even he had to admit defeat. After that he listened, and Mary-Jo came to the house for a few hours a day instead. At least when Mary-Jo was there, Casey felt a little more relaxed about going back to work.

Everyone around her seemed to consider her as much an invalid as Alex was, she grumbled to Sarah on their frequent visits to the Greys' home. Sarah wisely advised her to bide her time. 'They'll all get over it – as you will. Then things will all get back to normal.' she said, quietly. 'And the Press will leave you both alone sooner or later. They always do, when the next scandal breaks.' Weeks before there had been Press stories about her, simply because of the enormous publicity over the Keara ads, but Casey had been horrified by the enormous additional amount of coverage over the Adrian affair, even though most of the actual details had been kept from them. However, there was still endless speculation, and she knew only too well from a worried Chris that worse would follow when Adrian Shaw-cross finally came to trial. It had hurt her, and then infuriated her, when old and seemingly trusted friends had made hard cash from selling their stories about her to the papers. Even Colin Cooper had been run to ground and his tales of being infatuated with her had been plastered all over the front of one of the most lurid of the Sunday tabloids. '*I loved her and she ditched me!*' he had declared. It was a total fabrication, but Casey had read it before Alex could get to it, and she wept uncontrollably in his sympathetic arms at Colin's betrayal.

It was the closest they had been for many weeks, Casey was far too guilty about his injuries to attempt to get close to him. They spent hours together now she was in his house permanently. She had been given no chance to object to the move, much as she felt it was the wrong thing to do. Liz had given up the flat because of Casey's expected marriage, and anyway longed for the chance to move in with Robin, so Casey had no excuse on that score.

In some ways she loved being with Alex on a permanent-basis. They walked Griff in the park once he was able to, and played chess and backgammon on lazy afternoons when the weather dictated otherwise, slowly getting to know each other in a way they never had. She was endlessly solicitous as to his well-being, but reluctant to even try and make love, for fear, she declared, untruthfully, of exacerbating his still far from healed wound. Her fear stemmed far more from guilt than anything else but no way could she tell Alex that, however hard she tried over the weeks. Everything simply choked up inside her as she silently struggled to come to terms with all that had happened to her on the boat. In vain, Alex protested that the rest of his body worked perfectly but he recognized her fear and though it hurt, he wisely left it alone; accepting her careful embraces and knowing inside that she only had his best interests at heart. Casey always rushed home to him each evening after working, to be with him, knowing how bored he was when she wasn't there, but inevitably, they were in a sexual limbo, and as the weeks passed Alex grew more and more restive and anxious about her.

'I don't really understand what the problem is,' he groaned to Sarah on a visit to his half-finished Richmond house. 'She won't let me near her any more!'

They had settled in the partly furnished conservatory that he had had built and in the soft December sunshine Sarah unpacked the lunch she had brought from her own house.

'Alex!' she stopped what she was doing and came to drop into the white wicker chair next to his. 'What you have to remember is that Casey went through one hell of a trauma in those few days! She's bound to react to it.'

'Yes, I know.' Alex lifted Abby onto his lap, twirling her dark curls in his fingers, lovingly. 'But she won't give herself a chance to heal. She won't talk about it. She won't open up about it at all, and Chris can't – or won't – tell me what happened.'

'She *will* tell you – in time. After all, would *you* relish telling *her* something like that if it had happened to you?' Sarah looked sympathetically at him. 'But when that man comes to trial she'll have to say something. Has she tried therapy? They usually offer it to victims after that kind of event, don't they?'

'It's been offered. I said I'd pay for as much as she needed, but she won't hear of it,' Alex sighed. 'I can't get her to discuss anything, not even the wedding.'

'She's quite probably terrified that the same thing could happen again,' Sarah said, wisely. 'Surely you can understand that?'

'Of course I can! And don't you think I haven't tried to tell her? I don't care what she did on that boat – if anything!' Alex shifted in his chair awkwardly trying to shift Abby's weight into a more comfortable position for his arm. 'Sarah, I just want to be *married* to her! I think it would be the best thing for both of us, to get our lives back together, but it's as if she doesn't trust me any more.'

'Then we shall just have to do something about it!' Sarah grinned at him.

'Something about what?' Unheard by them, Nick had joined them, his soft loafers disguising his footsteps.

'Nick, this is serious!' Sarah smiled up at him as he bent to kiss her then lifted Abby from Alex's lap to kiss her. 'Alex is worried sick about Casey.'

Nick opened the wine bottle that Sarah had abandoned and poured it into the glasses she *had* managed to set out. 'Casey is very traumatized from the kidnapping,' he said quietly. 'And she will be for a while yet.'

'I can't get near her,' Alex said, 'And she goes into a blue funk every time I mention getting married.'

'But she loves you desperately,' Nick said. 'Any fool can see that! Just give her time, Alex. She's happy enough, living with you, isn't she?'

'I gave her no choice on that matter!' Alex replied with a grin. 'Lizzie moving in with Robin was a godsend, and with the Press on top of us it was the only solution. Even Casey could see that.'

Sarah went to finish unpacking at Nick's instigation and laid the rest of lunch out on the table. 'Alex?' She turned back, casually. 'Do Clare and Julian still live next door to you in Barbados?'

Puzzled, Alex nodded. 'Yes, but . . . why?'

'Well, it just occurred to me.' Sarah grinned, wickedly. 'If Casey needs a little nudge, well, I'm not too busy at the moment, and . . . well maybe there *is* something I can do to help things along a bit. But I would need Clare's help, and Liz's of course!'

'*Sarah*?' Nick and Alex spoke warningly in unison. They both knew Sarah's schemes of old! She was a practised match-maker, amongst other bright ideas.

'Don't you "*Sarah*" me like a pair of elderly

school teachers!' Sarah grinned unabashed at them. 'I've got a great idea, and *you* two are going to sit down and listen to it, *before* you start moaning!'

CHAPTER 25

Casey took a great deal of persuading that Barbados was a good place for them to go to for Alex to convalesce. Too far from his doctors, she objected, until finally he argued that he now had a clean bill of health from them, and that he was going, come what may. 'I need warmth and sun,' he declared. 'And a few weeks of Dora's cooking wouldn't come amiss, either!'

'Well, if you really are hell-bent on it?' Casey finally gave in.

'I most certainly am! And *you* are coming, like it or not!' He only just managed to refrain from threatening to make her go by force. It was a silly statement, but it had so almost jeopardized the whole exercise and he cursed himself, yet he prayed so often during the few days before they went that soon things would be back to normal for both of them.

He was exhausted by the time they landed on the island, and it was Casey who drove out to the villa this time, revelling in the freedom of the roads, empty of traffic at that time of the evening. She packed him off to bed, alone, almost the minute they arrived at the house, and took the opportunity while Alex's back was turned to make sure Dora knew exactly what Alex was allowed to do and not to do. Dora beamed. 'Bless you, Miss Casey,' she cried. 'I'll take care of him, never fear. He's in safe hands here.'

'Bossy witch!' Alex declared next day, and proceeded to do exactly as he pleased. Dora cooked them endless huge meals and fussed over them both, until even Casey began to relax and unwind. They lay by the pool and picnicked together on empty beaches, while daily, Alex grew stronger, and his skin, paled from illness, turned brown again in the sun. She learnt to handle the catamaran single-handed, since even Alex knew that was forbidden for a while, and finally entertained several neighbours for dinner with style and confidence.

It seemed no time at all before it was Christmas Eve. A beautifully warm, Christmas Eve, and Alex suggested they took a drive out to a beach on the Eastern side of the island. 'It'll be too rough for even you to swim, but I'm bored with the west coast,' he declared and simply loaded Dora's huge picnic into the Range Rover.

Casey was too relaxed to argue with him and even let him take the wheel. Alex's strength really had improved by leaps and bounds in the three weeks they had been on the island. Almost daily, she had watched the transformation from sick man to an energetic, dominant personality again, and her loving heart rejoiced at the sight.

Today, he seemed overjoyed to be alive. Laughing and teasing as he drove to his chosen beach, finally carrying the basket himself instead of letting her help him as she had been used to doing. They found a completely deserted beach washed by the frothy Atlantic waves, and settled happily in the shade of the over-hanging cliff to eat their picnic and lie together on the plaid blanket after it in complete harmony.

'I love you,' Alex murmured as Casey stretched in luxurious indolence.

'I do you,' Casey smiled and reached over to touch his bare shoulders, and then to run her fingers over the soft hairs of his chest. Very slowly, as if in a dream, Alex drew her into his arms and held her gently, seemingly for hours, until she finally fell asleep cuddled against him. It was pure luxury to feel her so relaxed after the trauma of his injuries had driven her away from him. Even here on the island, Casey had elected to sleep separately from him, in case, she said, she accidentally hurt him in the night. Alex had allowed it, simply because he had realized the reason for it, but it hurt him desperately that she still felt that way, almost three months since the shooting.

When she woke it was late afternoon and she smiled up sleepily, as Alex grinned down at her. 'I think it's about time we went,' he said, softly. 'Or Dora will start to get worried about us!' She was surprisingly reluctant to move and Alex leant over her for precious seconds to kiss her, before he finally, and regretfully, decided they *had* to move. A local family were on their way down the cliff path and very soon there would be very little privacy. 'Maybe it *is* time we went home, for something far more pleasant than supper,' he grinned at her. 'I feel fine today!' He drew her hand down between their bodies, leaving her in no doubt at all as to his fitness to carry out his threat, and Casey laughed with pleasure.

'Maybe, Alex,' she demurred.

'There's no maybe about it, my love,' Alex told her. 'I've had quite enough of being told I'm not yet fit! I give you due notice. From now on, it's business as usual!'

He drove back briskly, and Casey sat quietly beside him, her head in turmoil. Alex had declared his intentions, and to all intents and purposes his time in the villa had healed his physical wounds – but had it healed hers? She still had nightmares about Adrian touching her, waking almost every night in a cold sweat and shaking with fear. No way could she let Alex see that, she still needed time to get over that. Alex wanted her back in his bed, she knew, and deep inside her she wanted him too, but how could she face him when she knew her dreams were still filled with the cold reality of someone else torturing her?

But this afternoon Alex was so happy and cheerful that she knew that time was up. Tonight, she would spend the night in his bed, she decided, even as they drove back through the wrought iron gates of the villa. Maybe even before dinner? She had a good idea of what Alex had in mind! But she got a shock. Instead of guiding her to the room he used and that on their previous visit she had shared with him, Alex took her arm firmly and led her to one of the guest rooms.

'I have a surprise for you,' he announced as he opened the door. To her astonishment both Liz and Sarah stood in front of her and both grinning like lunatics at her surprised face. Alex swung her into his arms and kissed her thoroughly. 'In *exactly* one hour's time, *we* are getting married! Here in the house, it's all arranged! All you have to do is get dressed, darling. No cars, no journey of any description – and *definitely* nothing to worry about!' Gently, he propelled her towards Liz and Sarah and went off to shower and change himself, confident that the two girls would handle it.

Casey didn't know whether to laugh or cry. 'I don't believe it!' she gasped, eventually.

'You'd better!' Sarah threatened. 'It's taken me weeks to organize this! Now get into that bath, Casey! You're covered in sand and we really do only have an hour!'

'But I can't get married just like that!' Casey wailed. 'I need a dress – everything!'

'All sorted!' Sarah laughed. 'Marco made you a new one, and don't fret, it's completely different from the other one, deliberately so! We even thought of these!' With a flourish she produced embroidered shoes similar to those that Casey had been wearing that fateful day. 'Only they aren't quite the same,' she comforted. 'Marco had a friend copy them, and this time they have a special emblem on them. Look, Cinderella!' In the centre of the toe was embroidered a tiny mouse, and a pumpkin!

Numbly, Casey went to soak briefly in the bath they had waiting for her. Liz perched on the edge and handed her a glass of champagne 'to get her in the mood' and filled her in on the outfit they had organized for her. She would, infuriatingly, tell her nothing about the planned wedding except that it was all set up, simply that she had to hurry to keep them all to schedule. The three girls were all professionals, and a make-up and hairstyle presented them with no real problems. Sarah knew exactly what she wanted to do and Casey let her organize eveything in dumb resignation. She could, she discovered, be as forthright as Alex, given the opportunity!

By the time Alex reappeared, Casey was ready, and both Sarah and Liz melted away at his appearance, to dress themselves, so Sarah said. Alex, casual in an open-necked cream silk shirt and cream linen trousers, looked dazzlingly healthy to her and he smiled with pleasure at her own appearance. The silk dress was composed of many layers of softly coloured chiffon, varying from pale blue through lilac to white as it floated around her, and totally different from the first one, deliberately so, as Sarah had said. Made slightly A-line so that fittings were unnecessary, it was astonishingly comfortable to wear and Sarah had added a pretty circlet of flowers that she had created herself from garden blooms that afternoon, thus thoughtfully doing away with the need for a veil that Casey had dreaded.

Alex gently turned her so that he could see all of her and smiled as he did so. 'I have something else for you,' he said softly, and produced a gleaming string of pearls to carefully slip them around her neck. 'I knew you wouldn't want to wear those earrings again,' he said. 'So these are to wear instead.' He stepped back to admire her, as if he couldn't bear to take his eyes off her and then he reached for her hand. 'Shall we go and get married, my darling?'

Laughing with delight at her surprise, he led her down the wide staircase and through the hall into the loggia. There were no cars and no parting from him this time, as he had promised. Alex walked with his arm around her in a warmly protective gesture all the way. To her astonishment the loggia had all been rearranged during the day, and an awning now covered the swimming pool outside it, as protection from the night-time insects.

The entire loggia was full of scented white flowers, on tall pedestals and entwined around the columns, and dozens of candles lit the evening air. Small gilt chairs were arranged in rows where the normal wicker furniture usually stood and the beaming local minister in full regalia stood in front of a white cloth-covered altar. An extravagantly hatted Dora sat at a harmonium, with an ear-to-ear smile, and at a nod from the minister she launched into an astonishingly accurate wedding march. Staring round, Casey realized that everyone she would ever have invited was there. Her aunt and uncle, Alex's entire family, Robin, Joan, William, and even Moira, and Chris Booker and his wife were smiling at her from their place near the front, as Abby attempted to be the perfect flower girl and totally misjudged it, up-ending the entire basket over their feet, to her brother's lofty disgust, and Sarah's complete hysterics. Gripping Alex's hand, almost like life-support, Casey found herself being led between the rows of their beaming friends and relations to stand at the altar beside him, as Nick stepped forward to fulfil the role he had been expected to play at their first wedding.

The Reverend Sebastian Makepiece believed in the traditional prayer book service, and to *both* their astonishment, and their friends' great amusement, Casey found herself not only promising to love and honour, but also to obey! He boomed out the service, savouring every minute of it, and using every possible intonation to emphasize the full meaning of the words. By the end, it wasn't only Alex's mother who wept, there were tears in many eyes and certainly Alex himself had tears in his own as he hugged Casey to him afterwards. 'You may kiss the bride' had no place in the Reverend Sebastian's traditional service, but Alex did it anyway, nothing would have stopped him! There was no one else in the world apart from them at that moment as he held Casey in his arms briefly, before they were swept into the centre of the party.

It had to be the most perfect wedding, thought Casey dreamily as she finally took in all the incredible organization Sarah and Liz had done with Clare Sanderson's help. No wonder they had both been suddenly and mysteriously unavailable the last few weeks before she and Alex had left for Barbados. They had both been out here, she realized, looking after things for her. And Alex had kept the whole thing quietly to himself! Even today on the beach, planning that to the last detail simply to keep her out of the house. But all she could do was smile and know that despite her strong fears she was finally his wife. And she had promised to obey him too! Alex certainly wouldn't let her forget that in a hurry!

Deliberately, very little mention was made of their previous attempt to marry, either in the hilarious speeches both Alex and Nick made, or in the general conversation around them. It was as if no one wanted to break the happy spell that had been woven around them. Alex, it appeared, had organized that all their guests were staying at local hotels or with his many friends around the island – no mean feat at Christmas time! Only his brothers, and Nick and Sarah, were staying in the house, his parents had as many friends in the area as he had, and had made their own arrangements. So it was a surprise to Casey when Alex suggested she said goodbye to her aunt and uncle, almost the moment her special fireworks had been exploded over the bay in a glorious tribute of colour. 'Aren't we staying here?' she queried, as he took her hand.

'*No way!*' Alex grinned. 'I don't trust Robin – or my brothers – not one bit! Our room here is probably bugged knowing them. *We* are off!'

They roared away down the drive in a Range Rover festooned with flowers and tin cans. Casey hoped fervently that they weren't going far with the car in that state, and Alex soon granted her wish as he pulled off the road onto a narrow track. She knew it led to the sea but she gave a gasp of delight when he finally pulled up by a tiny beach house, perched above the palm-fringed silver beach. It was the most perfect and romantic spot in the world, she thought as he helped her out. The only concession he made to his health was regretting that he couldn't carry her over the threshold, but he had made up for it in every other way in the thoughtful preparations he had made.

'And these bits of the arrangements were mine alone,' he told her solemnly as he poured more champagne. 'Although the house itself belongs to Clare and Julian.' Casey looked around the candlelit room in delight. All it held was a muslin-draped bed, mosquito netting so that the windows could be opened to the night breeze, and the only lighting source was the candles Alex had lit as they had entered.

He opened the French windows and drew her out

onto the balcony where cane chairs had been left out for them. In no hurry, since they had as much time as they needed after all, Alex leant on the rail, idly contemplating the moonlit beach, and smiled. 'That walk on the beach is *still* my most precious memory of you,' he said.

Casey joined him and he slid an arm around her. 'No beach walk tonight,' she laughed. 'I love this dress too much to even try and risk it! Who designed it? Apart from Marco?'

'I . . . sort of did,' he admitted. 'It was how I dreamed you might look, and you looked exactly as I'd hoped – so very beautiful, darling.'

'It was a perfect wedding,' Casey sighed. 'Far better for being a surprise, I was getting into such a state about it.'

'Sarah was a brick!' Alex commented. 'Goodness knows how she found the time to come charging over here, with the new film coming up, but she did. We must certainly make sure she's asked to be godmother to at least one of our children!'

'Children!' Casey shivered. 'Alex – I need time for that one.'

'No, you don't!' Alex turned her to face him. 'I agree you have Nick's film, but after that, well, we have no real excuse, do we? I thought you were in agreement on that one?'

'I am – of course I am.' Casey gulped wildly at her wine for courage. 'It's just . . .'

'You're still worried about damaging my shoulder again, aren't you?' he accused. 'Casey, there's no need to worry any more. They're healed, my shoulder *and* my back. I'm quite fit again, and I want to make love to you, more than anything!'

'Yes, I know, and Alex – I want you too, I'm not so much afraid of that.'

'Then what *is* worrying you?' he demanded. 'Casey? Casey, you don't have to tell me if you don't want to . . . but . . . did that guy rape you? Is that the real problem?'

Slowly, Casey turned back into the bedroom and went to sit on the edge of the wide canopied bed. 'Alex . . .' He followed her and sat down beside her, his hands gentle on her bare shoulders as he turned her towards him. With a moan, Casey fell against him and began to cry agonized tears into his shirt. 'I – I felt so *dirty*, after I'd been all that time with . . . that man! After what I let him do to me. Oh – I talked him out of actually raping me – God knows how! But I let him touch me – I couldn't stop him – it seemed the easiest way to deal with him. But . . . I still feel so guilty about you,' she finally confessed, tearfully. 'You went through so much pain all because of me, and I let you down!'

'For heaven's sake, Casey!' Alex shook her in frustration. 'What happened to me was my own stupid fault, and no one else's! *I* took the flak jacket off, when I shouldn't have done! I was so sure of myself, and I made one hell of a mistake. I thought I was immune and I soon found I wasn't. I've learnt my lesson on that score. Chris gave me hell about it once he could argue with me, believe me! And I deserved it! I'll *never* be so arrogant again, that I promise you.'

'But you did it to save me,' she protested. 'You still went through all that just for me.'

'And I'd have gone through far worse, frankly!' Very carefully, he lifted the fading flowers from her hair. '*You* are my world, Casey,' he said, softly. 'My whole world. You're everything I will ever need.'

'Even after that man?' Casey shivered as she emembered the torture she had endured at Adrian's hands.

'Darling, he's *nothing*, not any more.' He kissed her, gently pushing her back until she was lying on the lacy pillows. 'I *know* you don't want to talk about those two days, and I respect that. I will listen, *when* you are ready, but until then, it doesn't *matter* to me what happened! Whatever you did, it was to stay alive and that is the most important thing of all! All I want to know is that you are here with me, and we're married, as we planned to be!' He ran his fingers over the gold ring he'd placed on her finger earlier, and she trembled at his light touch.

This was a moment they had not expected to see and they both realized it at the same time. At that point all she wanted to do was wrap herself around him as she had done on the beach that afternoon and with a sigh she did so, revelling suddenly in the warmth in his dark eyes as he began to unfasten the dozens of tiny buttons on the back of her dress. He undressed them both in a leisurely way, taking all the fear away, stroking and kissing every step of the

way until she was almost begging him to hurry –
'Please hurry, Alex!'

Alex wanted to keep it slow and easy but suddenly
he couldn't. The months of waiting and wanting
convulsed together in a whirl of need and with an
anguished cry he slid into her, hearing her cry out
too as he did so. For a moment then he was still,
looking down at her closed eyelids. 'Open your eyes,
Casey,' he ordered, sensually. 'Open them and look
at me!' Nervously, she did so, meeting the deep,
dark depths of his brown eyes and seeing the love
and need in them. 'I adore you, wife!' he added,
pressing a kiss onto the tip of her nose. 'And boy,
have I missed doing this!'

At first she slept, a deep contented sleep and Alex
watched over her for an age with a feeling of
complete peace with the world. He was almost
asleep himself when Casey woke, jerking upwards
with a harsh scream of pain. Her skin was damp and
clammy to his hasty touch when he grabbed at her in
alarm, convinced that their hideaway was being
invaded by his brothers at least – Alex's own
nightmare!

'Darling! *What is it?*' He pulled her into his arms
and felt her shaking with fright. Casey began to
wake up and cursed to herself. The nightmare of the
last few months was all too real; every time it
happened she prayed it would be the last time,
and it never was.

'Just a bad dream,' she whispered, wrapping her

arms around his neck for comfort. 'It's OK, Alex. Go back to sleep. They happen from time to time.'

'Only since October, though, am I right?' Alex replied. 'You've certainly never had a nightmare like that before, not when I was around, anyway.'

'I suppose so,' Casey allowed, as she shuddered at the memory the dreams recalled. 'Oh, Alex! Will I ever forget about him?'

'Yes, eventually,' Alex comforted, stroking her hair, gently. 'Once the trial is over – if he doesn't plead guilty, that is.'

'I can't bear the thought of it!' she confessed. 'Everyone knowing all those horrible things about me!'

'No one will judge you, Casey. Least of all me, I promise you! Look, it's almost dawn, shall I make some tea or something? Let *me* look after *you* for once, after all, *you've* been cosseting *me* for months.'

'*Is* there such a mundane thing as tea here?' Casey sat up, as he slipped from the tangled bed and put on a dressing gown to combat the chillier morning air.

'Naturally! I know your weaknesses by now.' He busied himself with the tray that had been supplied, and was quickly putting a cup of tea into her hands. Casey smiled at his solicitude and leant back against the pillows to drink it. How could she ever have thought Alexander Havilland was cold and rude? she wondered in astonishment.

'How civilized we are,' she commented. 'And on our wedding night too!'

'Only for a moment!' he promised her, and got

382

back into bed. For a while they leant against each other in a companionable silence, and then slowly – so very slowly – Casey began to talk about the two days of her life that had given her nightmares for all the months since. Alex listened, in complete silence, hiding the horror that welled up at the revelations of what she had endured at Adrian's hands. Once she started, it all began to spill out and she held nothing back, weeping as she stammered it out, until Alex could almost bear no more. Now, finally, he understood why she had rejected him for so long, and his loving heart ached for her.

'I don't blame you for any of it!' he assured her, finally. 'I think it's the bravest story I've ever heard, frankly.'

'Alex, I was so afraid you would hate me for letting him touch me!' she sobbed. 'You were always so suspicious and sarcastic about Robin – and that was for nothing!'

'I was a fool then!' Alex hated himself for his previously bigoted attitude. 'I'm not quite so quick to condemn now, and especially not for that. Trust me, Casey?'

And finally, she knew she could.

CHAPTER 26

'Happy Christmas, Lady Havilland!' smiled the receptionist as Casey hurried into the familiar foyer of Havilland Gracey.

'And to you, Karen,' Casey returned, quickly, grabbing at her almost two-year-old daughter before she disappeared off into the lift, intent on getting to her father's office as fast as she could.

'*See Daddy*!' Sophie demanded, trying to wriggle out of Casey's grasp.

'Yes, darling, but patience!' Casey laughed, and lifted her up to press the lift button. Sophie knew exactly which one to press to get them to the chairman's floor, and Casey smiled as the mirror-lined box swept them upwards. It was more than four years since she had first used that lift – and so much had happened to her since that fateful day!

The tacky costume had been replaced by Chanel from immaculate head to immaculate toe, an emerald-green bouclé suit that emphasized her vivid colouring and elegant height. However, she still checked her appearance with a nervous gesture as she got out of the lift; old habits were definitely hard to get rid of! Alex smiled as he strode towards the lift and saw her do it, having been warned of her arrival by reception, Casey would never change, he thought, lovingly, as he bent to kiss her, before he swept his little daughter up into his arms.

'Everything packed?' he asked as they walked along the corridor.

'All ready to go,' she assured him. 'William is waiting downstairs.'

'I just have to stop by the office Christmas party,' Alex said. 'Tony would never forgive us if we didn't see them before we go. And great news – he's finally persuaded Mary-Jo to marry him!'

'About time!' Casey grinned. She had been egging Tony on for months about that, ever since he had been promoted to assistant MD. Alex had done as he had promised and stepped sideways, not long after their marriage, to become chairman, thus letting his very able assistant take his place in the maelstrom. He still worked hard, but to Casey's delight he had cut back on his overseas visits and she now frequently went with him if he *had* to go. He was certainly loath to go without her. She was still not used to his knighthood and the title that went with it and Alex teased her gently every time she forgot her name! It had still been a proud moment though, when she had watched him receiving it from the Queen, almost as traumatic as Sophie's arrival. Alex certainly never let her forget *that* day!

From quietly having dinner with the Greys one

minute to writhing in agony on their bathroom floor the next, Casey had managed to give birth to her daughter in just under half-an-hour with both Alex and Sarah acting as midwives while Nick phoned desperately for help. Sarah had been four months pregnant herself at the time, spurred on by Casey's pregnancy she had said, and now their two little daughters played happily together at every opportunity. Nick laughed frequently to Alex and suggested that the next time he considered getting his wife pregnant, would he please keep her well away from Sarah, before *she* got infected with the broody bug again, since he was convinced he couldn't cope with any more children!

Their Christmas house-party in Barbados had become an anticipated event for both Alex and Casey – and the Greys and Faulkners who always came. This year Nick and Sarah had been away in Los Angeles for several months and Casey was looking forward more than ever to seeing them again. She had just finished a long stint in the West End a month before, and though she had never sought the kind of stardom Sarah had achieved, she worked as often as she wanted to do and had indeed become a respected actress on the London stage. The stage had always been her first love and now she had returned to it, with a Stratford season to look forward to in the spring. Alex, to his credit, had encouraged her, knowing that she would be lost without her work, and was loyally always there on first nights as her anchor. Alex was always there for her, loving and supportive, her rock, she often said, and particularly so during the nightmare of the trial when she was in the witness box for hours on end.

Adrian Shawcross, to their astonishment, had elected to plead not guilty, claiming that Casey had organized the whole thing with him to escape Alex! It felt as if her very guts were being torn out as she was then forced to relive her experiences in all their lurid detail, yet her very dignity had been her saving in the Press reports. They had taken her courage to their hearts and there had been nothing but praise for her in the newspapers, to her astonishment. Alex had sat determinedly through it all, comforting at every opportunity, and their marriage, far from being damaged by it all had seemed to strengthen in those few days, before Adrian Shawcross was sentenced to life-imprisonment, as Chris had confidently predicted.

She loved Alex desperately, as he did her. But though the rafters of their home frequently rang with their disagreements, Alex rarely needed to resort to the golf club to escape her wrath. Making up on the rows was part of the fun of it all, he declared. Apart, of course, from the incidental fact that Casey had turned out to be far too good a player herself, and frequently accompanied him!

To a man, the staff at Havillands adored Alex's wife. There was no petty jealousy from the women amongst them for her exalted position and the men competed good-naturedly for her attention. Since their marriage, Alex had relaxed, become warmer and more approachable somehow, and they all knew who was responsible for that. Casey knew everyone at the party and carefully made time to talk to as many of them as she could. Sophie was immediately swept off by Tony, her great friend, and was finally cornered by her mother, with a glass of wine clutched in her hand.

'Tony!' Casey chided with a grin. 'She's not even two yet!'

'Shame! Did you know she's going to marry me when she's three?' Tony grinned back.

'Not if M-J gets to hear of it!' Alex put in, overhearing them. 'Casey, we should go, planes don't wait, not even for us!' He scooped up Sophie and with a final farewell to the crowds of people he and Casey made for the lift.

'Disappointing,' Alex commented as the lift took them down again. 'No kissagram for the happy couple!'

'I thought you were dead against all that sort of thing?' Casey laughed.

'Oh, well, I was.' He smiled. 'Until . . . well . . . I fell in love with one! Funny, that green reminds me of it somehow.' He ran a hand over her elegantly clad shoulder. 'Whatever happened to that sexy little number? I don't suppose you still have it, do you?'

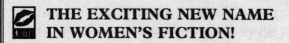

THE EXCITING NEW NAME IN WOMEN'S FICTION!

PLEASE HELP ME TO HELP YOU!

Dear *Scarlet* Reader,

As Editor of *Scarlet* Books I want to make sure that the books I offer you every month are up to the high standards *Scarlet* readers expect. And to do that I need to know a little more about you and your reading likes and dislikes. So please spare a few minutes to fill in the short questionnaire on the following pages and send it to me.

Looking forward to hearing from you,

Sally Cooper

Editor-in-Chief, *Scarlet*

QUESTIONNAIRE

Please tick the appropriate boxes to indicate your answers

1 Where did you get this Scarlet title?
Bought in supermarket ☐
Bought at my local bookstore ☐ Bought at chain bookstore ☐
Bought at book exchange or used bookstore ☐
Borrowed from a friend ☐
Other (please indicate) _____

2 Did you enjoy reading it?
A lot ☐   A little ☐   Not at all ☐

3 What did you particularly like about this book?
Believable characters ☐   Easy to read ☐
Good value for money ☐   Enjoyable locations ☐
Interesting story ☐   Modern setting ☐
Other _____

4 What did you particularly dislike about this book?
_____

5 Would you buy another Scarlet book?
Yes ☐   No ☐

6 What other kinds of book do you enjoy reading?
Horror ☐   Puzzle books ☐   Historical fiction ☐
General fiction ☐ Crime/Detective ☐ Cookery ☐
Other (please indicate) _____

7 Which magazines do you enjoy reading?
1. _____
2. _____
3. _____

And now a little about you –
8 How old are you?
Under 25 ☐   25–34 ☐   35–44 ☐
45–54 ☐   55–64 ☐   over 65 ☐

cont.

9 What is your marital status?
   Single ☐   Married/living with partner ☐
   Widowed ☐   Separated/divorced ☐

10 What is your current occupation?
   Employed full-time ☐   Employed part-time ☐
   Student ☐   Housewife full-time ☐
   Unemployed ☐   Retired ☐

11 Do you have children? If so, how many and how old are they?
   _____
   _____

12 What is your annual household income?
   under $15,000 ☐   or   £10,000 ☐
   $15–25,000 ☐   or   £10–20,000 ☐
   $25–35,000 ☐   or   £20–30,000 ☐
   $35–50,000 ☐   or   £30–40,000 ☐
   over $50,000 ☐   or   £40,000 ☐

Miss/Mrs/Ms _____
Address _____
_____
_____ Postcode:_____

Thank you for completing this questionnaire. Now tear it out – put
it in an envelope and send it, before 31 July 1998, to:

Sally Cooper, Editor-in-Chief

USA/Can. address
SCARLET c/o London Bridge
85 River Rock Drive
Suite 202
Buffalo
NY 14207
USA

UK address/No stamp required
SCARLET
FREEPOST LON 3335
LONDON W8 4BR
*Please use block capitals for
address*

THCIN/1/98

Scarlet titles coming next month:

THE MOST DANGEROUS GAME Mary Wibberley
Scarlet is delighted to announce the return to writing of this very popular author! 'Devlin' comes into Catherine's life when she is in need of protection and finds herself in that most clichéd of all situations – she's fallen in love with her bodyguard! The problem is that Devlin will leave when the job's over . . . won't he?

DANGEROUS DECEPTION Lisa Andrews
Luis Quevedo needs a fiancée in a hurry to please his grandfather. Emma fits the bill and desperately needs the money. Then she makes the mistake of falling in love with her 'fiancé' . . .

CRAVEN'S BRIDE Danielle Shaw
For ten years, Max Craven has blamed Alison for the death of his daughter. Now he returns home and finds his feelings for Alison have undergone a transformation. Surely he can't be in love with her?

BLUE SILK PROMISE Julia Wild
When Nick recovers consciousness after a serious accident, he finds himself married within days. Nick can't believe he's forgotten the woman he loves so passionately. Then little by little, he begins to realize that his beloved Kayanne thinks he's his own brother!